*For Sheila, my agent,
my support and my friend.*

Acknowledgements

My thanks as always to the wonderful team at Simon & Schuster who took my humble offering and turned it into this glossy tome. My gratitude in particular to Suzanne, Libby and Clare who kept me on the right track. To Michelle Connolly's Organic Eggs in Monaghan for the titbits on the wonders of egg farming. To Tony, Peter and Sean who keep me sane – well, almost! And to my wonderful mother for our telephone chats that always make me smile.

The Secrets
We Keep

Chapter One

When Erin Joyce closed the hall door behind her and set off down the drive she could hear PJ whistling as he watered the plants, Gracie playing hopscotch with an old shoe-polish tin, and the chatter of her German guests as they packed up the car in readiness for another outing tomorrow. As she turned into the lane the sounds receded and she was left with just the birdsong, the gravel crunching under her sandals and the distant hum of a tractor. She walked briskly, breathing in the fragrant summer evening. The hedgerow thinned as she rounded the bend and Erin could see the glistening water of the lough and the outline of Mark's boat moored near the shore. She knew that he would probably be onboard, preparing for a fishing trip the next morning. Business was good in July and though the weather had been erratic, it never affected the fishing. Mark would be kept busy through the summer months and well into autumn. Then he would take care of any maintenance work on the boat or house before he and Marguerite shut the restaurant for a few days and went to visit her mother in France.

Sometimes Erin forgot that Marguerite was French. She had been in Ireland so long and had cultivated a strange, lilting accent and a unique language. Ronan called it Franglais. It always made her customers smile. Mind you, just walking into Marguerite's restaurant was enough to make you feel happy. It was more like someone's sitting room than a formal dining room with its big squashy sofas in soft, pastel shades and old oak tables with glass vases of garden flowers. In the evenings, Marguerite or Sean would light small oil lamps, creating an intimate, romantic glow around each table. Even if the food wasn't marvellous – but it was – people would still be drawn to the restaurant simply because it was a lovely place to be. Erin rarely had the time to eat there during the summer season but at least once a week she would make the ten-minute walk to Dijon, which was named for Marguerite's home town, to join her friend for a glass of wine and a chat. They had known each other for nearly four years now, since Erin came to Dunbarra, and had been friends almost as long. Marguerite was the girlfriend that Erin never had before and they were close despite the fact that, at thirty-eight, Marguerite was seven years older than her.

Erin had not planned to come up tonight. Two new guests were arriving the next day and there was much to be done before then. But Marguerite had sounded distracted and anxious when she phoned and so Erin had immediately agreed.

When she finally turned on to the main road, such as it was, the restaurant loomed in front of her and she noted there were three cars out front. Not bad for nine o'clock on a Monday night.

As she pushed open the door, Erin paused to inhale the wonderful aromas of Marguerite's cooking.

'Well, good evening, Erin, how are ye?'

She opened her eyes and smiled. 'I'm fine, Sean. Duck on the menu tonight, then?'

'It is. Are you going to try some?'

'No, I've already had beans *sur* toast.' Erin laughed, crossing to the beautiful oak bar that ran along one side of the room and climbing up on a stool.

Sean stood with his two large hands planted on the counter and raised an eyebrow. 'Some wine, then?'

'Yes, please,' she said, combing her long, golden-brown hair back from her face with her fingers.

'Marguerite won't be long. She's just finishing off two main courses.'

Erin looked around the restaurant. There were five parties in all. Two businessmen at a centre table; a couple in the corner flirting madly; three older couples, local people, sipping coffee and liqueurs; a foursome arguing good-naturedly over desserts; and Erin's latest guest, a rather overbearing American woman, sitting alone at a table for two with just some wine and bread in front of her. 'What about Mrs Bell?' she whispered and nodded in the woman's direction.

Sean leaned across the bar and bent his head to hers. 'I think she's been stood up.'

Erin groaned. 'But it's her silver wedding anniversary! Her husband had some business in Dublin and said he'd meet her here at eight. I hope he hasn't broken down.'

'He probably got lost. Most people do.'

'I doubt it. I gave her very explicit directions earlier. Should I go over and talk to her?'

Sean frowned. 'Better not. It might just embarrass her.'

'Yeah, you're right.'

Marguerite Hayes emerged from the kitchen with food for the romantic couple. 'Erin! I'll be with you in a flash.' After ensuring they had everything they needed, she came over to join her friend.

Erin stood to embrace her. 'How are you?' They exchanged three kisses and Marguerite slipped on to the next stool. She looked tired and tendrils of hair clung damply to her forehead with the heat of the kitchen, but her dark eyes danced in her beautiful face and she was, as always, smiling.

'You only ever kiss me twice,' Sean grumbled with a wink at Erin.

Marguerite held up her hands, wide-eyed. 'But you must remember, I am married to a very jealous man.'

'My Mary's the same,' said the waiter, who was

portly, sixty-four and had just celebrated his fortieth wedding anniversary. 'Are you having a glass of wine, boss?'

Marguerite scanned the room, her eyes settling on Sandra Bell. 'I'd better stick with fizzy water for now, Sean.' She turned to Erin. 'So how have you been, my friend? Busy?'

'As always. Before I forget, I have a new crop of potatoes coming up tomorrow. Want some?'

Marguerite clapped her hands. 'Oh, *bien sûr*, please! And the watercress and courgettes?'

'I'll deliver them all in the morning,' Erin promised. 'You'll be pleased with the lamb's lettuce too. It's particularly sweet.'

'Good, it goes so well with the trout and I have a full house tomorrow night – businessmen from Belfast on some kind of bonding trip.' Marguerite rolled her eyes. 'Mark is taking them out for the day and then they're coming to me for dinner.'

'I have a German family staying who are interested in doing a bit of fishing.'

'No problem. Just give them Mark's card.'

Erin nodded. 'Will do.'

'We have quite the little cottage industry,' Marguerite laughed. 'Between you and the guest house and the market garden, Paddy Burke and his bread and cakes, Mark with his fishing trips—'

'And Ronan and his eggs,' Erin added. 'We're almost self-sufficient.'

'Speaking of Ronan,' Marguerite raised an eyebrow, 'How are things between you two?'

Erin grimaced. 'Better, I think. He certainly doesn't seem to be sulking as much.'

'I'm glad. Of course I still think you were crazy to turn him down . . .'

'Please don't go there,' Erin begged. 'You know how I feel about marriage and I was always completely honest with Ronan too.'

'You were,' Marguerite conceded. 'And I will say no more.'

Erin smiled. 'Good.'

'Tell me, are you fully booked at the moment?'

'Thankfully, yes.'

'Ah.'

Erin watched a frown pucker Marguerite's smooth brow. 'What is it?'

'I was hoping for a favour. There is someone I know who needs lodgings.'

'I will see what I can do to help. How long do they want to stay? Is it just the one person?'

Marguerite's eyes met hers. 'It's Sebastian, Erin.'

'Sebastian?' Erin stared.

'He needs a place to stay for a while.' Marguerite hurried on, 'I was hoping maybe you could put him up.'

Erin was dumbstruck. Why would Marguerite's half-brother and multimillionaire movie star, want to stay in her humble guest house? He stayed in his Mayfair penthouse when he was in London, the George V when he was in Paris and the Shelbourne when he was in Dublin. Mostly he divided his time between LA, where he was based, and New York, where his ex-wife and two kids lived. The only time Sebastian had visited Marguerite since Erin moved here he'd stayed in the luxurious K Club in Kildare and rented a helicopter to take him the twenty-minute flight to Dunbarra. Erin had met him only briefly. He was a very handsome man with the same dark eyes as his sister but there, Erin thought, the similarity ended. He didn't have Marguerite's warmth and he had a slightly pompous and condescending attitude that she found annoying.

'When is he coming?' she asked at last, realizing Marguerite was waiting for an answer.

Marguerite tugged absently at a loose thread on her chef's whites. 'He says he will arrive next week, but I have no idea how long he plans to stay.'

'I'm not sure I can help.' Erin shrugged feeling secretly relieved. 'The only room I'd have available is a tiny single and it doesn't even have an en suite. I'd have nowhere to put the rest of his –' Erin just managed to stop herself saying lackeys – 'team.'

'He is travelling alone,' Marguerite said quickly, 'and I don't think he'll care where you put him.' She paused and then looked straight at Erin. 'He's had some sort of a breakdown.'

'Oh, I'm sorry, Marguerite.' Erin put her hand on her friend's shoulder, her hazel eyes full of concern.

'I don't really know what has happened to him. He called a couple of days ago sounding so . . .' Marguerite wrung her hands, '*distrait*. He wanted to come and stay with me but, of course,' Marguerite gestured at the ceiling, 'there isn't room in our flat to swing a rat.'

'Cat,' Erin corrected her.

'Yes.' Marguerite nodded. 'So I thought of you. The Gatehouse is the perfect place. It will give him the peace and tranquillity he craves and he won't have to worry about fans or journalists following him to Dunbarra.'

'Don't be too sure,' Erin warned. 'There's no escape from the press any more. Surely the first place they'll look for him is with his family?'

'They don't know I am family. Maman never approved of us keeping in touch. It still upsets her to be reminded that Papa had an affair. She refuses to even talk about Sebastian and so, out of deference to her, he's never told anyone about us.'

Erin was surprised and gratified that Sebastian was capable of showing such consideration.

'Oh, Erin, please do this for me. I will feel much happier if Sebastian is close by, where I can keep an eye on him.'

Erin looked at the worry in her friend's face and realized she had no choice. She must make this work. Marguerite had done so much for her since she came to Dunbarra. 'Of course he can come. I will find somewhere to put him.'

Marguerite enveloped her in a warm hug. 'You are an angel!'

A scream from the other side of the room made them jump apart and Erin turned in time to see Sandra Bell drop her glass and burst into noisy tears.

She and Marguerite looked at each other and then hurried over to the woman's side.

'Mrs Bell, what is it?' Marguerite asked. 'Are you ill?'

The woman continued to sob loudly but didn't answer.

Erin crouched down and looked up into her face. 'Mrs Bell? Are you okay?'

Her hands shaking, Mrs Bell gave her mobile to Erin.

Erin looked from the American to the screen, puzzled. And then she saw it was a text message. She read it aloud.

'"Sorry Sandra. Not coming. Not today. Not ever. It's over."'

'Oh, poor Madame Bell!' Marguerite put a comforting arm around her shoulders. 'Cognac,' she instructed Sean, who'd been hovering nervously in the background.

'I'm so sorry, Mrs Bell.' Erin set the phone down. 'What a terrible shock.' The woman's eyes were red, her face blotchy and she clutched Erin's hand, making her wince.

'How could he?' she wailed. 'It's our anniversary.

And he didn't even have the balls to say it to my face. He ends our marriage with a text message.'

'It is not the behaviour of a gentleman,' Marguerite agreed. 'He is a shit.'

Erin shot her a look.

Marguerite shrugged, unrepentant. 'Well, he is.'

Sean appeared with a large cognac and quickly disappeared again.

'Is there anything we can do, Mrs Bell? Can I phone someone for you?' Erin asked as the woman knocked back the drink.

'Call me Sandra. There's no one here. My kids are both in the States. I'm all alone.' This realization unleashed another torrent of tears.

Erin patted the fleshy, beringed hand distractedly, wondering what on earth she could say to console her. 'I'll call the airline as soon as we get back to the Gatehouse and see if we can get your flight changed. I'm sure it won't be a problem.'

'Are you crazy?' Sandra looked horrified. 'I've told everyone about this romantic anniversary trip Jerry organized for us. I can't go back and tell them he dumped me. I'll be a laughing stock.'

'Of course you won't,' Marguerite soothed her. 'Your friends will be on your side. And surely you want to be with your family at a time like this?'

'No way.' Sandra was adamant. 'He's booked and paid for three weeks, hasn't he?'

Erin smiled politely. 'Yes.'

'Then I'm staying. I need time to figure out what I'm going to do and what I'll say to the kids. Oh, I miss my kids.' And she dropped her head on her arms and wept.

Marguerite slipped away to have a quiet word with the other diners, who were beginning to eye Sandra with a mixture of curiosity and irritation. Erin stuffed some napkins into Sandra's hand and helped her to her feet. 'Let's get you back to the Gatehouse.'

'But I haven't paid for the wine—'

'It's on the house, Mrs Bell,' Marguerite said, coming back to join them. 'And Sean will drop you both home.'

'Of course I will.' The waiter hurried over, rustling in his pocket for his car keys.

Sandra Bell nodded. 'Thank you.'

Marguerite smiled and gave Erin a quick hug. 'Thank you for your kindness, my friend. I'll be in touch with the details.'

'No problem,' Erin said with a bright smile. And linking her arm through Sandra's, she led her out to Sean's car.

Chapter Two

Hazel rinsed her brush in the jar of water and then dipped it into the azure blue. Gracie was sitting on the grass at her feet, arranging pebbles in a row. Hazel smiled at the deep concentration on her daughter's face then turned her attention back to the watercolour on the easel in front of her.

'That's nice.'

Hazel looked up at the man standing over her. 'Thanks, PJ.'

He put his head on one side and frowned. 'What is it exactly?'

She laughed and nodded towards the view in front of them. 'It's not a good sign if you have to ask.'

'You wouldn't want to mind me, girl. What I know about art you could put on the back of a postage stamp. But I like the colours.' He crouched down beside the child and smiled. 'And how are you today, young lady?' Gracie gave him a thumbs-up, making him laugh. 'Would you like to come and help me dig up some potatoes?'

Gracie looked at her mother and Hazel nodded. 'Thanks, PJ. Send her back if she's too much for you.'

'Ah, sure, she's a great little helper, so she is. You get on with your work. We'll be grand.'

Gracie jumped to her feet and put her hand in his.

Hazel watched as the two of them disappeared in the direction of the market garden. How lucky she'd been to stumble upon Dunbarra and the Gatehouse. If ever she was to rediscover her talent, surely it had to be here in this beautiful haven with its resident babysitter. Gracie normally shrank from people, especially adults, but she had taken to PJ instantly. Hazel knew it was because he hadn't bombarded her with questions as so many adults did with shy children. He'd waited patiently and it wasn't long before Gracie was shooting him curious glances and smiling when she heard him whistling. And she'd actually laughed out loud the day PJ had dropped the hose sending a spray of water all over the place, himself included. He'd smiled kindly as he'd shaken himself like a dog and Hazel knew it was all just a performance to amuse her daughter. Not many people took the trouble to make Gracie comfortable. After the initial inquisition – why doesn't she speak? Is she deaf? – most dismissed her. But not PJ.

Hazel judged PJ to be in his late sixties, early seventies. He was tall but slightly stooped and though he pretended to be a simple man, intelligence shone from his sharp, green eyes. A smile was never far from his lips and Hazel had never heard him raise his voice other than in song or laughter. Hazel had assumed that he was also a guest because he ate in the dining room with the other guests each morning and his room was along the hallway from hers, yet he was always working in the market garden and treated the guest house as his home. Also, Erin Joyce, their elegant and attractive hostess, treated him more like a beloved uncle than a paying guest. Perhaps he was.

PJ talked a lot about anything and everything and, though not normally a chatty person, Hazel was surprised to find she actually enjoyed his company. Whether it was because he never asked any searching questions or simply the kindness in those eyes, Hazel couldn't say. Whatever it was, she liked him and Gracie obviously adored the man. And she had learned that her daughter was a good judge of character.

Hazel turned her attention back to the canvas in front of her. She wanted to finish this painting this morning. She mixed some white with the blue and dabbed the brush across the top of the canvas in an effort to recreate the cloudy sky. She frowned in concentration and added some more white until she was satisfied with the effect. It didn't bother her too much that PJ hadn't recognized her painting as the view before them. Her aim wasn't to replicate the landscape but to attempt to capture its essence. With each day that passed, she felt she was getting closer to her goal. She mixed some black into the blue-grey mixture to create the darker hue of the lough in the distance. A small white dab on the horizon was enough to represent Mark Hayes's boat.

A shriek of amusement in the distance made her look up. Her daughter's laughter was a rare and precious sound but thankfully more common since they'd arrived in Dunbarra. Maybe in this peaceful, beautiful place she would talk again. Hazel prayed that it would be so. But she wasn't sure if she could afford to stay here much longer. They'd arrived almost five weeks ago now on what was supposed to be a short break to allow Hazel a chance to think and decide what to do next. But it was hard to leave Dunbarra and even harder to leave the Gatehouse. Still, Hazel realized she needed to find a more permanent base and a job, but the latter would not be easy given she had a four-year-old to look after.

The perfect scenario would be if she could turn her painting into a full-time occupation. Was it just a pipe dream or finally a real possibility? Hazel wasn't sure but she had been feeling more confident and optimistic about her art in the last few weeks. She thought of the tattered newspaper cutting in her wallet that, nearly six years on, she still carried everywhere.

Watch out for Hazel Patterson, a new and exciting young artist with a promising future. Focusing primarily on abstract landscapes, her work is colourful, vibrant and intense.

Time may have passed but if she had promise then, why not now? Surely it was like riding a bike? She looked around at the luscious, wild garden and then back at the old stone house with its ludicrous pink door. If she couldn't find inspiration here, there was no hope.

*

'Well, isn't it well for some?'

Mark opened one eye and looked up to see Ronan Masterson standing on the quayside watching him. He smiled, stood up and stretched. 'This is the first chance I've had to take a breather all day,' he protested.

'Of course it is.'

Mark used his hand to shield his eyes and appraised his friend. 'What are you doing all dressed up? Got a hot date?'

Ronan laughed. He was wearing an old tweed blazer over his cleanest jeans and he was wearing shoes instead of his usual working boots or wellies. 'Unfortunately not. I was in Mullingar for a meeting with my accountant.'

Mark groaned. 'I'd say that was fun.'

'You'd be wrong.'

Mark searched his face, his expression sober. 'Problems?'

'There are always problems with organic farming,' Ronan assured him but he was smiling.

'Well, now that you've got a jacket on why don't you bring Erin up to the restaurant for dinner?'

'I've already been knocked back, mate. She says she's up to her eyes. Two new guests arrived today and she also said something about looking after a deserted American.'

'Oh, that would be the woman who broke down at Dijon last night. Apparently the husband dumped her, and on their anniversary too. She's staying at the Gatehouse.'

'Poor Erin, no wonder she sounded so flustered.'

'There's more,' Mark said darkly.

'I'd love to stand here and listen to all the news –' Ronan smacked his lips together – 'only I'm awful thirsty.'

Mark grinned. 'Let me grab a shower and I'll meet you in the pub in an hour.'

Ronan climbed back into his jeep and drove the short distance to the Gatehouse.

Erin was putting down the phone when he walked into reception. She looked up in surprise and smiled. 'Ronan! What are you doing here? I told you I was too busy to go out tonight.'

'I'm fine, thanks. How are you?' he said mildly, his blue eyes twinkling with amusement.

'Sorry.' She gave him an embarrassed, apologetic smile as she reached up to kiss him. 'It's been a mad day.'

'I'll forgive you.' He produced a package from behind his back with a flourish. 'I was in Mullingar so I got this for you.'

She frowned as she opened the bag and then grinned in delight. 'A new cartridge for my printer! Oh, Ronan, that's great, thanks.'

He shook his head sorrowfully. 'You're easily pleased. Now I must go. I have a hot date.'

'Tell Mark I said hi,' she said, walking him to the door.

He laughed and kissed her again. 'See ya.'

'See ya.'

Erin stood watching as he went out to the car, then she waved at Hazel, who was sitting on the wooden bench at the bottom of the garden with her sketch pad on her lap. When the girl had been paying her weekly bill she had asked, yet again, to extend her stay. Between that and Sebastian coming to stay life was becoming very complicated; Erin wasn't sure where she'd put everyone. But a family from Cardiff had called this morning to cancel their booking so, with some juggling about, Erin could just about cater for everyone. The cancellation had filled her with fore-boding of the difficult times ahead. Already two other guest-house owners in the area had reported that business was way down on last year. Because of the

Gatehouse's lakeside location Erin hadn't had any problems but she knew it was only a matter of time. She sighed and turned to go back inside. She would have loved to enjoy the last of the sunshine but she still had beds to make up – her new guests were due within the hour – and a pile of ironing was also awaiting her attention. And she should really check on Sandra Bell again.

The woman had kept to her room most of the day but Erin had knocked a few times to deliver strong coffee and a light lunch. It wasn't a service she normally provided but it was the only way she felt she could help. She had no words of comfort to offer. At first Sandra had hardly spoken, but the last time Erin had looked in, she'd seemed inclined to open up. Erin had extracted herself with difficulty. She felt bad about it but she did have a guest house to run. Anyway, she was the last person in the world to offer advice on romantic problems and she had never been very good at the whole girly, heart-to-heart business. Marguerite would attest to that.

When Erin had first come to the Gatehouse as a guest she'd kept very much to herself. She'd spent her days wandering along the banks of the lough or in the garden watching PJ work or sitting on the bench where Hazel was just absorbing the wonderful stillness of the scene. Very occasionally she'd call into Dijon for an early, solitary dinner and find herself laughing when Sean flirted outrageously with her, and also opening up to Marguerite's warm, friendly nature. The relationship started slowly but, over time, she and Marguerite had become firm friends and Erin was glad to have the older woman in her life. But in those early days the only person she had really talked to was PJ. Sometimes she would accompany him to the pub and, as she sipped a glass of Guinness, he would talk about his love of gardening and give a humorous running commentary on everyone who came through the door. Days turned into weeks and though Erin knew she should have been out looking for a job and planning her future she couldn't bring herself to leave the Gatehouse. And then Ivy, the taciturn owner, announced that she was putting the business up for sale and, as soon as she got a decent offer, was retiring to Florida with her widowed sister. Erin was taken aback, as was PJ, and tentatively she asked him what his plans were.

'I'd like to stay, wouldn't you?'

'Of course, but how?' she'd asked.

'You could always buy the place.'

Erin had at first dismissed the suggestion but the more she thought about it, the more she realized that it wasn't such a bad idea. Her background was in the hotel business and she did need a job. And it would mean she could stay on in this wonderful place where she was happier than she had been in years. Three months later, Ivy was on a plane to America and Erin was the new and very nervous owner of a six-bedroom guest house.

Chapter Three

The day of Sebastian Gray's arrival dawned dull and grey. Erin hoped it wasn't a bad omen. She was ready for him but it didn't stop her running around like a mad thing, her 'to do' list in the back pocket of her jeans.

'I didn't know we were having royalty to stay,' PJ teased as she polished the mirror in the sitting room. He was in an armchair by the window, supposedly reading.

'Haven't you anything better to do?' Erin retorted, slightly out of breath.

He lowered the newspaper to look at her. 'That's no way to talk to your valued guests.'

Erin flopped into the chair opposite. She looked at him with worried eyes. 'This is never going to work, is it?'

PJ smiled. 'It will be grand, darling, stop worrying.'

'But what's he going to do all day?'

'Not your problem,' PJ pointed out. 'Make sure he's comfortable and give him a good breakfast and then leave him to his own devices. Doubtless he'll spend all his time with Marguerite or flying between here and Dublin or Shannon. We'll probably hardly see him.'

'I just wish I knew how long he was going to stay. Marguerite seems to have no idea.'

'Well, once he's paying, what difference does it make?' PJ said reasonably.

'I don't know. I just feel sure Sebastian Gray will disrupt things.' Erin picked distractedly at a fingernail as she talked and PJ reached out a hand to still hers.

'If it bothers you so much, why did you agree to let him stay?'

'I couldn't let Marguerite down,' Erin said simply.

'No, so now you must just make the best of it.'

She sighed. 'Yes. Well, I've put him in the cabin so at least if he's playing loud music or "entertaining", the other guests won't be disturbed.'

PJ frowned over his glasses. 'You're giving him your room? Are ye mad, woman?'

Erin shrugged. 'The only spare room I have at the moment is just too small; I couldn't put him in there.'

'And why not? If he'd wanted luxury he would have gone to a five-star hotel.'

'No, I think it will be better for everyone – me included – if he's under a separate roof.'

PJ grunted and went back to his paper. Erin pulled out her list and studied it. Most of her household chores were done but she still had several things to do in the garden. At times like this she wondered how wise it was to try to run two businesses at once. The market garden was only a small sideline but she supplied a range of organic vegetables to Marguerite, a few other restaurants and a popular greengrocer in Mullingar, so quality was all important. Erin was careful to keep her range small and select and also to go for more unusual varieties. Her specialities were seven different types of salad leaves that varied in texture and colour – the chefs loved that – and some of the more unusual herbs that rarely took to Irish soil. They required a lot of love and care and vigilance and, at the moment, she knew she wasn't paying them enough attention.

PJ folded his paper and stood up. 'Best get out and see to that garden.'

Erin looked at him in surprise. 'What about your nap?' PJ always had a quick snooze in the chair after lunch.

'Sure, how can I sleep with the racket you're making with all this bloody cleaning?' he grumbled.

'Sorry. But I've only the windows left and then I'll come and give you hand.'

'Windows.' PJ headed for the door. 'As if he'll even notice!'

Erin followed him outside and took the path around the side of the house to the cabin. She never really understood why it had been called that. It wasn't a quaint, wooden construction but a plain, stone chalet that Ivy had built for herself almost ten years ago. It had a bedroom, bathroom, galley kitchen and a small sitting room with a wonderful view of the lough. Erin was going to miss that but it would probably only be for a week, maybe two. She couldn't imagine Sebastian Gray staying in Dunbarra longer than that. The quiet life would surely drive him mad and he'd soon miss the buzz of his very public life.

Erin checked, yet again, that she'd left out enough towels and that there were spare pillows and blankets in the wardrobe. She'd lugged most of her belongings up into the small loft above. Marguerite and PJ would be horrified if they knew but Erin couldn't bear the thought of leaving her private possessions for Sebastian to snoop through when he got bored. She'd left the kitchen stocked with the basics and a colourful bowl of fruit sat on the counter. She'd thought of leaving a bottle of wine in the fridge but that seemed over the top. She didn't want to make Sebastian feel too welcome, just enough to keep Marguerite happy. She felt guilty for being so suspicious of her friend's brother. She found it hardly credible that such a rich and successful man was having a breakdown. What on earth had he to be sad about? Sure, his marriage had fallen apart but that had happened years ago now and, Marguerite told her, had been his own fault. So what could be troubling him so much that he'd had a breakdown? Perhaps he'd discovered his first grey hair or found a wrinkle or maybe one of his teenage girlfriends had dumped him. Bitchy, Erin told herself, smiling as she sprayed the front window and started to polish.

Finally satisfied that the cabin was as clean as she could make it, Erin locked up and checked her watch. There was still plenty of time before Sebastian and Marguerite arrived so she would easily get some gardening chores done. She stopped at the house to toss her polish and cloth into the hall, then crossed the lawn towards the market garden. She spotted Hazel Patterson down near the gate, bent over her easel, engrossed in her work. Even from here Erin could see the splash of red that represented the roses at the edge of the driveway. Although she mostly painted landscapes, Hazel had also painted the house from various angles and shyly presented Erin with her favourite. It was the view from the end of the lane where you turned off the road and caught a first glimpse of the glistening stone building with its pink door. Erin had hung it in the hall so it was the first thing people saw when they walked in. It always made her smile and many guests paused to admire it. She must tell Hazel to leave some business cards on the hall table. It was clear that the girl was short of cash. She never ate at Dijon and only occasionally visited the pub. She and Gracie mostly ate a large breakfast and then had sandwiches either in their room or in the garden. Erin had taken to giving them larger portions and putting an extra couple of rolls in the bread basket.

'Feeding the poor again?' PJ had commented one morning, from his table in the corner.

'No idea what you're talking about,' Erin had said, with a grin. PJ didn't miss much.

Erin passed under the archway, walked through the orchard and on into the vegetable garden. PJ was on his knees, working on a small area that had been sectioned off with pink ribbon. Gracie worked alongside him, a small, pink-handled spade in one hand and a fork in the other. 'Well, well, you two look busy.'

PJ looked up with a sheepish grin. 'I was just teaching young Gracie a bit about gardening. I thought it would be better if she had her own vegetable patch. I was going to mention it later. It's just a few spuds, carrots and lettuces and of course I'll look after it . . .'

'I think it's a great idea, PJ. What do you think, Gracie? Would you like to be a gardener when you grow up?'

Gracie thought for a moment then shook her head.

'No? So what would you like to be?'

Gracie moved her hands as if she were dabbing a brush in a palette and then painting.

PJ laughed. 'An artist, just like your mother.'

Gracie nodded.

'I'm sure you'll be as wonderful as she is.' Erin smiled. 'I'll leave you to it. I'm going to turn the compost, PJ.'

'No, you've enough on your plate today. I'll do it.'

'Are you sure?'

He winked at her. 'No problem.'

'Thanks, PJ.'

She wandered on down the garden, between the drills of vegetables, stopping every so often to check the moisture of the soil and look for signs of pests. Insects and snails were the biggest threat to the garden, to her whole business. It was a constant battle protecting young plants and vigilance was imperative. Life was easier for a gardener in July, though. Apart from watering, feeding and guarding the plants from predators, there was little to do. Each morning after breakfast, Erin would pick the vegetables and herbs that her customers wanted and once they were delivered, she could concentrate on her housekeeping. Nora Murray, a local woman, came in three times a week supposedly to help but she was incredibly unreliable and Erin did most of the chores herself.

The market garden brought in a nice little income which she'd tried to share with PJ, but he wouldn't take a penny, joking that she should be charging him for occupational therapy that kept him from premature senility. Erin knew what a proud man he was so she didn't argue with him but instead repaid him by cooking him meals, doing his laundry and adding a few extra comforts to his room, the largest in the house. He now had a small TV, a coffee-maker, kettle and a mini fridge. Erin had bought a soft, leather chair with a built-in footrest and positioned it by the large bay window that overlooked the front garden. She'd also bought him a small music system so he could listen to the radio or his beloved country and western music. He grumbled that she shouldn't be spending her hard-earned money on him but Erin knew he appreciated it and it made her happy to do it for him.

PJ had taught her everything he knew about gardening, including the tricks he'd picked up through experience. He had been a horticulturist in Dublin for many years and the breadth of his knowledge was truly impressive. He encouraged her to be adventurous and imaginative with her range of produce and though she'd been nervous at first, the positive feedback from the local chefs had given her the confidence to persevere. Now, many of the vegetables they grew were to order, resulting in a more profitable business.

Glancing at her watch, Erin realized that Marguerite and her brother would be here soon. She quickened her step and hurried back to the house, hoping that she would have time to tidy herself before they got here.

As it turned out it was almost two hours later before the taxi pulled up outside the Gatehouse. The house was quiet as PJ had gone to the pub to meet some friends,

Hazel and Gracie were watching a video, Sandra was in her room, and the two Dublin women had gone into Mullingar for the evening. Erin was tidying the kitchen when she heard the car. Wiping her hands, she rushed out to greet her new guest, glancing in the hall mirror as she passed. She had already changed into a clean, pink T-shirt and denim skirt and her long, golden-brown hair was tied back in a neat ponytail.

She opened the door and watched as Marguerite emerged from the car. 'Hi!' she said, injecting enthusiasm into her voice, but her smile faded as she saw the pinched expression on her friend's pale face.

'Hello, Erin. Sorry we're late.'

'No problem. Was it the traffic on the N4? It's always terrible on a Friday . . .'

She trailed off as Sebastian Gray got out of the car. She stared. Could this really be the same man? She would never have recognized him had they just met in the street. He looked thin and frail; his shoulders were rounded and slumped. His hair was cut close to his head like a convict's, and he had large, dark circles under bloodshot eyes. Erin wondered if he was on drugs. She didn't like the idea of having a drug addict under her roof but she couldn't renege on her promise now.

'Sebastian, you remember Erin Joyce?' Marguerite addressed him like a parent encouraging a shy child.

He lifted his head and looked blankly at Erin. 'Hi.'

She thought of the last time she'd met him and how

his eyes had sparkled and his whole persona had oozed charisma. 'Hello, Sebastian, good to see you again. Come on in and I'll make some coffee.'

He didn't reply.

'He's had a long trip and didn't get much sleep,' Marguerite said apologetically.

'Then I'll show you straight to your room.' Erin led them down the path. 'I've put you in the cabin. It's like a self-contained apartment but, of course, you're still welcome to use the facilities in the main house. Breakfast is served in the dining room between eight and ten.'

'But this is your apartment,' Marguerite hissed. 'I never expected you to give up your own bed, Erin.'

'It's fine, really. Sebastian will get more privacy and peace this way.' Erin smiled and opened the door, standing back to let them pass.

'Oh, this is perfect.' Marguerite put down the suitcase and waved at the view of the lough. 'Isn't it lovely, Sebastian?'

He looked out of the window, his face expression-less, and Erin wondered if he even knew where he was.

Marguerite's smile was strained. 'Thank you, Erin. I'll get Sebastian settled in and then come—'

'No. You go, Marguerite. I need some sleep.' Sebastian turned away and walked towards the bed-room.

'Are you sure? I could unpack for you.'

'I'll be fine.'

'Okay, then. Come over for some dinner later.'

Sebastian just gave a non-committal shrug and closed the door on them.

'I'm sorry about that,' Marguerite murmured as they left the cabin and went back to the house.

'Don't worry. Is he okay?'

Marguerite threw up her hands. 'Does he look it?'

Erin put an arm around her friend's shoulders. 'Let's get you some coffee.'

'He's hardly said two words since I picked him up at the airport.' They were sitting on the kitchen step and Marguerite was taking long drags on a cigarette. 'I asked him what had happened but he doesn't answer.'

'He *is* English: stiff upper lip and all that.'

'He's half French,' Marguerite reminded her. 'He's just not right, Erin. You can see that.'

Erin nodded. She looked at her troubled friend and then decided that it was best to be straight. 'Could he be on drugs?' she asked.

Marguerite gave a tired shrug. 'He's an actor and lives in Hollywood so I suppose it's a possibility. Oh, Erin, I am so worried. Perhaps I should call a doctor.'

'Let's wait and see how he is when he wakes up. Jet lag messes around with your head and body clock, even when you're in the whole of your health.'

'Whole of your health – such a funny phrase,'

Marguerite said with a wan smile. 'But you are right. I will wait. And let Mark talk to him too and see what he thinks.'

'Good idea.'

'Will you join us for dinner?'

Erin couldn't imagine anything worse. 'I don't think that's a good idea. Sebastian doesn't seem in the mood for company. Maybe in a few days, when he's settled in . . .'

Marguerite nodded. 'Of course you are right. I suppose I am just looking for moral support.'

'You have Mark. Try not to worry. I'm sure everything will be fine.' Erin patted her hand and went to get them more coffee. She hoped that she sounded more convincing than she felt. She had been taken aback by Sebastian's appearance but was now more concerned by his lethargy. He was like a different man. She carried the mugs back outside and sat down carefully.

'He's so thin and gaunt and lifeless,' Marguerite said, echoing her thoughts. She took her mug and turned it round and round between long fingers. 'There is nothing in his eyes, Erin. Did you notice? They are dead.'

Erin had noticed. She shivered. 'Didn't he tell you anything at all?'

'When he came into the arrivals hall he just hugged and thanked me and said that he'd have cracked up if he'd stayed in LA.' Marguerite's gaze drifted to the hedge that screened the cabin from them. 'Perhaps he already has.'

'Of course he hasn't,' Erin retorted. 'He'll be fine after a couple of weeks in Dunbarra.'

'I hope no one recognizes and pesters him,' Marguerite fretted.

Erin thought it was unlikely that anyone would think this shell of a man was the assured and handsome Sebastian Gray, but she didn't think that was what her friend needed to hear. 'If anyone recognizes him they will take great pleasure in pretending they don't,' she said instead. 'It's the Irish way.'

Marguerite laughed at that. 'So it is.'

'Just take each day as it comes,' Erin advised.

'I don't suppose I have much choice.'

Chapter Four

'And he wins again!' Ronan tossed the squash racket into a corner, mopped his brow with a towel and took a long drink from his water bottle.

'I let you win,' Mark assured him, breathless, a sheen of sweat on his broad brow.

'Sure, you did.' Ronan laughed, patting his friend's ample stomach before leading the way back towards the changing rooms. 'You need to get back in shape.'

'I'm in great shape,' Mark retorted with a grin. 'You just got lucky.'

'Yeah, lucky, that's me.' Ronan said grimly and stepped into the shower.

'You're really worried about the farm, aren't you?' Mark said as they were dressing.

'I've had better years, Mark,' Ronan admitted. 'I'm under a lot of pressure from the retailers to cut my prices but I have wages to pay and feed to buy. I may have to let at least one person go.'

'That bad?' Mark looked at him in concern. Ronan had only five staff, all local people, and making someone redundant would send a shock wave through the small community of Dunbarra.

'So my accountant says, and we're not even sure that will be enough. He seems to think that people won't be able to afford the luxury of buying organic eggs.' He took the towel and roughly dried his short, thick crop of blond hair.

'He's wrong. People will put their health first,' Mark said, ever the optimist.

'Yeah, sure they will,' Ronan said without conviction as he zipped up his bag and slung it over his shoulder. 'How about a quick pint?'

Mark sighed. 'Better not. I've a six o'clock start in the morning.'

'Come on, then, I'll drop you home and say hello to Marguerite. Maybe Erin will be there.'

Mark patted half-heartedly at his unruly, fiery mane before following Ronan outside. 'She won't be. She hasn't come over since Sebastian arrived. I can't say I blame her. It must be hard enough living with the guy without seeing him during her time off too.'

'So how is your brother-in-law?' Ronan frowned at Mark across the bonnet of the jeep. 'Or is that half-brother-in-law?'

'No idea, but either way he's a right misery guts. We don't see much of him but, when we do, he just hangs around the place saying little or nothing and staring into space. It gives me the creeps, to be honest.'

Ronan started the jeep and guided it out through the narrow lane and on to the main road. 'Is he all there, do you think?' He tapped the side of his head.

Mark sighed. 'That's the million-dollar question. He's changed so much. He used to be very entertaining and charming, although he did tend to overwhelm people.'

'He certainly doesn't do that any more.' From what Erin had told him, Sebastian Gray was a silent, brooding and gloomy presence.

'No,' Mark agreed. 'Still, at least he's not holed up in the room all the time. Erin says he goes out walking a lot, at all hours of the day and night.'

'Why don't you take him fishing?' Ronan suggested. 'The change might do him good.'

Mark turned startled eyes on him. 'You're suggesting I take an unhinged man out on to the lough? Have you taken leave of your senses?'

Ronan laughed. 'Well, when you put it like that maybe it's not such a good idea.'

'Do you think Erin is coping with him okay?' Mark asked. 'Marguerite's feeling very guilty for foisting him on her but, honestly, Ronan, we had no idea he was in such a bad way.'

'She knows that and she's fine,' Ronan said, although this wasn't entirely true. Erin had been a bag of nerves since her infamous guest had arrived. 'Any idea how long he plans to stay?' he added lightly.

Mark shook his head. 'I'm afraid not, but if Erin

wants her room back I'm sure we can find somewhere else . . .'

'Hey, it's nothing to do with me, Mark,' Ronan assured him as he guided the jeep into Dijon's car park.

Mark shot him a curious look. 'You're a strange pair, do you know that?'

'What's that supposed to mean?' Ronan protested but he was smiling.

'You've been dating for – what, two or three years? – and anyone can see that you're perfect for each other. Would you not propose to the woman and have done with it?'

'How did a beautiful woman like Marguerite end up with a blunt, tactless eejit like you?'

'You know I'm right,' Mark said, unabashed. 'You're pushing forty, man.'

Ronan put self-conscious fingers up to his greying sideburns. 'Excuse me, I won't be thirty-nine for another six months.'

Mark stopped as they reached the door of the restaurant. 'Stop avoiding the question. Are you going to ask her, or what?'

'What makes you think I haven't already?' Ronan replied with a sad smile.

'Did you know that Ronan had proposed to Erin and she'd refused him?' Mark asked his wife later as they got ready for bed.

Marguerite, who was sitting at the dressing table, met his eyes in the mirror. 'When did he tell you that?'

'So you knew! My God, woman, you tell me nothing.' Mark climbed into bed, shaking his head in disgust.

'I'm sorry, *chéri*, but she told me in confidence.'

'But why did she turn him down?'

Marguerite went back to massaging cream into her face and neck. 'I don't really know.'

'You do but you're not telling me.' He sighed and plumped up the pillows under his head. 'That's okay. I don't want to know anyway but she needs her head examined. Ronan's a good man and he's mad about her.'

'What difference does it make? He doesn't have to put a ring on her finger for them to be a couple.' Marguerite climbed into bed beside him and planted a kiss on his chest.

He put his arm around her and pulled her close. 'He's missing out on this, that's what difference it makes.'

'Did Ronan say anything about Sebastian?' Marguerite asked.

'What do you mean?'

She frowned. 'I don't know, but I don't think Erin is too happy about having him stay. I've hardly seen her since he got here. And when I call she seems . . . guarded.'

'She's probably just busy. She has a full house at the

moment, doesn't she? Ronan says he hasn't seen much of her either.' He closed his eyes and yawned.

Marguerite trailed feather-light kisses down his stomach. 'Oh, poor darling, are you very sleepy?'

Eyes still closed, Mark smiled and pulled her closer. 'Not any more.'

'You're good.'

Hazel looked up, startled to find Erin's new, reclusive guest looking over her shoulder. He'd been here almost two weeks but this was the first time he'd talked to her. Gracie moved closer to her mother and Hazel rested a reassuring hand on her head. 'Thanks.'

He nodded and then fixed his gaze on the water. It was a grey day and the clouds in the distance looked dark and menacing. The water was like glass. 'It's cool here,' he said.

'Yes.' Hazel handed her daughter a sketchbook and pencil and Gracie settled down at her feet to draw.

'Do you sell your work?' he asked, looking back down at the canvas.

She pulled a face. 'I wish.'

'I'll buy it.'

Hazel's eyes narrowed in suspicion. 'Pardon?'

'I said I'll buy it.'

'You haven't even asked me how much.'

He shrugged. 'How much?'

She stared at him. 'I'm not sure. It's not even finished yet . . .'

'There's no rush. I'll be around for a while.' He turned away and strode on down the track, hands deep in his pockets and his head down.

What a weird guy, Hazel thought. She touched her daughter's cheek. 'You okay, Gracie?'

Gracie nodded but kept drawing. Hazel's eyes returned to the canvas in front of her. It was exciting to think that it might be as good as sold, although she was afraid to get her hopes up. She knew nothing about this man other than he was a fellow guest. He was handsome, but he did seem very slightly unhinged. He was hurt or damaged, she could tell. There was a haunted look in his dark eyes and he didn't seem comfortable in his own skin. Hazel wondered if he could even afford to buy her painting. She could easily charge two hundred euros for a canvas this size, two-fifty if he wanted it framed, but if he could afford that he'd probably forget that he'd made the offer. She got the impression that by tomorrow he'd have forgotten he'd even talked to her, he had that vague, distracted air about him. It was best if she assumed that he wouldn't buy the painting. But Hazel couldn't help herself, she was already spending the money. She could take Gracie into Mullingar for the new shoes she so badly needed. They might even visit the cinema . . .

Gracie was having her nap later that afternoon and Hazel was reading when her landlady knocked with clean towels. Hazel stepped out into the hallway and smiled. 'Thanks very much.'

'No problem. Anything else you need?'

'No. Though I was wondering . . .'

'Yes?'

'Do you know anything about the guy staying in the apartment at the back of the house?'

Erin visibly stiffened. 'Why?'

'He expressed an interest in buying one of my paintings. I wasn't sure if I should take him seriously or not.'

Erin was looking at her now, her expression a mixture of curiosity and surprise. 'I didn't realize you'd met.'

'We haven't really. He just came up behind me when I was working this morning and said he liked the painting.'

Erin shrugged. 'I'm sure he wouldn't have said it if he didn't mean it, but he could easily afford it, if that's what you're asking.'

'Okay, thanks, Erin.' Hazel went back into her room and sat down in the chair by the window. That had been odd. If this man was a stranger, like Erin had implied, why had she been so cagey? Who was this mystery man and why had Erin Joyce been so obviously ill at ease discussing him? Perhaps PJ might know. He seemed to know everything and everyone.

*

As it turned out she didn't even have to ask. It was PJ who brought up the subject the following day and in rather a strange way too. She and Gracie were in the garden sharing their picnic of cheese rolls and scones with him, when Sebastian emerged from the cabin and walked right past them without even saying hello. Gracie had immediately sidled closer to PJ.

He snorted. 'I won't disagree with ye, darling.'

'What do you mean? Who is he, PJ?' Hazel blurted out before she could stop herself.

'His name is Gray. Apparently he needs a break from life.'

She watched PJ with interest. 'You don't like him.'

'I don't know him,' he admitted.

'But you don't like him,' Hazel repeated.

The man sighed. 'He doesn't belong here and it's not right that Erin's given him her room.'

'I didn't realize,' Hazel said. She had never given much thought as to where Erin lived. She hadn't asked and Erin certainly hadn't volunteered the information. Each day she greeted them with an enormous tasty breakfast, the weather forecast and news of any local events. Then she got on with her chores and left them to their own devices.

PJ dusted off his hands and stood up. 'Well, young Gracie. Shall we go and do a bit of work?'

'You don't have to look after her—' Hazel started.

'Ah, sure, she looks after me,' he said, his face creasing

into a smile as the little girl put her hand in his.

'Thanks, PJ. Bye, sweetie. Be good.'

Erin was washing the porch and front step when Sebastian breezed by and headed down the drive. She opened her mouth to call out to him, but he seemed oblivious to her so she closed it again.

'He's a strange one, isn't he?'

She looked up to see Sandra standing in the doorway, staring after him.

'I wonder what he's hiding.'

Erin squeezed out a cloth and dragged it across the tiles. 'What makes you think he's hiding something?'

'He's a man, isn't he?' Sandra's mouth twisted into a bitter smile. 'He looks vaguely familiar. I feel I know him from somewhere.'

Erin put a bit more elbow grease into her work and said nothing.

'Attractive, though,' Sandra continued. 'Those dark, smouldering good looks do it for me every time. If I was five years younger – okay, maybe ten . . .'

Erin laughed and stood up.

'About the right age for you, though.' Sandra eyed her appraisingly.

'I'm not interested.'

'No, I don't suppose you are. You've got that dishy farmer to keep you happy, haven't you? He's a big man; I've always loved big men.' Erin stared and Sandra laughed. 'Sorry for being so inquisitive, but I don't have much else to do so studying the locals has become a bit of a hobby. Ronan Masterson is quite a catch. There aren't exactly many eligible men in Dunbarra' – she pronounced it Doone-barra – 'although the guy with the boat is quite easy on the eye.'

'He's married,' Erin said, worried by the calculating look in the woman's eye. It looked as if Sandra was not only getting over Jerry's defection; she was in the market for a replacement.

'To the talented and lovely Marguerite.' Sandra sighed. 'Yeah, pity.'

Dear God, Erin thought, does she know everything about everybody?

Sandra seemed to read her mind. 'Paddy Burke is a great baker and an even better talker.'

Erin smiled, picked up her bucket and started back towards the kitchen.

'I could do with some towels,' Sandra called after her. 'And I think you need to get the plumbing checked. The water wasn't very warm this morning. I couldn't have my bath.'

Erin bit her lip and then turned to offer an apologetic smile. 'No, the plumbing is very old and unreliable. If you want a bath, you have more chance if you do it very early, before the other guests get up.'

Sandra's eyes widened in horror. 'You're kidding, right?'

Erin suppressed a grin. 'I'm afraid not. That's why you won't find the Gatehouse in any of the brochures.

We can't offer the standards they demand. And,' she added stiffly, 'our prices do reflect that.'

'Jeez,' Sandra said, going upstairs. 'I only asked for a bath.'

Erin went into the kitchen and banged the bucket down, sloshing water everywhere. 'Damn,' she muttered, wishing Sandra would go home.

Initially Erin had been sympathetic but the woman's many complaints and inordinate interest in everyone else's business was beginning to grate. Erin couldn't believe she knew about Ronan. But then given how much time Sandra spent in Paddy's café, the pub and the restaurant, it wasn't surprising she'd heard some of the local gossip. At least she didn't seem to know who Sebastian actually was, which was something. Erin emptied the bucket into the sink, dried the floor and put on the kettle for a much needed cup of coffee. It was ironic that she'd felt sorry for Sandra and suspicious of Sebastian Gray and it was turning out that the abandoned woman was the difficult customer while Sebastian was proving to be quiet and unobtrusive, no trouble at all. He usually came into breakfast at precisely eight every morning, before the other guests were up and about. He would offer her a weak smile and then eat his food – scrambled eggs and bacon.

What had happened to turn him into this silent shadow? Erin could understand why Marguerite was so distraught. It was hard to watch someone in such despair and feel so useless. Erin felt drawn to him now as she never had when he was here before, and she was uncomfortably aware of how much she'd like to be the one to take the pain from his eyes. But Sebastian wasn't talking to anyone, including his sister. Although he spent some of his evenings at Dijon, he still hadn't divulged the cause of his breakdown. It was driving Marguerite to distraction. At first she'd been delighted when he'd started going out for long walks, seeing it as a sign of progress. Now, when he disappeared off for hours at a time, she was convinced he would be discovered floating in the lough.

Mark, Ronan and Erin were all under orders to keep their eyes peeled and make sure he didn't do anything stupid, but Sebastian just seemed to walk and walk, pausing only to stare out across the water as if searching for answers. He didn't talk to Erin save for the few words they exchanged over breakfast. Marguerite couldn't drag anything out of him. Erin suspected that the only person Sebastian had actually initiated conversation with was Hazel, and she was embarrassed to find herself jealous.

Chapter Five

Ronan looked at his watch, cursed and hurried over to his second-in-command. 'Vincent, I have to go. Can you manage without me?'

'I'll try,' Vincent Hamil said drily and waved him away.

Back at the house, Ronan showered and pulled on clean jeans and a shirt. His hair was still damp when he jumped into the jeep twenty minutes later, but it would have to do. He'd been nagging Erin to take a proper night off for weeks and now, when she'd finally agreed, he was late.

He swung the jeep into the drive and saw Erin sitting on the steps, looking stunning in a beautiful green dress, her hair a glossy, golden-brown curtain around her shoulders. Sebastian Gray stood looking down at her and she was smiling up at him. Ronan pulled up right beside them, sending pebbles scattering. Sebastian turned and stared.

Ronan nodded briefly as he climbed out, then smiled at his girlfriend. 'Sorry, Erin, I was delayed. Ready to go?'

'Yes.' She stood up but she was shooting him filthy looks. 'Ronan, meet Marguerite's brother, Sebastian. Sebastian, this is Ronan Masterson.'

Ronan held out his hand but Sebastian was already turning away. 'Nice to meet you,' he mumbled and started down the path towards the cabin.

'Nutter,' Ronan mumbled as he held the door open for Erin.

'Ronan!'

He climbed in beside her and grinned. 'Well, he is. So what were you two talking about?' he asked, trying to keep his voice light.

'He was just saying how special the light is at this time of the evening.'

Ronan's lips twitched. 'The light?'

'The light,' Erin said, smiling.

'Nutter,' Ronan repeated. 'When's he going home?'

'No idea. Why?'

'I don't like the idea of you having a space cadet like him on the premises. And it's not fair that you had to give up your own home.'

'One, he's not a space cadet, he's Marguerite's rather troubled brother. Two, I have a full house of people to protect me, including PJ and a very athletic German man. Three, you're just fed up because I'm sleeping in a tiny room in the centre of the house and there's no way you can come and visit.'

'One, I love Marguerite but her *half*-brother is nuts,' he insisted. 'Two, I think the world of PJ but I'm not sure he'd afford you much protection, and what's this about your German guest being athletic?'

Erin was laughing now.

'And three, yes I do miss our nice cosy evenings in the cabin. Tonight, you can come back to my place.'

'Oh, Ronan, I'm not sure. I need to be up early to get started on breakfast.'

'I'm a farmer,' he reminded her. 'I get up early too.'

'We'll see,' she prevaricated.

Ronan knew what that meant but he'd persuade her otherwise before the night was over. 'Fair enough,' he said. 'And may I say you are looking particularly stunning tonight.'

Erin smoothed down her dress. 'It's probably too glamorous for dinner in Mullingar but it's been stuck in the wardrobe since I got here, and as it is such a lovely evening . . .'

Ronan put a hand on her thigh. 'Beautiful,' he agreed, searching with his fingers till he found the slit in the skirt and her smooth bare leg underneath. 'Really gorgeous,' he murmured. 'Are you sure you're hungry?'

She laughed and pushed his hand away. 'Starving!'

Twenty minutes later they had ordered their food and were sitting back enjoying a glass of wine.

Erin shot him a guilty look. 'We shouldn't really have any. You're driving and we both have to be up early.'

'Will you lighten up, woman? A half bottle won't hurt. One of these days we must get someone else to do the morning shift and have a real night off.'

Erin closed her eyes. 'Now that would be bliss.'

'We'll do it,' he promised her.

Erin looked at him in disbelief. 'I won't hold my breath.'

'We will,' he insisted. 'Anyway, tell me more about the nutter.'

'Stop calling him that. If Marguerite ever heard you she'd be very upset. She's so worried about him, Ronan.'

'Mark says he just hangs around the place like a bad smell.'

'I wouldn't put it quite like that but I know what he means. The only person he's talked to is Hazel. He said he was interested in buying one of her paintings, so he can't be completely bonkers.'

'She is quite good. She's been with you ages, hasn't she?'

Erin nodded. 'Yes. She keeps extending her stay. She says she finds the scenery inspiring, hasn't painted so much in years.'

'It's the wonderful light in the evening,' Ronan said, straight-faced.

Erin rolled her eyes. 'You're a real comedian.'

'You do realize you have a houseful of people and you don't know when any of them are going home?'

'Not true. Sandra will be leaving on Saturday, the

Dublin girls on Sunday, and I should be able to move into an en-suite room then.'

He wriggled his eyebrows suggestively. 'Does that mean I might be able to sneak up to your room occasionally?'

'If you play your cards right.' She laughed.

Ronan was unconvinced. 'Unless, of course, some other lost soul rolls up on the doorstep in the meantime.'

'That's what I like best about this place,' Erin said. 'People come and then they don't seem to want to leave.'

He smiled. 'A bit like you. Are you glad you stayed?'

'Oh, yes.'

'Is that because of me or Marguerite?' Ronan said, watching her closely.

She held up her hands. 'You've got me.'

It wasn't quite the answer Ronan was looking for but he knew better than to pursue the matter.

Their starters arrived and Erin asked for a jug of water.

Ronan sighed. 'So my evil plan of getting you drunk and having my wicked way with you is foiled again.'

She laughed as she broke up her roll and buttered it. 'Lord, I'm hungry and this fish looks wonderful. Speaking of fish, are you going out on the boat with Mark on Sunday?'

'I'm not sure. He may have a party coming up from Cork for the day and he doesn't know if there'll be room for me too.' Ronan shrugged but he was disappointed. He loved fishing. It was the one thing that made him forget all about the farm for a while, and a day out on the lough, particularly in summer, was a great treat. But Mark couldn't afford to turn business away so that often meant disappointment for Ronan. 'If I can't go out on the boat I might just take the rod up to Lyons Point instead. You could come with me. We could bring a picnic and a bottle of wine and make a day of it.'

She made a face. 'Sorry, not a hope. Laundry to do, beds to make.'

'Just occasionally it would be nice if our time off coincided,' Ronan complained. 'Maybe we should sell up and get more normal jobs.'

'I can't see you at a desk,' she teased.

'Me neither. But I wouldn't mind more sociable hours.'

'Take on more staff and then you can work what hours you like.'

'Take on more? I'll be lucky if I can keep the ones I've got,' Ronan said under his breath.

'Well, I can't really complain. When the season is over I'll have plenty of time to relax.'

'Are you going to stay in Dunbarra for Christmas this year?' He hadn't planned to ask that now, but it was as good a time as any. Every year Erin spent

Christmas in Dublin with her mother, leaving PJ to look after the Gatehouse and Ronan at a loose end. He was a bit put out that she could leave him so easily after they'd been together – sort of – for nearly three years.

'Probably,' she said, her attention on her food.

'I think you must have a secret boyfriend up there, you know that?' As soon as the words were out of his mouth he knew he shouldn't have said them. Her whole attitude changed and he could almost feel the coldness in her eyes.

'I don't have a boyfriend in Dublin or anywhere else,' she said pointedly.

He smiled and touched her hand. 'Glad to hear it. So tell me, what is the attraction?'

She put down her cutlery and looked at him with a mixture of annoyance and frustration. 'Ronan, I hardly see my mother from one end of the year to the other. Don't begrudge me spending Christmas with her.'

'And one of her boyfriends,' he murmured. 'I mean you can't possibly enjoy it; you always come back in a bad mood. If she's not alone, why can't you stay here and have some fun with me instead?'

'Ronan, most people spend Christmas with their family.' She shrugged. 'You do what you have to do.'

He didn't. His parents had assumed he would stay in County Clare and work in the family butcher's but Ronan couldn't wait to leave. He'd grown up over the shop and his childhood memories were tinged with the smell of blood. The idea of spending his adult life in the same environment was completely abhorrent. He wanted to go to college and make his own way in the world. His mother was devastated when he announced this, his father furious. He thought they'd come round when he graduated at the top of his class and got a job in the government food development authority, in their research department. They didn't. After ten years as a civil servant Ronan decided to go into farming but he couldn't face livestock production – the childhood memories were still too painful. And he had never been turned on by crops. It had to be eggs. The organic poultry market had finally taken off in Ireland, but organic eggs were still hard to come by and expensive. Always fond of a challenge, Ronan decided this was the business for him.

He kept in touch with his parents, of course, but he used his business as an excuse for not visiting. They didn't seem too bothered. They had their heir in his little brother, Paul, who had married and provided them with three grandchildren. Ronan, black sheep of the family, was surplus to requirements.

'Ronan?'

He looked up to see Erin studying him. 'Sorry?'

'I was just saying why are you thinking about Christmas, it's months away.'

He shrugged and smiled at her. 'No idea.'

As they walked back to the jeep, his arm around her bare shoulders, Ronan tried to persuade Erin to come home with him. 'I even changed the sheets,' he murmured, kissing the soft skin at the nape of her neck.

She turned in his arms and stretched up on her tiptoes to kiss him fully and thoroughly before pulling back to look at him. 'You are so unimaginative,' she teased.

He frowned. 'I am?'

She pressed her gorgeous body against his. 'You are. We don't really need a bed, do we?'

He smiled slowly. 'So what did you have in mind?'

She kissed the edge of his mouth. 'It's a lovely night and there's a very private little spot just behind the Gatehouse . . .'

'You want to do it outside?' He was surprised at her daring but more than a little turned on.

'It's very secluded,' she assured him, 'and it's late – everyone will be tucked up in bed by now.'

He kissed her hungrily. 'Then what are we waiting for?'

It was the flash of green that caught Sebastian's eye. He was sitting on the bank, smoking, when he saw it in the distance, and then he heard a man's voice followed by a giggle. He smiled slowly as he recognized the woman's voice. Well, well, well. Who'd have thought that his very prim and proper host could be such a naughty girl?

Chapter Six

Erin stared speechless at the distraught woman in front of her. She'd just finished hoovering the dining room – Nora had phoned in reporting some family emergency that prevented her from coming in today – when Sandra had appeared in the doorway and made her request.

'I don't mind if you have to move me to a smaller room,' she was saying now, a desperate look in her eyes, 'but please don't ask me to leave.'

'I'll have to check the bookings,' Erin said, playing for time. 'But this is a really busy period. You know there's a lovely guest house just the other side of the village . . .'

'Oh, no, I want to stay here.' Sandra looked alarmed. 'I can't face strangers, not after everything that's happened.'

Erin nodded, knowing Ronan would tell her she was a complete wimp. 'I'll see what I can do.'

'What choice did I have? She was devastated at the thought of leaving. She's very fragile, you know,' Erin said to PJ later as they worked side by side in the garden.

He chuckled and said nothing.

'What?' Erin sat back on her heels and wiped an arm across her brow.

'She didn't look too fragile in the pub last night when she was making eyes at Paddy Burke.'

Erin gaped at him. 'No! You're mistaken. She just enjoys having a good gossip. It's a great distraction for her.'

'She looked like she was definitely distracting Paddy!' PJ hooted with laughter.

'I can't believe it.' Erin shook her head in disbelief. 'So Paddy's the real reason she wants to stay. But then why wouldn't she agree to move to the other guest house? It's just as close to town and her beloved Paddy and she'd be out of my hair.' Erin returned to her weeding with a vengeance. 'I feel a total eejit now. I'll give her two more weeks and she's out.'

'Two?'

Erin sighed. 'Once I told her she could stay, she paid me in advance – in cash.'

PJ chuckled softly. 'Poor old Paddy won't know what's hit him.'

'Do you think he fancies her?' Erin grinned.

'Are ye joking me? He just likes her because she's as big a gossip as he is.'

'Ain't that the truth?' Erin muttered. 'She seems to know everything about everyone. I think it's the only reason she wants to stay, it's certainly not for the service. I get the feeling our Sandra is used to at least five-star treatment. I've no idea how she ended up in Dunbarra in the first place.'

A couple of hours later it was Marguerite's turn to stare, her knife paused over the chopping board. 'You're letting her stay on? But I thought she was driving you around the corner.'

'She is,' Erin said, not bothering to correct her.

'You are a very kind woman,' Marguerite said, scraping the peppers into a bowl and wiping her hands on her apron.

'No, I'm spineless. You won't believe it, but PJ says Sandra has the hots for Paddy.'

Marguerite looked puzzled. 'The hots?'

'Fancies him,' Erin explained.

'Funny, I thought she had her eye on Sean.'

Erin frowned. 'But he's married.'

'And so he is a safe one to flirt with,' Marguerite said with a smile. 'And you know Sean. He's full of that special Irish charm, and heavy-fisted with the compliments. All women love that, especially the ones that are single and over fifty. She has been hurt and she is lonely. Paddy and Sean make her feel that there is hope, that perhaps she is still attractive.'

'You're probably right, you usually are. And you certainly know more about romance than I do. Anyway, enough about her, how are you doing?'

'Okay. Busy.' she shrugged.

'And Sebastian?'

Marguerite's expression clouded. 'Now I am sure that you know more about that than I do.'

'I'm afraid not.'

'I suppose he talks a little bit more,' Marguerite conceded, 'and seems slightly more interested in his surroundings.'

'I've noticed that too. He's become almost chatty over breakfast. He was asking me this morning about the local wildlife. What?' Erin asked, when her friend burst out laughing.

'Oh, *chérie*, I'm afraid he was teasing you.'

'I don't understand.'

Marguerite wiped her eyes. 'He saw you and Ronan the other night enjoying the – ah, view.'

A flush crept up Erin's neck and into her cheeks as realization dawned. 'He saw us?'

'I think he heard more than he saw,' Marguerite said, her dark eyes blinking mischievously.

'No!' Erin groaned. 'How am I going to face him?'

'For goodness sake, Erin, he lives in Hollywood. I'm sure he's experienced much more *risqué* behaviour.' Her lips twitched. 'But I'm impressed that you are so adventurous. Perhaps there is hope for you two after all.'

Erin scowled. 'Stop, Marguerite, this is not funny.'

'Oh, but it is.'

'I am so embarrassed.' Erin put her head in her hands.

Marguerite sobered. 'I am sorry, Erin, but it cheered me up enormously to hear him tease you in such a way. He sounded like his old self when he told me the story. For the first time I thought that, maybe, he could get better.' Her voice wobbled.

'Of course he'll get better.' Erin reached out and squeezed her hand. 'And if laughing at me helps then I suppose I can live with that.'

Soon afterwards, Erin kissed her friend goodbye and left the restaurant. She still felt mortified that Sebastian had seen her and Ronan rolling around in the grass like a couple of teenagers. And, at the same time, the thought of Sebastian watching them made her heart beat a little faster. That's totally perverted, she told herself. Ronan would probably be horrified if he knew that Sebastian had seen them. But what he didn't know wouldn't hurt him.

As she neared the Gatehouse she saw Sandra hurrying out in rather impractical sandals and a flamboyant red dress. 'Hi Sandra,' she said as they came abreast.

'Hi Erin,' Sandra said, looking up. 'I was miles away. Thinking about Jerry, the lousy schmuck.'

Erin thought of what PJ and Marguerite had told

her about Sandra's antics and had to bite back a smart comment. 'Off into town?' she asked.

Sandra nodded. 'It puts in a couple of hours. And I can go online at the café and talk to my son.'

Erin frowned. 'Paddy's got a computer?'

'Two. It was actually my idea,' Sandra told her. 'There can't be that many locals with access to the internet. It's a great money-spinner.'

'Yes, I suppose it would be,' Erin agreed, wondering why no one had thought of it before. 'Although I'm amazed Paddy agreed. I don't think he even possesses a mobile phone.'

Sandra gave a throaty laugh. 'Oh, we took care of that last week.'

'You're really making your mark on this town, aren't you, Sandra?'

The woman shot her a sharp look and then glanced at her watch. 'Better go.'

'Yes, you don't want to keep Paddy waiting. Have fun,' Erin called after her.

Sandra stopped and looked back. 'Oh, by the way, could you please change my pillows? The ones I have are very lumpy; they're playing havoc with my neck.'

'I'll take care of it straight away,' Erin said through gritted teeth and watched as the woman tottered off on her spindly heels.

'Hello, Erin.'

She spun around, startled as Sebastian Gray

emerged from the bushes. 'Do you have to creep up on people like that?'

'I'm sorry.' He looked completely taken aback and embarrassed, and turned to leave.

Erin grabbed his arm. 'No, Sebastian, wait. I'm sorry. That was very rude.'

'No, I frightened you, I'm sorry.' He looked past her, shifting from foot to foot.

'Are you on your way to Marguerite's?' she asked.

'Not tonight.'

They walked together towards the house and Erin was struck again by how much he'd changed. It was hard to believe that this awkward, nervous man at her side was the ebullient Sebastian Gray. 'What will you do for dinner?' she asked.

He looked at her with a hint of a smile. 'Now you sound just like my sister.'

'Sorry.' She laughed. They walked on in silence for a moment and then she decided to take advantage of his good mood. 'She's worried about you.'

He sighed and nodded. 'I know.'

They stopped at the front steps of the Gatehouse.

'Why the pink door?' he asked.

'The previous owner picked that colour. She was a very grumpy, cantankerous woman and it seemed incongruous that she would choose such a frivolous colour. I couldn't bring myself to change it.' Erin watched his face transform with a smile. He really was incredibly attractive.

'That's nice. And did she name it too?'

Erin was too distracted by his mouth to hear the words. 'Sorry?'

'Did she name it the Gatehouse?'

'Oh, no.' Erin shook her head. 'It's always been called that. This was the original gatehouse to Dunbarra House, which apparently stood up there.' She pointed to the hill in the distance. 'There was a fire at the start of the twentieth century and it was razed to the ground. The Gatehouse was empty for many years after that. Eventually a local entrepreneur bought it and restored and extended it. He sold it to my predecessor, Ivy McDonald. That would have been about twenty years ago now. After her children married and her husband died, Ivy started to take in guests. I don't think she needed the money. She just couldn't stand being alone in the house.'

'I thought she was grumpy and cantankerous,' he said.

'She was,' Erin assured him, smiling. 'But she was still human.'

'So is she dead now too?'

'Nope. She's sunning herself in Florida.'

He nodded. 'Heaven's waiting room. And the market garden?'

'That was all PJ's idea.'

'The old guy?'

She grinned. 'Don't let him hear you call him that.'

'So where do you come in?' Sebastian asked.

'I suppose I was in the right place at the right time,' Erin said. 'She wanted to retire and I'd fallen in love with the place.'

He watched her, his dark eyes showing a spark of interest. 'I'd say there's a lot more to it than that.'

She held his gaze. 'Would you?'

He smiled. 'I'll see you later.'

Erin watched him go and then called after him before she lost her nerve. 'I'm having lasagne for dinner. There's plenty in the pot, if you're interested. PJ had to go out,' she added hurriedly.

'What time?'

She shrugged. 'Eight?'

'See you then,' he said, and disappeared down the path to the cabin.

The phone was ringing when Erin walked into the house and she ran to answer it. 'The Gatehouse.'

'Hi, Erin.'

'Oh, hi, Ronan, how's it going?'

'Great. Can I tempt you down to the pub for a pint and some dinner?'

'Oh, no, Ronan, sorry, not tonight.' She hesitated. 'I've just invited Sebastian to dinner.'

'You did what?'

'Well, when I say dinner, it's only lasagne. PJ was supposed to be staying in but now he's going out and I just bumped into Sebastian and he said he wasn't going up to Marguerite's tonight so I just asked him.' She finally stopped, realizing she was babbling.

'I see,' was Ronan's rather cool reply.

Erin sighed. 'I regretted it the moment the invitation was out of my mouth. It'll probably be hard going.'

'It was kind of you,' he said quietly.

'Well, he is Marguerite's brother. And she's my best friend. Why don't you ask Mark to go to the pub with you? Marguerite's got a full house tonight so he's probably at a loose end.'

'Maybe.'

'Do,' she urged.

He was silent for a moment, and then: 'I have to go into Mullingar in the morning for a few things, want to come?'

'What time?' she asked.

'About ten?'

'Could you make it ten-thirty?'

'Sure.'

'Excellent. See you then. Goodnight, Ronan.'

'Goodnight, Erin.'

She put down the phone and stared at it. Ronan wasn't happy and was it any wonder? She'd probably sounded as guilty as sin. And why, for God's sake? She'd just offered a guest a meal. But she knew, if she was honest with herself, it was more than that. She was fascinated by Sebastian Gray. If he had arrived with a fanfare and been the loud, overbearing man she remembered, she wouldn't have given him the time of day. But his dark, troubled presence in her home was harder to ignore. She had primed herself to dislike the actor and to make it clear that she was unimpressed by his fame. Instead, Erin found herself wanting to comfort him, to drive the haunted look from his eyes, and be the one to make him laugh again.

She shrugged off the ridiculous notion. They weren't Cathy and Heathcliff; Sebastian was just a guest and would be gone soon. But now she'd offered him a meal so she'd better get on with it. She went into the kitchen, turned on the oven and took the pre-pared lasagne from the fridge. She washed some salad leaves, made a dressing and then slid the lasagne into the oven. Realizing that she had another thirty min-utes before Sebastian arrived, Erin went upstairs to change. She picked out a dress to wear and then stared guiltily at it. It was one she'd usually only wear if she was going out to dinner. Shoving it back into her wardrobe, she pulled out a blue, sleeveless top with a mandarin collar and a pair of faded jeans but she still applied a little make-up, and, after only a moment's hesitation, left her mane of golden-brown hair loose around her shoulders.

Once she'd checked the lasagne and laid the table, Erin took an open bottle of wine from the fridge, poured herself a glass and went to sit on the step out-side the back door. The garden stretched out before her and she breathed in the smell of aromatic herbs mixed with the lavender that PJ had planted in pots either side of the door. This truly was the most wonderful place on the planet and it was her home. Erin didn't think she'd ever get used to the fact. She might be greeting a guest, or making a bed, or walking down to Dijon with a basket full of fresh vegetables and it would hit her. She owned the Gatehouse. She was a part of the Dunbarra community. She belonged.

Chapter Seven

'Hi.'

Erin stood up and smiled. 'Come on in. Dinner won't be long. Can I get you a glass of wine?'

'Sure.' Looking decidedly ill at ease, he went outside and lowered himself on to the step.

She poured the last of the bottle into a glass and took it out to him.

'Thanks.' He moved over to make room for her.

Erin sat down, acutely conscious of his shirt brushing her bare arm.

'It's lovely here,' he said. 'It makes me feel almost normal.'

'I'm glad.'

'If only it could be like this all the time.'

'I'm sure it can.'

He said nothing.

She put a hand on his arm. 'If you want to talk . . .'

'Has my sister put you up to this?' Sebastian demanded.

Erin snatched her hand back as if she'd been burned. 'Of course not.'

'I'm sorry.'

'It's okay,' Erin mumbled and stood up. 'I'll just go and check on the food.'

He grabbed her hand and looked up at her, his eyes sad. 'I mean it. I really am sorry.'

'It's okay,' she relented. 'I hate it when people pry too.' She went inside, lifted the lasagne out of the oven and then cut up a baguette. As she was serving up, Sebastian came in.

'Can I do anything to help?'

She nodded towards the rack in the corner. 'You could open another bottle of wine. If you fancy some, that is.' Her eyes met his. 'No pressure.'

'I'm sorry. I should have brought some wine.'

'You didn't know you were coming to dinner until an hour ago,' Erin retorted, losing patience with him.

'Right now you're wondering why you invited me at all, aren't you?' he said, a twinkle in his eye.

'No, right now I'm wondering if you're going to open the wine.'

He laughed aloud this time. 'I'm sorry for being such a lousy dinner companion. Maybe I could treat you to lunch or a meal at Dijon someday to make it up to you.' He made a face. 'On second thoughts, we wouldn't get any peace there. Perhaps the pub?'

'Let's just eat,' she suggested. Sebastian's moods were mercurial and she doubted he'd follow through on his invitation, if indeed he remembered even making it.

'You have quite a good selection,' Sebastian said, looking through the contents of her wine rack.

'Most of them are presents from guests or from your sister,' Erin said as she added dressing to the salad.

'Marguerite has good taste but she is a bit of a snob when it comes to new world wines.'

'She is, isn't she?' Erin laughed.

'But she's not here, so let's live dangerously.' He pulled out a bottle of South African Merlot.

Erin ladled the lasagne on to two plates, sat down and waited as he opened the wine with deft fingers. 'Did you spend much of your life in France?'

'None.' He poured. 'My father thought it best to keep his mistress in a different country.'

'Oh.'

'Try it.'

She took a sip of the wine and nodded. 'Lovely.'

He sat down opposite her and smiled. 'Thank you for this.'

'You're welcome.'

Sebastian tasted the food. 'This is delicious. Yes, my father was a salesman for Renault. He came to England, to Portsmouth, to my mother, four or five times a year. When she first told him she was pregnant he wanted nothing more to do with her. He changed his mind when he found out I was a boy.

Don't get me wrong, he adored Marguerite, but he'd always wanted a son and apparently his wife couldn't have any more children. So he was pleased, even though his son was going to be an English bastard.'

'You sound bitter,' Erin observed.

'No, not at all, I'm just telling it as I see it. I loved my father although he was quite a weak and selfish man. I thought he was perfect when I was small but as I got older I came to see his faults. I also realized that he'd destroyed my mother's life. She spent her days either waiting for him to visit or grieving that he'd left.'

'That's sad. Did you know all along that you had a half-sister?'

'Oh, yes, he talked about her all the time and showed me photographs. I kept asking him to take me to France to meet her or bring her to visit us but he said it wasn't possible.'

'Because his French family didn't know you existed.'

He looked at her, his eyes thoughtful. 'You and Marguerite must be close.'

'We are.'

He continued with the story. 'No, they didn't find out about us until after my father's death. It was rather cruel and spineless of him, don't you think? The first his wife knew of his affair was when she saw that he'd left a third of his estate to my mother and me.'

'Marguerite says her mother was devastated and that she has never really recovered.'

Sebastian sighed. 'And ironically it was the start of the most contented period of *my* mother's life. She was able to be truly independent for the first time. And now she's married to a very gentle, unassuming sort of man, as different from my father as you could get.'

'Is she happy?'

'Very.'

'Do you get to see her much?'

'Yes, she lives in London and I visit her there a couple of times a year. Then she flies to New York to see the children and comes occasionally on to stay with me in LA.'

Erin watched him as he talked. This was the most normal she'd seen him since he came to Dunbarra. There were even moments when she caught a glimpse of the man she'd first met. The confidence and ego were still there, if more subdued.

He glanced up and caught her watching him. 'What?'

Erin flushed. 'I was thinking that you seem much more relaxed tonight. It's nice to see you smile.'

'I don't have much to smile about,' he replied, looking annoyed. 'You just made me forget for a while.'

'Forget what?' she asked and then held up a hand. 'No, don't answer that.'

His expression softened and there was even a hint of a smile in his dark eyes. 'You've been very kind and I'm an ungrateful and obnoxious guest.'

'No, you're not, but . . .'

'Go on.'

'Must you always be so dramatic?'

'I am an actor,' he pointed out.

'So you are,' Erin laughed.

'Or I was.' His eyes darkened again and he gazed moodily into his wine.

'Tell me about your children,' Erin suggested. Surely that was a safe topic?

And yes, his expression changed again. It was like the sun coming out from behind a cloud. 'Jess is nearly nine and so sweet and very pretty,' he told her, a note of pride in his voice. 'And Toby is a very wild seven-year-old.' He gave a rueful shrug. 'A chip off the old block, I suppose.'

'You must miss them.'

There was another flicker of annoyance in his eyes when he answered. 'I do see them quite often.'

Erin laid down her knife and fork and looked at him. 'Look, Sebastian, I'm just trying to make conversation. It's what people do over dinner. Perhaps I should just stick to the weather.'

He held up his hands and rolled his eyes. 'I'm sorry . . .'

'Just don't jump down my throat all the time. I'm not trying to pump you for information. You're my guest and Marguerite's brother. I have no hidden agenda.'

His eyes held hers. 'So do all your guests get this treatment?'

Erin blinked. Was he flirting with her now? It was impossible to keep up with this guy. Perhaps he was on something. 'No, they don't,' she admitted.

'So why me?' Again there was a slight challenge but there was also something else, a definite spark of interest.

Erin felt her pulse quicken although common sense told her to keep her distance, for many reasons. 'Because you're Marguerite's little brother.'

'Oh.'

He looked disappointed and Erin couldn't help smiling. 'And you looked like you could do with a good meal.'

He glanced down at his lean frame. 'I have lost weight. I just forget to eat a lot of the time. It doesn't seem that important any more.'

'You see, there you go again.' She shook her head.

'Excuse me?'

'You make these dramatic remarks and then get annoyed when I react.' She raised a hand as he opened his mouth. 'And don't apologize again.'

He sat back in the chair with his wine and stared beyond her, through the open door, at the garden, still bathed in sunshine. 'It's been a while since I've had a proper conversation with anyone. I'm afraid to talk,' he admitted, his voice so soft Erin had to lean forward to hear him. 'I feel if I say what I'm feeling, if I put it into words, then there will be nowhere to hide. This is a wonderful hiding place. It's so peaceful. Not just Dunbarra but this house, the garden, the water.' He looked back at her, his eyes suddenly crinkling with an unexpected grin. 'The views over the lough are especially beautiful at night, don't you think?'

Erin felt the colour flood her cheeks but she couldn't help smiling. 'I think so.'

'Yes, very beautiful.' His eyes held hers for a moment and then he looked away again. 'And it's nice to be near Marguerite. Our father would be so happy that we'd found each other and had become friends.'

'Who found whom?' Erin asked. Perhaps Marguerite had told her but she couldn't remember.

'I came to France after my father died and we'd been told about the inheritance. That's almost fourteen years ago now. I wanted to meet Marguerite and tell her that I was sorry.'

'It wasn't your fault.'

'I know but I thought it must be very hard to suddenly find out that you're not an only child. We had to meet in secret, of course. To this day Marguerite's mother won't even acknowledge that my mother or I exist.'

'That's understandable,' Erin said, in case he was even thinking of criticizing Marguerite or her mother.

He nodded. 'Of course. But I'm delighted Marguerite didn't feel that way. It wasn't easy that first time we met but both of us were curious to find out about our father's other life. After that we kept in touch, through cards and emails. I got married, she got married, the children came along. We talked about getting together but, of course, we didn't.' His expression darkened. 'And then Jess got sick, meningitis. I thought we were going to lose her. I was sick with worry, as was Vanessa, my ex-wife. Jess made a complete recovery but it was after a very anxious few weeks.' He smiled. 'Marguerite called every day. She even offered to come to New York to look after Toby or take him home with her so that we could spend all of our time with Jess.'

'That doesn't surprise me. Marguerite has a huge heart.'

'Yes. So, after that, we grew closer and though we don't see each other that often, she knows she has only to pick up the phone if she needs me.' He gave a humourless laugh. 'Except it seems that I'm the one who needs her.'

Erin put her hand over his. 'Things will work out.'

'You think so?' Sebastian stood up. 'I should go. Thanks for dinner.'

'No problem. I'd better get back to work anyway. I have to water the garden.'

'I don't know how you do it all. Your life makes mine seem so superficial.'

'We're not that different. We both look after people. I take care of their basic physical needs and you distract them and give them something to dream about.'

He put a hand on her bare arm and bent his head to kiss her cheek. 'You're a lovely lady, Erin.'

She kissed him back, conscious of the roughness of his unshaven cheek under her lips. When he pulled back, he didn't take away his hand. 'I really would like to buy you that lunch or dinner.'

'There's no need . . .'

'But I'd like to,' he said, an urgent look in his eyes. 'I don't suppose there are many restaurants in these remote parts?'

'There's a lovely one, White's, on the far side of the lake. It's quite expensive and formal, though.' Erin trailed off, her eyes drifting to his creased T-shirt and ragged jeans.

'I promise to dress appropriately,' he teased, obviously amused. 'I'll even shave – for you.'

Erin felt herself redden again. 'I'm honoured,' she said and moved away from him towards the door.

'So, when? Tomorrow night?'

She hesitated. Going out to dinner with Sebastian would draw a lot of comment and speculation and Ronan would not be impressed at all. 'Lunch would suit me better, but are you sure it's a good idea? What if someone recognizes you?'

'Don't worry about it.'

'But—'

'Do we need to book?'

'Probably not .'

'Great. See you out front at twelve-thirty.'

She smiled. 'Okay, then.'

He touched her cheek. 'I'll look forward to it.'

Erin stood for a moment after he was gone and put a hand to her cheek. What a strange evening. She wasn't sure what to make of Sebastian; he seemed a mass of contradictions. One minute she felt full of sympathy for him, for there was obviously a huge weight on his shoulders. The next she wanted to scream at him for his irritability and brusque manner. But throughout their meal, however unpredictable his mood, she couldn't deny that she found him hugely attractive. It was a bad idea to have lunch with him. What on earth would Ronan say? Of course he didn't need to know. And then she remembered their arrangement. They were going into Mullingar together at ten-thirty. There was no way she would get back in time. She'd have to cancel lunch, which was probably just as well.

Chapter Eight

Service was over and Marguerite was cleaning up.

Mark came up behind her, placed his huge hands on her shoulders and started to knead the base of her neck with his thumbs.

Marguerite moaned and leaned back against him. 'Oh, that feels good.'

'Do you realize it's our anniversary soon?' he murmured, nuzzling into her hair. 'We should do something.'

'Twelve years!' Marguerite sighed. 'And it has gone so quickly.'

'You were the most beautiful bride,' he said turning her round to face him.

'It's easy to be beautiful when you're twenty-five.'

'You're just as beautiful now. In fact, no, you are more beautiful.'

'And you, *mon cher*, need glasses.'

'I mean it,' he assured her. 'But you also look tired. Come to bed.'

'I need to finish up here first.'

'It can wait until morning and then Sean can help you. He has too easy a time of it by half.'

'He's not getting any younger,' Marguerite protested.

'He's well able to reel in a ten-pound fish or sink a few pints in the pub,' Mark retorted. 'Come to bed.'

Marguerite smiled and took off her apron. 'Okay, then. It's been a long night.'

'You need more help in the kitchen.'

'Maybe.' Marguerite was too tired to argue. Mark was right but she hated the thought of sharing her kitchen. She had her own peculiar ways and the thought of teaching them to someone – *alors*! Most of her recipes weren't even written down. She had learned to cook alongside her mother and grand-mother and everything they'd taught her was in her head. And anyhow, how did you teach someone to use just the nose to recognize when a joint of lamb is ready? To taste a dish and realize immediately what ingredient would turn it from a plain meal into a splendid one? How did you teach someone a genuine love of good food or a passion for perfection? Marguerite wasn't sure it was possible.

'Are you coming?' Mark had locked up and was leaning in the doorway waiting for her.

Marguerite flicked off the lights and followed him up to the flat.

'Coffee?' Mark asked as she collapsed on to the sofa and kicked off her shoes.

'No, but some hot chocolate would be nice.'

'Was Sebastian in tonight?' Mark asked as he poured milk into a saucepan. He had been out on the boat and had only just returned as the restaurant was closing.

Marguerite frowned. 'No. I called but he said he was busy. Busy.' She made a face and pulled her feet up underneath her. 'Doing what, please tell me?'

Mark smiled. 'He does seem a lot better, though.'

'You think?'

'Sure.'

'But he still won't talk to me, Mark.'

'He'll talk when he's ready.'

'But it's been weeks. I thought he'd have gone home by now. I'm sure Erin did too.' She sighed.

'Has she said something?' Mark said as he poured the steaming chocolate into two mugs and set them carefully on the small table in front of the sofa.

Marguerite leaned forward, dipped a finger in her mug and sucked it. 'Erin is not saying much about anything.'

'Maybe there's nothing to say.'

'She must have some sense of how he is by now.'

He smiled. 'Then stop fretting and ask her.'

Marguerite looked at him for a moment and nodded. 'I will.'

Hazel stood up slowly and winced. While she worked she never noticed the discomfort of sitting hunched over the easel. But, when she stopped, she quickly became aware of the dull ache that crept through her body. She did some stretching and groaned as her joints creaked in protest. It wasn't surprising really. She had been working at a frenetic pace. But though she felt exhausted she was also exhilarated. She looked at the canvas with pride. It had been worth it. She'd crept out of her room at first light this morning, careful not to disturb Gracie, and gone out to the garden. She had gasped at the scene before her. The water was grey, a low mist hanging over it. The only hint of dawn was a line of orange along the horizon, and so the fields and hedgerows were a myriad of muted browns and greys. They exuded a feeling of peace and serenity that was almost tangible.

'You've excelled yourself.'

She jumped at the voice in her ear. It was Sebastian Gray and he was staring in admiration at the painting.

'I'm sorry, did I give you a fright?' He gave a self-deprecatory smile. 'I seem to do that a lot.'

She smiled. 'It's okay. I just thought everyone was still in bed.'

He shrugged. 'I don't sleep much. My mother says it's the sign of a guilty conscience. But then that's because she thinks in my line of work I probably have a lot to feel guilty about.'

Hazel smiled and then set about cleaning her brushes. 'What do you do?'

Sebastian looked taken aback. 'I'm an actor.'

'Wow, really? How exciting. I'm sorry, are you very famous?' she said, realizing he wasn't impressed that she hadn't recognized him. 'I don't watch much TV and the only movies I see are animated ones.'

He laughed. 'You're probably better off. Everything I've been in lately has been violent or bordering on pornographic. Anyway, my sister tells me that I am virtually unrecognizable at the moment.' He put a self-conscious hand to the stubble on his chin.

'Is Erin your sister?'

'No!' He seemed amused at the idea. 'Marguerite Hayes, the lady who runs Dijon. Well, she's my half-sister. We have different mothers.' He put out a hand. 'I'm sorry, I never even introduced myself properly. Sebastian Gray.'

'I know. It was on the cheque.'

'Of course!' His smile was pained. 'Now I'm truly crushed. You knew my name and still didn't recognize me.'

'Like I said, I don't get out much,' Hazel said, feeling terrible.

'I'm joking. It's a pleasant change to be around someone so untouched by the world of movies. Now, are you going to tell me who you are? You're not some hugely famous artist, are you?'

She laughed. 'Hazel Patterson, and no, I'm no one important.'

'Never say that.' He told her and, looking past her at the painting, he added, 'And you may not be famous but if you keep producing art like this then it's only a matter of time. You've captured the atmosphere of this place perfectly.'

She glowed at his praise. 'Do you really think so?'

'Without a doubt.'

'Thank you, that means so much to me.'

'I think I'm going to have to buy this one too. Or is it a commission?'

'No, it's for sale,' Hazel whispered, feeling faint.

'You seem to be working very hard. Every time I look out of my window, or go for a walk, there you are. Have you an exhibition coming up?'

If only, Hazel thought. 'No. I haven't painted in years so I'm just trying to get back in the saddle, I suppose.'

'Why did you stop?'

She looked away from the intensity of his gaze. 'I'm not sure.'

He smiled and backed off immediately. 'Well, I must go. Let me know how much,' he called over his shoulder.

'Pardon?'

He stopped and looked back at her. 'The painting? Have a think about the price and let me know.'

'Oh, okay, thanks. I'll drop a note through your door.'

He waved a hand in acknowledgement and disappeared down the path towards the lough.

Hazel smiled happily as she put away her things, slung the large, paint-stained bag over her shoulder, tucked the easel under her arm and carried the wet canvas carefully back to the house.

As she let herself in the front door, the smell of breakfast hit her nostrils and her tummy rumbled. This economizing was getting out of hand. She had only bought chips for Gracie's supper last night, taking barely a handful for herself. No wonder she felt slightly dizzy and light-headed. If she sold Sebastian Gray this painting, though, it would keep them going for another while. But not long. Hazel had done her best to conceal the fact that her funds were limited but knew that she hadn't succeeded. PJ always treated her and Gracie to a pastry or an ice cream if he met them in Dunbarra and Erin's breakfasts were increasing in size every day. Hazel felt embarrassed and ashamed of her impoverished status but it was only temporary. She would find someone to sell her paintings and at the rate she was producing canvases she would be able to buy Gracie anything she wanted. Perhaps Sebastian Gray would buy them all. Strange man.

What was a famous, attractive and obviously troubled actor doing hanging around here? Hiding, perhaps. She could relate to that. And though he always seemed miserable, this morning he had been almost animated, but he had definitely been irked that she didn't know who he was.

Hazel let herself quietly into the bedroom and set the easel down by the window. She studied the canvas with a critical eye. It was unquestionably her best yet and the fact filled her with excitement. Turning to the bed, her eyes softened as she looked at Gracie's little heart-shaped face; it was flushed with sleep, the pink lips parted slightly. She was so incredibly beautiful and precious. 'It's all for you,' she whispered. 'I'll never let you go.'

Erin was scrambling eggs when she heard the door of the dining room open. Eight o'clock precisely, it had to be Sebastian. She'd go straight out there, take his order and tell him that their lunch date was off. She didn't want to and had been sorely tempted to phone Ronan to cancel the trip into Mullingar, but common sense prevailed. Ronan was a constant in her life; a warm, rich part of an otherwise almost humdrum existence. Sebastian, on the other hand, was an exciting interlude, but no more. He'd recover from whatever trauma had brought him here and then he would return to his own life. And yet – she stared into space as she stirred the eggs – just once wasn't she entitled to a little excitement? She was thirty-one, single and living in the middle of nowhere. It was unlikely that she'd ever get invited out by another attractive famous man. Would it be so wrong of her to go? It was only lunch. There was an undeniable attraction between them. She hadn't imagined the interest in his eyes. But she knew he was only looking for temporary distraction and she wasn't willing to provide that. Of course she wasn't. So what harm was there in going out for a meal together? Ronan was the answer to that question. Ronan wouldn't see it as harmless. Ronan knew her better than that. She couldn't do it, not without hurting him.

'Hello? Anyone home?' Sebastian called from the dining room.

Erin pulled the pan off the heat, picked up the coffee pot and hurried to greet him. 'Sorry, I'm running a bit late this morning. Your usual?'

He nodded and smiled. 'Please. Are we still on for lunch today?'

Erin hesitated. Here was the perfect opportunity to make an excuse, apologize and cancel the date. Instead she smiled and poured him some coffee. 'Sure.'

Ronan took it quite well really. But then why wouldn't he? She hadn't told him the truth. She'd just said that something had come up and she'd fill him in later. Ronan, used to things 'coming up' in both their lives, said that was fine. Erin hummed as she made breakfast. Full fry-up for PJ – a weekly treat. Poached eggs on toast for Hazel. Cereal and honey on fresh rolls for Gracie. Grilled bacon and tomato for Sandra, or omelette, or just fruit – depending on her mood. The latest guests, a young couple from Liverpool, were having the works. They came down at the last minute so Erin would have been late if she had been going into Mullingar with Ronan. That made her feel slightly better. He hated to be kept waiting. He was an organized man who never wasted time. He even managed to make Erin feel disorganized. If he was stuck in traffic, he'd make a phone call. If he was going into town, he'd have a list. And he would have checked out prices and availability online beforehand. It was why his business was a success. Organic farming was an expensive and precise science. Paying too much for feed or fertilizer added hugely to costs. As for recycling, Erin sometimes felt Ronan had invented it. And when he and PJ got together, it was slightly scary how often compost was a favourite topic of conversation.

The dining room emptied except for the loving couple feeding each other toast. Erin cleared the tables around them with gusto, hoping they'd get the hint. She wanted to get all her chores done this morning. Just in case she was late back, which she wouldn't be. But . . . just in case.

Chapter Nine

'Will I do?'

Erin had emerged from the Gatehouse to find Sebastian waiting for her. His dark hair had grown and didn't look as severe, and his cheeks had filled out a little. But it was his clothes that really took Erin's breath away. He was wearing a simple sand-coloured linen suit, a white, open-necked shirt and beautiful shoes. And he was clean-shaven. He looked as if he'd just stepped out of *The Great Gatsby*.

'I thought you'd be in disguise,' she teased him.

He held up a finger then produced a pair of horn-rimmed glasses and adopted a foppish pose.

Erin clapped her hands, laughing. 'Very impressive.'

'You look lovely,' he said, tucking away the glasses.

'Thanks.' Erin had dithered ridiculously over what to wear. She had finally settled on a white lacy top and matching skirt, with wedge sandals. The girls Sebastian usually dated probably spent more on their make-up than she had on her whole outfit, but then, she reminded herself, this wasn't a date.

At first Erin pretended she hadn't noticed the fidgeting and sighs but she couldn't ignore them any longer. His earlier bonhomie had given way to silence as soon as they sat down, and he was looking completely miserable again. He hadn't needed to wear the spectacles. The restaurant was deserted except for some customers of a vintage who wouldn't recognize Sebastian even if there was a neon sign over his head. Perhaps that was the problem. Maybe he was actually hoping to be recognized. Erin put down her menu.

His eyes met hers and he sighed again, shaking his head. 'I'm so sorry, Erin. I promised myself today would be different. I was so looking forward to our lunch but—'

'If you want to go, that's perfectly fine. I understand.' Her voice was sharper than she intended but she just felt so disappointed.

'Do you?'

'You're obviously going through a difficult time at the moment.'

He gave a harsh laugh that drew some looks. 'Difficult. You have no idea.'

She swallowed hard and forced a smile. 'Then let's go.'

'No!' He clenched his fists, closed his eyes for a

moment and then sat up straighter in his chair. 'I can do this.'

'It's not a test, Sebastian.'

'No, it's just lunch and we're going to enjoy it. I can't keep hiding away in the Gatehouse, lovely as it is. I have to surface sometime. And I can't think of a better time or better company. Let's order.'

His smile was full-on but Erin wasn't convinced. 'Are you sure?'

'I'm sure. Bring your best champagne,' he called to the waiter who'd been hovering nearby, pretending not to listen.

'Oh, I don't think so,' Erin said, alarmed by the flamboyant gesture.

'Please?' There was a faintly desperate look in his eye. 'Shouldn't I celebrate my coming out? This suit alone demands champagne, never mind your pretty dress.'

Erin smiled. 'Okay, then.' The waiter left and Erin picked up her menu again. 'So have you seen anything you fancy?'

'I have.'

She looked up to see his eyes twinkling back at her. 'Oh, please!'

'I'm sorry, was that very corny?'

'Absolutely,' she said but she loved the insecurity in his eyes. It made him much more attractive than the brash, conceited man she'd first met.

'I'm a little out of practice,' he admitted. 'It's a long time since I took a beautiful woman out.'

'I find that hard to believe.' She dragged her eyes from his and looked down at the menu. 'If you like fish, I'd recommend the trout. It will have been caught in the lough. The venison is also from a local producer.'

He picked up his menu. 'And do you provide the vegetables?'

'No. They order some produce off me occasionally but I can't provide the quantities they need on a regular basis.'

'Why don't you expand? You have the space.'

'Now you sound like your sister.'

He grinned. 'We're an interfering family, I'm afraid.'

She laughed, pleased that he'd relaxed again. 'I think I'll have the venison steak.'

'That sounds good, although I am tempted by the trout.'

'If you like, we could share the fish platter starter and then both have the venison,' Erin suggested.

'That's an excellent idea.' He closed the menu and picked up the wine list. 'Now let's find something fruity to go with venison.'

'I'm not having wine and champagne. I've a guest house to run,' Erin said, amused but irked that he thought she could just write off the whole day for him.

'I'm annoying you now,' Sebastian said, his eyes sharp.

'No, of course you're not.' She gave a helpless shrug. 'We're just from different worlds.'

He looked at her in dismay. 'I don't know anything about you, do I? Not a thing. Tell me everything,' he commanded.

Erin was saved by the arrival of the waiter but as soon as they'd ordered, Sebastian took up exactly where he'd left off.

'Come on now. Tell me about Erin— Lord, I don't even know your surname.'

'It's Joyce, and there's nothing much to tell. I'm originally from Dublin; I came to Dunbarra on holiday, fell in love with the place and stayed.'

'And that's it?' He looked unconvinced.

'Pretty much.'

He shook his head sadly. 'It would never make a movie. Every script needs a broken heart somewhere along the line.'

'So is that why you're here? To get over a broken heart? Or did you do the breaking?'

His expression darkened. 'I don't want to talk about it.'

'I'm sorry, I was just being flippant.'

He stared into the distance in silence. Erin was about to apologize again, anything to bring back the smile, but then he started talking.

'Her name was Marina,' he said softly, his voice trembling slightly. 'She was special and different from the women I usually met.' He smiled. 'Not tanned all over, no boob job, no Botox. Marina was as real as they come. Usually people in Hollywood only want to know you for one of two reasons,' Sebastian explained. 'Because you're rich or because you can introduce them to someone who'll make them a star. But not Marina. She wasn't interested in money or fame. She was the most straightforward, honest person you could meet. That was a major part of the attraction. Not that she wasn't beautiful,' he added quickly. 'She was lovely. It's just that she was so ordinary it was extraordinary, if you know what I mean.'

Erin nodded. 'So she wasn't an actress.'

He shook his head. 'A set designer and one of the best in the business. She loved her work, kept me waiting many times because of it.'

The waiter arrived with their fish platter and set it down between them but Sebastian didn't seem to notice. Erin watched as a variety of emotions crossed his face. Whoever this Marina was, he was obviously crazy about her.

'She didn't want anything from me,' he continued. 'In fact, she didn't want anything to do *with* me in the beginning. She hated the fact that I was famous, that people came up to me in restaurants or photographers followed me around. I told her that these things weren't my fault, they came with the job. Eventually she agreed to go out with me.' He smiled. 'I wore a wig and a fake moustache and took her to a terrible burger bar in the middle of nowhere. We had a brilliant night.'

Erin smiled. She had never seen him so natural or heard him talk so openly and honestly.

'We were inseparable after that,' he went on. 'I was absolutely crazy about the girl.'

Lucky girl, Erin found herself thinking.

'I couldn't wait to introduce her to everyone I knew and, because she hated the public attention, I invited them all to my home to meet her. They loved her as much as I did and she fitted in immediately. Everything was perfect.'

Erin looked at him over their untouched food. 'What went wrong?'

He sighed. 'One of my friends introduced her to coke. It didn't bother me at first. I mean everyone does it at some time or another in LA. But I soon realized she liked it a little too much.'

'Is there a problem with the food?'

Erin looked up to see the waiter hovering.

'No, it's fine, thanks,' she said, picking up her knife and fork. 'Sebastian?'

He looked blank for a moment and then picked up his cutlery but made no attempt to eat. 'She started to change very quickly after that,' he said when they were alone again. 'I soon realized she was using a lot more than she was letting on. Sometimes she was full of life and energy and positively insatiable. Other times she'd be withdrawn and moody and want to sleep all day. I became really concerned, though, when her work started to suffer. Marina had always been such a conscientious person and now she was turning up late for work, sometimes not going in at all. I'd seen the signs before and I knew she was hooked. I asked her to get help but she wouldn't listen. She told me I was possessive, that I was smothering her. After a few more arguments, she left.'

'Have you seen her since?' Erin asked.

'Just once.' Sebastian looked up, his dark eyes full of pain. 'When I went to identify her body.'

'Are you okay?' Erin asked. Lunch had been abandoned and they were now sitting on the patio at the back of the restaurant, drinking the champagne. You could just about see the rooftop of the Gatehouse from here. Erin was going to point it out to Sebastian but she didn't think he'd care. She didn't blame him.

'I'm sorry.' He gave her a weak smile. 'Some lunch this turned out to be.'

Erin picked up a piece of bread roll and smiled. 'Bread, wine and a sunny afternoon, what more could you ask for?'

'Good company, a decent meal and no hard-luck stories? I have to snap out of this. There's nothing I can do for Marina now.'

'No,' she agreed. 'But first you have to stop blaming yourself. You tried to help her. There's nothing more you could have done.'

'How do you know that? How can I ever know that?' He shook his head in despair and stood up. 'I'm sorry, but I need to get out of here.'

She stood too. 'No problem. I'll ask the waiter to call us a taxi.'

'No, you go ahead. I'll make my own way back.'

Erin looked at him in alarm. 'But Sebastian, it's at least an eight-mile walk.'

'I don't mind. I need to be alone right now. Don't worry about me, I'll be fine.' And he turned on his heel and disappeared around the side of the restaurant.

Erin was still staring after him when there was a discreet cough from the doorway. She turned to see the waiter watching her.

'I'm sorry, Ms Joyce, but I wonder if you could settle the bill?'.

Erin thought of the vintage champagne Sebastian had so recklessly ordered and groaned inwardly. Not only had she not been fed but she'd been stuck with an almighty bill, and the cab fare home. 'Of course,' she said and followed him inside.

The final straw was the sight of Ronan's jeep in the driveway when she got back. Erin played for time as she fumbled in her purse for the fare. Perhaps she could creep inside unnoticed; Ronan was probably out at the back with PJ. But as she stepped out of the car she looked up to see the two men walking towards her. 'Hi,' she said, with a limp wave.

'Hello, there.' Ronan eyed her curiously. 'You're looking very glamorous. Where were you?'

Erin fiddled with her hair and avoided PJ's knowing look. 'I had a meeting in White's.'

Ronan's eyes widened in delight. 'Excellent. Are they going to increase their order?'

'They're thinking about it,' Erin prevaricated, feeling even guiltier. 'I'd better go and change. I've so much to do.'

'Me too, I'll call you later.' Ronan called after her.

'Great.' She turned on the steps and smiled.

In the safety of her room she sank down on to the bed and dropped her head in her hands. Dear God, now not only did she have to live with the guilt of lying to Ronan, there wasn't even anything worth lying about. Her stomach rumbled loudly and she stood up, changed into jeans and a T-shirt and went downstairs in search of something to eat.

PJ walked in as she was wolfing down a cheese sandwich. 'Good lunch, then,' he said, filling the kettle.

'I didn't have lunch,' she mumbled between mouthfuls.

He raised an eyebrow. 'Ah, so our illustrious Mr Gray has become your new business partner, then.'

Erin wiped her chin and stared at him.

He smiled sadly.

'It was completely innocent,' she said stiffly.

'So no reason for secrets, then. Cup of tea?'

'No, thanks, I've got work to do.' She hurried to the door.

'Erin? Be careful.'

She met his eyes and smiled briefly. 'Relax, PJ, there's nothing to worry about. Sebastian is just another lost soul looking for a sympathetic ear.'

He shrugged. 'If you say so.'

She spent the rest of the afternoon working in the market garden while watching out for Sebastian. Worried when there was no sign of him, she made a few furtive trips to the cabin to see if he'd returned and even asked Hazel if she'd seen him. It was almost seven when his hunched frame finally passed the door and she was able to breathe a sigh of relief.

Chapter Ten

Marguerite was just serving up the last dessert of the evening when Sean shuffled in. 'Please don't tell me someone wants more,' she begged.

He smiled. 'No, no, you can relax.'

'You get off home,' she said, taking in his slumped shoulders and the dark bags under his eyes.

'I was hoping for a quick word first.'

Marguerite noted the uneasy expression in his eyes and nodded. 'Sure. You take this out to table three. I'll get cleaned up and be straight out.'

'Will you have a glass of wine?' he asked as he carried the plates towards the door.

'Definitely,' she said and went into the small staff loo to clean her hands and release her hair from its tight knot. When she went into the restaurant, Sean was sitting at the bar, his head bent. Marguerite climbed on to the stool next to him. 'You look like the weight of the universe is on your shoulders.'

'You mean world not universe.'

She raised an eyebrow. 'I know what I mean. Now tell me, what's wrong?'

'Me and Mary have been talking.' He smiled. 'Well, to be honest, she's been doing all the talking.'

'And?'

Sean sighed. 'She wants me to slow down. That old fool of a doctor told her I shouldn't be on my feet so much, what with the arthritis.'

Marguerite's brow knitted in concern. 'I didn't know you were having problems.'

'Ah, it's just a few aches and pains. Who doesn't have them, especially at my age?'

It was Marguerite's turn to sigh. 'So you want to retire.'

'No!' He looked horrified. 'I'd crack up in the house all day and Mary would go mad with me under her feet. I was just wondering if there was any way we could reduce my hours. I know you're finding it hard to manage as it is but I thought we could hire someone to job-share; a strong young lad who could do the heavy work and wouldn't mind working late nights.' He gave a nervous laugh. 'With a bit of luck I might have him trained in before I'm ready for the knacker's yard.'

'Don't talk like that,' she admonished. 'Mark has been saying the same thing. He said we should get someone who could help in the kitchen and out front and give us both a break.'

Sean's face lit up. 'That would be ideal.'

'Only where in Dunbarra are we going to find such a person?' Marguerite pointed out.

'I'm way ahead of you,' Sean told her. 'My son says that we should advertise on the internet; everyone does that now. That way we can reach a huge audience in minutes. Imagine, Marguerite, you could have a new employee in a matter of days.'

'Then that's what we'll do,' Marguerite told him. 'But I know nothing about the internet. Do you think if I drafted the advert, your son could do the rest for me?'

'He'd be happy to,' Sean assured her. 'Why don't you do it now while I finish cleaning up?'

Feeling trapped but helpless in the face of Sean's enthusiasm, Marguerite smiled. 'Good idea.'

Marguerite was astounded at the speed and number of replies there were to her advertisement. Sean arrived in every morning, clutching a handful of CVs that his son had printed off for him. Feeling less than enthusiastic, Marguerite dutifully read them all and was almost relieved that none of the applicants suited their requirements.

Preoccupied with this new task that had been added to her already heavy load, it was several days before she finally got a chance to visit Erin. She didn't call to warn her friend that she was coming; some instinct telling her that Erin would put her off. As she walked the short distance to the Gatehouse,

Marguerite kept her eyes peeled for Sebastian. He had not been in touch for a few days and she was worried. She couldn't believe he'd been here for so long and not opened up to her. It hurt. She was also a little embarrassed and guilty that he was still resident in the guest house. She knew that Sebastian would pay handsomely for inconveniencing Erin but that didn't make it right. When Marguerite had asked her friend to take him in, she'd thought it would be for just a week or two. Now she wasn't sure when Sebastian would be ready to leave. He showed no interest in returning to LA. Marguerite had suggested that perhaps he should go and visit the children, maybe even take them on holiday, but he'd dismissed the idea out of hand.

There was no one around when Marguerite got there and she went out to the garden in search of Erin or Sebastian. Hearing the sound of voices coming from the orchard, she changed direction and walked through two rows of apple trees before finally discovering Erin and PJ. 'Hello, you two.'

'Marguerite.' PJ beamed at her. 'Looking *très belle* as usual.'

'*Merci, monsieur*,' she said, kissing him on both cheeks.

Erin smiled too, but it seemed a little strained. 'This is a nice surprise.'

'I was hoping for a chat.' Marguerite hesitated. 'But if it's a bad time . . .'

'We were just finishing up,' PJ assured her, looking at his watch. 'I have some things to do before I go out.'

'Want a coffee first?' Erin offered.

He shook his head. 'I'm sure you don't want an oul fella like me listening in on your gossip.'

'We don't gossip,' Marguerite admonished him.

'If you say so.' He grinned and strolled away with a wave of his hand.

Marguerite took Erin's arm and they headed back towards the house. 'How are you?'

'Okay. You?' Erin led the way into the kitchen and washed her hands.

'Fine. Okay. The same.' Marguerite wandered around the kitchen, stopping to inspect the pots of herbs on the broad window sill. 'Is Sebastian around?'

Erin turned. 'I don't know. Did you want to see him?'

'Not especially but I haven't seen him in a while. I'm worried about him. Every time I think he is making progress, he seems to get down again.'

'Well, it can't be easy for him,' Erin said vaguely, filling the kettle.

'Why do you say that?'

'Pardon?' Erin busied herself fetching milk and sugar and taking two mugs from the cupboard.

Marguerite's eyes narrowed. 'What can't be easy?'

'Nothing.'

But Marguerite saw that Erin wouldn't meet her eyes. 'We have known each other too long, my friend. Tell me what's going on.'

'We have talked,' Erin admitted, abandoning the coffee and sinking into a chair. 'But I can't really say any more than that.'

'That is ridiculous, you must tell me. How else can I help him?'

'There's nothing you can do to help,' Erin assured her. 'Try not to worry. He hasn't done anything wrong, Marguerite. It's nothing like that.'

'I'm glad to hear that, but if it's not so big a deal you can tell me, right? I'm his sister,' she added, her voice sharp.

Erin pulled her hands away and massaged her temples. 'It's not up to me.'

'Please, Erin,' Marguerite begged, tapping her foot impatiently on the tiled floor.

'Okay. In a nutshell: he was in love, she died. It was a drugs overdose.'

The foot-tapping stopped. 'She died?'

'Her name was Marina.'

Marguerite searched her tired brain. 'He never mentioned this girl to me. There was a Rachel and a Savannah, no Marina. When did all this take place?'

Erin shrugged. 'It's the reason for his depression so I assume it must have been recent.'

'I suppose so. Oh—'

'What?' Erin said worriedly as Marguerite put a hand to her mouth.

It took Marguerite a moment to put her fears into

words. 'It wasn't his fault, was it? Please tell me Sebastian didn't give her the drugs.'

'No, of course not.' An expression of doubt crossed Erin's face.

'What?' Marguerite pushed.

'It was a friend of his that introduced Marina to cocaine,' she admitted. 'So I think maybe he does feel responsible.'

'I must go and talk to him.' Marguerite stood up and moved swiftly towards the door but Erin was there before her.

'Then he'll know that I betrayed his confidence. You might scare him away and what good would that do?'

Marguerite hesitated.

'Sebastian came here because of you, Marguerite. He will talk to you, I'm sure of it. Just give him time. I think he's actually still in a state of shock.'

'Then why did he talk to you? In fact,' Marguerite's expression was cool, 'when did this cosy *tête-à-tête* take place?'

Erin reddened. 'Over lunch last week.'

'Go on.'

'We went to White's.'

Marguerite stared at her. 'You and Sebastian went out to a restaurant together.'

'He was just saying thank you for dinner—'

'Lunch? Dinner?' Marguerite put her hands on her hips and shook her head. 'And tell me, have you two had breakfast in bed, Erin?'

'Is it any wonder I didn't talk to you?' Erin said wearily. 'You're completely overreacting.'

'And, I wonder, would Ronan overreact too,' Marguerite threw back. She gave a grim smile when Erin's eyes slid away from hers. 'Oh, Erin.' Marguerite pushed past her friend and walked out.

Erin hadn't told Ronan, of course she hadn't, but, she reasoned, there was nothing to tell. Why make him suspicious and jealous when he had no reason to be? But if it was all so innocent, why did she feel so guilty?

She was still sitting at the table, staring into space, when there was a gentle tap on the door. Hazel stuck her head in. 'Sorry to bother you. I was just looking for PJ.'

Erin looked up at the clock and got slowly to her feet. 'He'll be gone by now but he's usually back by five.'

'Where does he disappear off to? Has he a girlfriend tucked away somewhere?' Hazel joked.

Erin looked at her without smiling. 'He visits a sick relative.'

'Oh, I'm sorry,' Hazel murmured, feeling terrible, but Erin had already turned away and was bending to empty the washing machine. 'I'll leave you to it,' she said and backed out of the room.

Making her way through the quiet guest house she went into the sitting room to check on Gracie. The child had fallen asleep in front of *Barney*. Hazel settled a cushion under the small head, turned off the TV and crept out of the room. Going out through the front door she sat down on the steps and pulled a sketch pad and pencil from her bag. She wasn't in the mood for drawing though.

She had made an appointment to meet the owner of a gift shop in Mullingar next week but as soon as she'd put the phone down, Hazel regretted it. She'd been hoping to have a word with PJ about it, he had a knack for making her feel better and he might be able to give her some tips about how to handle the interview. She was also hoping that he'd look after Gracie. It wouldn't look very professional arriving at a business meeting with a four-year-old in tow. Still, she could ask him this evening or tomorrow, there was no rush. Hazel chewed on her pencil and scanned the garden for something worth drawing. There wasn't much of a view from this aspect but she didn't like to wander too far from Gracie. She had just started to sketch the trees that lined the driveway when a flash of colour caught her eye. She turned her head and saw a woman stride by, her face averted. Hazel recognized the cloud of dark hair and small trim figure of the lady who owned the restaurant down the road. She seemed upset. That was strange, Hazel knew that she and Erin were friends but Marguerite obviously hadn't been visiting her. And then she remembered that the woman was Sebastian Gray's sister. She looked around to see the man himself standing at the side of the house, smoking and staring after his sister, a slight smile on his lips. As if he'd felt Hazel's eyes on him, he turned his head and looked straight at her.

Embarrassed at being caught out, Hazel bent her head over her pad, letting her hair fall down to hide her burning cheeks.

'Working on something new?'

She looked up to find him standing over her. 'Not really, just waiting for Gracie to wake up from her nap. I'm not very good on detail.' She waved disparagingly at her work.

'Don't put yourself down or you'll never be a success.'

'I'm not interested in being a success, just surviving.'

'Everyone is interested in success,' Sebastian insisted, sounding irritable.

'Not me. I'm only interested in earning enough so I can look after my daughter.'

'I care about my kids too,' he retorted with a scowl. 'I've got to go.'

'I'm sorry, I didn't mean to offend you,' she said but he was already walking away.

Hazel sighed. Now she had managed to insult not only the most attractive man she'd met in years but her only customer as well. Turning the page she started a new sketch, her pencil moving quickly, deftly across the page. She started with the short cap of dark hair and broad forehead, then the strong line of his nose, the cleft on the right side of his chin and the sexy curve of his lips. The image was in her head and she felt a compulsion to get it down on paper but she heard Gracie stir, and with a sigh she shoved the pad back into her bag and went inside.

'Hello, beautiful,' she said softly, reaching for her daughter and smoothing her hair. 'What do you say we get out the play dough?'

The child yawned and nodded, smiling. Hazel fetched the play dough box and they took it out to the bench on the front lawn. When Gracie was busy making flowers and dolls with the soft dough, Hazel pulled out the sketch pad again. She made a few changes, rubbed out some lines and added others. It was a good likeness and she was pleased with it, though the eyes weren't quite right. The shape and size were accurate but something was missing. It was his expression, Hazel finally realized. That's what was wrong. She worked on the portrait for nearly an hour. But try as she might she just couldn't capture what it was she'd seen in Sebastian's eyes.

Chapter Eleven

It was a dismal Monday morning and after making some deliveries for Erin, PJ decided to stop off in Dunbarra and treat himself to a coffee before getting back to work. Sandra was perched on a stool at the counter in Paddy Burke's coffee shop gossiping when PJ walked in. He stood quietly by, unnoticed, and listened in for a few moments.

'Erin doesn't come from around here, does she?' Sandra was asking.

'No, no, she's a Jackeen.'

'I'm sorry?' Sandra looked at the old woman in confusion.

'A Dubliner,' the pensioner cackled.

'Oh, I see. What brought her here?'

Paddy put a muffin in front of her and shrugged. 'I don't know. Maybe she was looking for a suitable guest house to buy.'

'No, no.' The pensioner was emphatic. 'Erin was here for a couple of months as a guest before Ivy put the Gatehouse on the market.'

'You're right, of course.' Paddy nodded. 'I'd forgotten that.'

'A couple of months?' Sandra raised an eyebrow. 'That's some holiday. Did she know anyone around here, have any relatives maybe?'

PJ reached behind him and pushed the door closed, making the three at the counter look round. He smiled broadly. 'Good morning, everyone, how are we all this fine day?'

Paddy looked past him at the darkening sky outside. 'You're in a good mood, PJ, or your sight is failing – one or the other.'

'Well, there's no point being miserable, is there?' PJ slid on to a stool at the other end of the counter. 'I'll have a white coffee and some of your apple crumble, please, Paddy. So, ladies any plans for the day? Dorothy, I didn't expect to see you this morning. Isn't it your day to do the church flowers?'

The woman's gaze flew to the clock on the wall and she stood up and tugged on her coat. 'It went completely out of my head. Thanks, PJ,' she said and hurried out through the door.

PJ met Sandra's chilly stare and smiled. 'Have you tried Paddy's apple crumble, Mrs Bell? It's wonderful.'

'She's tried everything,' Paddy said happily and then reddened. 'My cakes, I mean.'

PJ smiled at the other man's mortified expression. 'So, Mrs Bell, how long more are you planning to stay in Dunbarra?'

'I haven't decided,' Sandra said, shooting Paddy a flirtatious smile. 'But I'm in no hurry to leave.'

PJ thought Paddy was going to pass out with embarrassment and yet he seemed really taken with this brash woman. Not that he'd ever do anything about it. Paddy was a consummate bachelor, as Mrs Bell would find out eventually. But PJ found it hard to believe that she was seriously attracted to the shy, simple man. It was much more likely that he was no more than a source of information. But what was all that about? Why would a worldly woman like Sandra Bell be so interested in the people of a small town like this? And why was she looking for information on Erin? 'You must be missing your children,' he said to her, smiling his thanks at Paddy, who had put his food and steaming coffee in front of him.

'Of course I am,' she snapped, 'but they understand that I need time alone.'

'Of course.' PJ turned his attention to his food.

'Sandra's like one of us now,' Paddy said with shy affection. 'Dunbarra is full of people who came for a holiday and then didn't leave.'

'Oh, who else?' Sandra asked immediately, her eyes alight with curiosity.

'It happens all over the world,' PJ said before Paddy could answer. 'Many city folk are eventually drawn to the quiet of the countryside. It's this burn-out phenomenon.'

Paddy leaned on the counter and nodded. 'Do you know, PJ, I think you have a point.'

'So who else burned out and found their way to Dunbarra?' Sandra persisted in an attempt to get the conversation back on track.

'Old Clive Mulvany,' PJ said. 'He used to run a jeweller's in Cork, a very successful one too.'

'That's right.' Paddy agreed. 'He came up here for a spot of fishing, and a few weeks later he'd sold up and bought a cottage by the lake.'

'Who else?' There was an edge to Sandra's voice.

PJ ignored the question. 'Ivy, of course, did the opposite.'

'She did!' Paddy gave a hoot of laughter.

'Who's Ivy?' Sandra asked.

'She owned the Gatehouse before Erin,' Paddy explained. 'She retired to Florida.'

PJ immediately realized his mistake. In his attempt to put a stop to Sandra's nosiness he'd led the conversation right back to Erin.

'And Erin Joyce took over.' Sandra shot him a triumphant look. 'How long ago was that, Paddy?'

Their host frowned. 'It's a few years ago now, eh, PJ? It wasn't that long after you moved here yourself, was it?'

'I don't remember,' PJ muttered, concentrating on his crumble.

'So you're a relative newcomer yourself, Mr Ward.'

'Sure, he's another Jackeen. Isn't that right, PJ?'

'Paddy, this bloody machine isn't working!' An old guy in the corner started banging the keyboard off the table.

'Ah, Seamus, don't do that, it's brand new,' Paddy groaned and hurried over to stop him.

It was PJ's turn to flash Sandra a smug grin as he wiped his mouth on a napkin, dropped a few euros on the counter and stood up. 'I did enjoy our chat but I have work to do.'

'Tending someone else's garden,' she said with a saccharin smile.

He gave a small bow. 'Goodbye, Mrs Bell. Have a nice day.'

PJ left, knowing that his attempts to thwart Sandra's curiosity had completely failed and, if anything, he'd now drawn attention to himself as well. Still, what difference did it make what the woman found out? She would be gone soon enough and he for one wouldn't miss her.

Marguerite had finally found four candidates that she thought were worth interviewing. They still didn't look that good on paper but Sean was getting increasingly anxious and she felt she needed to do something constructive. But it wasn't going well. Marguerite tapped her pen against the page in front of her and then frowned over her glasses at the pimply youth on the other side of the desk. 'You don't have much experience, do you?'

He shrugged. 'I help the Ma a bit. I do a great fry-up.'

Marguerite blinked and looked back at the page. 'And you're sure that cooking is what you want to do?'

'Well, I was going to be a brickie—'

'Excuse me?'

'A builder,' he explained. 'But with the credit crunch there isn't much work in the building trade. But as the Da says,' he grinned, 'people will always need feeding.'

Marguerite forced a smile and stood up. 'True. Well, thank you for coming in.'

'So have I got the job?' he asked, standing too.

'I have a couple of other people to see,' Marguerite said, though she knew she should just have said no, not in a million years.

There was one more person to see, a girl this time, but, from their brief conversation on the phone, Marguerite didn't hold out much hope. She had sounded young, cocky and very vague about her background; it would be another waste of time. Marguerite dropped her pen, fell back in her chair and massaged the bridge of her nose. She really wasn't in the mood for this, not at the moment. She kept reliving her argument with Erin and subsequent *tête-à-tête* with her brother but she was as confused and upset as ever. Confused as to how her brother had been involved in such an intense and unhappy relationship and not mentioned a word of it to her. Upset that he had confided in Erin, someone he barely knew. And upset that Erin had kept the truth from her. What could she do to help if he still insisted on keeping her very much at arm's length? Marguerite had gone over and over the subsequent conversation with Sebastian, but she still didn't understand.

It took an age for Sebastian to answer the door that day and when he did, she pushed past him and stood in the centre of Erin's small sitting room. 'I've just talked to Erin,' she said without preamble. 'She told me a very sad story about you.'

He stood looking at her, eyebrows raised. 'A story?'

'Well, you tell me, Sebastian. Perhaps I've got something wrong. Tell me about this girl, Marina.'

'If Erin has told you then what more is there for me to say?'

'Well, let's start with you telling me when this tragic girlfriend came into your life. Was it before Rachel or Savannah or maybe after Diane? Or perhaps you were seeing them all at the same time?'

He looked away. 'I've never claimed to be an angel.'

'No,' Marguerite agreed. 'It seems you are just like our father. But your new *amie*, Erin, seems to think that this Marina was the love of your life.'

'She was,' he said, sounding tired and defensive.

'Then explain to me, please, why you would two-time her. Explain to me why you never mentioned her to your only sister. Explain to me why you've been here for weeks now and said nothing.'

'Please don't, Marguerite. This isn't about you or us. I came here because I needed to escape all of that. I came so that I wouldn't have to talk.'

'Yet you told Erin.'

'It just came out; I didn't plan it.'

'And it "just came out" over dinner, did it? Or perhaps over lunch?'

'Why are you being like this, Marguerite?' He flashed her a look of irritation. 'Why are you so angry?'

Marguerite flopped into a chair. 'I don't know. I suppose I'm hurt that you didn't tell me first. Unless this is a fabrication in order to get into my friend's bed.'

'You have a very low opinion of me, don't you?' Sebastian said with a reproachful look. 'Perhaps you think I lost two stone just to win the affections of a woman I didn't even know.'

Marguerite felt dreadful, realizing the truth of his words. He had been a mess when he got here and something terrible must have happened to him to cause such a dramatic change in his appearance and character. She reached out her hand and grasped his. 'Of course not, I'm sorry. It's just hard for me to understand.' She searched his face with worried eyes. 'You've changed so much.'

'And you didn't think I had a heart to break.'

'I know you have. I've seen you with Toby and Jess.' A shadow crossed his face at the mention of his children. 'I'm sorry, Sebastian. Forgive me?'

He nodded.

'Why don't you come back to Dijon for some lunch? Then we can talk properly.'

It was like a shutter coming down. Sebastian shook his head. 'No, Marguerite, not today. I'm too tired.'

'Then I'll go.' Marguerite hopped to her feet and went to the door.

He put out a hand and said he was sorry, but Marguerite felt hurt and excluded and on the verge of tears, and she left quickly.

Later she had told Mark everything. Saddened, he'd accepted Sebastian's explanation without question. But then he was a man, he would. She wasn't so sure. She would have loved to talk to Erin about it, but she still felt hurt by her friend's behaviour and wasn't quite ready to make peace.

'Mrs Hayes?'

Marguerite sat up and blinked at the vision in the doorway. 'Yes?'

'Rai Price. I came for the interview.'

'Of course, please come in.' Marguerite gestured to the chair opposite and watched in fascination as the girl crossed the room.

She had a pixie-style haircut dyed various shades of

blonde and red. Her large green eyes were lined heavily with kohl. She wore a very short denim skirt over opaque purple tights that encased long and slender legs. Her smile showed off perfect white teeth and she held out a hand heavy with rings. 'Nice to meet you.'

'And you.' Marguerite took the hand, surprised and pleased at the gesture. 'Have you brought your CV?'

The girl grimaced. 'Yeah, but I'm afraid it's rather short.' She rummaged in her backpack, pulled out a transparent folder and handed it over.

Marguerite glanced at the single page inside. The girl was nineteen, had attended a very good school in Dublin, although no mention was made of how she had done in her exams, and just a single paragraph covering her work experience. She read it, reread it, looked up at the girl, then back at the CV and then back at Rai again. 'You've been training under Conor O'Brien at Chez Nous?'

Rai shifted in her chair. 'Sort of.'

Marguerite sighed. It would have been too good to be true to have a candidate trained by a Michelin-star chef. 'Were you just waitressing? Only I need someone who can cook too.'

There was a blaze of anger in the beautiful eyes. 'I can cook!'

'Okay, then. Perhaps you would like to tell me in more detail about your experience as this isn't much help, is it?' Marguerite tossed the CV on to the table.

'No,' Rai admitted reluctantly. 'Sorry, I just find it a bit embarrassing.'

Marguerite watched her and waited.

Rai sighed. 'Look, he's my stepfather.'

'I don't understand.'

'Conor O'Brien, head chef of Chez Nous, is my stepfather. Price is my mother's name.'

'Go on,' Marguerite said, intrigued as to why the stepdaughter of one of the most respected chefs in the country wanted to come and work for her.

Looking like a sulky teenager, Rai explained. 'I wasn't doing very well at school so Dad said if I wasn't prepared to do the work, he wasn't prepared to pay the fees. He made me leave after my junior cert and start as an apprentice in his kitchen.'

'So you've been working with him, for – what, maybe three years?'

Rai nodded. 'It will be three in October.'

'And you want to leave?' Marguerite stared at the girl. Was she completely mad?

'We don't get on. He still treats me like a kid and won't listen to any of my ideas.'

'He does have a reputation to maintain.'

'But I'm good,' Rai protested, 'really good.'

'And modest, it seems.'

'I know food.' Rai leaned forward and tapped her heart. 'It's in here. Don't write me off because I'm young. If Stephanie West had done that Dad would never have got his start.'

Marguerite knew this was true. Stephanie West had bought out her boss more than ten years earlier and put his sous chef, Conor, in charge of the kitchen. Within a year, they had won back their Michelin star. 'So why apply for a job in a little restaurant like this? Your dad could have got you a position in any of Dublin's best restaurants.'

Rai scowled. 'I don't want or need his help. I want to do what he did, start at the bottom and work my way up.'

'Then you've come to the right place,' Marguerite laughed. 'There are only me and Sean running things here. We do whatever needs doing. Cooking, waiting tables, unblocking toilets—' she looked the young girl straight in the eye – 'everything.'

Rai just smiled. 'That's cool.'

Marguerite had planned to discuss the candidates with both Mark and Sean but she knew there really was no choice; the other applicants had been useless. Rai was different although her strong personality might cause problems. But there was only one way to find out. 'The job is yours if you want it,' she told a delighted Rai. 'But make no mistake: you will be starting at the bottom. You will do what Sean or I tell you without argument.'

'I can do that if you promise to teach me,' Rai told her. 'I'm not afraid of hard work but I want to learn.'

'Then we should get along just fine. I'll pay you ten euros an hour and it will be thirty to forty hours a week; it varies from day to day, as you can imagine, but I will give you as much notice as I can.' She frowned. 'Where are you going to stay? Commuting from Dublin would not be practical.'

'Don't worry,' Rai told her. 'I'm happy to move down here.'

Marguerite's eyes widened. 'I've told you the salary. I'm not sure you could afford a reasonable place . . .'

'Dad will pay once he knows I'm working and in a kitchen too.'

'I must warn you that I've never shared my kitchen before and it's something I've resisted, but Sean, my restaurant manager, is not getting any younger and needs to reduce his hours and that is why your time will be divided between the kitchen and front of house.'

'Okay.'

'You must wear whites in the kitchen and a white blouse with black trousers or skirt when you're front of house, but I will pay for the clothes. Is that okay?'

'Cool.'

Smiling, Marguerite stood up and held out her hand. 'Welcome to Dijon.'

Chapter Twelve

Hazel never did talk to PJ about her interview. She had almost cancelled a number of times and then decided to go through with it. And she wouldn't tell PJ. Imagine his surprise when she told him that she'd brokered a deal for her work unaided. He would be so impressed. Except he wouldn't. Because it hadn't worked out that way at all.

Hazel sat across from the unsmiling shopkeeper and wished she hadn't come. He was looking at the canvasses with a mixture of confusion and distaste. She felt sick and humiliated and wanted to run and hide. Gracie wasn't helping. Usually such a good child, she had been mewling and testy since they'd got here and the shopkeeper seemed as unimpressed with her as he was with the paintings.

'You said on the phone that your work was based on the local scenery,' he said now, his voice accusing.

Hazel forced a polite smile. 'Yes, I'm living in Dunbarra and all these paintings were inspired by the surrounding countryside.'

He looked from her back to the paintings, a sceptical expression on his face. 'Really? Well, I was looking for something more traditional. My customers are mainly tourists who want to take home a reminder of their holiday, not a piece of modern art. These are far too big anyway.'

'I do have some smaller pieces . . .'

He stood up. 'Yes, but like I said, they're a bit too abstract for my customers.'

'Well, thank you for your time,' she said, putting the canvases back into her portfolio and blinking back tears. She quickly hustled Gracie outside, kept walking until they got around the corner, and then she slumped against the wall, letting the tears flow. It was several moments before she became aware of her daughter tugging on her sleeve. 'What is it, Gracie?'

The child pointed at the ice-cream sign outside the newsagent's across the road.

'You want ice cream?' Hazel glared down at her. 'Only good girls get ice creams, Gracie, and you haven't been a good girl at all. Don't you understand?' she said, her voice rising. 'If I don't sell some of my paintings soon we're going to have to go home, and you know what will happen then, don't you?'

Gracie looked up at her with frightened eyes and Hazel was filled with remorse.

'Oh, I'm sorry, darling, I'm so sorry.' She crouched down and gathered the child into her arms. 'Mummy isn't really cross with you, just a bit sad.'

Gracie put out a hand and touched her cheek, her eyes round with concern.

Hazel kissed the little fingers and smiled. 'Come on, let's both have a huge ice cream, it will cheer us up. In fact, I think we might even go to the cinema too. What do you think of that, Gracie?'

The child clapped her hands in delight and hugged Hazel.

Hazel hugged her back, and closed her eyes tight. 'I love you, sweetie. Don't ever let anyone tell you otherwise. You hear me?'

On Saturday evening Erin and Ronan sat at a table in the pub eating shepherd's pie and drinking lager.

'You're very quiet,' Ronan commented. 'Everything okay?'

'Yes, fine.' She forced a smile but she was lying; she felt miserable. She was worried about Sebastian, he was even quieter these last few days and hardly opened his mouth. And she and Marguerite weren't talking. It was the first time they'd fallen out and Erin hated it.

'You never told me how dinner went with your famous guest.'

'Fine.' Erin wasn't fooled by his teasing tone. Ronan was obviously unhappy that she'd invited Sebastian to dinner. How would he feel if he knew the rest? Not that she was going tell him. She'd decided it really wasn't worth the hassle. She'd already said that she was in White's on business and she couldn't admit that she'd lied, even though it had been completely innocent.

'Did he tell you why he's here?' Ronan was asking.

Erin wondered how to answer this without lying again. 'Not really.'

'So what did you talk about?' Ronan persisted, his tone more impatient.

'His kids and Marguerite mainly,' she told him and congratulated herself that this was true.

'Oh.' He finished his dinner and sat back in his chair, his eyes on her face.

Erin pushed away her plate and put a hand to her temple. 'You know, I have a bit of a headache. Do you mind if we go?'

'Of course not,' he said with a tight smile and stood up. 'I'll go and get the bill.'

When they pulled up in front of the Gatehouse, Ronan went to get out but Erin put a hand on his arm. 'It's okay, you stay there. I need to go straight up to bed; sleep is the only thing that's going to sort out this headache.'

She leaned over and kissed him. 'I'll call you tomorrow.'

Erin watched him drive away and was about to go inside when, on impulse, she took the path around the side of the house to the cabin. It was about time she apologized to Sebastian and explained why she'd told

Marguerite. She stood at his door for a moment before knocking gently. Sebastian opened it almost immediately. He said nothing, just stood looking at her, waiting.

'I came to see if you were okay. And to tell you that I'm sorry.' He stood back to let her in. Erin walked past him into the sitting room. 'I didn't intend to tell Marguerite anything. But she knows me so well, it's hard for me to hide anything from her.'

'That's Marguerite.' A faint smile touched his lips as he sat down. 'You know, I don't think she believes me. She said you'd told her "my story".'

Erin perched beside him and patted his hand. 'Of course she believes you. She's just hurt because you didn't tell her.'

'I don't have the energy to care what she thinks or how she feels. I'm sorry if that makes me sound hard.'

'Of course it doesn't. You're grieving. She'll come round, don't worry. She loves you, Sebastian.'

He looked at her, his eyes bright with tears. 'I wish that made me feel better but it doesn't. Sometimes . . .'

'What?' she prompted.

'I don't know. I just don't see the point in going on.'

'Don't say that.' Erin took his face between her hands and looked into his eyes. 'Don't ever say that. I know you feel bad now but it will get easier.'

'Will it?'

'Yes, yes, it will.' Erin let go of his face and put her arms around him. After a moment she felt his body shake with silent tears. She held him this way for what seemed like hours, patting his back and whispering reassuring words in his ear. Finally his breathing evened out and she settled back against the cushions with him cradled in her arms. Despite the cramp in her arm caused by his weight, Erin felt her eyelids grow heavy and she drifted off to sleep.

Erin woke to the sensation of a hand massaging the base of her back. She groaned in pleasure and then smiled as the hand moved around to her front and slipped under her top. Erin held her breath as the fingers started to caress her breast. Ronan had never woken her up quite like this before . . . Her eyes flew open and she saw that it was Sebastian Gray that was lying in her arms, his eyes shut. She watched in fascination as his hand continued its gentle massage under her top. Did he even realize he was doing it, she wondered, or perhaps he was dreaming and thought she was Marina. She debated whether to wake him or to just move his hand. She did neither. Instead she closed her eyes and let her head fall back against the cushion. She would move in a minute. But he shifted suddenly, and she held her breath thinking he must have woken and realized that he was making love to the wrong woman. Erin could have cried out in frustration. She looked up to find him standing over her. His eyes held hers as he pulled her to her feet, opened her shirt and pushed it off her shoulders. She stayed motionless and let him. Then he was removing her bra and only when it had joined her top on the floor did he let his gaze drop to her bare breasts. He looked back at her face and smiled, and without a word he took her hand and led her into the bedroom.

Careful not to wake Sebastian, Erin slipped out of the bed, gathered her clothes and went into the sitting room. Pulling on her shirt, she shoved her bra into her pocket and quickly let herself out of the cabin. Her pulse racing, she hurried round to the front of the house and put her key in the lock with trembling fingers. When she was safely inside, she leaned against the hall table and let out a long, ragged breath.

'Someone's up late.'

Erin jumped and she stared into the darkness until her eyes found the figure on the stairs.

'Sorry if I startled you,' Sandra whispered. 'I was just getting myself some water.' She raised her glass for Erin to see. 'Did you have a nice evening?'

'Yes, thank you,' Erin whispered back.

'Good. All work and no play as they say. Goodnight, then.'

'Goodnight,' Erin said, and she watched the woman's progress up the stairs. When Sandra had disappeared and Erin heard the click of her door closing, she ran up to her own room, went inside and locked the door. Flopping down on the bed she stared up at the ceiling and blinked several times, hardly able to believe what had just happened.

She wondered how Sebastian would feel about it when he woke up. Had it been her he was making love to or had she just been a poor substitute for Marina? There had been no tenderness in their coupling. If anything it had been almost aggressive. Sebastian had been impatient, even rough, and Erin had responded to him in a way she never had with any man before. Her love life with Ronan was often passionate and equally often gentle, but what had happened tonight made Erin feel like an animal. It had been frantic, thrilling and instinctive. She and Sebastian had seemed to read each other exactly right and do and move in the way the other wanted. There had been no kissing, Erin realized, her fingers going unconsciously to her lips. Kissing, she'd always thought, was the difference between making love and having sex. But of course it had just been sex. And she had enjoyed it and not once thought of Ronan. Tears filled her eyes. What did that make her?

Not bothering to undress, Erin climbed under the covers and shut her eyes. However she felt she still had to be up at seven to get breakfast; to get *his* breakfast.

But Sebastian never appeared the next morning. Erin was about to abandon her post and go to check on him when PJ arrived and commented on That Eejit out walking in the rain in only a T-shirt. Erin heaved a sigh of relief but then started to worry in case he was on his way to throw himself into the lake because of her. Realizing that the toast was burning, Erin cursed, threw out the blackened bread and put some fresh slices in the toaster.

PJ asked. 'Everything okay?'

'Fine.' She turned her back on him and cracked an egg into the pan.

'Did you have a nice evening?'

Erin stiffened. 'Sorry?'

'Didn't you go out with Ronan?'

'Oh, yes. Yes, it was fine although I had a bit of a headache so I came home early.'

'Better now?' he asked.

'Not really.'

'Go back to bed after breakfast,' he advised.

'Maybe I will. Come on, yours is ready.'

A couple of moments later when Erin carried his tray through to the dining room, Sandra was standing talking to him. Erin was surprised. Sandra was usually one of the last guests down to breakfast. 'Good morning.' She smiled, praying the woman wouldn't mention their meeting in the early hours.

'Good morning, Erin, how are you today?'

'Fine, thanks. What will you have for breakfast?'

Sandra frowned. 'Something light, I think. I didn't have a great night. I just tossed and turned after I went back to bed. What time was that, Erin?'

Erin felt a flush creep into her cheeks. 'About two, I think.'

'I don't know how you run this place with so little sleep.' She laughed. 'I'd never be able to do it.'

PJ was looking on with interest as he munched his toast. Erin avoided his eyes. 'Maybe some fresh fruit and toast?' she suggested to Sandra.

'Yeah, fine; and a large mug of very strong coffee, please.'

'Coming up,' Erin promised and escaped to the kitchen.

'Are you sure you're all right?'

She whirled round to see PJ standing in the doorway. 'Yes, fine. Did you want something?'

'You forgot the sugar,' he said, fetching a bowl himself and going back into the dining room.

'Sorry,' Erin called after him. She put on some toast for Sandra. All she needed now was for Sebastian to walk in and make some lewd reference to the night before. Even though the door was closed, Erin could hear Sandra's voice and she hurried with the breakfast. PJ would not be impressed that the woman was interrupting his favourite meal of the day. It was unusual, PJ didn't often take a dislike to people – he was the most affable and easy-going of men – yet she knew he didn't like Sandra. It was also clear to Erin that he didn't trust Sebastian. Perhaps she should trust his instincts. The toast popped up and Erin arranged it in a basket, and with that and the fruit in one hand and the coffee pot in the other, she took a deep breath and went into the dining room.

It turned out it was Hazel and Gracie that Sandra was now talking to. PJ was hidden behind his newspaper. Hazel wasn't saying much, she looked very down, and Gracie was cowering behind her mother.

'Breakfast,' Erin announced with a smile and she set Sandra's breakfast down on a table at the far side of the room. Hazel shot her a grateful smile. Once she'd made sure that Sandra had everything she needed, Erin went over to her. 'Good morning. The usual?' she asked, tweaking one of Gracie's plaits.

'Please,' Hazel replied but her face was tense. 'Sit up, Gracie,' she said, pulling her daughter from behind her and pushing her into a chair. 'If you don't, Erin won't bring you your Rice Krispies.'

'Of course I will.' Erin smiled at the child. 'Sure, she's the best little girl in Dunbarra, aren't you, Gracie?'

This resulted in a shy smile from the child but a glare from her mother and Erin quickly left..

'I could do with some more of the low-fat spread,' Sandra called after her.

Later, when Erin emerged with cereal for Gracie and poached eggs for Hazel, it was to find Sebastian leaning against the wall chatting to them. Immediately she felt a rush of embarrassment at the memory of last night and jealousy at the intimate way

Sebastian was talking to Hazel. 'Good morning,' she said with a tight smile as she set down their food.

He smiled at her. 'Good morning, Erin. Did you sleep well?'

Erin felt her cheeks flame. 'Fine, thanks, and you?'

'Very well.'

'The usual?' she asked.

'I'm quite hungry this morning for some reason,' he said. 'I think I'll have the full Irish breakfast.'

'Coming right up.' Erin turned to go back into the kitchen.

'Erin?' Sandra called and she froze.

'Yes?'

'The spread?'

'Oh, yes, of course, sorry.' Erin dived into the kitchen grabbed a handful of portions and dropped them on Sandra's table. 'This is going to be a long morning,' she muttered to herself as she went back into the kitchen to make Sebastian's breakfast. By the time she served Sebastian, PJ, Hazel and Gracie had finished and left and Sandra was in the hall talking on her mobile phone.

'How are you?' Sebastian asked, his voice soft.

'I'm not sure,' she admitted with a nervous smile. 'You?'

'The same,' and then he winced. 'Sorry, that didn't sound very gallant. It was great, it's just—'

'You really don't have to explain.' Erin smiled and carried her tray back into the kitchen. Alone, the smile quickly disappeared and she banged down the tray and flopped into a chair. Okay, she hadn't expected Sebastian to bring her flowers but he didn't have to look quite so relieved that she'd let him off the hook.

There was a rap on the kitchen door and Ronan stuck his head round it and smiled at her. 'Good morning.'

She jumped to her feet, startled. 'What are you doing here?'

He came over and kissed her. 'I was worried about you. Are you feeling any better?'

'I'm fine,' Erin assured him and turned away to stack the dishwasher. 'Do you want a coffee?'

'Please.' He took her seat and helped himself to a piece of leftover toast.

'I can make you some breakfast,' she offered, half out of guilt.

'I already ate,' he admitted with a grin.

'How come you're not twenty stone? You must have hollow legs.'

There was another knock and Sandra poked her head in.

'Oh, sorry to interrupt—'

'That's okay.' Erin crossed the room so that she was standing between Sandra and Ronan. 'What can I do for you?'

'My phone's on the blink. Could I use yours? It's not to the States, I just need a taxi . . .'

'Of course, no problem.'

Sandra leaned around Erin to smile at Ronan. 'Isn't she lovely?'

'She is.' He smiled.

'Although you really shouldn't be keeping her out so late when she has all of us to look after.'

Before Ronan could respond, Erin hustled Sandra back into the dining room and was relieved to see that Sebastian had left. 'I'll call a cab for you, Sandra. Would you like it straight away?'

'Please.'

'Anything else?' Erin asked.

'Not a thing,' Sandra said and went upstairs humming.

Erin made the call and then went back into the kitchen.

Ronan looked up as she walked in. 'What was she talking about?'

Erin shrugged. 'No idea. She's always coming out with these strange comments. She drives PJ around the twist.'

Ronan glanced at the clock as he stood up. 'I'd better get going, I have some deliveries to make.'

'On a Sunday?'

'It's just another day in the egg business,' he laughed. 'See you tonight.'

She blinked. 'Tonight?'

He shook his head, smiling. 'Mark and Marguerite invited us to dinner, remember?'

Erin was at a loss for words. She had forgotten all

about the invitation that had been made long before she and Marguerite fell out over Sebastian. 'I'm not sure that's still on,' she said eventually.

He frowned. 'Oh? Why not?'

'Marguerite and I had words,' she admitted. 'I think she's still annoyed with me.'

'Over what?'

'Something silly.'

'Call her and sort it, Erin.' He bent his head to kiss her. 'She's your best friend.'

'You're right, I will,' Erin promised.

Chapter Thirteen

Hazel was sitting in front of a blank canvas, staring out over the water, when PJ appeared beside her.

'Can I join you? Only it seems ages since we've had a chat.'

He opened a bag and pulled out three cheese rolls, a packet of crisps, bottled water and some juice for Gracie. 'I thought you might be hungry,' he said. 'You didn't eat much at breakfast. Where's Gracie?'

Hazel nodded towards the bench in the distance where Gracie sat with an arrangement of teddies around her.

'A picnic!' PJ laughed. 'Looks like I timed that well. I'll just go and give her this.' He hesitated and looked down at Hazel, a frown furrowing his brow. 'If that's okay?'

Hazel nodded. 'Sure. Thanks.'

She watched as the man went down to Gracie and presented her with the food. Gracie smiled in delight and proceeded to break the roll into small pieces and divide it out. PJ said something, laughed, patted her head and then came back to join Hazel. He put a roll and bottle of water down in front of her. 'Thanks,' she said, 'but I'm not really hungry.'

He looked at her, his kind eyes full of concern. 'What is it, Hazel? You're not yourself these days. Why aren't you painting?'

'I've decided to pack it in.'

'That's a shame. Why would you do that?'

'Because I'm not any good, that's why.'

He laughed. 'What a load of rubbish.'

She tried to smile though tears pricked her eyes. 'You don't even like my paintings.'

'Yes, I do,' he insisted. 'I may not always understand them, admittedly, but I love the colours. Your paintings are full of life and warmth, Hazel.' He smiled, his eyes crinkling at the corners. 'Like you. I think you're very talented, But sure, if a rich and famous man like Sebastian Gray loves your work why would you care what a *culchie* like me thinks? Now tell me, what has you so down?'

'I had an interview in a shop in Mullingar last week. I was hoping they'd agree to sell my paintings but the owner hated them.'

PJ frowned. 'Which shop?'

'The Lucky Leprechaun.'

PJ stared at her in disbelief. 'You took your wonderful paintings to that chancer, Mick Flaherty?'

'You know him?'

'Not personally but he doesn't have the best reputation. If you'd told me you were going to see him I would have saved you the bother.'

'Oh, well, it was just an idea.' Hazel shrugged and opened her water and took a sip. 'Thanks for this.' She felt tears threaten again. Why had this man taken her under his wing? Was it pity? She was beginning to think so. It was probably also why Sebastian Gray had bought two of her paintings. They saw a young, single woman with a mute child and they felt sorry for her.

PJ watched her with kind eyes. 'You know, there's a gallery on the Dublin side of Mullingar that would be a more fitting setting for your work. I know the lady that runs it. If you like, I'll take you there this afternoon.'

'No, I can't.' Hazel shook her head. All of her enthusiasm and optimism seemed to have withered and died. She didn't think her paintings were all that good and she didn't feel she could cope with another rejection, especially in front of PJ.

'So what are your plans, love?' PJ asked, his voice soft, eyes kind. 'Are you going to stay in Dunbarra or will you return to Dublin?'

Hazel felt panic bubble up inside. 'I'm not sure.'

'You should think about settling down somewhere, Hazel' He looked at her and smiled. 'There are worse places than Dunbarra, and we have a great little school. I know the principal. Gerry's a good man and knows how to make every child feel special.'

'I have to go,' Hazel mumbled and began to gather up her things. 'Come on, Gracie,' she called. She could see from her stance that Gracie wasn't impressed that her picnic was being interrupted.

'I haven't finished my lunch yet.' PJ gestured to his half-eaten roll. 'If you like, Gracie can stay here with me for a while.'

'No, it's time for her nap,' Hazel said, her tone sharper than she'd intended.

'Then at least let me take you to that gallery this afternoon and introduce you to Niamh. You'll like her; she's very down to earth.'

Another wave of panic threatened to engulf Hazel and blindly she tugged her bag over her shoulder and went to fetch Gracie. 'Come along, darling, it's time to go.'

'Well?' PJ looked at her.

'Okay.'

His face split into a happy smile. 'See you out front at three?'

'See you then. Thanks, PJ.' And dragging a reluctant Gracie along behind her, Hazel hurried back towards the guest house.

'Marguerite? It's me, Erin.'

There was a pause before her friend replied. 'Erin.'

'Marguerite, I'm sorry, you know I am. What can I do to make this right?'

There was a sigh and then Marguerite answered

sounding more like herself. 'I'm sorry too, Erin. I overreacted. But I've been so worried about Sebastian and you knew that . . .'

'I should have said something but I thought it was more important that Sebastian was at least talking to someone.'

'You're quite right, my friend.' A small pause. 'Has he said anything else?'

Erin was glad this was a phone call and Marguerite couldn't see the guilt on her face.

'No,' she said. After all, talking hadn't really been on the agenda last night.

'Still, at least he's agreed to come to dinner with us tonight. That's a good sign, no?'

Erin groaned inwardly. 'About tonight, I'm not sure it's such a good idea . . .'

'No, please come, Erin. I want to know everything is okay between us again.'

'It is but—'

Marguerite cut in. 'I think Sebastian is only coming because you'll be there.'

Erin wasn't sure whether to be thrilled or horrified by this information. 'When did you invite him?'

'Today, why?'

'Oh, no reason.' What was he up to? How was she going to sit at a table with both him and Ronan present?

'So you will come?' Marguerite pressed.

'Okay, then. But one thing, Marguerite . . .'

'Yes?'

'Please don't mention any of this in front of Ronan. He seems a little jealous of Sebastian and so I haven't told him anything about our conversation or the fact that we went out to lunch.'

There was another pause and then Marguerite responded, sounding slightly disapproving. 'Erin, it's not a good idea to try to keep things from him; this is a small town.'

'I know. I've been stupid.'

'Don't worry about it, Erin. Put it behind you. We will have a lovely evening, I just know it.'

'I'll look forward to it,' Erin lied.

'*Au revoir* my friend.'

Erin put down the phone glad that she and Marguerite were friends again but dreading the night ahead. She would have to be very careful what she told Ronan, and how, and she would need to pay Sebastian as little attention as possible. She toyed with the idea of going to see him and warning him to behave himself but that could prove even more embarrassing. He probably had casual sex all of the time and last night meant nothing. She was surprised to find that, apart from the feelings of embarrassment and humiliation, she was also jealous of a dead woman. Marina must have been something special to capture the heart of a wild boy like Sebastian. And that was part of his attraction, Erin realized. He was unavailable in the real sense of the word and therefore a challenge.

But not one she was going to take up, she told herself. She'd behaved disgracefully and been unfaithful to the most important man in her life. It would not happen again. There would be no more *tête-a-têtes*, no more deep conversations and no more intimate meals. If he needed a shoulder to cry on Sebastian could go to his sister. Erin was no longer offering a counselling service, or any other service for that matter. She was going out with Ronan and she was lucky to have him. She needed to remember that.

PJ sat waiting in his car. It was ten past three and there was still no sign of Hazel. He thought of going upstairs and knocking on her door but maybe he was being too pushy. It was none of his business if Hazel decided to stop painting. But the thought made him sad. He was afraid that if she gave up on her art there was a danger that she might give up on everything. It was such a shame. She'd blossomed over these last couple of months and was positively buzzing with happiness some days – until she'd met that fool Flaherty. In one fell swoop he'd destroyed her confidence and turned her back into a shy, nervous mouse. 'Gobshite,' PJ muttered. But he probably hadn't helped the matter by quizzing the poor girl about her future. 'Two gobshites,' he said, shaking his head and climbing out of the car. He went back into the house and was halfway up the stairs when the idea popped into his head. What harm could it do? No one would probably even notice. And if it wasn't to be then no one would be any the wiser. Not stopping to think of any cons, PJ, retraced his steps and, taking the painting off the wall, hurried back out to his car.

Erin was working on her accounts at the kitchen table when there was a clatter in the hall. She was about to go and investigate when PJ walked in. 'Hi, what was the noise?'

'Noise?' He looked blank.

Erin eyed him suspiciously. 'What are you up to?'

'Nothing. Any news?'

She shrugged. 'Not really. Other than I'm going to Marguerite's for dinner tonight with Ronan and,' she sighed, 'Sebastian's going to be there.'

He leaned against the door jamb. 'Oh. And is that a problem?'

'Maybe.'

'Erin?'

She looked back up at him. 'Ronan doesn't like him. I think he's jealous.'

'I see. And has he reason to be?'

Erin bit her lip and nodded.

'Oh, Erin,' he groaned.

'Don't say it like that,' she protested. 'It was a mistake. It won't happen again.'

'Does Mr Gray know that?'

'He's not interested in me,' she assured him.

'Yet you're worried about tonight.'

'Sebastian's unpredictable. When he's miserable he's fine but when he's in good humour he can be a bit of a rogue.'

'So you're afraid he'll try to stir it with Ronan just to amuse himself?'

'Exactly.'

PJ pulled himself up to his full height. 'Want me to talk to him?'

'No!' Erin looked at him, horrified.

'Then you should. Tell him to behave or he's out.'

'Perhaps you're right.'

'I am.' He put a hand on Erin's shoulder. 'Ronan's a good man, Erin. He's really good for you. I'll never understand why you don't marry him and—'

'Don't start,' she warned.

'Okay, okay, I won't. But don't mess it up, that's all I'm saying. Not over someone like Gray.'

'Don't worry, I won't,' Erin promised.

He nodded, satisfied. 'Good. Now, I don't suppose you've seen Hazel, have you?'

'No, why?'

'Oh, I just wanted a quick word.' He frowned. 'She hasn't gone out, has she?'

'I've no idea where she is, but if I see her I'll tell her you're looking for her.'

'No, don't do that,' he said hastily.

'What are you up to?' Erin eyed him curiously.

He winked. 'Never you mind. I'll be in the garden if you need me.'

Erin sat there after he'd gone outside, debating what to do. Half of her dreaded the thought of confronting Sebastian; the other half was glad of an excuse to go and see him. As the day wore on, last night's visit to the cabin grew more surreal but the tenderness of her breasts was proof that she hadn't imagined it. And though she felt embarrassed and guilty, she was also filled with the suppressed excitement that only an illicit liaison could trigger. Logic told her that PJ was wrong and she should stay well away from Sebastian Gray. But she knew she wouldn't.

Sebastian opened the door, a towel around his waist and a razor in his hand. 'Hi.'

'Hi.' She concentrated on looking into his eyes. 'Sorry. Bad time.'

'I'm under instructions from Marguerite to clean up my act for dinner tonight.'

Erin smiled.

'Come in.' He stood back.

She looked around. 'I'd better not.'

'We need to talk but it's probably not a good idea to do it on the doorstep, certainly not with me looking like this.'

'I suppose not.' She stepped into the cabin and sat down in the armchair furthest away from him.

He looked at her in amusement. 'Why don't you make us both a coffee while I finish shaving?'

'Sure.' She stood up again and went into the small kitchen. As she waited for the kettle to boil she wandered back into the sitting room. Glancing into the bedroom she caught sight of the tousled bed and she had a flashback that made her flush. She hurried back into the kitchen. She shouldn't have come, she realized. She considered just leaving but that would only make things more awkward tonight. She carried the mugs through to the sitting room, set his down on the table and, cupping her own between her hands, she sat down to wait for him.

'You look deep in thought.'

She jumped, slopping hot coffee on to her jeans.

'Shit, sorry!' Sebastian grabbed a cloth from the kitchen and brought it back to her.

He went to dab at her jeans but Erin snatched the cloth away from him and did it herself.

'Are you okay?' he asked, crouching down in front of her.

Erin wished he'd move away. She could smell the lemony scent of his aftershave and feel his breath on her cheek. 'Fine.' She gave him a bright smile that she hoped said she was completely in control.

'How are you?' he asked, his eyes searching hers.

'Fine,' she squeaked. 'You?'

He winced slightly. 'Feeling a bit guilty.'

Great. His girlfriend was dead and he still felt he'd been unfaithful.

'I took advantage of you,' he continued.

Erin stared. 'What? No, of course you didn't. I'm not sixteen.'

He smiled. 'You're lovely.'

'But you're right, it shouldn't have happened.'

His lips twitched. 'Shouldn't it?'

'You know it shouldn't,' she said but she couldn't hide her smile.

'It was very nice though.'

'Nice isn't the word I'd use.'

'Oh? What word would you use?' he murmured and leaned over to kiss the hollow of her neck.

'Stop!' she gasped.

He looked into her eyes. 'Do you really want me to?'

'Yes,' she insisted, pushing him away. 'Please sit over there.'

Obediently he stood up and crossed over to the sofa and picked up his mug. 'There, is that better?'

'Yes. Look, I'm not quite sure what happened last night but of course it shouldn't have. I'm in a relationship.' He opened his mouth to reply but she held up her hand. 'No, please, let me finish. We are going to dinner at Marguerite's tonight and I don't want it to be awkward.'

'Why would it be?'

'Ronan's a jealous kind of guy. Please don't do or say anything to upset him.'

He nodded. 'Okay.'

'Okay?' She eyed him suspiciously.

'Anything else?'

'Please listen, I'm not joking. This is my life you're playing with. Last night was great but I need more than that. I have more than that. I have Ronan.'

He looked at her, his eyes thoughtful. 'Yes, but does he have you?'

'Sebastian, please don't mess this up for me. I know that you miss Marina—'

His expression hardened. 'So you think that I'm jealous that you have a partner and I don't?'

'No, of course not,' she said quickly.

He stood up. 'You have nothing to worry about, Erin. I'll be on my best behaviour.'

Erin stood too and looked up into his proud, cool eyes. This hadn't gone the way she wanted, but then, what exactly had she wanted? 'Please don't be like this Sebastian. I just wanted to avoid any awkwardness later.'

'And you have.' He opened the door and, with a helpless shrug, Erin walked through it. She had achieved what she'd set out to do, or had she? Whether Sebastian stuck to his word or not she felt she was in for a difficult evening.

Chapter Fourteen

Erin was a bag of nerves that evening as she waited for Ronan. So much so that she'd poured a large glass of wine and was knocking it back in the kitchen when he walked in.

'One of those days?' he laughed as he came to kiss her.

'You could say that. You look well.' He was wearing a brown cord jacket over a white shirt and jeans and looked healthy and handsome.

'You don't look bad yourself.' Ronan stepped back so that he could take a good look at her.

'What, this old thing?' Erin smiled. It was a simple dress but it was a designer brand and very well-cut, and its rich ruby colour made Erin's skin glow. She wore high black sandals and had slipped on a cropped black cardigan as there was a chill in the air. 'Would you like a drink?' she asked.

He looked at his watch. 'We should go.'

'I suppose.' Erin drained her glass.

'You don't seem keen. Haven't you and Marguerite made up?'

'Yes, but I'm still not looking forward to the evening. I think it will be difficult and awkward with Sebastian there.'

'I'm surprised he agreed to come. It's the first time he's shown any interest in socializing since he got here. Well, except for his dinner with you.'

'Don't start that again, Ronan.'

'Just joking. Should we ask the VIP if he wants a lift?'

Erin stared at him. The thought of being in the jeep with both Ronan and Sebastian filled her with dread but it would look very odd if they didn't offer him a lift. 'I suppose we should. You start the car and I'll get him.'

Erin hurried round the side of the house and knocked on Sebastian's door but there was no answer. 'He seems to have left already,' she told Ronan as she climbed into the car.

'Then we'd better get going. I'm sure someone like Sebastian Gray is not used to being kept waiting.'

'He's not like that,' Erin said, irritated.

'Oh?' He shot her a sidelong glance. 'You've changed your tune.'

She shrugged. 'He may be famous but he's still just a man, and he has problems just like everyone else.'

He said nothing and they drove the rest of the way in a tense silence. When he pulled up outside Dijon he came around to open her door.

'Let's try to make this a pleasant evening, Ronan,' Erin pleaded, taking his hand, 'for Marguerite's sake.'

He kissed her and smiled. 'Sure.'

There were still three parties in the restaurant when they got there. Sean was serving and Mark was behind the bar. 'Hello, there,' he said, coming around to kiss Erin and shake Ronan's hand. 'I'm afraid Marguerite's running behind schedule.' He nodded towards a table of six by the window. 'They arrived late,' he murmured, 'and have been a total pain in the arse since they got here.'

Erin laughed. 'No problem, we can wait.'

'Have a seat,' Mark said, going back behind the bar and producing a bottle of chilled white wine.

Ronan climbed on to a stool beside Erin. 'So where's the main man?'

'Sebastian? He hasn't got here yet.'

Erin frowned. 'I did knock on his door to offer him a lift but there was no answer.'

'He's probably just gone on one of his marathon walks first,' Mark said, filling three glasses. 'Cheers.'

'*Sláinte*.' Ronan touched his glass against Erin's.

'Mmmm, lovely.' Erin looked up as Sean went bustling past to the kitchen, looking flushed. 'Tell Marguerite she doesn't have to bother with dinner, Mark. We could easily make do with cheese and dessert, couldn't we, Ronan?'

Mark laughed at Ronan's disappointed expression.

'Don't worry, it's all taken care of. Marguerite had it all prepared before they arrived.'

Ronan smiled broadly. 'She's a great woman, I've always said so.'

Sean reappeared, two plates in one hand and a basket of breads in the other. 'Something to keep you going,' he said, setting it on the bar between them.

Ronan dived on the rolls. 'Sean, you're a lifesaver. So how is your brother-in-law?' he asked Mark between bites. 'Are we in for a difficult evening?'

Mark pondered the question. 'I don't think so. He seems to have relaxed a bit, wouldn't you say, Erin?'

She coughed as some wine went down the wrong way. 'I suppose so.'

'He's very relaxed with Erin,' Ronan said with a meaningful look at Mark.

'Oh?' Mark looked from him to Erin.

'Ignore him,' she advised. 'You promised to behave,' she said to Ronan.

'And I will but he's not here yet. When's he going back to the US?'

'Ronan!' Erin hissed.

'It's only Mark, he doesn't mind.'

'I don't mind, Erin.' Mark grinned. 'And I probably will heave a sigh of relief when he goes if it means Marguerite will stop worrying about him.'

They chatted over their wine while Marguerite and Sean finished serving their guests and then Sean seated them at the table in the centre of the room. Marguerite came out to say hello, glancing anxiously from her watch to the door. 'I'm sorry about this, my friends; I don't know where Sebastian has got to.'

'Give him five minutes and then serve,' Mark said. 'I don't know about the rest of you lot but I'm starving.'

Sean came over to Marguerite's side. 'Want me to stay and serve this lot, chef?'

'I think I can manage them, Sean, but you're welcome to eat with us, if you like – there's plenty.'

'Ah, no, Mary can never go to sleep if I'm not there.' He winked at Erin. 'She looks forward to a nice cuddle.'

'Too much information,' Mark said and received a flick from Sean's cloth.

'I'll just give the stragglers their bill, then, and I'll say goodnight. Enjoy yourselves.'

'We'll try,' Erin said with feeling. She'd had two glasses of wine since they got here and she was beginning to feel a little woozy. She reached over to take a piece of bread, hoping it would soak up some of the alcohol. She was chewing on it when Sebastian walked through the door, causing her to choke and cough.

'Have a drink,' Mark suggested.

'Some water, please.'

'Hello, everyone, sorry I'm late.' Sebastian stood beside her and she was acutely aware of the smell of his aftershave and his unbelievable magnetism. He wore a simple black jacket over a white T-shirt and black jeans. Erin couldn't tear her eyes away from him but Sebastian hadn't even glanced in her direction. She wondered if anyone else had noticed. She looked across the table at Ronan, to find him watching her.

'Here.' Mark handed her the glass of water and then poured Sebastian some wine. 'You've met Ronan Masterson, haven't you, Sebastian?'

'Yes, briefly.' Sebastian reached over to shake Ronan's hand.

'How are you?' Ronan said, sounding stiff and formal.

'Fine, thanks. Where's Marguerite?' Sebastian asked Mark.

'Getting ready to serve up; we'd almost given up on you.'

'I'll go and say hello,' Sebastian said, and glass in hand he disappeared into the kitchen.

'He seems normal enough tonight,' Ronan said.

'Shush, Ronan,' Erin hissed with a nervous look at the kitchen door.

'Calm down, Erin, he can't hear me,' Ronan retorted, an edge in his voice.

Erin bit her tongue. If she started annoying him the evening would go steadily downhill. 'Sorry,' she mumbled.

'Will you two stop?' Mark said with an easy smile. 'You're here to enjoy yourselves. Forget about

Sebastian. He'll be a lot more relaxed if we all just treat him the same way as anyone else.'

'It would be easier if he behaved like everyone else,' Ronan muttered.

Erin opened her mouth to rebuke him but was silenced by the challenge that glittered in his eyes. She would have to be careful, she realized. Ronan was more observant than she'd given him credit for. She abandoned her water and had some more wine. Maybe if she loosened up a bit she would behave in a more natural manner and allay his suspicions. 'So Mark, do you have a trip lined up for tomorrow or can you relax and enjoy a few drinks?' she asked.

'I'm taking a party out in the afternoon so I'll be able to have a lie in.'

Erin rolled her eyes at Ronan. 'Wouldn't you just kill for a lie-in?'

'I'm having one.' He grinned at her. 'Vincent said he'd come in early tomorrow.'

'He didn't!' Erin was scandalized.

'He did!'

'So I'm the only one getting up at the crack of dawn?' she groaned.

'Not so.'

Erin looked round to see Marguerite and Sebastian had come out of the kitchen. 'What do you mean, Marguerite?' she asked.

'I called and talked to PJ. He's put up a notice saying that breakfast doesn't start until nine tomorrow. I hope you don't mind me interfering, *chérie*, but I thought you deserved an extra hour in bed.'

Erin stood up to embrace her friend. 'You are an angel, thank you. I don't know why I haven't thought of doing it before.' She shot Sebastian a nervous smile. 'But your brother might object. He always has breakfast at eight.'

'Pah!' Marguerite laughed. 'He'll be under the covers until midday after tonight, won't you, *mon frère*?'

Sebastian smiled at Erin and his eyes were gentle. 'It's no problem. I think you deserve a rest.'

'Absolutely,' Mark agreed. 'And trust me, you don't want someone with a hangover cooking your breakfast.'

'Who says I'll have a hangover?' Erin protested.

Mark promptly filled her glass. 'I do.'

They all laughed and Erin thought maybe everything would be all right after all.

Marguerite served them seafood chowder followed by confit of duck and roasted vegetables. The conversation was relaxed for the most part and moved from the tourist business in Ireland to the success of Erin's market garden and Ronan's eggs.

'It's been quite profitable,' he said, in response to a polite query from Sebastian, 'but I foresee hard times ahead. The credit crunch will see to that.'

'So what will you do?' Sebastian asked.

Ronan shrugged. 'Ride it out, I hope.'

Sebastian frowned. 'Shouldn't you have a Plan B? Aren't there other areas you could branch into?'

'Possibly,' Ronan acknowledged.

He was looking defensive now, Erin knew the signs. She decided maybe it was time she showed some solidarity. 'It's easier said than done,' she told Sebastian. 'There's a lot involved from both a commitment and a financial point of view when you choose the organic root. Switching to a different product wouldn't be easy and would probably damage your reputation as a conscientious farmer.'

Sebastian looked sceptical. 'A good reputation isn't much use if you're out of business.'

'Perhaps I'll take up acting,' Ronan said with a cool smile. 'There seems to be good money in that business.'

'There are more out-of-work actors than there are rich ones,' Sebastian assured him.

Ronan nodded. 'So I believe. Still, the movie world has to be a lot more glamorous than farming.'

'It has its moments,' Sebastian agreed.

'Have you a new film coming out?' Mark asked.

'Yes, it comes out in the States before Christmas but it will probably be spring before it hits Europe.'

'Is it another violent blockbuster?' Marguerite asked, shaking her head.

'Or bonkbuster?' Mark said with a wink.

'Both, of course,' Sebastian said with a humourless smile. 'But it will probably be my last for a while.'

Marguerite looked at him, her eyes concerned. 'Oh, why is that?'

Sebastian looked uncomfortable. 'I'm just working on something else. I'd prefer not to talk about it; it's early days.'

'So it's true: actors are very superstitious.' Mark smiled at him.

'I'm afraid so.'

Erin leaned forward, interested. 'Do you have any rituals you have to go through before you go on set?'

'I touch wood,' he admitted.

'That's not so weird,' she said, disappointed.

He laughed. 'I worked with one actress who walked off set because someone sent her flowers.'

'I don't get it,' Mark said.

'Fresh flowers are considered bad luck, but that's usually just on stage. I think she was actually looking for an excuse to go back to her trailer and her bottle.'

Ronan finished his meal and wiped his mouth on a napkin. 'Marguerite, that was magnificent – as always.'

She blew him a kiss and smiled. 'I am glad you enjoyed it.'

'Yes, Marguerite, your cooking gets better and better,' Sebastian agreed.

'Of course it does. That's because she works so hard,' Erin said with an affectionate smile at her friend.

'For your information, I've just hired an assistant.'

'That's wonderful news!' Erin exclaimed.

'I was almost giving up hope.' Marguerite. said. 'All the applicants were useless. It was very depressing. But then this young girl came in and I think she will actually be perfect.'

'Touch wood.' Sebastian tapped the table.

Marguerite laughed and tapped it too. 'She trained in Chez Nous.'

'The Michelin-star restaurant in Dublin?' Erin asked.

Marguerite nodded. 'Her stepfather is the head chef.'

'Are you sure she realizes what the job entails, Marguerite?' Mark asked.

'I made it very clear that she would have to turn her hand to everything. She seems fine with that. Apparently she wants to work her way up and prove herself just the way her stepfather did. Anyway, I'm happy to give her a chance. The other people I interviewed were,' she shuddered, 'terrible.'

'I am sure it will be a great success,' Erin said raising a glass to her friend, 'and if she takes even some of the burden off you then it will be.'

'With two chefs in the kitchen you'll be real competition for White's,' Ronan told her.

Marguerite laughed. 'Oh, I don't think so.'

Sebastian frowned. 'White's?'

'It's an haute-cuisine restaurant over the other side of the lake,' Mark explained.

'Ah, yes, of course.' He nodded.

'You know it?' Ronan shot him a curious look.

Sebastian met Erin's eyes. 'I've heard of it.'

Erin felt her cheeks grow hot as Ronan's eyes found hers. 'Dijon is much nicer than White's,' she said with a bright smile and stood up. 'Excuse me.'

Marguerite was waiting for her when she came out of the loo. 'I'm sorry about that, Erin, but I'm sure Ronan didn't notice.'

'Oh, I think he did. I think that was Sebastian's intention.'

Marguerite's eyes were sharp. 'No, of course it wasn't. Why would he do such a thing?'

'Why indeed?' Erin murmured.

'What are you going to do?'

'I don't know. I'll have to wait and see. If Ronan asks it's probably better that I tell him the truth.' Or part of it anyway, she added silently.

'That would be best.' Marguerite embraced her.

Erin smiled and hugged her back. 'I am so glad you've found someone to help out here.'

'She could be a blessing but she may bring trouble too. She's very attractive. In fact,' Marguerite put her head on one side, 'maybe I should fix her up with Sebastian. He always liked his women young and it would keep him out of your hair and stop Ronan feeling jealous.'

'I don't think Sebastian is ready for another relationship yet, do you?'

Marguerite's eyes twinkled. 'Who said anything about a relationship? *Mais, non*, perhaps you are right. If he broke her heart she would leave and then I would be back to step one. Now, let us go and make some coffee.'

Chapter Fifteen

Hazel stayed very still, kept her breathing steady and waited until she heard the door close before she opened her eyes. She sighed as she looked down at Gracie sleeping on the sofa beside her. She couldn't avoid PJ for ever, but his concern was beginning to overwhelm her. She could still see the excited look on his face when he'd told her about the gallery owner's interest. He'd wanted to pile her, Gracie and all of her paintings into the car, there and then, and take them into Mullingar. Hazel had wanted to run and hide.

Poor PJ was completely bewildered but she didn't know how to explain. Since then she'd been avoiding him like the plague, much to her daughter's chagrin. And now, deprived of her friend, Gracie was growing tired and discontented in Dunbarra. It was time to move on. Hazel had felt safe and cocooned in the Gatehouse but now she was feeling stifled and the old familiar and sickening feeling of panic was threatening to engulf her. She needed to find somewhere

where no one knew her and wouldn't care what she did or didn't do. But the thought of leaving was equally frightening.

Hazel's breath came quick and shallow and when she put up a hand to push her hair back, her forehead was damp with sweat. With a quick glance to check Gracie was still asleep, Hazel slipped silently out of Erin's sitting room and went out to sit on the front step. She forced herself to breathe naturally and finally the feeling of panic began to abate. When she opened her eyes it was to see Sebastian standing a short distance away watching her. 'Oh, hi,' she said, hoping her voice sounded more normal to him than it did to her.

'Hi.' He came over and lowered his long frame on to the step below her. 'I haven't seen you painting in a while.'

'I'm not in the mood.'

He nodded his understanding. 'That's the worst about doing something creative for a living. If you're not feeling inspired you just can't work.'

She peered at him through her hair but didn't respond.

'You need a break from here,' he said, his eyes lighting up. 'Let's go out.'

'I don't think so.'

'Oh, come on, live a little.'

She grinned, infected by his good humour. 'Where would we go?'

'We could go out on the lake or go and see an obscure subtitled movie. We could go to the pub and get drunk . . .'

'I have a daughter to look after,' she pointed out.

'The old man will look after her,' he said, dismissing the excuse with a wave of his hand. 'Come on, what do you say?'

Hazel knew that PJ would be delighted that she was going out and would readily agree to look after Gracie for a couple of hours, but something told her it would be best not to mention that she was going out with Sebastian Gray. 'Okay, then.'

'Great!' He stood up. 'You sort out your babysitter and I'll phone a taxi. Meet you on the main road in twenty minutes.'

That suited Hazel perfectly but she did wonder why he didn't want to advertise that they were going out together. As soon as he was gone she was having doubts about the excursion, but what harm could it do? She needed a break and Gracie would be only too happy to escape from her morose mother for a few hours and spend some time with her beloved PJ.

As Hazel went in search of the man, she realized she was a little envious of him and his easy relationship with her daughter. In fact, she was jealous of his easy way with everybody and how he seemed so comfortable in his own skin. Hazel couldn't ever remember feeling like that. There was a period after she'd left school when her whole life lay before her and the possibilities and opportunities had seemed boundless and exciting. And she would never forget her euphoria when she'd got that amazing review for her work. There was the night Dessie had asked her to marry him and then, of course, there was the night she had Gracie. But though that had been the most special night of all, Hazel remembered the terror that followed when she realized that she was now responsible for another human being, twenty-four, seven.

She found PJ in the orchard and his face lit up when he saw her.

'Hello, love, where's Gracie?'

'Having her nap. I was just going to wake her. I was wondering . . .'

'Why don't you leave her with me for the afternoon?' he suggested. 'I could do with some help.'

'Well, I did want to go out for a while.'

'Off you go. I'm sure you could do with a break.'

She smiled. He was such a good man. 'If you're sure you wouldn't mind . . .'

'And why would I mind? That child of yours is a little darling. It's a pleasure to have her around.'

'Thanks, PJ.' She went off to wake Gracie, who lit up with happiness when she heard the plans for her afternoon.

'I won't be long,' Hazel promised PJ when she delivered her daughter to him.

'Take as long as you like. We'll be fine, won't we?' He winked at Gracie.

Sebastian was standing by a taxi waiting for her. 'I thought you'd changed your mind.' He opened the door for her and she clambered in.

'Where are we going?' she asked.

'We could visit an art gallery and then go on to the cinema.'

'No art gallery,' she said.

He shot her a curious look but just shrugged. 'Then it's straight to the cinema.'

In the foyer of the small cinema they argued over what they should see. Sebastian fancied the horror movie but Hazel wanted to see a comedy. In the end they had to settle for a second-rate romance as there was nothing else on for at least an hour.

'Who could possibly fall for her?' Sebastian complained of the leading lady. 'She does nothing but whine and play with her hair.'

Hazel laughed. 'He's not exactly a great catch either.'

They ate popcorn, drank cola and ridiculed the lame performances and weak storyline but still Hazel felt the tears well up at the soppy ending.

'Are you okay?' Sebastian asked, his eyes shining in the darkness.

'Yes,' she sniffed. 'Sorry.'

'Love means never having to say you're sorry.'

Hazel giggled at his puppy-dog expression. 'You're mad.'

Sebastian gave a solemn nod. 'I know. We have a lot in common.'

Finally the credits rolled.

'That was terrible,' he said.

'Terrible,' Hazel agreed, blowing her nose.

'Did you enjoy it?'

She nodded. 'Absolutely.'

He laughed. 'Come on, let's find a pub.'

'I should get back,' Hazel said with a glance at her watch.

'Nonsense, you can't go back in this state. Anyway, I'm hungry, aren't you?'

'After all that popcorn? No, I'm stuffed.'

He patted his stomach. 'That was just an appetiser.'

'How can someone so skinny eat so much?'

He made a face. 'I'm making up for lost time. I'd better be careful or I'll end up at the other extreme and out of work.'

'What happened to you?' she asked when they were sitting on stools at the bar of a tiny, gloomy pub that smelled of damp.

Sebastian looked into his pint. 'The usual.'

'A woman?' she ventured, surprised at herself. She couldn't remember the last time she'd been interested enough in another person to ask.

He nodded. 'She died.'

'I'm sorry.' She put her hand over his.

'Thanks.'

'Were you married?'

'No.'

'If you don't want to talk about it . . .'

'No, it's okay. But it's still hard.'

She nodded her understanding and waited.

'It was a drugs overdose. I watched her fall apart in front of my eyes but I couldn't help her.'

Now it was Hazel's turn to stare into her drink. 'You can't help someone unless they want to be helped.'

'So everyone keeps telling me,' he said, sounding weary, 'but it doesn't make it any easier.'

'I know.'

'Do you?' He looked at her.

'I've been through a similar experience.'

'I'm sorry.'

'Oh, no one died,' Hazel assured him. 'Not yet anyway.'

'Is that the reason you came to Dunbarra?' he asked.

'Yeah. You?'

He smiled. 'Yeah.'

'But you will go back, won't you? To acting I mean.'

'I suppose so. What about you?

Hazel lowered her head. 'I'm not sure.'

'I wish you'd stop doing that,' he sighed.

'What?' she said, puzzled.

'Hiding behind your hair. What exactly are you hiding from?'

'Everything? Everyone?' She stood up. 'I have to go.'

'No.' He grasped her hand. 'I'm sorry. I didn't mean to upset you. Please stay.'

Hazel hesitated. The feel of his hand warm and firm, holding hers, had a calming effect and she sank back down on to the stool. 'Well, just for a little while.'

He smiled. 'Talk to me about your painting. When did you know it was what you wanted to do?'

She thought about it for a moment then shrugged. 'It never occurred to me to do anything else.'

His face lit up immediately and Hazel thought how handsome he was.

'That's exactly how I feel about acting,' he said. 'When the camera starts to roll it just transports me to a different place.' He gave a short laugh. 'If only I could stay there. Then, when I did something wrong, I'd just have to do another take to make it right.'

Hazel gave a wistful sigh. 'That would be nice.'

'I'm not a great fan of real life,' Sebastian carried on.

Hazel sighed again. 'Me neither.'

He smiled and signalled to the barman. 'Let's drink to that.'

When they came out of the pub, Hazel squinted up at the sky. 'What happened?' she asked, swaying slightly. 'Where did the sun go?'

Sebastian grinned. 'It's night-time, Hazel.'

'No!' She gaped at him. 'But it can't be.'

'It is.' He tugged her towards the taxi rank.

'Oh my God, what will PJ say?'

'Probably "Where were ye two eejits?"'

Hazel started to giggle. Sebastian was a very good mimic. PJ might well be annoyed with her but he'd get over it. He'd told her to enjoy herself, after all. And it wasn't that late. She tried to look at her watch but it was hard to focus. 'What time is it?'

'No idea,' he said, helping her into the back of a taxi.

'Oh, God,' Hazel groaned as the driver did a U-turn, 'I don't feel very well.'

The taxi driver braked. 'Are you going to puke, woman?'

'No, she's fine,' Sebastian told him, 'but if she does have an accident I'll pay to have your car cleaned, okay? It needs it anyway,' he added quietly for Hazel's benefit.

The driver glared back at Hazel but drove on.

'Just take some long, deep breaths,' Sebastian whispered in her ear. 'You'll be fine.'

It was only a twenty-minute journey, Hazel reminded herself, closing her eyes and digging her fingers into the seat. She could surely manage twenty minutes. Oh, what had she been thinking, having all of those Bailey's coffees? What would PJ say? She was a truly awful person and a terrible mother.

'We're here,' Sebastian said, and after pushing one hundred euros into the taxi driver's relieved and grateful hand, he helped her out of the car.

As she stood there swaying, the door opened and Erin was looking down at her.

'Hi Erin,' Sebastian said cheerfully. 'Sorry we're a bit late.'

'Sorry, I'm sooo sorry,' Hazel sang then she giggled and hiccupped, and leaning into the flower bed she promptly threw up.

Chapter Sixteen

Erin closed the door gently and went downstairs.

'How is she?' PJ asked.

'Out cold. She's going to have a serious headache in the morning.'

'Is Gracie okay?'

Erin smiled. 'Fast asleep. She didn't even budge when Hazel collided with the dressing table.'

PJ shook his head. 'What on earth was she thinking of, getting into such a state?'

'I doubt she was thinking. Where's Sebastian?'

'Fecked off home as soon as you took her upstairs,' PJ said with a disapproving scowl. 'I told you he was one to watch. I hope he hasn't got his sights set on Hazel now. That girl isn't able for the likes of him.'

Erin looked at him, feeling a mixture of irritation and amusement. 'PJ, she must be almost thirty and a mother. I think she can look after herself.'

'I wouldn't be so sure.'

After PJ had retired to bed, Erin made herself a mug of coffee and took it out to the back step. It was a cool night, and there wasn't much light left in the sky but the air was still and filled with the perfumes from the garden. Erin usually enjoyed these moments of solitude, which were rare when you were running a guest house, but tonight she felt troubled. What was Sebastian Gray doing messing around with Hazel and how had the girl got so drunk given that Sebastian seemed merely merry? She wondered what else they'd got up to. The thought of Sebastian making love to Hazel triggered serious pangs of jealousy and she wondered if that had been his intention.

They hadn't really talked since the day of the dinner party. Sebastian had tried to apologize for his comments about White's restaurant in front of Ronan but Erin had been too angry to listen and too scared of someone seeing them together to hang about. She had avoided him since and maintained a formal distance when serving breakfast. He hadn't seemed to notice, which was very annoying. The flirting had ceased as quickly as it had started and it was as if the events of last week hadn't happened. Which confirmed what Erin had thought to begin with: that she could have been anyone, Sebastian didn't care. It could just as easily have been Hazel. For all she knew he'd had her too.

It was a humiliating thought. Erin felt cheap and stupid. She'd taken such a risk and for what? She might well lose Ronan because of her foolishness. He hadn't made any reference to Sebastian's comment about White's restaurant but Erin knew he hadn't missed it or its significance. She'd hardly seen him since. Any time she invited him over or suggested going out, he made excuses. Erin wondered if she should just confront him, but if he asked her outright if something was going on what would she say?

For the moment maybe it was best just to lie low and perhaps this episode with Hazel would help take the heat off. She'd have to make sure Ronan got to hear about it. PJ could take care of that. Or she could tell Marguerite. That would kill two birds with one stone. Marguerite would be happy that Erin was keeping her informed and she would tell Mark, who would in turn tell Ronan. Erin sighed and leaned her head against the door frame. Life was complicated. At least, it was since Sebastian Gray had come to town. And yet, despite everything, when she thought of their brief time together . . .

Her eyes flew open and she jumped to her feet. Why was she thinking like this? The rat had spent the afternoon getting another woman drunk. Sad, she told herself, and going inside she locked the back door, washed her mug and went upstairs to bed. She paused on the landing to look out of the front window and a flash caught her attention. It was someone lighting a cigarette. Judging by the position, they were sitting on the bench at the bottom of the garden, looking up at the house. It would be Sebastian. Was he hoping to catch a glimpse of her or of Hazel or was he thinking of Marina? Erin turned and went back downstairs. If she slipped out of the back door and came around the side, it would look as if she were just coming back from the garden. It would be a chance meeting, no more, and it would give them an opportunity to talk in private.

Not giving herself time to examine her motives, Erin slipped on her boots, grabbed a torch and went outside. She skirted the house, walked around the greenhouses and then came back through the orchard. She was almost halfway across the front lawn now but it seemed that Sebastian still hadn't noticed her. She jerked the torch up a little and gave a small cough, ashamed and embarrassed at her own desperation.

'Erin?'

She forced herself to start and spin round. 'Sebastian! What are you doing out here at this hour?'

'Thinking. You?'

'I just wanted to check the temperature gauge in one of the greenhouses. It's been playing up lately and—' She stopped. 'But you don't want to know about that.'

'How's Hazel?'

Erin stiffened. 'Sleeping it off.'

'You're annoyed.'

'Of course I'm annoyed! I run a guest house not a babysitting service.'

'I thought PJ was minding the child.'

She couldn't make out his expression but she could hear the amusement in his voice. 'PJ agreed to mind Gracie for the afternoon not the rest of the day.'

'I didn't hear him complain.'

'Do you think it's responsible behaviour to go off and get drunk and leave your child with strangers in a strange place?'

He came closer and studied her, his eyes thoughtful. 'What exactly are you cross about, Erin: the fact that Hazel got drunk, stayed out so long, or was with me?'

'Don't flatter yourself,' Erin retorted and started to walk away.

Sebastian turned her back around to face him. 'You're jealous.'

Erin could see his white teeth flash in the darkness. 'Don't laugh at me.'

He pulled her close, kissed her hungrily, then drew back just far enough so he could look into her eyes. 'I'm not laughing now,' he whispered.

Erin slid a hand up into his hair, pulled his mouth down to hers and kissed him back, dignity and pride abandoned. As Sebastian responded and his hands moved up under her shirt, Erin knew she should pull away now. She should say goodnight and go to bed and think of Ronan. But she didn't. Sebastian drew back again and led her in silence out of the garden and on to a trail that led down to the lake. She knew exactly where they were going. It was to the spot where she and Ronan had made love that night. It seemed the ultimate betrayal. But she knew she wasn't going to object. In fact, she couldn't remember ever feeling so turned on. When they reached the clearing and Sebastian turned to face her, she pulled her shirt over her head and stepped into his arms.

'No, not like that, like this.' Impatiently Sean showed Rai yet again how he wanted the tables laid. She'd been in the place only a few days but she was already trying to do everything her way.

'I used to work in a Michelin-star restaurant,' she reminded him with a glare, 'and we always put the butter knife on the plate.'

'Good for you, but at Dijon we don't,' Sean snapped.

'Whatever,' Rai mumbled.

Sean counted to ten and smiled. 'I know that you'd prefer to be in the kitchen, love, but you knew that the job involved serving as well.'

She nodded. 'Yeah, sorry. I don't mind serving, it's laying tables and clearing them I hate.'

His eyes widened in surprise. 'Isn't that strange and they're my favourite parts of the job.'

Rai made a face. 'Funny.'

'What's not funny is that we open in ten minutes, so get a move on, please,' Sean told her and went out to the kitchen.

Marguerite looked up. 'Is everything okay?'

'Fine.'

'Is Rai behaving herself?' Marguerite pressed.

'She'll learn, don't worry. Need any help back here? I know a certain young lady who'd be only too happy to help.'

'Maybe later.' Marguerite still shrank from the idea of sharing her kitchen. Sean helped out all the time but he didn't get in her way and he never got involved with the cooking. He could reheat, he could prepare vegetables and he could follow her instructions to the letter but that was all and that was the way Marguerite liked it. Rai was different. Already she had seen the way Rai watched her; maybe she was getting paranoid in her old age but she always felt the girl was on the verge of saying, 'That's not the way I'd do it.' But she could feel and understand the girl's frustration and if she wanted to keep Rai then she'd have to allow her into the kitchen.

'Marguerite?'

She looked up and realized Sean was waiting for an answer. She sighed. 'If you can manage without her this afternoon then she could work on the desserts for this evening.'

Sean's smile seemed one of relief. 'I can manage. I'll send her in and you can give her the good news yourself.'

He went off whistling and Marguerite realized that he too was probably finding it hard to adapt to having someone else in the place. They had worked together for so long that they knew each other's ways, respected each other and knew when to talk and when to keep quiet. It was one of the reasons that Dijon was a success, and if Rai didn't fit in then this just wouldn't work.

The girl herself almost bounced through the door, her face alight with expectation. 'Sean said you wanted me?'

'Yes.' Marguerite nodded. 'I wondered if you'd like to work on the desserts for tonight's menu.'

'Are you kidding?'

'No. Are you up to it?'

'Sure. Maybe I could make a chocolate parfait or there's my plum crumble—'

Marguerite watched as the girl started to run through recipes in her head and smiled. 'Why don't you have a think about it and we'll discuss it after lunch.'

'Cool.' Rai beamed at her. 'And thanks, Marguerite, you won't be sorry.'

Marguerite watched Rai disappear through the door. 'I hope not.'

Rai moved quickly and silently between the tables, smiling and helpful when dealing with customers and silent and watchful when she wasn't. Sean looked on with some relief. It looked as if Marguerite had found a gem and a sparkling one too. The prim white blouse, black skirt and flat pumps couldn't detract from the girl's beauty and Sean had noticed some of the male clientele watching her with interest. He hoped that Rai's looks wouldn't prove a problem. It was all within her control, of course. You could flirt with customers – he always had – but you had to know when to draw the line, when it was in danger of getting out of hand and when it was time to back off. Rai was young and probably well used to men's attentions but did she know how to handle herself professionally? Time would tell. For now, Sean planned to keep a close eye on her and any potential troublemakers. Dijon's proximity to three upmarket hotels meant that many of their customers weren't local. Some were tourists but most were business people attending conferences or salesmen entertaining clients. As a result, Sean was used to dealing with the unknown. The best dressed and most distinguished guests could turn out to be the ones who got drunk and became boisterous. The quiet, reserved lady could also be the one dancing on the table at the end of the night and flirting with anything in trousers. For all his advancing years, Sean still got the occasional proposition; if only Mary knew. He chuckled to himself.

'What's so funny?' Rai asked, coming to lean on the bar.

Sean continued to polish glasses. 'You wouldn't believe me if I told you, love. So did you get a job in the kitchen?'

A smile lit up Rai's face. 'Yeah, I'm on desserts for tonight's service.'

'Good for you.'

'Any advice?' she asked and then laughed at his look of surprise. 'I'm not so full of myself that I can't take it. What do you think would impress Marguerite?'

He considered the question. 'Good pastry,' he said finally, 'or ice cream. She keeps her menus simple but she serves only the best. If you can do the same, you'll be on to a winner.'

'Thanks, Sean.'

'No problem. Now clear table seven and take table three's order.'

'Yes sir!' Rai saluted with a grin and sped off to his bidding.

Chapter Seventeen

Mark and Ronan were finishing off the coq au vin and washing it down with a bottle of burgundy.

'Did you manage to get your mites problem fixed? Are the birds laying better?' When there was no reply, Mark looked around to see what was distracting his friend. It was Rai Price. 'Pretty, isn't she?' he said, with a grin.

'What?' Ronan looked blank.

Mark laughed. 'It's okay, I won't tell Erin that you were eyeing up birds of the non-feathered variety.'

'I was not. She's probably young enough to be my daughter.'

Mark looked back at Rai, who was casting speculative looks in their direction. 'I don't think that would bother her, somehow.'

Ronan followed his gaze and was alarmed when he caught Rai's eye and she smiled. 'She's probably wondering why two old geezers like us are eyeing her up.'

Mark grinned. 'Ah, so you admit it.'

'Would you just shut up?' Ronan muttered, and concentrated his attention on finishing his dinner.

'Was everything okay for you?'

Ronan had only just laid down his cutlery when Rai was at his side. 'Yes, lovely as always. My compliments to the chef.'

'And mine,' Mark echoed, with a wink.

Rai grinned and handed them the dessert menu.

'Nothing for me, thanks,' Mark said.

'No, I'm full too.' Ronan handed back the menu.

Her face fell. 'Oh, please, you must.'

Sean appeared out of nowhere. 'Rai, if they don't want dessert then they don't want dessert.'

Rai ignored him. 'I could put a little of everything on one plate and you could share,' she suggested.

Mark looked at Ronan and then back at Rai. 'I think we could manage that.'

The girl lit up like a Christmas tree. 'Cool.' She took their menus and sped off in the direction of the kitchen.

Sean cleared away their plates with a sigh. 'I'm afraid she's a little too eager. Marguerite finally let her into the kitchen today and she's dying for some feedback.'

'Marguerite let her cook,' Mark marvelled. 'Which dishes?'

Sean's eyes twinkled. 'Why don't you taste them and then you can tell me?'

Mark pretended to shudder. 'That could get me into a lot of trouble.'

'No more than you deserve.' Ronan laughed.

Rai arrived back within minutes and set down a plate between them with three small desserts on it. 'I hope you like them,' she said, hovering for a moment before retreating reluctantly into the kitchen.

'The poor girl looks a nervous wreck,' Ronan said, 'but I don't know why, it all looks great.'

'She cares,' Sean told him.

Mark tried some of the ice cream. 'This is very good.'

'Lovely.' Ronan tried the apple tart next and smiled at Mark as he ate. 'This is definitely your wife's handiwork.'

Mark tasted it. 'Yes, I think you're right.' Then he turned his attention to the crème brûlée. 'I'd say that Rai made this,' he announced.

Ronan tried some too, unaware of Rai peeking anxiously at the two of them from the kitchen doorway. 'I don't know who made it but it's great.'

'Marguerite will be pleased.' Sean smiled broadly.

'You think?' Mark looked doubtful.

'Absolutely. She's only going to be happy letting Rai cook if people can't tell the difference.'

Marguerite emerged from the kitchen with Rai as they finished eating. 'Well?' she asked, sitting down and looking expectantly at the two men.

'I feel very intimidated,' Ronan said, exchanging a worried look with Mark.

'I promise I won't bar you,' Marguerite laughed. 'So you can be honest.'

Rai stood behind her, her eyes darting from one man to the other.

'Oh, lads, will you put the girl out of her misery,' Sean begged.

Ronan smiled. 'Well, I liked all of it.'

'Me too.' Mark nodded.

'Liked?' Rai's nostrils flared.

'Loved,' Ronan amended as Sean looked on, amused.

'But which dishes do you think I made?' Rai said, her voice full of exasperation.

'I'm honestly not sure,' Mark admitted. 'The only dish I'm certain about is the apple tart; Marguerite definitely made that.'

'Definitely,' Ronan agreed. 'But it was all very good.'

Marguerite looked round at Rai. 'Congratulations.'

'Thanks.' Rai smiled.

Mark looked from one to the other. 'Well, come on, then. Tell us. Were we right?'

'Nope!' Sean laughed.

Ronan frowned. 'I don't understand.'

'Rai made everything,' Marguerite explained.

'Really?' Mark looked incredulous. 'Even the apple tart?'

Rai nodded, her smile growing.

'Congratulations,' Ronan said, 'you are a very talented girl.'

'So does this mean you're retiring?' Mark looked hopefully at his wife.

'What do you think?' She laughed. 'But perhaps I will have a little more time on my hands if Rai takes on more of the cooking.'

'I'd love to!' Rai looked delighted.

'But you won't be in the kitchen full-time,' Sean warned and then a flicker of doubt crossed his face. 'Will she?' he asked Marguerite.

'No,' his boss assured him. 'This is still a small business so, Rai, you must help out front when you're needed.'

'That's cool,' Rai said.

'This will work out well for all of you,' Mark pointed out. 'Rai gets the experience she wants. Marguerite, you have more time to manage the restaurant, and that relieves some of the pressure on Sean.'

'True. And I'm going to manage right now. Get back to work, you two, while I entertain my customers,' Marguerite said with an imperious wave of her hand.

Laughing, Sean and Rai went into the kitchen and Marguerite turned back to Ronan and Mark. 'So now tell me the truth. Were you really impressed or were you just being kind?'

'We were very impressed, sweetheart,' Mark promised her. 'We were both convinced the apple tart was yours.'

'And I thought you'd probably made the ice cream

too,' Ronan added. 'She's very good for one so young.'

Marguerite shrugged. 'Some are just born with a gift; I think Rai is one of them. I watched her make the tart and it was all instinct. She didn't measure anything, she didn't need to.'

'I just hope she can stay the course,' Mark fretted.

'She's stubborn and she has a temper,' Marguerite acknowledged. 'She and Sean have already had words on a few occasions but I think that will settle as they get used to each other. I doubt she will stay with us for more than a year, though. She is a restless creature and an ambitious one. Even if I put her in charge of the kitchen, Dunbarra won't hold her interest for long.'

Mark looked disappointed. He was making plans for their extra free time together and Marguerite was already predicting Rai's departure. 'Then is there any point in taking her on?'

Marguerite was amused at her husband's dismay. '*Bien sur!* The customers will like a new face around the place and if the men don't come for the food, they will come to see her.'

Ronan laughed. 'She is pretty.'

'She seems to think you're not so bad either,' Marguerite said, her eyes twinkling with mischief.

Mark punched his arm and winked. 'I hope Erin doesn't catch her making eyes at you.'

'Ah feck off, you.' Ronan shoved his friend away,

embarrassed. The mention of his girlfriend had sobered his mood. These days he doubted Erin would notice or care if he had sex with Rai in the middle of the restaurant. Conscious of Marguerite's shrewd eyes on him he shrugged and smiled. 'It's not my fault if I'm irresistible.'

Erin was sitting in her usual spot on the back step drinking a beer when PJ arrived back from the garden. 'Not going out tonight?' he asked as he pulled off his boots.

She shook her head.

'There's a good film starting soon, why don't you watch it with me?'

'No, thanks all the same but I think I might have an early night and read my book.'

PJ gazed down at her, his eyes soft. 'He's not worth it, you know.'

She looked up at him. 'Who isn't?'

He smiled. 'If you change your mind, you know where I'll be.'

He patted her shoulder and Erin covered his hand with hers. 'Thanks. Goodnight.'

When she was alone, Erin pulled her cardigan tighter around her and stared miserably into the garden, oblivious tonight to its beauty. She'd screwed up. She'd screwed up big time. Ronan was still giving her the cold shoulder and she'd hardly set eyes on Sebastian since their night 'al fresco'. He'd gone back to being distant and morose. She had a theory that he lost himself in sex and then felt guilty afterwards that he'd been disloyal to Marina's memory. It was sweet in a way but also rather annoying. How could he hold her in his arms, kiss her and make love to her one night and then behave as if it had never happened? Not that she cared. She didn't love him or anything like that and they obviously had no future, but his coolness made it hard for her to remain professional and serve him breakfast every morning. Sometimes she felt like tipping his eggs over his head but she still had a modicum of dignity left and she planned to keep it. Sebastian, for his part, was sometimes vague, sometimes grim but never flirtatious. The only time he seemed in anyway animated was around Hazel but, ironically, the girl seemed unaware of his interest and attention.

She was another worry. The girl seemed to have totally withdrawn into herself. If it wasn't for Gracie, Erin didn't think she'd ever come out of her room. And she never painted any more. She just sat staring into space while Gracie played close by. But it was obvious the child was affected by her mother's mood. She didn't smile as much and she only seemed happy when she was with PJ. Erin was worried that PJ was getting too involved in their lives.

Erin stood up, threw the empty bottle in the crate by the door and locked up. She was crossing the hall to the stairs when the front door opened and Sandra walked in. 'Hi, Sandra, did you have a nice evening?'

Sandra scowled. 'It could have been better.'

'Were you at the pub?'

'No,' Sandra retorted and didn't offer anything else. 'I don't suppose you have any whiskey, Erin? I'd be happy to pay for it.'

Erin knew there was half a bottle of Scotch but it was PJ's favourite. 'Sorry, no. I could let you have a bottle of red wine. I have white but it isn't chilled.'

'Red will do,' Sandra said ungraciously.

Erin retraced her steps and took a bottle of Californian Merlot from the rack, fetched a glass and carried them back into the hall. 'It's a screw top so you don't need a corkscrew.'

'Great, just add it to the bill.'

'It's on the house.'

Sandra looked surprised and a little suspicious. 'That's very kind, are you sure?'

Erin smiled. 'Sure. Goodnight, Sandra.'

''Night.'

Erin waited until she heard the other woman's door click before going into the sitting room in search of her book. There was an elderly couple from Devon sitting watching a sitcom and after a brief chat Erin said goodnight and went upstairs. She paused outside PJ's room and then decided to let him enjoy his film in peace. Instead she went into her room and locked the door. This week she was staying in the large double room at the front of the house that had an en suite. She went through to the bathroom, undressed and ran a bath, hoping there would be enough hot water to fill it. She poured in some of her most expensive oil and fetched her book. She wished now that she'd brought up a glass of wine too and decided to nip down and get one. Tugging her robe from the hook on the door, Erin belted it tightly around her waist and hurried downstairs. In the kitchen she selected a bottle of Bordeaux, took down a large crystal glass – she deserved pampering – and was on her way back upstairs when the doorbell rang. Cursing under her breath, she went down again, and peered out through the glass in the top of the door and was surprised to see Ronan looking back at her. Putting down the wine, Erin quickly opened the door. 'Hi!'

'Hi.' He took in her appearance. 'Sorry, I didn't realize it was so late.'

'It's not. I just decided to have an early night and a bath. Oh, God, the bath! Come in,' she called to him and sped back upstairs. For once Erin was grateful that the plumbing in the house was so ancient. The bath was only half full. She turned off the taps and went into her room to get dressed again. But Ronan was waiting there, holding the wine. 'I don't suppose we could share?'

Erin smiled. 'We could.'

'What about your bath?' he murmured, putting down the glass.

She watched him cross the room to stand right in front of her. 'It can wait.'

Ronan pulled on her belt and her robe fell open. 'Oh, I've missed you,' he groaned reaching for her.

'I've missed you too,' Erin said, and sliding her arms around his neck, she pulled his head down to hers.

Chapter Eighteen

It was five to eight before Erin came down to get breakfast. She hated being late but at the same time she couldn't keep the smile off her lips. It was a long time since she'd been woken up in such a wonderful way. Her body was still tingling from Ronan's touch. She thought of him now upstairs in her shower and had to banish the thought immediately. If she didn't keep her mind on the job at hand then no one would get fed this morning. She took out bacon, eggs and sausages and then put rolls into the oven to warm. She was just whisking eggs when she heard someone coming into the dining room. Sebastian.

Armed with the coffee pot, she went in and greeted him with a warm smile. 'Good morning, Sebastian, did you sleep well?'

He looked up, surprised. 'Not bad. You seem very chirpy this morning.'

'Do I? So what can I get you, your usual?'

He took a sip of coffee and nodded. 'Please.'

'Coming right up,' she said going back into the kitchen, humming. She put on the bacon and then, after heating a little oil in a pan, she poured in the eggs. She was just plating up Sebastian's breakfast when Ronan walked in.

'Hey, sexy,' he said, rubbing up against her and snaking his hands around to cup her breasts.

She squealed. 'Are you crazy. Stop that.'

'That's not what you said earlier,' he said but he moved away and helped himself to coffee.

'I wasn't holding a pan earlier,' she reminded him, laughing, before opening the door with her hip and carrying in Sebastian's breakfast. 'Here you go.'

'Thanks,' he grunted.

Erin went back into the kitchen and was immediately grabbed again by Ronan. 'Stop!' She wriggled out of his grasp. 'Sit down and let me make you some breakfast.'

'Aren't I allowed to mix with the guests?' His tone was light but Erin knew this was a challenge. She looked him straight in the eye and smiled. 'Sure. Take a seat, sir, and I will make you the best breakfast in town.'

Ronan smiled back and took his coffee into the dining room. Erin had to fight the urge to follow him or, at least, listen at the door. When she carried in Ronan's breakfast five minutes later it was to find him sitting at Sebastian's table. She hesitated before putting down the plate.

'That looks great, sweetheart, thanks.' He took the plate from her.

She set down the toast and risked a quick look at Sebastian. He met her eyes but she couldn't read his expression. 'I'll go and get more coffee,' she said, taking his empty plate.

'Thanks, Erin, that was lovely.'

By the time she'd refilled their cups three more guests had come down for breakfast so she didn't have time to worry about what Ronan and Sebastian were discussing. She was aware, though, that they were talking and both men seemed reasonably relaxed. Twenty minutes later PJ walked in. 'What's going on? How come Ronan's here? Is everything okay?'

'Everything's fine. Ronan dropped in last night after you went to bed and he stayed over.'

'Oh, I see.' He smiled. 'I'm glad.'

'Yeah, me too.'

'But what are you doing letting him have breakfast with yer man?' He jerked his head in the direction of the door.

Erin sighed. 'I know, but there wasn't much I could do about it. I came out with Ronan's breakfast and he was sitting with Sebastian. I could hardly tell him to move.'

'Let's hope they're just discussing the weather.'

'Why don't you go and join them?'

'Oh, no.'

'Oh, please, PJ. You can steer them away from any dodgy topics. It won't be for long. Sebastian finished his breakfast ages ago and Ronan will have to get back to the farm soon. I'll make you a full breakfast,' she wheedled.

He sighed. 'Make sure there're mushrooms and black pudding, and my egg is runny,' he told her before going into the dining room.

Moments later the door opened again and Ronan came in. 'Thanks for that, Erin, it was lovely. I'd better get going or Vincent will be sending out a search party.' He bent his head to kiss her. 'We have to do this more often,' he murmured, his eyes warm.

'We do.' Erin smiled in relief. Conversation had obviously been all above board. Thank you, Sebastian.

'I'll phone you later,' he promised and kissed her again before leaving through the back door.

Erin finished PJ's breakfast and carried it in. He was alone at the table, reading a newspaper. 'Here you go. Anything to report?' she whispered so the couple at the next table couldn't hear.

He shook his head. 'Sebastian was leaving by the time I came in but it all seemed quite civilized.'

'Thank goodness for that.'

He shot her a reproving look. 'So let's keep it that way. Stay away from that man, Erin, do you hear me?'

'I am not a child, PJ,' she retorted.

'No, but you're not too old to heed some common sense,' he shot back.

She scowled and turned to leave.

'Some more coffee would be nice, and don't forget my toast,' he called after her.

When she came back again, Hazel and Gracie were sitting at their usual table. Hazel's head was stuck in a book and Gracie was looking longingly in PJ's direction. Erin went over and smiled at them. 'Good morning.'

Gracie smiled back but Hazel barely looked up. She was looking a little rough, with her hair tousled and a paint stain on her shirt. Also, Erin noticed, the hand holding the book shook slightly. 'Will you have your usual?' she asked.

'Please,' Hazel replied while Gracie watched her mother with sad eyes.

'Fine.' Erin turned away and met PJ's concerned gaze. She shrugged. She had no idea what was wrong with Hazel and she didn't really want to know either. But her heart went out to Gracie. The poor little girl seemed miserable. She quickly prepared their breakfast and when she carried it back inside, Gracie was on PJ's lap, chewing on a piece of toast.

'Gracie! Come and sit down for breakfast,' Hazel called, her tone shrill.

Gracie clambered down and reluctantly came back to her mother.

'You mustn't bother PJ when he's having his breakfast,' she berated her daughter as Gracie climbed back into her chair.

'Oh, he doesn't mind,' Erin said and received a glare for her trouble. 'Enjoy your breakfast,' Erin said and gave the child a sympathetic smile before returning to the relative peace of her kitchen.

After breakfast, PJ went for a walk along the lakeside path. It was a beautiful morning and the views were breathtaking, but he was so preoccupied that they were lost on him. He was worried about Hazel and yet powerless to help. She didn't open up to him any more but she didn't seem to talk to anyone else either. In fact, she seemed totally isolated in the world. He'd asked once about Gracie's father but Hazel clammed up as soon as he mentioned him. And with each day that passed since she stopped painting Hazel became more despondent and unpredictable. She only talked when she had to and then most of her responses were monosyllabic. PJ felt frustrated and helpless, a feeling he was all too familiar with. But surely this time he could do something to help or, if not, find someone else who could. But there was no one—

He stopped dead in his tracks as the idea came to him. It was a long shot and not one he relished, but the girl needed help and he was out of ideas. The worst that could happen was nothing, so it had to be worth asking. He turned and retraced his steps, deciding he'd better act now before he changed his mind.

Sebastian looked bemused when he opened the door.

'Sorry for bothering you. Could I talk to you for a moment?' PJ said stiffly. 'It won't take long.'

'Sure.' Sebastian stood back to let him in.

PJ shuffled in and stood in front of the fireplace. He waited until Sebastian had shut the door. 'It's about Hazel.'

'Hazel? We just went to the pub, she had one too many—'

'What?' PJ scratched his head. 'Oh, no, it's nothing to do with that. The thing is, I need your help.'

Sebastian sat down and gestured to PJ to do the same. 'I'm intrigued.'

PJ perched on the edge of a chair and leaned forward, his elbows on his knees. 'You must have noticed how withdrawn she's become.'

Sebastian shrugged. 'She's always been quiet.'

'That's just it, you see, she hasn't. She was like a mouse when she first arrived and then she changed completely and was full of fun, but now she seems to have plummeted to the depths of depression. It seems to be linked in some way to the fact that she's not painting. There must be something troubling the poor girl.'

'Perhaps,' Sebastian acknowledged. 'But what does that have to do with me?'

PJ bristled at the man's detached air and he had to swallow hard to stop himself telling the actor exactly what he thought of him. 'You've spent some time with her; I thought that maybe she'd confided in you.'

'She didn't.'

'Did she not tell you anything about her husband or family?'

'Nothing specific.'

PJ sighed. 'Damn. I thought if we had a name or address then we could make contact with her family and get them to come and see her.'

'You can't just meddle in someone's personal life like that. You have no idea what their relationship is like.'

'I assure you it's not something I'd do lightly, but I'm really concerned about Hazel. And I hate to say it, but I'm worried for Gracie too.'

'Hazel wouldn't do anything to hurt her own child PJ.'

'No, of course not. Not intentionally.'

Sebastian shrugged again. 'Well, I wish I could be more help but, like I said, she didn't tell me anything about her family.'

'You could always talk to her and see what you could find out—'

'I don't think so.' Sebastian stood up.

'Oh, for God's sake, man,' PJ said, losing patience. 'I bet she was only too happy to listen to your problems. Would it be too much to ask that you put someone else's needs before your own?'

'I think you should go now.' Sebastian went to the door and opened it.

PJ realized his temper had lost him the little bit of advantage he'd won. 'Look, I'm sorry. I can't explain it but I have a very bad feeling about her and I want to do what I can to help. Please, just try to talk to her?'

Sebastian seemed on the point of refusing but then he hesitated. After a moment he nodded. 'I'll try but I wouldn't hold out much hope.'

'You can only try. Thank you, thank you very much indeed. I appreciate it.' PJ smiled gratefully and walked out of the door and then turned. 'Do it as soon as possible, there's a good lad.'

'I'll do it when the opportunity presents itself, okay?'

'Fair enough and thanks again.' PJ went down the path not knowing if he'd done the right thing or not. But now all he could do was sit back and see what happened.

Hazel trudged along the road back to the Gatehouse, Gracie shuffling along behind her. She was sulking because Hazel hadn't bought her an ice cream, but when Hazel had spied the American woman in the coffee shop she'd quickly dragged her daughter away. As a result, Gracie had started to whinge and cry and Hazel had lost her temper. Now Gracie wouldn't walk with her or look at her and Hazel felt a mixture of irritation and guilt. She had been very hard on the child lately but Gracie had to learn that her mother wasn't made of money. With her savings dwindling at an alarming rate Hazel knew she wouldn't be able to stay at the Gatehouse much longer. And though she'd be glad to escape PJ's concern, Erin's questioning looks and that American woman's nosiness, Hazel was terrified of leaving. How wonderful it would be to be invisible. What a huge relief it would be if she could just disappear.

'Hazel, wait.'

Hazel turned to see Sebastian jogging to catch them up. Her first instinct was to continue walking, but that would seem very rude and anyway he was not the sort of man who was easily put off. She stood waiting for him and Gracie pressed her small body against her leg. 'Hi,' she said when he reached them.

He smiled. 'Hello, there.' He put a hand out to touch Gracie's head but she shrank from his touch.

'Gracie!' Hazel rolled her eyes at Sebastian. 'Sorry, she's in a mood.'

'That's okay. So how are things?' he asked, falling into step beside her.

'Fine.'

'I haven't seen much of you since our day out. You're not annoyed with me, are you?'

Hazel shook her head. 'No, of course not.'

'So it's just a coincidence that you've hardly said two words to me since.'

Hazel wondered why he cared. 'Yes. Sorry.'

'And you're not painting.'

She shook her head again. 'No.'

'That must hurt.'

She looked at him then. 'Everything hurts.'

'Yes, I have days like that but it's more than that for you, isn't it?'

Hazel said nothing. She didn't want to talk, not like this anyway.

'Would you prefer me to mind my own business?'

She smiled faintly and nodded.

'Fair enough,' he said and they walked in silence for a while. 'I was thinking of visiting Dublin. You're from there, aren't you?'

'Yes.'

'So any recommendations as to where I should stay?'

She glanced at him, amused. 'I doubt I've ever been in the kind of hotels you go to.'

'Okay then, where should I visit?'

She shrugged. 'It depends on what you're interested in.'

'I don't really know but I feel ready to step outside Dunbarra. I'd prefer not to do it alone, though.' He stopped and turned to her. 'Why don't we go together?'

'What?' She frowned and shook her head. 'No, absolutely not.'

'Why not? Don't you want to go home?'

'Home.'

Hazel looked down at Gracie who was clinging to her side and looking up, her eyes wide. 'What did you say, Gracie?' she said, crouching down to look into her daughter's face.

Gracie, looking surprised, swallowed hard and put a hand to her throat. Then she opened her mouth and said it again: 'Home.'

It was barely a whisper but it was the first word Hazel had heard Gracie say in a very long time. 'Oh, my darling, well done.' She pulled Gracie into her arms and hugged her tightly.

Sebastian stood looking down at them. 'So is that a yes?'

They sat in a corner of Paddy Burke's coffee shop and drank lattes while Gracie played games on a children's website. Hazel drummed the table with her fingers as Sebastian went on and on about Dublin. 'I can't do it. I can't go back,' she blurted out finally.

'Why?' Sebastian asked unruffled by her outburst.

She looked at him for a moment and then turned her eyes on Gracie. 'Because if I do, I'll lose her. She'll be taken away from me.'

'Why?' he repeated.

'Because my husband doesn't think I'm a fit mother.'

'That's rubbish. You're a great mother.'

Hazel smiled slightly. 'Thanks for the vote of confidence.'

'So why do you think he wants to take her away from you?'

Hazel shrugged, not meeting his gaze. 'Des was always a bit envious of how close Gracie and I are. And as our marriage started to break down, that envy turned to resentment.'

'Are you divorced?'

'No. He doesn't want one and I can't afford it.'

'But if you formalized your arrangement then you wouldn't have to worry about losing Gracie,' Sebastian pointed out.

'Des would probably win custody if it went before a judge.'

He nodded his understanding. 'What is it – drugs? That's why you understood about Marina.'

'No!' Hazel looked at him, appalled.

'Then what?'

'I have the opposite problem. I *won't* take my medication.'

'What's wrong with you?'

Hazel kept her eyes on her coffee. 'I get down.'

'Don't we all?' he quipped.

'No, I mean really down.'

'How down? Have you tried to—?' He stopped.

Hazel dropped her head further, unable to meet his eyes.

He leaned across the table and lowered his voice even more. 'Hazel, it's nothing to be ashamed of. But you should really take the medication. Then your husband could never take Gracie away.'

'It's not that simple.' Hazel felt her eyes start to fill. 'I can't paint when I'm on medication. And if I can't paint then . . .'

He looked confused. 'So you *are* taking your medication.'

She shook her head, tears flowing down her cheeks.

'I'm sorry, you've lost me.'

'That man hated my work.'

'What man? Hazel?'

She wiped her eyes and rummaged in her pockets for a tissue. 'I went to a shop in town and showed this guy my paintings. He hated them.'

Sebastian burst out laughing. 'And that's what's got you so down? Jeez, Hazel, is that all?'

'I knew you wouldn't understand,' she cried, jumping to her feet and knocking over her chair in the process. 'You're just like everyone else. You think I overreact, think I'm mad. Well, maybe you're right. Maybe I am.'

'Hazel, please, sit down.'

But Hazel couldn't sit here any longer. She couldn't listen to him tell her that everything would be okay when she knew it wouldn't. She was halfway out of the door when he called her again, making heads turn and people stare. She spun around to face him. 'What?' she screamed.

He nodded towards Gracie. 'Aren't you forgetting someone?'

Chapter Nineteen

Marguerite was paying a rare visit to the Gatehouse thanks to Rai. Erin made coffee and marvelled at the difference in her friend. She seemed brighter and happier, even younger. She smiled while Marguerite filled her in on the girl's progress and the hiccups along the way.

'She and Sean still rub against each other the wrong way sometimes.'

Erin giggled. 'You'd better not tell Mary that.'

Marguerite frowned. 'What's so funny?'

'Don't mind me; I'm just being juvenile.'

Marguerite shook her head. 'Anyway, Sean thinks that Rai is a little too attentive with the male customers.'

Erin laughed. 'Then they should make a great team – Sean's a professional flirt. Is she attractive?'

'Didn't Ronan tell you?' Marguerite's dark eyes widened. 'She's stunning.'

'I didn't even know he'd met her,' Erin said as she set two mugs of coffee on the table and then opened the box of muffins that Marguerite had brought.

'He certainly did. In fact, he was one of the men that she kept fluttering her eyelashes at.'

'No!' Erin didn't know whether she was amused or shocked. 'But I thought you said she was only nineteen.'

'Well, *exactement*, but Rai is not your average teenager. She has the body of a girl but the mind of a woman.'

'Oh, really?' Erin retorted.

'You have nothing to fear,' Marguerite assured her. 'Ronan was mortified. Anyway, I think Rai has a hidden agenda.'

Erin frowned. 'Oh?'

'*Oui*, I think she believes that if she misbehaves out front I will let her spend more time in the kitchen just to maintain the peace.'

'Ah, I see, very clever.' Erin smiled.

'She is clever and gifted. Her pastry is as light as a feather. One day she will be a great chef and have her own restaurant somewhere cosmopolitan and chic.'

'Good, but in the meantime she'd better keep her claws off my man.' Erin swallowed a mouthful of her bun. 'Still, I'm glad you finally hired someone. You work so hard.'

'Are we talking about me or you?'

'PJ does all the real work,' Erin said with a grin, 'and Nora, of course.'

'Pah! That woman just makes work for you. I don't know why you keep her on. Sebastian says he came in one day and she was sitting on his sofa watching television.'

Erin's eyes widened. 'No!'

Marguerite nodded. 'Yes! Get rid of her and find someone young and energetic like Rai.'

'I couldn't do something so cruel; Nora's like part of the furniture.' She pulled a face. 'And, if I fired her, word would be all over Dunbarra within hours and there'd be a posse out to get me.'

'A what?' Marguerite wrinkled her nose.

'The locals would not be impressed,' Erin explained.

Marguerite shrugged. 'I wouldn't care. She is a drain on your pocket. You are way too soft, Erin.'

'Rubbish, I'm as tough as they come – ask Ronan.'

'Ronan would not agree.' Marguerite's eyes twinkled. 'He seems like a very satisfied man at the moment.'

'You think so?' Erin smiled.

'I'm happy for you, *chérie*, I'm happy for you both. It seems Sebastian did you a favour in the end. A little jealousy is not such a bad thing.'

Erin reddened, feeling terrible. If Marguerite knew the truth, what would she think? Would they still be friends or would she be horrified by her duplicity? Still, she was finished with Sebastian and things were better than ever with Ronan. Everything had worked out fine. Okay, she had to admit she was a bit miffed that Sebastian seemed to have lost interest in her, but it was for the best . . .

'You're miles away, what are you dreaming of? Not my brother?' Marguerite laughed.

Erin forced herself to laugh too and hoped Marguerite wouldn't notice that it was ever so slightly hysterical.

'I am very grateful you took him in, Erin. The Gatehouse seems to have done him good.'

'Well, it's certainly working from the privacy aspect. According to PJ's newspaper the other day, Sebastian is on set in New Mexico!'

'Yes, that was the story Sebastian's agent put out to keep the press off his back.'

'But surely it's only a matter of time before they realize that's a lie.'

'Maybe but by then he'll be back in L.A. At least, we hope so.'

'Do you think he'll go home soon?'

'He hasn't said anything, but then,' Marguerite sighed, 'he doesn't talk to me. Why is that, Erin?'

'I really don't know but try not to take it to heart. He wouldn't have come here if he didn't feel close to you. He told me all about how great you were when Jess was sick. It meant so much to him. He loves you, Marguerite. It may not always seem like it but hey,' Erin shrugged and smiled, 'he's just a man.'

Marguerite's smile was sad but resigned. 'I suppose you are right. Mark wants to take me to see Maman but I wouldn't like to leave if Sebastian is still here.'

'That's ridiculous. You must go. Sebastian can take care of himself. And like you said, he's so much better.'

'Maybe.'

'No maybe, Marguerite,' Erin said firmly. 'It's time you put Mark first. He's had to be on a back burner while you fretted about Sebastian or the restaurant. You need to spend some time together. In fact, you should extend your break and have a few days in Paris too; I'm sure Mark would enjoy some time alone with you.'

'Has he said something?'

'Nothing.' Erin grinned. 'But it's not rocket science.'

'Even after all these years I don't know what you're saying half the time. Ah, but it would be nice to visit Paris,' Marguerite admitted. 'It must be two years since I was last there.'

'I think it's a great idea.'

'Perhaps you and Ronan should join us.'

Erin looked at her in mock horror. 'Go to Paris, the most romantic city in the world, as a foursome?'

Marguerite chuckled. 'Okay, perhaps that is not the best idea. But you should take your own advice. A holiday is exactly what you and Ronan need.'

'Maybe in October or November, if Ronan is interested.'

'I think it is safe to say that he would be interested.' Marguerite's eyes twinkled mischievously.

'You need to get a move on and empty that dish-washer,' Sean said.

'I don't have time for that,' Rai retorted. 'I'm getting ready for lunch.'

Sean's usually genial face settled into stern lines. 'No, *we're* getting ready for lunch and *I'm* in charge. You'd do well to remember that.'

'I'll get to it in a minute.'

'See you do,' he said and went back into the restaurant, shaking his head. That girl was a mixed blessing. There was no doubt she could cook and Marguerite was already looking more relaxed, but she had a tough side that made Sean feel uneasy. And what kind of a bloody name was that anyway? It sounded like something out of one of those silly American soaps and yet the girl was from the north side of Dublin. He'd bet any money it was fake. He'd told Marguerite she should check that Rai was who she said she was but she'd laughed, saying that Rai's cooking spoke for itself. And that was true, she was a natural. And why would she lie just to work in a little restaurant in the middle of nowhere? He was being ridiculous but then Mary always said he took contrary notions, more so as he got older. He should cut the girl some slack and accept that she seemed to know what she was doing and was a hard worker. Maybe he should go back into the kitchen and empty the dishwasher; he'd do it for Marguerite. But Rai was young and strong and it wouldn't kill her. Instead he pulled up a stool and settled himself at the bar to polish the cutlery and read the racing pages. Maybe having an extra pair of hands around wasn't all bad.

Sandra took a sip of her skinny latte and smiled with pleasure. It had taken her three weeks to teach Paddy how to make it the way she liked it but now he was an expert. If she closed her eyes she could almost imagine she was back home; if it wasn't for the accents and the cold, that is. The locals kept talking about how lovely the weather was but there was always a cool breeze and it rained at least once a week; the Irish were strange people.

'You should've been in earlier, Sandra; you missed all the commotion.'

Sandra looked up at his animated expression and smiled. Paddy was a simple man who loved life and lived for gossip but she had become quite fond of him. 'Oh, yes? Was George Clooney in with his latest girlfriend?'

'No, why would you think that?' Paddy frowned.

'Never mind, Paddy. What did I miss?'

'That girl from the Gatehouse was in along with that film-star fella.'

'Erin and Sebastian?' Sandra's ears pricked up.

'No, no, the girl with the child.'

Sandra's eyes widened. 'Hazel?'

'That's the one. She seemed very upset.'

'Oh?'

He leaned across the counter and lowered his voice, although Sandra would bet he'd probably told every other customer here already.

'They sat over at the corner table while the little one played on the computer,' he told her. 'They seemed very deep in conversation altogether. I didn't know they were close at all.'

'Me neither,' Sandra muttered. 'Then what happened?'

'She looked as if she was crying and he was trying to comfort her. But the next thing she stood up and knocked over her chair and she said that he was just like everyone else and then she stormed out and he had to call her back.'

'Why?'

'Well, hadn't she completely forgotten the poor child?'

'Oh, wow. And what happened then?' Sandra urged.

Paddy shrugged. 'She came back, took the little one by the hand and dragged her outside and Gray paid the bill and followed. Now wasn't that strange?'

'It was,' Sandra agreed. 'It certainly was.'

Chapter Twenty

PJ waited anxiously to hear from Sebastian, but though they'd crossed paths a number of times, the actor hadn't said a word. The man was very unpredictable altogether. One day he was down and hardly opened his mouth. The next he was chatty and quite charming. But then he had come here because he was having problems; PJ wondered what they were. He could ask Erin but he wasn't sure he wanted to acknowledge their obvious connection. She seemed happy with Ronan for the moment and he didn't want to remind her of her mistakes. Hopefully Gray was a minor indiscretion and one that was firmly in the past.

Taking his cap and jacket off the hook by the kitchen door, PJ went out to the garden. He smiled when he saw Gracie waiting for him. 'Good morning, darling, how are you?' This had become a habit over the last few days. Hazel went back to bed after breakfast and Gracie came out to the back garden to play. PJ didn't know if Hazel realized that Gracie trailed him around all morning. If she did she didn't comment. But then she hardly spoke at all any more and she didn't seem to really care what Gracie was up to. It worried and appalled him and he knew that Erin was not happy with the situation. She felt that Hazel was using them, especially him, and she wanted to say something. But PJ didn't think Hazel was doing it consciously, that was the problem. He felt she was really sick and he was grateful that she was here and that he could keep an eye on Gracie. He'd heard from a couple of people in the village that Hazel had walked out of the coffee shop and left the child behind. He'd made light of it because there were some people who wouldn't think twice about calling social services. Hopefully he would get help for her and everything would work out all right for both mother and daughter. In the meantime he'd be keeping a close eye on Gracie. But he would need Erin to take over when he was out. She would complain that she had enough to do, but she'd do it. He would have to warn her, though, not to say anything to Hazel. A wrong word and he knew the girl might leave, and that was a scary prospect, especially for Gracie.

The child in question was standing patiently, waiting for him to come out of his reverie. 'What am I like, Gracie, standing here daydreaming? That won't get the work done, will it?' She shook her head and he laughed. 'How would you like to learn how to transplant some lettuces?'

Gracie nodded enthusiastically.

'Good. Let's go!'

Erin, coming out of the house to hang out the washing, was in time to see the two disappear into the garden. She frowned as she started to peg the clothes to the line. Hazel was undoubtedly holed up in her room again. Erin was feeling increasingly nervous about having that woman under her roof, but at a loss as to what she could do about it. PJ had taken a liking to both mother and daughter and would be furious if she turned them out. It was a very tricky situation. Erin wondered if all guest houses got the strange mix of people she did.

This led her thoughts to the rather irritating, demanding and very curious Sandra Bell. When would the woman go home? Any time Erin broached the subject Sandra gave her the run around. And she couldn't exactly make a big deal of it because the season was drawing to a close and there were two free guest rooms; Sandra could stay on indefinitely if she wanted. Erin groaned as she took a peg from her mouth. What on earth was keeping her here? It certainly wasn't the scenery. The only time she put a foot outside was to go to the village or into Mullingar. And what about the husband? Though Sandra had seemed desolate initially, apart from the odd barbed comment about the treachery of men she seemed to have completely forgotten him. Weird, given they'd been married for twenty-five years. Could it be possible that she really had fallen for Paddy? Erin couldn't credit it. They were such an improbable pair, and though Paddy might be enjoying the attention, Erin doubted he would ever date a woman never mind marry her. Poor Sandra could well end up broken-hearted all over again. Erin shook her head and went back to the job in hand. At least Sandra was planning to take herself off to Dublin for a few day to 'see the sights'. That would be a welcome respite. In fact, it should be a quiet week all round. Apart from an Italian couple, who would arrive midweek, she had only PJ, Hazel, Gracie and Sebastian to look after.

She finished hanging the clothes and took her empty basket back inside. She'd go into the village now and do her shopping and maybe treat herself to a coffee and a cake at Paddy's. She would normally drop into Dijon and have a cuppa there, but Marguerite and Mark had left for France yesterday. It was the first time they'd gone away and left the restaurant open. But Erin knew that Marguerite had put a lot of work into making sure things would run smoothly in her absence. Several dishes had been made in advance and frozen and all Rai would have to do was defrost and heat them through. The menu had been pared back to three choices of starter, main course and dessert. One of the starters would of course be soup and Marguerite had left three choices in the freezer.

'A monkey could run the place,' Mark had told Erin when she'd phoned to wish them *bon voyage*. 'She's left nothing to chance.'

'Well, that means she'll relax and enjoy her holiday more,' Erin had pointed out.

Pulling her hair into a ponytail, Erin slipped on a sleeveless jacket, took her purse and basket and left the house. She did all her daily shopping in Dunbarra and a monthly shop in the cash and carry. Usually she drove into the village, dropping off produce en route, but there were no deliveries to be made today and she fancied a walk. The morning was much cooler and there was a distinct hint of autumn in the air. Erin even noticed some leaves along the driveway. Though she loved the changing colours of the countryside at this time of year she dreaded the cold, dark winter mornings that lay ahead. For the next couple of months she and PJ would be busy harvesting, protecting plants from the cold weather, and planting lettuces, tomatoes and spring vegetables in the tunnels. Then life would quieten down for a while and they could concentrate on any maintenance required both in the garden and in the house.

Erin shopped at a relaxed pace in the small supermarket and then went into Paddy's to enjoy her treat.

She took her coffee and cream cake to a table by the window and opened out the newspaper. She didn't actually want to read it but, as the coffee shop was deserted, she knew Paddy would be over for a gossip if she didn't have something to occupy her. She was halfway through her cake when he loomed over her with his shy smile.

'Is that okay for you, Erin?'

Her mouth was full so she just nodded and smiled.

'Good, good. You deserve a break. Sure, I hear you're very busy down at the Gatehouse.'

She nodded again, wishing he'd go away.

'You've still got quite a houseful of guests, haven't you?'

Erin put down her cake. 'Not that many; it's beginning to quieten down now and of course Sandra is off to Dublin tomorrow.'

'Yes. It won't be the same without her, will it?' He sighed.

'It won't,' Erin agreed honestly.

'But you still have that Mr Gray and the girl and her little one.'

'Yes.' Perhaps she should have just gone home and made her own coffee.

He sat down and leaned into her. 'They were here the other day, you know, the three of them.'

Despite herself Erin felt her ears pricking up. 'Oh?'

He glanced around in a conspiratorial fashion even though they were alone. 'She got very upset, she did.'

'Gracie?'

'No, no, the mother. She even ran out of the place and left the poor child behind; can you believe that?'

Erin shrugged and smiled. 'Well, I think I'd forget my head sometimes if it wasn't screwed on.'

Paddy wasn't to be diverted. 'Her and Gray were quarrelling, they were. I could tell. What do you make of that fella, Erin?'

'I don't really know him that well.'

'Oh?' He frowned. 'I thought you were close.'

Erin looked at him sharply. 'Why's that?'

He quickly rose to his feet, a red flush creeping up his neck. 'Look at me interrupting your elevenses. You enjoy your cake, Erin, and just shout if you need more coffee.'

'Thanks.' Erin popped a piece of cake in her mouth and looked back down at her newspaper. But the cake seemed tasteless and the newsprint swam before her eyes. Now that things were back on track with Ronan, the last thing she needed was Paddy spreading gossip about her and Sebastian. It was easy to figure out who he was getting his information from. And though that was all she should be worrying about, Erin couldn't help wondering why Sebastian and Hazel would be arguing. Had Hazel feelings for Sebastian and he'd rejected her? It would explain the girl's recent depression certainly.

What the hell was he up to? Surely he realized that Hazel wasn't exactly stable. But then Sebastian didn't seem to think much beyond his own little world. He'd discarded her too and, despite everything, that hurt. Though their liaison had been brief, it had been powerful and passionate and Erin had really thought there was a connection between them. The last time they'd been together, that night by the lake, had been incredible and yet he'd given no sign that he wanted to repeat it. Of course it was a relief, but she was only human. No woman liked to be dumped, which in effect was what had happened. But she could take it. Hazel wasn't as strong and now seemed to be unravelling. Sebastian was out of order. He couldn't play around with someone so obviously vulnerable and then walk away. It wasn't just Hazel he was hurting either, it was Gracie. As a father himself, he should know better.

And while all these thoughts ran through her mind, Erin knew what really bothered her was the fact that he hadn't pursued her. She was happy with Ronan and glad that things were good between them again but she'd expected Sebastian to fight for her especially after the night Ronan had stayed over. She'd thought he'd be jealous, or at least indignant that she had chosen a farmer over a film star, but he hadn't reacted at all. There had been no teasing twinkle, no *double entendres*, nothing. He seemed to hardly notice her these days. Yet again, Sebastian had managed to make her feel like a cheap tart and she didn't like it.

Draining her coffee mug, Erin folded her paper, tucked it into her bag and stood up.

Paddy looked up in surprise. 'Are you off already, Erin? Can I not get you another coffee?'

She shook her head and smiled. 'Thanks, Paddy, but it's time I got back to work. See you soon.'

'Bye, love, take care.'

Erin marched back to the Gatehouse at a much faster pace than she'd left it. The beauty of the morning no longer captured her attention; she was in a bad mood and annoyed at herself for feeling that way. As she approached the house, it was almost a relief to see Sebastian coming towards her. She wanted to confront him and it was better that there were no prying eyes around.

He looked up and saw her and smiled, raising his hand in greeting. Erin didn't respond and his smile faded, to be replaced by a puzzled frown.

'Hi, Erin, everything okay?' he asked when they drew level.

The polite enquiry just added fuel to the fire. 'As if you care.'

'Pardon?' Sebastian looked completely bewildered now.

'You are some operator, Sebastian,' she hissed. 'You ignore me from one end of the week to the other unless, that is, you're in the mood for some extracurricular activities.'

'My recollection is that our activities were a result of our mutual feelings,' he said, obviously amused.

'Feelings? I doubt you even have feelings.'

His expression sobered. 'Erin, I'm sorry if I've upset you—'

'You haven't upset me, you've annoyed me. You are irresponsible, thoughtless and cruel and you disgust me.'

'Strong words, Erin. Don't you think you should at least tell me why you're so angry?'

'I'm talking about Hazel.'

'Hazel?' Again he looked puzzled.

Erin gave him a pitying look. 'You're not in LA now, Sebastian. Dunbarra is a small place and word gets around. Especially words about you and Hazel having a public disagreement in the coffee shop and her running out in tears.'

'Oh, I see.' Sebastian nodded in understanding. 'But you've got it completely wrong.'

Erin looked at him in disbelief. 'Oh, come on!'

He shrugged. 'You can believe what you want to believe, Erin, but I assure you the argument you're referring to was not some lovers' tiff.'

Erin hesitated. 'Then what?'

'I'm sorry but I don't discuss other people's private business.'

Erin reddened at the obvious dig. 'Why on earth would she want to confide in you?' she blurted out, realizing as she said it that she sounded petulant and childish.

'Why, indeed.' He smiled.

Erin clenched her hands in frustration. This had not

gone the way it was supposed to at all and, rather than being upset, he seemed amused by her attack. 'Perhaps it's time you went home, Sebastian.'

'Erin, you're hurting my feelings.' And, his eyes twinkling, he put up a hand to tug her ponytail.

Erin felt as if a bolt of electricity had shot through her from head to toe.

'You know you'd miss me if I left,' he said softly, moving closer.

Erin held her ground and looked him straight in the eye. 'I'd survive.'

'Ah, so you *would* miss me. I'd miss you too.' He moved even closer, his eyes going to her lips.

'I've got work to do,' Erin muttered and made to move around him, but he put up an arm to block her way.

He looked at her, serious now. 'There's nothing going on between me and Hazel, Erin. I've stayed away from you because I thought that was what you wanted; you and your boyfriend are obviously getting on so much better. I'd like nothing better than to see more of you.' His lips twitched. 'Perhaps I could have phrased that better.'

'You could,' she agreed, but her anger had dissipated, and when he slipped his hand into hers she didn't pull it away. 'I'm sorry, I shouldn't listen to gossip.'

'You shouldn't, but I can understand you jumping to conclusions.'

Chapter Twenty-One

Back at the house, Erin whirled around the place, putting her shopping away, answering phone messages and making sure that Nora was cleaning bedrooms rather than watching *This Morning*. When she'd established that everything was in order and PJ had left for the afternoon, she retired to her room to examine her wardrobe. She had no intention of changing into anything special that would give Sebastian the wrong idea. Instead she changed her sweatshirt for a new pink T-shirt. It was rather low-cut so she added a pink coral necklace and left her hair loose. Pink lipstick and a spray of perfume and she was ready. She swapped her trainers for a pair of white pumps and tied a white sweater loosely around her shoulders. That was better. Now she knew she looked good but casual. Meeting her own eyes in the mirror she paused, guilty. What was she playing at? Why was she doing this? It wasn't too late. She could just not bother turning up. But that would be rude and make their relationship intolerable. It would be much better if she went to meet him and cancelled. Yes, that was definitely the answer.

When she arrived at the beauty spot, there was no sign of Sebastian. She fervently hoped he hadn't decided to walk here or she'd have a long wait. She got out of the car and crossed over to the wall to enjoy the view. This was a much quieter and untamed part of the lake. The land surrounding it was rocky, the trees were tall and there were no houses for miles. It was a haven for birds and wildlife, though, and had many different trails that led both sides of the lake. It had been a while since Erin had been up here and she drank in the wild beauty and enjoyed the silence. It would be nice to write off the afternoon and follow one of those paths; maybe another day.

A long, piercing whistle made her turn her head and she saw Sebastian standing down near the water, beckoning to her. 'I can't stay, Sebastian,' she called but he obviously couldn't hear her. 'Shit,' she mumbled. She went back to lock the car and then picked her way down the uneven path towards him, wishing she'd kept her trainers on. She was slightly breathless by the time she reached him and more than a bit irritable. 'Why on earth did you drag me down here? I don't have time to go to lunch and stroll around the lake.'

'Which is why I thought a picnic would be a good idea,' he replied, waving a hand at the bags around his feet. 'This way you don't have too far to go, we don't have to worry about bumping into anyone and we can enjoy the nice weather.'

'Oh.' Erin looked at him, wondering if his picnic would actually involve food or if he had other activities in mind.

'I picked a choice of sandwiches because I wasn't sure what you liked; I have a bottle of red wine – I couldn't get any chilled white, there's some water to keep you sober and fruit for afters. How does that sound?'

She smiled. 'It sounds lovely.' And it did. The day had grown warmer, there was no wind and the place seemed to be deserted. But she still wondered if he was up to something. The thought, rather than bothering her, excited her.

'Come on, then.' He picked up the bags. 'I've found a nice spot for us to eat.'

'It won't be very comfortable,' Erin pointed out. 'If you'd told me what you were planning I could have brought something for us to sit on.'

'Don't worry, you'll be comfortable.'

Erin followed him down the track for almost five minutes before he turned off and led her through some undergrowth until they emerged into a clearing, right on the edge of the water. The view was incredible and the only sounds came from the birds and the gentle lap of the water. Erin gasped as she looked around her. 'How did you find this place?'

'I think I know these trails better than any local at this stage.' Sebastian put down the bags and came to stand next to her. 'Lovely, isn't it?'

'Lovely.'

'So maybe this wasn't such a bad idea?'

She looked at him, shrugged and smiled. 'Maybe not.'

He turned to his purchases while Erin took off her sweater and folded it to sit on.

'No need for that.' He pulled out a colourful padded rug and tossed it to her.

'Where on earth did you get this?'

'It was on sale in that enormous supermarket outside Mullingar.'

Erin laughed and shook out the large blanket that was waterproof on one side. 'Were you in the scouts?'

'How could you tell?' He saluted and produced a selection of sandwiches and set them down beside her along with two bottles of water and then opened the wine with the corkscrew attached to his penknife. He produced plastic glasses and napkins from another bag and sat down next to her. He poured the wine and handed a glass to her. 'Cheers.'

'Cheers,' Erin said, taking a tiny sip and setting it down. 'Thank you, this is nice.'

He looked at her. 'Yes, it is.'

Erin stretched out on the rug, leaned on one arm and unwrapped a turkey sandwich. They ate in silence, looking out over the water and Erin was overcome with a sense of peace and well-being. It was ridiculous that she lived in this beautiful place and took so little time to enjoy it. She would make more of an effort to get out and about, she decided. 'Thank you for bringing me here, Sebastian.'

'Sometimes you need to stop and smell the roses, don't you think?'

She nodded. 'That's just what I was thinking. Still, at least I spend almost half my day outdoors, which is something.'

'You've created a very special place in the Gatehouse, Erin.'

'I wish I could accept the credit for that but the truth is, it was special when I got here.'

'And that's why you end up with deadbeat guests like me and Hazel.'

'I never called you deadbeats,' Erin protested, laughing.

'No, but that's what we are.'

'You're worried about her,' Erin said, pleased that he cared but jealous too.

'No, I only worry about me.'

'I don't believe that.'

He studied her, his expression thoughtful. 'Really?'

She met his eyes. 'Really.'

'Interesting.'

'But you are quite strange,' she teased.

He gave a wry grin. 'I've been called worse.'

They lapsed into a companionable silence again as

they finished their lunch. Erin couldn't remember feeling this comfortable with him before and, looking at Sebastian, she thought he seemed just as relaxed.

He turned his head and caught her watching him. 'What?'

She shook her head. 'Nothing. I was just thinking this is nice and you seem much happier than you were when you first got here.'

He shrugged. 'That wouldn't be hard. And what about you, Erin? Are you happy?'

Erin flushed. 'I suppose so.'

'Tell me about your life before you moved to Dunbarra.'

'I told you already, and it was so interesting you've forgotten.'

'I haven't forgotten. You said you were originally from Dublin, that's it. Why so reticent, Erin? You're not on the run from the police, are you?'

'Nothing so exciting.' She laughed.

'So?'

She sighed. 'I had a row with my mother, I had problems in work and then I lost my job. I needed to get away for a while and I ended up here.'

'What did you fight with your mother about?'

'After my father died she turned into this rather desperate and embarrassing man-eater. I decided to move out.'

'So don't you two talk any more?'

Erin shrugged. 'Sure, we go through the motions but we're not close.'

'And what did you work at?'

'I was the assistant manager in a business hotel. Why on earth do you want to know all this?'

He looked into her eyes. 'Because I want to know all about you.'

Her pulse quickened at his tender, sexy smile. 'Then shouldn't you be asking me about my taste in music or books or my feelings on politics or religion . . .'

'Okay, then, what music *do* you like?'

'I love every kind of music but particularly blues.'

'Really?' He grinned delightedly. 'Going to a dark cellar bar full of smoke and listening to jazz or blues used to be one of my favourite hobbies.'

'Used to be?'

He scowled. 'It's just not the same since the no-smoking regulations came in.'

She threw back her head and laughed. 'I know what you mean.'

'You have a lovely laugh,' he said, turning on his side to face her.

Erin was immediately conscious of his proximity and acutely aware of how completely alone they were in this beautiful place. He stretched out a hand and touched her cheek. She steeled herself not to turn her head and kiss it. 'I was coming here to tell you I'd changed my mind about going to lunch with you,' she told him.

'Yet here you are,' he said, his hand moving into her hair.

'You'd gone to so much trouble it would have been rude to cancel.'

'So you're only here because you're a well-mannered young woman.'

'That's right.'

'Well, I'm very impressed. And have you enjoyed your lunch?'

'It was lovely.'

'So where are your manners?' he scolded. 'Aren't you going to say thank you?'

'Thank you.'

He looked affronted. 'That's it? I go to all this trouble and I don't even get a peck on the cheek?'

She leaned towards him and placed a prim kiss on his cheek. 'Thank you,' she whispered in his ear.

He turned her face so that their lips touched. 'That's better,' he murmured before kissing her again a lot more thoroughly.

Erin knew that it was wrong, but when he started to push her back on the blanket she let him and welcomed the feel of his weight on top of her. As his hands and mouth started to caress her body, she stared up into the branches above them and realized that this was exactly why she had come here.

Afterwards he lay with his head in her lap and she stared out at the water.

'What are you thinking about?' he asked. 'Or should I say who?'

'What,' she confirmed. 'I was thinking that every time I leave you I feel cheap and dirty.'

His eyes widened and he sat up. 'That's awful.'

'Yes.'

'But why?'

Her smile was sad. 'I suppose I'm an old-fashioned girl, Sebastian. I'm involved with someone else and I don't like betraying him, and for what? You couldn't even call this an affair.'

'You want to be romanced, is that it?'

She detected a derisive note in his voice and immediately moved away and started to tidy herself. 'I don't want anything, don't worry.'

'Oh, no, don't go getting all prickly,' he said with an exaggerated sigh. 'Why must women be such extreme creatures? One moment you're sexy, passionate sirens and the next you're all pious and prim.'

She scrambled to her feet and stared down at him. 'How dare you?'

He stretched out on the blanket, linked his hands behind his head and closed his eyes. 'Go on back to your farmer, Erin. And when you need some more excitement in your life, you know where to find me.'

'You bastard,' she muttered and stumbled back down the path as fast as her flimsy pumps would allow.

Chapter Twenty-Two

Erin was digging potatoes with a vengeance when Hazel appeared looking nervy and unkempt. She was the last person Erin wanted to see – well, the second last. 'Hi, Hazel, can I help you?'

'Where's Gracie?'

Erin bristled at Hazel's accusing tone. This girl was pushing her luck. 'I'm afraid I have no idea.'

'Isn't she here with you and PJ?'

'PJ took Gracie back up to your room before he went out.'

'But she's not there,' Hazel's voice had risen.

'Calm down, Hazel. I'm sure she's around here somewhere. She'd never venture outside the Gatehouse on her own, would she? She never has before.'

'No,' Hazel agreed.

'So let's split up and find her. She's probably fallen asleep in a corner somewhere.' Erin checked her watch. 'She usually naps after her lunch, doesn't she?'

Hazel stared, her expression a mixture of horror and shame. 'I didn't realize it was so late. I haven't given her any lunch. I've been sleeping . . .'

Erin smiled. 'Then if she's hungry and tired she's definitely curled up somewhere. You look around the house and I'll check the sheds and greenhouses.'

Hazel stood motionless, her hand over her mouth.

'It will be fine, Hazel,' Erin said, adopting a firm voice like a teacher with a young child. 'Go on now, we'll find her in no time and then you can make her the most enormous lunch she's ever had.' Erin watched until Hazel had disappeared into the house and then headed for the largest barn, where they kept all the tools including the pink plastic ones that PJ had bought Gracie. It was a large sprawling building with bags of fertilizer and insecticides stacked everywhere. Children shouldn't be allowed anywhere near any of this stuff and the realization filled Erin with trepidation. But the child wasn't allowed into the market garden without PJ, and she knew that. She always waited in the kitchen garden for him; she knew the rules. Erin just hoped that she hadn't decided to break them or, if she had, that there wouldn't be any consequences. She shivered at the thought and started to pull the barn apart, calling the child's name.

After a fruitless search of the entire garden and orchard, Erin hurried back across the lawn towards the house, sick to her stomach. As she got closer,

Hazel burst out of the front door and her face told Erin everything she needed to know.

'You didn't find her?' Hazel said, sounding frantic.

Erin shook her head. 'No, but I'm sure she's fine.'

'How are you sure?' Hazel cried. 'How could she be all right? She's only four and she's completely disappeared.'

'Hazel, calm down; you're no use to her if you get yourself in a state.'

Hazel burst into tears. 'Oh, God. Erin, what are we going to do? She could be anywhere.'

'Nonsense, she's too small to have got far.'

'But someone might have taken her, or she might have gone down to the lake.' She collapsed into Erin's arms and began to cry hysterically.

Erin held her tightly. Of course the thought of Gracie and the lake had occurred to her too. There were several areas in the grounds where there was access, but only with effort; Gracie would have had to intend to get to the water, which was, of course, a possibility. She gripped Hazel firmly by the arms and looked into her face. 'Hazel, pull yourself together, you have to think. You need to go to all the places where you've taken Gracie, especially the spots she liked most. I'm going to phone Ronan and Nora and ask them to come over and help search.'

'Should we call the police?' Hazel whispered.

'Maybe.' Erin didn't see the point in lying. 'But not

until we are absolutely sure she's not in the house or grounds.'

'I've searched the house,' Hazel reminded her.

'You weren't able to go into the other bedrooms. Gracie could have sneaked into one. I'll go and check that now. So are you okay, can you do this?'

Hazel nodded. 'Call me if you find her, won't you?'

'I'll scream my head off.'

Erin went inside and phoned Nora.

'She'll turn up, love, don't worry,' was the reply. 'I'd come and help if I could but I'm on my way to the doctor.'

'Never mind, Nora. See you tomorrow.' Erin quickly hung up before Nora started to relate all her symptoms. She hesitated for a moment before calling Ronan. It was such a cheek, given that she'd been with Sebastian only a couple of hours ago. But this was about Gracie not about her. Ronan was a good man and he'd want to help. Putting her guilt on a back burner she dialled his mobile number.

Ronan was in the jeep. 'Will I come over or do you want me to drive around?' he said immediately, when she had filled him in.

'Drive around, I think, though she'd hardly have gone far.' Unless someone took her, Erin thought.

'How long has she been gone?' Ronan asked.

'PJ dropped her back to her room around twelve. No one's seen her since.'

'Phone him and double-check the time, Erin. I'll check the main roads in the immediate vicinity. Is Sebastian there?'

Erin hesitated. 'I'm not sure, why?'

'Ask him to help, for God's sake. He probably knows the trails around the lake as well as any local.'

'Yes, I suppose he does.' Erin closed her eyes, feeling sick with shame. 'I'll see if he's in.'

'Try not to worry, Erin.'

'I'm more worried about Hazel, she is completely distraught.'

'It will be fine, Erin, you'll see.'

'Oh, God, Ronan, I hope so.'

Erin hung up and, realizing that Ronan was right, she went down the path and knocked on Sebastian's door. She felt a mixture of relief and frustration when there was no reply. In the distance she could hear Hazel calling to her daughter. No luck yet, then. Erin went into the house, fetched her bunch of keys and started a systematic search of the house. She doubted Gracie was there, though. If she'd come inside she'd have gone to the sitting room or into the kitchen where PJ sometimes brought her for milk and biscuits. The child had always seemed obedient and shy so Erin thought it unlikely she'd venture into the room of a stranger; still, she had to check.

It took only fifteen minutes for Erin to satisfy herself that Gracie was definitely not in the house. She went in search of Hazel and caught up with her in the orchard.

'Have you found her?' were Hazel's first words.

'No.'

Hazel shook her head. 'I don't understand. She's never done anything like this before. You see how she is. She hardly ever leaves my side unless it's to be with PJ.' Her face brightened. 'Maybe she's with him, Erin.'

Erin shook her head. 'I doubt it, Hazel. PJ wouldn't take her out without permission.'

'He might have,' Hazel insisted.

Erin took out her mobile phone and rang PJ's number. 'I'll ask him.' But all she got was his answering service. 'Sorry, Hazel, but he has his phone switched off.' Erin quickly left a message asking PJ to contact her, and rang off.

'I bet they're together. I'm sure of it!' Hazel's eyes shone with relief.

'I really don't think so, Hazel.'

'But you don't know. They could have gone somewhere together, and his battery might have died or his phone could be broken.'

Erin sighed. 'Hazel, PJ is visiting someone in a nursing home, that's why his phone is switched off and he would never have taken Gracie there, I promise you.'

Hazel's shoulders slumped. 'Then where is she?'

Erin took her hands. 'We'll find her.' Her mobile rang and she put it to her ear. 'Yes?' It was Ronan.

'Erin, any sign of her?'

'No.'

'I've been up and down the road a few times but I can't see her. Did you find Sebastian?'

'No.'

'Then I think you'd better call the guards and let them know what's happened. Also you could phone the coffee shop and the pub and we'll organize a proper search party. Tell them to meet up in Dijon's car park.'

'Do you think that's necessary?'

'It doesn't look good, Erin, and the longer it goes . . . well, I just think we should get as many people out looking for her as possible.'

'I'll get right on it.' Erin shoved her phone in her pocket and put an arm around Hazel's shoulders. 'Ronan thinks I should phone around and get more people out searching.'

Hazel nodded. 'Yes, yes, please do that.'

'I'll call the police first—'

'Oh God,' Hazel moaned, closing her eyes.

'I'm sure she's safe, Hazel, but they're the experts in situations like this and they'll know what to do.'

'But she's here, she must be.' Hazel started back down towards the lake. 'And I'm going to find her.'

Erin watched helplessly as she strode away. She wanted to go with her but Ronan was right: she had to call in some reinforcements. First she phoned the local Garda Station and explained the situation.

She waited impatiently as they put her on hold. After what seemed like an eternity a deep male voice came on the line and asked her all the same questions the policewoman had just asked. Erin exploded. 'I already told someone all of this! Now, there's a little girl lost. Are you going to help me find her, or not?'

'I know you're worried, Miss Joyce, but please try to stay calm. I need to ask you some questions. The more information I have now, the more effective we can be.'

Erin closed her eyes and nodded, even though he couldn't see her. 'Yes, I'm sorry.'

She listened carefully as he went through a number of points and answered him as best she could. Then she went in search of Hazel. Inspector Geraghty had said he'd organize the search party so she didn't have to phone anyone else. He'd asked that she take care of Hazel, find a recent photo of Gracie and provide them with a piece of clothing that belonged to the child. The last request made Erin shiver.

The Inspector had quizzed Erin extensively and, feeling guilty, she had told him of Hazel's recent moods and withdrawal from everyone including her daughter. But what could she do? She had to tell him everything.

Back outside she took the track that Hazel had taken earlier, listening and watching as she went. She stopped abruptly at the sound of crying. Following the sound, she found Hazel on her knees near the water's edge, her head in her hands. 'Hazel?'

The girl looked up, her face tortured. 'We're never going to find her, Erin. She's gone.'

'Of course she isn't,' Erin said firmly. 'Now come on, we need to go back to the house. The police want a photograph and something Gracie wears a lot. You also need to tell them exactly what she was –' Erin paused – 'is, wearing.'

Hazel allowed Erin to lead her back towards the house but she was silent and her steps were heavy.

'You mustn't give up,' Erin said softly as they climbed the front steps. 'You have to believe that she's out there and that we are going to find her; you have to, Hazel.'

Hazel's eyes filled with tears but she nodded and started to go upstairs.

As Erin stood watching her, her mobile phone rang and Hazel whirled around, hope lighting up her eyes. Erin looked at the phone. 'It's PJ. Hello, PJ?'

'I got your message, Erin. What's wrong?'

Erin shook her head at Hazel and, with a strangled sob, the girl ran on upstairs.

'PJ, Gracie is missing.'

'What?'

'No one's seen her since you left. Can you remember what time that was?'

'I'm not sure – no, wait, it would have been about

ten to twelve. When I got into the car the midday news was just starting.'

'And how was she this morning, PJ? Did you notice anything different about her?'

'Well, she didn't want to go back up to Hazel, to be honest,' he admitted. 'But I told her that she couldn't come with me and she couldn't wander around on her own. I saw her to her room, Erin, and she definitely went inside. That's the God's truth.'

'No one is questioning that, PJ,' Erin told him when she heard the anguish in his voice. 'I'm sure she'll turn up soon. Is there anywhere you can think of that she might have gone?'

PJ made a few suggestions but they were all places that she and Hazel had checked. 'After that, it's just the trails by the lake.'

'Yes. We're checking them next. The police are organizing a search party.' As she spoke, a squad car sped through the gate and squealed to a halt outside the door. 'Look, I have to go, the guards are here.'

'I'll be home as quick as I can,' he promised.

Erin brought Inspector Geraghty and the young policeman, whose name she had already forgotten, into the living room and sighed as the questions started again. 'It's her mother you should really be talking to,' she told them. 'I'll go and get her.'

'In a minute, Miss Joyce. We'd like to talk to you first. Who else is staying here at the moment?'

'There's an American woman; but she's gone to Dublin for a few days. There's an Italian couple who went out straight after breakfast and they're not due back until late. And there's another man; he's not here at the moment either.'

The two guards exchanged a look.

'Oh, no,' Erin shook her head, 'it's nothing like that.'

'Nothing like what, Miss Joyce?' the Inspector asked politely. 'What is the name and nationality of this guest?'

Erin looked him in the eye. 'He's English, lives in the US and is a half-brother of Marguerite Hayes, the proprietor of Dijon restaurant. His name is Sebastian Gray.'

The young police officer looked up from his notebook. 'The actor?'

Erin nodded.

The Inspector raised an eyebrow at his subordinate.

'He's one of the big names in action movies today,' the lad explained.

'And he's here on holiday?' Geraghty asked Erin.

'Yes.'

'Has he mixed with your other guests, in particular Ms Patterson?'

'Yes, a little. Hazel – Ms Patterson – is an artist and he's bought some of her work.'

'Does he talk to the child?'

Erin didn't like the way this was going at all.

'No, he's not really into kids; it was Hazel he was interested in.'

Again Geraghty's eyebrow went up. 'Indeed?'

'I meant her art,' Erin protested. 'Look, you are barking up the wrong tree. Gracie has been very down lately because her mother is down. She has probably just wandered off and got lost. Possibly she ran away, but I doubt it.'

'Who else are Ms Patterson and her daughter friendly with?'

'PJ Ward. He's a long-term guest here. He helps me with the market garden. He's very fond of Gracie and she follows him around a lot.'

Inspector Geraghty frowned. 'I think I know him. Tall man, late sixties? He's been here a few years now?'

Erin nodded. 'That's him. He was the last person to see Gracie. She spent the morning in the market garden with him and then he dropped her back to her room.'

'And where is he now?'

'He's gone to visit a relative in a nursing home.'

'Which nursing home?' the Inspector asked.

Erin told him. 'But he phoned just as you came in and he's on his way back; he should be here any minute.'

The Inspector nodded. 'You've been very helpful, Miss Joyce. Could you get Ms Patterson now, please?'

'Sure.' Erin went out into the hall to find Hazel

halfway down the stairs, one of Gracie's tops clutched tightly against her breast.

'Hazel, the police are here.'

'She took her teddy,' Hazel told her, tears sliding down her face. 'Harvey, the teddy she sleeps with; she took him.'

Erin held out a hand. 'Come and tell the police, Hazel. The sooner they have all the information they need, the sooner they can bring her home.'

Moments later the young policeman left with the clothing and photo. Several other cars had arrived and there were now three excitable dogs straining on their leashes and sniffing eagerly around them. Erin should have felt relieved to see them but it just reminded her of television coverage about abducted children. Those stories rarely had a happy ending. Surely that couldn't happen here in Dunbarra. As she stood staring out at the strangers crowding her driveway, she saw PJ's car turn in the gate. He drove around the other vehicles and pulled up right at the door, emerging from the car with a broad smile.

'Panic over. Look who I found!' he said, and lifted Gracie out of the back seat.

'Hazel! PJ's found her!' Erin screamed, before hurrying down the steps. But as she approached the car, she was pushed firmly to one side and PJ was surrounded and hustled into a police car.

Chapter Twenty-Three

It was several hours and a lot of questions later before PJ was released. Gracie was interviewed by a social worker, a policewoman and a child psychologist and finally, when the police were satisfied that she was telling the truth, they packed up and left. PJ was delivered home an hour later. He was pale and shaken and suddenly looked old and frail. Erin made tea while Ronan put a large whiskey into his hand.

'How's Hazel doing?' PJ asked after a moment.

'She's fine now that Gracie's here. They're both dying to see you.'

'Maybe later. They thought I'd taken her,' he marvelled, almost to himself.

'Don't take it personally,' Ronan told him. 'They were just following procedure.'

Erin nodded. 'I think they were suspicious of Sebastian too. I suppose they have to look on everyone as a possible suspect, and as neither of you were here you were top of their list. But they know you're completely innocent, PJ. Gracie told them everything.'

PJ looked at her, baffled. '*Told* them? But sure, how could she do that?'

Erin smiled. 'Well, that's the good news. She's talking.'

'I didn't think she could.'

'It seems she only stopped talking a few months ago after some kind of trauma. Hazel said she started again a few days ago but it was just a word here and there. The only reason she spoke up today was because Hazel told her you might be in trouble and Gracie wasn't going to let that happen. She adores you.'

PJ wiped his eye. 'I'd never harm a hair on her head, you know that, don't you, Erin?'

Erin crouched down at his feet and took his hands. 'Of course I do! No one who knows you would ever think you capable of hurting a fly, never mind a child.'

'So what did she say?' he asked.

'Well, apparently she was upset that you were going out. Then, when she went into her room, Hazel was still asleep and she couldn't wake her. So she took her blanket and teddy and hid on the floor in the back of your car.'

PJ shook his head. 'I can't believe that I didn't discover her until I was halfway home, and then it was only because she sneezed.'

'She fell asleep before you'd even got into the car,' Erin told him. 'When she woke, you weren't there – you must have been in the nursing home. She didn't know where she was and she was too afraid to get out so she just curled up on the floor again and waited.'

'Thank God she did,' Ronan said, 'or this day might not have had a happy ending.'

PJ flinched. 'I don't know what I would have done if something had happened to her and it was all my fault.'

'It wasn't, PJ,' Ronan said. 'Now stop beating yourself up about it. She's home and safe and that's all that matters.'

'Why don't you go up and see them?' Erin urged. 'It will make you feel better.'

PJ got slowly to his feet and made for the door. 'Then I think I'll go on into bed, Erin. It's been a long day.'

'This has taken a lot out of him,' Ronan remarked when they were alone.

Erin collapsed into a chair. 'I know. I just hope he can bounce back.'

'It may take some time. How are your other guests?'

'Thankfully there was no one around. Sandra is in Dublin and my Italian couple were out for the day.'

'And where's the resident celebrity?'

Erin closed her eyes and faked a yawn. 'I've no idea. That's why I'm sure he was Geraghty's main suspect. It didn't help that I told him Sebastian spends most of his days wandering the trails around the lakes.'

Ronan laughed. 'Well, it wouldn't.'

'I am so relieved that no one else was involved. I don't think I could have continued to live here if anything sinister had happened.'

'Well, it didn't,' Ronan said. 'All's well that ends well, as they say. Hazel must be a very happy and relieved woman.'

'You'd think so, wouldn't you? But she seems as miserable as before. The only difference is that she won't let Gracie out of her sight for more than a minute.'

Ronan rose to his feet. 'She's probably still in shock. It's been an awful day.'

'You can say that again,' Erin said with feeling as he pulled her to her feet.

He folded her into his arms and kissed the top of her head. 'Go to bed, you're exhausted.'

She walked with him to the front door. 'Thanks for everything you did today, Ronan.'

'I wasn't much use.'

She kissed him. 'You were here when I needed you; that was enough.'

'And I always will be, Erin, you know that.'

Erin sighed as she watched him run down the steps, climb into his jeep and drive away. She really didn't deserve the guy, and instead of counting her blessings she was doing everything to destroy what they had – and with a cold-hearted bastard like Sebastian Gray too. She should be sectioned. But, thankfully, she'd been lucky and Ronan didn't suspect anything. Maybe it was time she started to trust him. Maybe it was time she settled down and started to plan a future with him. Maybe it was time she stopped behaving like her mother.

Erin closed the door and went into the kitchen to make some tea and hot chocolate. Putting the drinks and a plate of biscuits on a tray, she took it up to Hazel's room. She knocked gently and a moment later Gracie opened the door and offered her a shy smile.

'Hello, there! I've brought you some hot chocolate, would you like that?'

Gracie nodded, and held the door wide open to let Erin in. Hazel and PJ were sitting at the small table by the window and she set the tray down between them.

'I was feeling a bit useless so I thought I'd bring you some tea. It's what everyone does at times like this, isn't it?' she joked.

PJ patted her hand. 'Thanks, darling.'

Hazel said nothing.

Erin shot a concerned look at PJ and then looked back at Hazel's blank expression. 'How are you feeling, Hazel?'

'Fine.' Hazel lifted Gracie on to her lap and pulled the hot chocolate closer. 'Be careful, darling, it's hot, and when you're finished it's time to sleep.'

Erin backed towards the door. 'I'll say goodnight, then. But I'm just across the hall. If you need anything, just ask.'

Hazel nodded but her eyes were fixed on her daughter.

PJ smiled and nodded his thanks. 'Goodnight, Erin.'

Erin never heard the alarm the next morning and arrived downstairs only minutes before Sebastian. She put on a pot of coffee and went in to see him. 'Good morning,' she said with a nod.

He looked at her, an amused look in his eyes. 'Good morning.'

'I'm afraid breakfast will be a bit late this morning; I slept in.'

'Ah, Ronan stayed over again, did he? You must be tired.'

She decided to ignore the sarcasm. 'Gracie went missing yesterday and gave us all quite a fright. We had to call in the police.'

'Did they find her?'

Erin was relieved to see a look of concern in his eyes; maybe he wasn't a total bastard. 'They didn't have to look. PJ was going out for the afternoon and she wanted to go with him, so she hid in the back of his car and fell asleep. He only discovered her on his way home.'

'I'm so glad.'

Erin pulled a face. 'It wasn't exactly a happy ending, though. The police jumped to the wrong conclusion and hauled PJ off to the police station. Thankfully, hearing that her friend could be in trouble, Gracie decided it was time to speak and told them the whole story.'

'Ah, so she spoke again.'

Erin's ears pricked up. 'You've heard her talk before?'

'Just once.' He didn't elaborate. 'So did they release PJ?'

'Yes, but he was very upset.'

'I'm not surprised. It's not nice to be accused of something you haven't done.'

'No. Anyway, I just wanted you to know the full story because I've no doubt there will be all sorts of inaccurate versions going around.'

'Well, thank you for that, and if I hear any such stories, I will correct them.'

She softened at the kindness in his eyes. 'Thanks. Well, I'd better go and make your breakfast.'

'Erin?'

She turned back. 'Yes?'

'I really enjoyed yesterday up until the point when we started to argue again. And I'm sorry about that too. I don't know why I said those things.'

Erin studied him. He looked genuinely contrite. 'You weren't very nice but I probably overreacted. We're bad for each other, Sebastian. I think it's best if we stay away from each other for the remainder of your visit.'

'I don't believe that's what you want.'

She shrugged. 'I want everything but I can't have it. What I do know is that I'm not very proud of myself at the moment and I don't like that feeling.'

'That's just your Catholic guilt,' he teased, 'but if you want me to stay away from you then that's fine. You know where I am if you change your mind.'

'I do but I won't. Now I'll go and make your breakfast.'

It was almost an hour later before Hazel and Gracie appeared. Erin made a fuss of them, loading their table with food of every kind. The Italian couple came over to ask after Gracie, and Sebastian joined them for a cup of coffee too. But there was no sign of PJ. He rarely slept late but Erin supposed it wasn't surprising after the awful experience he'd had. Once she'd made sure all her other guests were happy, she took a cup of tea upstairs and tapped gently on his door.

'Come in.'

She found him sitting by the window, wearing his dressing gown. 'Oh, you're up. I thought you'd decided to have a lie-in.'

He shook his head. 'I couldn't sleep.'

Erin set down the tea in front of him and noted the dark circles under his eyes. 'Would you like me to bring your breakfast up?'

'I don't feel that hungry.'

Erin sat down beside him. 'Are you still upset about yesterday?'

He chuckled but his eyes were sad. 'I can't say I enjoyed being taken off in a Garda car and questioned at the station for hours. Why is it that even when you're innocent, there's something about being in a place like that, that makes you feel guilty?'

Erin smiled. 'I feel like that every time I'm around a copper; it must be the uniform.'

He nodded and stared out of the window.

'Drink your tea; it's getting cold.'

He took a sip but she knew it was only to keep her happy.

'Well, Gracie is in fine form this morning. The experience doesn't seem to have done her any harm. In fact, it's probably done her a lot of good. She's talking now and Hazel is more attentive than she has been in weeks.'

'That's good.'

'Do you know why Gracie stopped talking in the first place? Did Hazel ever tell you?'

He shook his head and stood up. 'Maybe I'll go back to bed after all.'

'Good idea. You do that and I'll make you something nice when you get up.'

'Thanks, darling.'

She reached up to give him a quick hug. 'See you later.'

Gracie ran to meet her when she walked back into the dining room. 'Is PJ coming?'

Erin smiled at the sound of the sweet little voice. 'Not yet, pet, he's having a lie-on this morning.'

Gracie's face crumpled with disappointment. Hazel came over to join them. 'Is he okay?' she said, slipping an arm around her daughter.

'He didn't sleep very well and he's still a bit shaken, I think. I'm sure he'll be fine after he's had some rest.' Erin looked down at Gracie. 'So what are you two going to do today?'

'I promised Gracie we'd spend the morning in the gardens with PJ but that will have to wait. Why don't we go for a walk, Gracie? We could go up as far as the field with the ponies.'

Gracie didn't look very impressed.

'That's a good idea,' Erin said, feeling sorry for Hazel. 'If you like, I could give you some carrots and sugar lumps to feed them.'

Gracie brightened at that. 'Okay.'

'You run upstairs and brush your teeth and I'll be with you in a minute,' Hazel told her. 'Is PJ really all right?' she asked Erin when they were alone.

'I think he's just upset. He can't believe that anyone would think he'd hurt a child, let alone Gracie. He adores her, Hazel.'

'I know that. Do you think I should go and see him?'

'Not now. He was going back to bed and I think he'll feel a lot better after a sleep. I tell you what, why don't you come back here for one o'clock and we can all have some lunch together? I'm sure he'd like that.'

Hazel's face immediately relaxed into a smile. 'Oh, that would be great, Erin. Gracie will be so pleased.'

Erin smiled too. 'Then that's what we'll do.'

When PJ came downstairs he was still very withdrawn and Erin wondered if lunch was such a good idea after all. But though he was quiet to begin with, Gracie soon worked her magic on him, and by the time the meal was over he seemed like his old self. But then it was hard not to smile, listening to Gracie's excited chatter; she was a different child from the one that had been creeping around the place recently. Hazel too seemed happier. She didn't say much but she followed her daughter around with her eyes and she touched Gracie at every opportunity. Erin wondered what it would be like to love someone like that. When PJ finally rose to go outside, Gracie immediately begged to go along.

'That's up to your mother,' he told her.

'It's fine,' Hazel said, much to Gracie's delight, 'but you must do whatever PJ says and no running off, do you hear me?'

'I promise, Mummy.' Gracie hugged her and then skipped off after PJ.

'She seems no worse for her adventure.' Erin remarked.

'No, she's fine; it's just the rest of us that are reeling.'

'You must have been so scared.'

'I was. I kept thinking: what if she's gone too near the lake?' Hazel shivered.

'I can't say the thought didn't occur to me,' Erin admitted. 'Still, she's safe and talking; you must be delighted about that.'

Hazel smiled. 'Yes.'

'Why did she stop, Hazel? Do you know?' Erin could almost see the shutter come down.

'She got a fright. Doctors said there was nothing we could do but wait; they said she'd talk again when she was ready.'

'And she has!' Erin smiled and began to clear the table. Hazel obviously wasn't comfortable talking about this, or talking about this to her, and Erin wasn't going to pry.

'I think I'll go and join Gracie and PJ. Would that be okay?'

'Of course.'

'Okay, then, see you later, and thank you for everything, Erin.'

'You're welcome.'

Later, when Erin went out with her basket to pick beans, she smiled at the sight of Hazel on her knees next to her daughter, pulling weeds. At this rate she'd have to put them both on the payroll. Maybe she should start marketing the Gatehouse as a haven for gardening therapy; it might catch on.

Humming to herself, she went down the rows of vegetables thinking that, given how horrible yesterday had been, today wasn't turning out so bad. She was particularly happy to have made her peace with Sebastian and she knew that staying away from him was the right thing to do, the only thing to do. She just hoped she could manage it.

Chapter Twenty-Four

PJ thought a lot about what he should do next. His first instinct was to mind his own business and do nothing. After his visit to the police station last week, he was quite happy to live a quiet live and avoid any sort of bother. But he couldn't ignore the uneasy feeling in his gut. And then Paddy had blurted something out and that had been that; he knew he couldn't pretend that everything was okay. In fact, Paddy had come out with two gems and neither of them had impressed PJ. But for the moment he'd concentrate on Hazel. And so here he was, standing outside the cabin, waiting for Sebastian Gray to return from breakfast. He never had reported back on his chat with Hazel and PJ now knew there had definitely been 'a chat'. Paddy had told him about the little scene in the coffee shop. For Hazel to get that upset, Sebastian must have touched a nerve. He needed to know exactly which one and if Sebastian had found out any more information. PJ wasn't comfortable sneaking around like this but

Hazel was getting worse and Sebastian was his last hope before doing something drastic like searching the girl's room. He heard Sebastian's footsteps on the path and turned to greet him.

'Good morning, PJ, how are you?' Sebastian nodded, and made to go past.

'Fine, thanks. Could we talk, please?'

Sebastian paused and then turned to unlock the door. 'Sure.'

PJ followed him inside and though Sebastian offered him a chair, PJ chose to stand in front of the fireplace.

'What can I do for you?' Sebastian sat down and looked up at him expectantly.

'You never told me how your conversation with Hazel went. I was wondering if you found out anything.'

'Not much. Anyway, it's immaterial now, isn't it? She seems fine.'

'She's far from fine,' PJ said bluntly.

Sebastian frowned. 'Why do you say that?'

'She's becoming more withdrawn every day.' PJ shook his head. 'I thought she was going to be okay. She was so relieved when Gracie turned out to be safe and sound, and happy that the child was talking again but something's just not right.'

Sebastian said nothing for a moment and then nodded. 'Okay. She has a medical condition – depression,

I think. She won't take the medication because when she takes it she can't paint.'

'So she's taking it now? Well, that's something, although it doesn't seem to be helping.'

'She isn't taking it. At least she wasn't when we talked. She's not painting because some idiot didn't want to buy her paintings.'

'She told me about that and I took one of her paintings to a friend of mine who owns a gallery, and she was crazy about it. She wanted to give Hazel a show but the girl wouldn't hear of it. I really don't understand her.'

'I think I do. She's afraid of losing Gracie to her husband. If her work got any coverage in the press he'd be able to trace her to Dunbarra.'

'That might not be such a bad thing. And Gracie might be better off with her father for the moment.'

'That's not really your call to make.'

'So what do I do? Sit back and watch the girl self-destruct? And what about Gracie? That child is as sharp as a tack; she senses Hazel's moods and she is definitely affected by them.' PJ closed his eyes briefly. 'I think I'll go to the police.'

'What?' Sebastian stared at him.

'They may be able to trace Hazel's husband.'

'That's a really bad idea. You have no idea what the guy is like. You don't know why he and Hazel even broke up; he could have been abusing her, hurting the child . . .'

'Do you think so?'

Sebastian sighed. 'No, but I don't know and, the point is, neither do you.'

'What should I do?' PJ sank on to a chair.

'Perhaps you need to tell her what you're thinking of doing.'

PJ looked at him as if he were mad. 'But sure, then she'd just take Gracie and run, and that would be disastrous. At least while she's here we can keep an eye on her.'

'I don't know what else to say. Maybe you should talk to a doctor or a psychiatrist and get some advice.'

PJ brightened. 'That's a good idea. Do you have any more details about her illness or her medication?'

'Sorry, no. But—'

'What?'

Sebastian sighed. 'I think she may have attempted suicide at some stage.'

'Jesus, Mary and Joseph!' PJ crossed himself.

'So you see that whatever you do, PJ, you must handle this very carefully.'

'Yes, I see that.' PJ nodded, feeling immeasurably sad. 'But I also see that I definitely can't ignore it either.' He stood up and crossed to the door, then turned back to Sebastian. 'There's one other matter.'

'Yes?'

'I'm very fond of Erin,' he said, making sure his

voice was quiet and measured. 'Don't hurt her in any way.'

'Or what?' Sebastian looked at him, amused.

PJ wasn't sure what to say to that but the other man's expression was enough to give him further cause for concern. 'Just don't do it, Mr Gray,' he said finally, and with as much dignity as he could muster, he walked out, closing the door quietly behind him.

As he crossed back to the garden he wondered how and when he should broach this thorny subject with Hazel. He noticed that she was brighter in the mornings and seemed to grow more morose as the day progressed; so first thing, then. And he should do it as soon as possible, for Gracie's sake at least. The poor wee thing had revelled in her mother's attentions after her escapade last week, but as life settled down again and Hazel grew distant, Gracie got more anxious and clingy. Whereas she usually wanted to be in the garden as much as possible with him, lately she seemed torn between spending time with him and staying with her mother. And it wasn't as if they were doing anything exciting. Hazel either planted Gracie in front of Erin's television or left her to her own devices. It was heartbreaking to watch. He'd talk to her first thing in the morning. He'd ask Erin to keep an eye on Gracie and, if it was dry, he and Hazel could go for a walk. If not they'd have to use the sitting room. There were only a couple of other guests at the moment and, thankfully, Sandra Bell was still in Dublin. Having such a private conversation with that bloody woman in the building would be impossible. He had to give a lot of thought to what he would say to Hazel, he mused, as he went into the barn, but he felt better already that at least he'd come to a decision.

'PJ?'

He went back to the door when he heard Erin call. 'Over here,' he shouted back. He watched her walk towards him, his smile of greeting fading as she drew closer. He could tell even at this distance that it was something bad and he had a pretty good idea what. But he didn't know for sure until she got here. As long as she was walking towards him he could pretend everything was just fine. For a few more precious seconds . . .

And then she was in front of him, her eyes bright with tears. She reached out and took his hands in hers. 'I'm so sorry, PJ. She's gone.'

PJ told Erin about Isabelle the night that she signed the contract to buy the Gatehouse. He hadn't planned it, but after some wine she had got quite emotional and told him about how her father had died and her mother had gone off the rails. She'd told him that this was the happiest she'd been since, and that if it wasn't for him she would never have had the courage to take over the guest house. PJ had been touched. He had contributed a relatively small amount of money to the venture but Erin said his gardening expertise was worth more than cash to her. It had been a lovely evening and, before he knew it, he was telling her about Isabelle. She was the only person in Dunbarra he'd told before or since. Though many people knew that he had a sick relative whom he visited often, he'd led them to believe it was a distant aunt; that they were merely duty visits. He never let on that the woman he visited every week was his wife and the love of his life.

'Are you okay?'

He looked over at Erin, who was driving him the thirty miles to the nursing home. 'I'm grand.'

'The nurse said she went in her sleep; she wouldn't have known any pain.'

'It's a blessed release,' he said, more for her sake than anything else. Why did people say that? What was blessed about dying? But then Isabelle probably wouldn't agree. She had been the most vibrant person he had ever known, and when she'd been diagnosed with Alzheimer's she'd been horrified. The thought of losing her mind, of losing control – it had terrified her. She'd tried to make him promise to help her on her way when she became a burden but he'd refused point-blank. And he pointed out that when she went gaga she wouldn't be any the wiser, so what was the problem.

That had been more than ten years ago now and he realized that they were lucky she'd stayed well for so long. It was only four years ago that she'd started to go downhill; but once the decline started, it was rapid. A year later she had to go into the nursing home and that's when he decided he had to sell their home and get away from everything he'd once shared with her. There was a long and difficult road ahead and he knew he would only be able to face this living hell if he found some way to escape it, at least occasionally.

'Nearly there,' Erin said, patting his hand.

He nodded and smiled at her. What would he do without Erin? He'd told her she didn't have to come with him but she wouldn't hear of it. And not only was she bringing him to the nursing home, she insisted that she was staying for the funeral too.

'You'd do the same for me,' she'd told him and, of course, she was right.

They'd limped through that first year at the Gatehouse together and then walked. And this last couple of years he'd actually started to feel normal again. There were moments when he even forgot about Isabelle, forgot about the nursing home. But now he had to face the fact that she was gone, that this part of his life was over. He let out a small, involuntary gasp and immediately Erin's hand was gripping his.

'It's going to be okay, PJ. You're going to be fine.'

'Of course I am.'

She swung the car into a parking spot outside the nursing home and turned off the engine. 'Ready?' she asked.

He took a deep breath. 'I'm ready.'

It was late that afternoon before they finally checked into a hotel. PJ carried their overnight bags upstairs while she followed with a suit carrier. He tried to get the key into the lock but his hands were shaking so much that eventually she put a gentle hand on his arm and he stood back and let her open the door for him

'Can I get you anything?' she asked.

'No.'

'I'd better make a few phone calls.'

PJ's face darkened. 'Don't tell them anything, Erin.'

'But PJ—'

'No, Erin, I mean it. I've kept it a secret all this time. I'm not going to ruin it now. When this is all over I'll be able to go back to Dunbarra and carry on as before. I don't want special treatment or funny looks. And I certainly don't want sympathy.'

Erin stared at him. 'But PJ, how do I explain this? What do I say to Ronan? Everyone is going to think it odd that I've come with you to the funeral of a distant relative.'

But PJ couldn't deal with her dilemma. He shrugged and started to close the door. 'Tell them you came because you were worried about me. Tell them it was an elderly aunt and I'm in charge of her estate. I really don't care what you say, Erin.'

In her room, Erin went over her story in her head before she phoned Ronan. Even so she knew her boyfriend was more than surprised that she'd left her guests high and dry to take PJ to a funeral.

'So are you driving back tonight?' he asked.

'No, I thought I'd stay.'

'But what about the guest house?'

'There're only Sebastian, Hazel and Gracie there at the moment so I was going to get Sean to ask Rai to help out. I'm sure a young girl like that would be glad of the extra money.'

'It's very good of you to go to such trouble for PJ.'

'Well, I feel sorry for him; he's got no one else.'

There was a moment's silence. 'You're right. Look, give me the details and I'll do my best to come along. Paddy would probably like to come too.'

'No!' Erin exclaimed, cursing herself for putting the idea in his head. 'It's a private affair, Ronan. In fact, there isn't even going to be a proper service; she wasn't a religious woman. It will just be a few prayers at the graveside. Anyway, I need a favour.'

'No problem.'

'I need you to harvest and deliver my vegetables, if that's okay.'

'Of course.'

'There's a note on the board in the shed with all the details.'

'Fine. So when will you be home, tomorrow?'

'I'm not sure. I think PJ has a few legal duties to take care of and I don't want to leave him.'

He seemed to accept that. 'Okay, then. Pass on my condolences to PJ, will you?'

'Sure. Bye, Ronan, and thanks.'

The call to Sean was, thankfully, a lot easier. He accepted her story without question and, after a few words with Rai Price, he put the girl on the line. Erin quickly introduced herself and explained the situation.

'I'd be happy to help,' Rai told her.

'I really appreciate it,' Erin said with feeling and quickly talked Rai through her kitchen, larder and guests. She finished by promising the girl a generous salary for cooking breakfast for the next two or three mornings. 'I'm not sure yet when I'll be back,' she explained.

'No problem.'

Erin sighed. 'I wish Nora was more like you.'

'Who?'

'My cleaner. She's not the most reliable worker but if she lets me down, the place is unlikely to fall apart I suppose.'

'I'll have a word and if she can't look after things, I'd be happy to help.'

'Rai, if you ever get fed up working at Dijon, you've got a job at the Gatehouse.'

Chapter Twenty-Five

Rai heard someone come into the dining room and bounced through the door to say hello. She pulled up short when she saw the man sitting at the corner table, a newspaper spread out in front of him. 'Hi,' she said in a timid little voice that Sean wouldn't have recognized.

He glanced up and smiled in a slightly puzzled way. 'Hello. Where's Erin?'

'She had to go away.'

He frowned. 'Away? Where to? Will she be gone for long?'

'I don't know where she's gone but she won't be back for a couple of days, so I'm afraid you're stuck with me.' She gave an apologetic shrug.

He smiled slowly. 'I think I can live with that. What's your name?'

'Rai, Rai Price.'

'That's not very Irish,' he teased.

'No, my mother was a bit of a hippie. She always had to be different.'

He laughed. 'I like it.'

Rai smiled. She'd be quite happy to stand here looking at him all day. He was gorgeous. And when he smiled, her insides turned to liquid. What on earth was Sebastian Gray doing in a place like this?

'Is there a problem?'

'Sorry?'

'Can't you cook scrambled eggs and bacon?' he asked.

'Yes, yes, of course! I'm sorry, but I've never cooked for anyone famous before; it's a bit daunting.'

'I assure you we're the same as everyone else.'

'I'll go and make it straight away.'

'Any chance of some coffee?'

'Sure,' she said, speeding into the kitchen to get the coffee pot. In her haste, she spilled some on her hand and yelped.

'Everything okay?' he asked when she returned.

'Fine.' She concentrated hard on holding the pot steady as she filled his cup. How could she ever live with herself if she scalded Sebastian Gray? And he'd think she was a total idiot, although he probably thought that already.

Never had so much effort or care gone into preparing a breakfast before. Rai smiled, thinking her dad would be impressed. She carried the food through to the dining room and set it in front of Sebastian. She stood waiting for him to try it.

He looked at her warily as he folded his newspaper. 'That's great, thanks.'

'No problem,' she said, not budging.

He picked up his knife and fork and tried the eggs. He nodded his appreciation. 'Very good. Tell Erin there's no need to rush back.'

Rai beamed with delight. 'Good. I'll leave you in peace to enjoy it. Just shout if I can get you anything else.' She had difficulty staying in the kitchen while he ate, and she couldn't resist peeking through the door at him from time to time. She was sorely tempted to take his photo with her phone – her mates would be so impressed – but he'd freak out if he saw the flash and then both Erin and Marguerite would fire her. She quickly cleaned the kitchen and sat at the table to wait for the other guests to come down. She'd been hoping that they ate early so she could get in and out quickly; that would be easy money. Now she was quite happy to stay here until it was time to go to Dijon. Just being in the same building as Sebastian Gray was enough to make up for any inconvenience. She hoped Erin would stay away all week; if she called, she'd tell her so. Well, she might not put it quite like that.

It was strange to be working for someone she'd never met. Just looking around this kitchen, though, Rai had a picture in her head of what Erin would be like. Probably around Marguerite's age or older; organized – the kitchen was neat, clean and practical; and married, but with no kids. Strange that neither Erin nor Marguerite had family, she mused. Perhaps they couldn't have kids or maybe they were more interested in career than family. Rai could understand that. She had no plans to have children either. Well, not for ten years anyway. She planned to be running at least one restaurant before she settled down. Unless, of course, Sebastian Gray fell madly in love with her and whisked her off to a mansion in California. Then she might be tempted to fill it with babies. They'd have beautiful children together, she thought dreamily. He was fairly old, in his mid-thirties, but still young enough to have kids, just. She frowned in concentration as she tried to remember what she'd read about him. He was divorced and already had kids, or one anyway, and there had been numerous girlfriends, but she was pretty sure he hadn't married any of them. So, she thought, sneaking another peek at him, there was a vacancy. Not that he'd be attracted to her looking like this, she glanced down at her kitchen whites. Tomorrow she'd dress up a bit; something tight and low-cut was called for. And her hair, she had to do something with her hair! What were the chances of finding a decent hairdresser in a place like this? But then she was Dijon's only cook at the moment so even if Nicky Clarke had a place in Dunbarra she wouldn't have time to pay him a visit. She'd just have to do a DIY job—

'Excuse me, any chance of some breakfast?'

Rai looked up to see a woman glaring at her from the doorway. 'Sure. Sorry, I didn't hear you come in.' The woman didn't reply just disappeared back into the dining room. 'Snotty cow,' Rai muttered, following her. The woman sat at the other end of the room with a little girl who was looking at her with large curious eyes.

'Who are you?' she asked, in a thin, squeaky voice.

Rai smiled. She was kind of cute and a lot nicer than her mother. 'I'm Rai. And who are you?'

'I'm Gracie. Where's Erin?'

'She had to go away for a couple of days.' Rai turned her attention to the mother. 'What can I get you?' she asked politely. After taking the order she stopped by Sebastian's table. 'Can I get you anything else?' she asked, noting with pleasure that he'd cleaned his plate.

'No, thanks.' He stood up and put his paper under his arm. 'Maybe I'll see you tomorrow?'

She smiled suggestively. 'I certainly hope so. But if not you can come and eat lunch or dinner in the restaurant where I work. It's called Dijon, do you know it?'

Hi nodded, smiling. 'I know it. So you're cooking there?'

'Head chef,' she told him.

'Really?' He looked impressed.

She nodded. 'So come in and try one of my specials.'

He raised an eyebrow. 'How can I refuse?'

Rai went into the kitchen, beaming. Excellent! Now he knew where she worked they had a future. There had definitely been a glimmer of interest in his eyes, despite her plain clothes; that was a good sign. She hummed happily as she prepared the other breakfasts. It was just cereal and breads so she'd be out of here in no time and she could go home and do her hair. And she'd wear something nice under her whites today in case he did pop in. What a difference a day makes, she thought, shaking her head. Yesterday, the only thing that excited her was the food she was cooking. Today, there was more to distract her; she paused and closed her eyes, and he was some distraction. Imagine coming to the arsehole of nowhere and finding a rich superstar like Sebastian Gray sitting at her breakfast table; it had to be destiny. The very least she could get out of this was a compliment to Marguerite or Erin about her food, but she was planning on getting a whole lot more.

'Where is PJ?' Gracie said for what seemed like the tenth time, in a whiny voice that was really beginning to grate on Hazel's nerves.

'I told you, he had to go away for a couple of days.'

'But we were supposed to be planting onions today. Now what am I going to do?'

'Read or play with your dolls,' Hazel said, only half listening.

'Why don't we go down to the lake, Mum? We could paint. You haven't painted in ages.'

'No, not today, it's too cold.' Hazel shivered.

'We could dress up warm.' Gracie pressed her hands together. 'Oh, please, Mum.'

Hazel sighed. She felt bone weary and longed to crawl back into bed, but with both PJ and Erin away she couldn't leave Gracie unsupervised. Hazel felt irrationally angry with PJ for disappearing without even telling her. It was frightening how much she'd come to depend on him. 'We'll go for a walk and you can bring your drawing book,' she said, relenting.

'Great!' But Gracie put her head on one side. 'And what about you, Mum? Will you bring your sketch pad?'

'Okay, then.' Hazel gave her daughter a wan smile. She was in no mood for drawing and she knew that she wouldn't be able to even if she tried.

'Yes!' Gracie beamed at her, delighted, and started to gather up the leftover bread and spreads to take with them.

Hazel watched her with sad eyes. The poor child was so easily pleased. She deserved so much more than Hazel was giving her. She deserved a mother – no, parents – who could give her the life she deserved, not this nomadic existence. PJ was the only one who was providing Gracie with any kind of stability but, as she'd found out yesterday, she couldn't rely on him to be there whenever she needed him. He was a good, kind man but he was a stranger, and Gracie was not, and should not, be his responsibility.

'Come on, Mum!'

She looked up to see her daughter hopping impatiently from one foot to the other. She smiled and stood up. 'Okay, darling.' And taking Gracie's hand, Hazel resolved to make this a very special day, one for her daughter to remember.

Ronan was filling up at the petrol station just outside Dunbarra when a station wagon stopped beside him and beeped the horn. He turned and smiled when he saw Marguerite and Mark waving at him. 'You're back!' he said as they climbed out of the car and came over to say hello.

'How are you, Ronan?' Marguerite stretched up to kiss him on both cheeks.

'Not as good as you, you look wonderful. Good holiday?'

'Marvellous. You must bring Erin to Paris, Ronan. Mustn't he?' she said, putting an arm through her husband's.

'You must,' Mark said, squeezing her to him and kissing her on the lips.

'Oh, please.' Ronan pretended disgust. 'It's too early in the day for that kind of carry-on.'

Mark laughed. 'So have we missed anything exciting?'

'Not really, other than we had a missing person – oh, and Erin has stolen your chef.'

'Sorry?' Marguerite said.

'PJ's old aunt finally died and she took him to the

funeral so she asked Rai to do breakfasts while she was away,' he explained.

Marguerite frowned. 'I thought it was an uncle he used to visit.'

'I thought it was an old neighbour.' Ronan laughed.

'So why has Erin gone with him?' Mark asked. 'I didn't think she ever left the Gatehouse.'

'PJ must have been upset,' Marguerite deduced.

Ronan nodded. 'Erin said he was. I didn't see him myself; they left in quite a hurry. Also, I think PJ is the executor.'

'So Rai is working at the Gatehouse. Sebastian will be pleased.' Mark winked at Ronan. 'I'm sure he'll enjoy her, er, food.'

Ronan laughed as Marguerite belted her husband.

'I hope he behaves himself,' she said.

'She's well able to take care of herself, that one,' her husband replied.

Marguerite looked at him in surprise. 'I thought you liked her.'

'I do. What's not to like? All I'm saying is that she's not exactly the shy, retiring sort.'

Ronan nodded in agreement. 'I almost feel sorry for your brother, although she's probably exactly the kind of woman he likes.'

'And the right age group too,' Mark quipped, earning himself another thump.

'But what's this about a missing person?' Marguerite asked.

'It turned out to be a fuss over nothing. Gracie, the little girl staying at the Gatehouse, went missing and we were all in a right panic for a couple of hours. But it turned out that she'd hidden in PJ's car and fallen asleep. He went off to visit this aunt not even realizing she was there.'

'*Mon Dieu!*' Marguerite shook her head. 'Her poor mother must have been distraught.'

'She was. And then poor old PJ got taken down to the police station for questioning. I can tell you, he wasn't the better of that.'

'And now a death in the family. Poor PJ. No wonder Erin went with him. Ronan, come and have dinner with us tonight and you can tell us everything. I'm not back on duty until tomorrow.'

'Yes, come,' Mark echoed. 'We're dying to bore someone with our holiday photos.'

'I can live with the photos but I can't handle you two groping each other all evening.'

'Ah, he's missing his woman.' Mark pulled a face.

'We'll behave ourselves, promise.'

Mark grabbed her around the waist and pulled her to him. 'Speak for yourself.'

She pushed him away, laughing. 'Settle down, my darling, the holiday is over.'

'Yes, settle down,' Ronan agreed, 'you're making me queasy.'

'Eight o'clock,' Marguerite told him, 'and don't be late.'

'No, don't – we'll be going to bed around nine.'

'Mark, stop,' Marguerite admonished but she was laughing.

With a wave, Ronan turned away. 'I'll see you later, but do me a favour and have a little siesta first.'

'Great idea,' Mark called after him and the two climbed back into the car, giggling.

'Lucky bastard,' Ronan muttered and went in to pay for his diesel.

Chapter Twenty-Six

Erin set her bag down in the hall and went into the kitchen. She had only been away for four days but it felt like much longer. She wouldn't have been able to stay even that long if it hadn't been for Rai Price. As usual Nora had let her down and Rai had immediately agreed to take on the housework as well. Considering Marguerite was away this was no mean feat and Erin was deeply grateful. She couldn't wait to meet the girl who'd saved her bacon. Erin grinned at her choice of words.

'What are you looking so happy about?' PJ asked, coming through the door and reaching for the kettle.

She shook her head. 'Nothing worth sharing. Why don't you go and have a lie-down?'

'I want to check on the garden.'

'I can do that.'

'No, I want to,' he said. 'Please, Erin, no special treatment.'

'Okay.' She held up her hands.

'Would you like some tea?'

She nodded. 'Please. Well, it looks like they got on okay without us.'

'Are there deliveries to be made?' he asked.

'No, Ronan did them this morning.'

'He's a good man.'

'Yes.' Erin looked at PJ. 'We need to agree on what we are going to say to people.'

He dropped tea bags into two mugs of boiling water and carried them to the table, then fetched the milk and sugar. 'Just keep it simple, Erin. My aged aunt – ninety-eight – died. I'm the only surviving relative and I had to look after her estate.'

'Yes, but it will seem odd that I went with you, so I'm afraid I'm going to have to say that you were very upset.'

He actually smiled at that. 'Why, because she was cut down in her prime?'

'Very funny. Well, have you got any better ideas?'

'No. But just remember to add that she left me a few bob so I'm fine now.'

'Are you really sure that you want to keep all of this to yourself, PJ?' Erin said gently. 'Don't you think it will be harder for you to grieve?'

He looked at her in surprise. 'But I'm not grieving, Erin. I grieved when Isabelle was diagnosed. I grieved when she started to forget what a cup was for. I grieved when she no longer recognized me. And I grieved when I put her in that damned nursing home. Now, finally, it's over. Now I can honestly say that I feel relieved and happy that Isabelle's pain – and mine – is over.'

'You're amazing.' She squeezed his hand. 'But just remember that if you ever do want to talk about her, I'll be here.'

He smiled. 'You're a good girl. Thank you for coming with me. It was a lot harder than I'd imagined and it would have been worse alone.'

'No problem.' Erin drained her mug and stood up. 'I'm going upstairs to change.'

He stood too. 'I'll get to work. But do me a favour, Erin. If anyone asks, I'm out for the rest of the day. I'd just like a bit of time to settle back in.'

'Sure.'

As Erin crossed the hall she heard a car pull up and she retraced her steps thinking it might be Ronan. When she opened the door it was to see Sandra in a heated discussion with a taxi driver. Erin turned to go back inside but Sandra had spotted her.

'Erin, does ninety euros sound like an exorbitant amount of money to you or is it just me?' she called.

The taxi driver rolled his eyes and Erin smiled. 'Welcome back, Sandra, did you have a nice time?'

'Lovely. There's eighty,' she shoved the notes into the man's hand, 'and you're not getting another cent.'

With a muttered curse, the man climbed back into his cab and drove away.

'No offence, Erin, but the cab drivers in this country are robbers.'

'What, all of them?' Erin said mildly.

Sandra grinned, unabashed. 'Well, maybe not all. So have you been away too?' she added, nodding at the bag in Erin's hand.

'Not really. So what did you think of Dublin?'

'It was okay but one city is much like the rest. So where did you go?' Sandra asked, her eyes sharp.

'To a funeral.'

'Oh, I'm sorry, not anyone close, I hope?'

'No, no, and she was a grand old age.' The phone rang and Erin could have punched the air. Instead she offered Sandra an apologetic smile. 'I'd better get that.'

Sandra sighed irritably. 'I suppose so. Let's catch up later.'

'Let's.' Erin smiled and hurried inside. Grabbing the phone, she took it into the kitchen just in case Sandra decided to hang around. 'The Gatehouse.'

'Welcome home.'

'Ronan! Hi. We just got in.'

'How's PJ?'

'Tired and a bit sad. I think losing his last surviving relative reminded him of his own mortality, and none of us likes to dwell on that, do we?'

'No, I suppose not.'

'So how are things here? Any problem with deliveries?'

'None.'

'Ronan, thank you, you've been great. I really appreciate it.'

'No problem.'

'So, no news? Didn't I miss anything?'

'You've only been gone four days.'

'I suppose.'

'But Mark and Marguerite are back.'

'Ah, you see, something did happen. Did they have a good time?'

'Fantastic. They both look brilliant and are behaving like newly-weds.'

Erin laughed. 'Oh, really?'

'Yes, I had dinner with them last night and the way they were going on it nearly put me off my food.'

'But not quite?'

He laughed. 'Not quite. I'm glad you're back, I've missed you.'

'Me too.'

'Can we have dinner together?' he asked.

'That would be lovely. Where shall we go?'

'I have an idea, leave it with me. Pick you up about eight.'

She smiled. It wasn't like Ronan to spring surprises. She'd have to go away more often. 'Perfect, see you then.'

When she hung up, Erin got changed and had a wander around. She was pleased to see that everything was dust-free, neat and tidy. Back in the kitchen she read the note that Rai had left her. It gave her a brief report on what she'd missed and ended with a list of items she thought were running low, including eggs. Erin had better call Ronan back and get him to bring some over later and then she'd have to nip out and stock up at the supermarket in Dunbarra before it closed. But first she called each of her customers, apologized for being away and wrote down their fruit and vegetable orders for the next few days. Then she called Dijon and Marguerite answered.

'Welcome back,' she said.

'Erin, hello! Welcome back to you. How is PJ?'

'Tired and emotional but he'll be fine. Listen, I can't wait to hear all about your holiday but I'm in a bit of a rush now. I just wanted a word with your wonderful new chef.'

'Yes, I heard you'd stolen her away from me.'

'She's been marvellous, Marguerite. Not only did she cook but she kept the place spotless too.'

'Here, tell her yourself.'

Erin waited while Marguerite fetched Rai.

'Hello?'

'Rai, hi, how are you?'

'Fine. You're back, then?'

Erin frowned. The girl sounded almost disappointed. 'Yes, and I just called to thank you for all your hard work. I don't know what I'd have done without you.'

'Any time,' Rai replied. 'I'm always glad of the extra experience and, of course, the money comes in handy too.'

'I'll remember that,' Erin promised. 'Anyway, I just wanted to let you know that I'll drop over your wages later.'

'That's great, thanks.'

'I'll look forward to finally meeting you.'

'Yeah, me too.'

'See you later, then.'

'Okay, bye.'

Erin hung up, smiling. Rai sounded so young yet she was obviously hugely capable. Marguerite really had been very lucky to find her. With another glance at the clock, Erin realized she'd better get moving or the supermarket would be shut. After a look in the cupboards and fridge, she grabbed her bag and keys and hurried out to the car. She was just about to drive off when Hazel and Gracie appeared round the corner and Gracie came running to greet her. Erin wound down the window to say hello to the child.

'Oh, you're back!'

'I am.' Erin smiled at Hazel. 'Hi.'

'Is PJ back too?' Gracie asked.

'He certainly is. Have you missed him?'

She nodded. 'Where is he?'

'He's gone out for the evening but you'll see him tomorrow.'

Gracie's face fell.

'Come on.' Hazel put a hand on her daughter's shoulder. 'Let's go into town and get some chips and I'll buy you an ice cream for dessert.'

'With sprinkles?' Gracie asked.

Hazel smiled. 'With sprinkles.'

'Can I give you a lift?' Erin asked. 'I'm going in to the supermarket.'

'That's okay, thanks. We enjoy the walk.'

When Erin returned it was to see Gracie playing alone in the front garden. She looked around for Hazel and spotted her at the side of the house. She was listening intently to something Sebastian was saying. He looked up and spotted Erin and she turned and hurried inside. She wasn't going to let him think she was interested in who he was with. Anyway, she wasn't. If he and Hazel were getting together – well, good luck to them. Although PJ would not be happy. She quickly put the groceries away and went out to the garden to check on him. He was nowhere in sight and the barn and sheds were all locked up. Going back inside she noticed his wellies by the door and realized he must be in his room. Perhaps she'd just take him up a tray before she went out and that way he wouldn't run the risk of meeting anyone. She'd make him a nice omelette, she decided; but first she'd go and get ready for her date. She was really looking forward to seeing Ronan and that alone was enough to make her smile.

After she'd showered, done her hair and applied her make-up, Erin threw on a tracksuit and went downstairs to cook PJ's supper. When she took it up to him twenty minutes later, PJ was sitting in his chair watching TV.

He looked up and smiled, but his eyes were red. 'You shouldn't have bothered, darling.'

Erin set down her tray and perched on the bed. 'Are you okay?'

'I'm grand.'

'Gracie and Hazel were asking for you.'

'Were they?'

'Gracie was disgusted that she had to wait until tomorrow to see you.'

PJ picked up his cutlery and started to eat. 'Aren't you eating?'

'Ronan's taking me out to dinner.'

'That's nice.'

Erin sighed at the lack of interest in his voice. 'Is there anything else I can get you?'

'No, you go and enjoy yourself.'

She stood up. 'Goodnight, then.'

'Goodnight, darling.'

When she got outside, Hazel was hovering on the landing, waiting for her. 'Is everything okay?' she asked.

'Fine.'

'Is PJ there? Do you think I could see him for a moment?'

'I'm afraid not. He's exhausted and having an early night.'

A look of panic crossed Hazel's face. 'Do you think he'll be up and about tomorrow?'

Erin smiled. 'Of course he will.'

Hazel seemed relieved. 'Would you ask him to come and see us first thing?' she asked. 'I don't mean to be a pest but Gracie is really dying to see him.'

'He's missed her too,' Erin assured her. 'I'll pass on the message.'

Hazel held out her hand. 'Thank you, Erin. Thanks for everything.'

Erin took her hand, surprised. 'No problem.'

Hazel nodded, smiled and disappeared back into her room.

Erin stared at the closed door for a moment and then, with a shrug, went to her own room to change.

When Ronan pulled into the drive, Erin was ready and waiting. He got out of the jeep and stood staring at her.

Erin held out her hands. 'Will I do?'

'You look incredible,' he said and then he looked down at his white shirt and blue jeans. 'I feel a bit underdressed.'

She glanced at his broad chest, his lean body, and smiled. 'You look just fine to me.'

He held out his arms and she walked into them, holding up her face for his kiss. They were standing right under Sandra's window and Erin hoped she was watching.

Ronan stepped back, his hands linked loosely around her neck. 'I've missed you.'

'I'm glad to hear it. So where are you taking me?'

His smile faltered. 'I may have to go to Plan B. That dress demands an audience.'

'You're the only audience I'm interested in,' she assured him.

'Then Plan A it is,' he said, holding the door open for her.

Erin was so busy telling Ronan about Hazel's odd behaviour that she didn't notice where they were going until he pulled into the farm. Her voice trailed away and she looked at him. 'You're cooking?'

He laughed. 'No, I wouldn't do that to you.'

'Good! You had me worried. So what exactly is Plan A?' she asked.

He held up a finger. 'Patience, my darling, patience.' He led her into the house and through to his rarely used dining room.

She smiled when she saw the table laid with silver cutlery, crystal glasses and a single red rose across her crisp white napkin. 'This is lovely. So what's for dinner, a number twenty-two with fried rice?'

'Nothing so crass,' he berated her. 'Sit down and prepare to be amazed.'

'Is it okay if I pour the wine?'

'Be my guest,' he said, going through to the kitchen.

She had just set the carafe down when he reappeared with a large dish. 'I detect Marguerite's hand in this.'

He smiled. 'You're too clever for me.' He took the lid off the dish with a flourish. 'Bourguignon à la Dijon.'

'Oh, lovely,' she said faintly, marvelling that after all this time, Ronan didn't know that she detested mushrooms. And it wasn't as if she could pick them out. In Marguerite's version of the dish they were finely chopped and it was impossible to avoid them. Her stomach rumbled. She was starving but she didn't know how she was going to eat this. 'Any vegetables?' she asked hopefully.

'Salad,' he said. 'I'll go and get it. I thought vegetables would be a bit too heavy.'

'Yes,' she said wistfully, thinking she'd kill for a couple of baby new potatoes drowned in melted butter with a sprinkling of parsley and black pepper.

He returned with some fresh green leaves and Erin's spirits dropped further. Not even a spring onion or tomato to fill her up.

'Come on, eat up before it gets cold,' he urged. 'Marguerite wasn't sure you liked this dish but I told her she was wrong.' His brow furrowed. 'She was, wasn't she?'

'Of course, this is lovely.' Erin picked up her fork and, spreading the stew across her plate, she speared a tiny piece of meat and put it in her mouth.

Oblivious, Ronan told her about his evening with Marguerite and Mark and their holiday. Erin was glad he was too focused on his story and his dinner to notice her trying to hide food under the salad. She was also relieved that he wasn't quizzing her about the funeral. And so what if she didn't get to eat? She could always make a sandwich later.

Ronan polished off his dinner and was helping himself to seconds when he noticed her meal was barely touched. 'You're not eating.'

'Sorry, I'm not really hungry,' Erin lied.

He threw down his napkin. 'Marguerite was right, wasn't she?'

Erin bit her lip and nodded.

'I am so sorry,' he groaned. 'Why didn't I listen to her?'

'It doesn't matter,' Erin said, just grateful that she didn't have to eat any more.

'The good news is that I do have your favourite dessert.'

She laughed. 'Oh, thank God. I'm so hungry I was ready to start in on my napkin.'

'And the better news is that you can relax and enjoy it and the wine and not have to worry about getting up early.'

She frowned. 'What do you mean?'

'I've arranged for Rai to do breakfast again tomorrow.'

'What?'

'Well, she managed fine for the last few days, so why not one more? You deserve a night off.'

'I've just had three,' she reminded him.

He shook his head. 'Going to a funeral and looking after an elderly man does not count as time off.'

Her lips twitched. 'I'd like to see you call PJ "elderly" to his face.'

'I wouldn't dare. So,' he smiled at her, 'how do you feel about spending an entire night, Ms Joyce?'

'Feed me some dessert and I'll think about it.'

Chapter Twenty-Seven

It took a lot for PJ to drag himself out of bed. It would be so much easier to stay under the covers and sleep. With sleep came oblivion. On the other hand when you woke, you thought everything was okay for a few seconds and then reality started to kick in. Isabelle hadn't been part of his day-to-day life for a long time now but she had still been the centre of his universe. He structured everything else around his phone calls and his visits to her. He heard something on the news and he imagined her reaction. He cultivated a new breed of tomato and he longed for her to taste it and give her opinion. He held young Gracie's soft hand in his and he wondered, if he and Isabelle had had a daughter, would she look like her mother. And now, he wondered, what was the point? What reason did he have to get up in the morning? And what eventually persuaded him into the shower was the thought that Erin needed him. She'd been so kind and understanding these last few days, and there was a lot to do in the garden as a result of their absence.

He steeled himself to go downstairs and face the inevitable questions and sympathies. He was surprised and relieved, though, to find the dining room empty. 'Where is everybody?' he asked, going into the kitchen. He pulled up short at the sight of the girl sprawled in a chair, reading a magazine.

She smiled and jumped to her feet. 'You must be PJ. Hi, I'm Rai.'

He smiled. 'The amazing young lady who held things together in our absence. Thank you. But where's Erin?'

'She stayed over at Ronan's last night and he asked me if I could cover for her so that she could have a lie-in.'

'That was a good idea. And very kind of you.'

She shrugged. 'It's no problem. So, what would you like for breakfast?'

'Just some cornflakes, toast and coffee, please.' He patted his stomach. 'I've been eating full fry-ups these last few days and I need to purge the system.'

She immediately started to put a tray together. 'Sorry for your trouble, by the way.'

'Thanks.' He grinned. 'Isn't that the most ridiculous phrase?'

'Mad,' she agreed.

He rested against the table and folded his arms. 'So you work up at Dijon?'

'Yeah.'

'Do you like it?'

'Most of the time, though I'm not keen on cleaning up.'

He laughed. 'Who is? But you love to cook, I hear.'

'Yeah, it's cool.' The toast popped up and she put it into a rack and poured his coffee.

'That's grand,' PJ said, going to pick it up.

'Hey, are you trying to do me out of a job?' she chided.

He backed off, hands up. 'I wouldn't dream of it,' he said, and held the door open for her. 'The table in the corner,' he told her and followed her down the room. 'So has everyone eaten or are they all sleeping in this morning?'

She set out his breakfast, put the tray under her arm and stood back. 'Mr Gray has eaten but the other guests haven't come down yet.'

PJ looked at her and frowned. 'Hazel and Gracie aren't up?'

'Well, if they are, they haven't eaten. Enjoy your breakfast.' Rai told him and disappeared back into the kitchen.

Perhaps she's painting down at the lake, he thought, looking out at the misty morning. It was the kind of weather that would appeal to Hazel. The thought that she might be working again cheered him up. In the midst of his own trauma, he'd forgotten his plan to talk to the girl; perhaps he wouldn't have to say anything after all. Feeling slightly happier, he tucked into his cereal. He was halfway through when Sandra Bell bustled in.

'Good morning,' she called.

''Morning.' He nodded and bent his head over his breakfast.

Not surprisingly, she came straight over. 'I was sorry to hear of your bereavement.'

'Thank you.'

'Was it your sister?' she asked.

'My aunt.'

'Oh, so she was old then.'

'She was.'

'Well, that's easier. Good of Erin to go with you,' she observed, watching him.

'Very good,' he agreed and turned his attention back to his cereal. Thankfully she got the message.

'I'll leave you to enjoy your breakfast,' she said and stalked off to her table just as Rai came out to serve her.

'Who are you?' Sandra asked.

'Rai,' the girl replied with a pleasant smile. 'I'm standing in for Erin this morning.'

'Oh, okay. I'll have an omelette,' Sandra told her, 'and I need some very strong coffee. That child woke me at the crack of dawn with her crying. I think I'm going to have to ask Erin to move me to a different room. I mean, I know this is just a bed and breakfast, but I should at least be able to count on getting a night's sleep.'

PJ was up and out through the door in an instant.

'PJ, is everything okay?' Rai called, hurrying after him.

'Oh, God, I hope so,' he muttered, taking the stairs two at a time. He stood outside Hazel's door and listened. Sure enough, he could hear Gracie sobbing though it was nothing like the racket Sandra had described. He knocked on the door. 'Hazel? Hazel, it's me, PJ.' There was no reply but Gracie stopped crying. 'Gracie, are you okay, darling?' PJ tried the handle and was relieved when the door opened. Gracie was sitting in the corner of the room, her eyes red and swollen. He crouched down and held out his arms and she ran into them, crying. 'It's okay, darling, everything's okay,' he said, stroking her hair and scanning the room at the same time. 'Where's your mum?'

'I don't know,' she hiccuped. 'I woke up, and it was still dark, but she wasn't here.'

It was after nine now and it got bright around five-thirty; Hazel had been gone for some time. His eyes were drawn to the closed bathroom door. He should check, just in case, but not in front of the child. 'I'm going to take you down to Rai for some breakfast, darling. How does that sound?'

Fresh fat tears slid down the little girl's cheeks. 'I can't.'

'Why not, sweetheart?' he asked, pulling out his handkerchief and dabbing her cheeks. She dropped her head and mumbled something he couldn't make out.

He lifted her chin with his finger and smiled into her eyes. 'Gracie, there's nothing to be afraid of, no one is angry with you, no one is going to fight with you. Now tell me, darling, what's wrong?'

She chewed on her lip for a moment and then whispered her answer. 'I'm wet.'

'What?' He frowned and then caught sight of the damp patch on her pyjamas. 'Oh, is that all? Sure, that's no problem, darling; everyone has accidents.'

'Mummy says only babies wet themselves.'

'Yes, well, this will be our little secret, okay? Mummy need never know.'

Gracie brightened and the tears stopped. 'Really?'

'Cross my heart,' he promised. He saw a little pink tracksuit on a chair by the bed. 'Now, if I go into your bathroom, do you think you could put these on?'

She nodded, sticking her chin out with pride. 'I always dress myself.'

'Sure, you're a grand girl altogether.' He beamed at her and stood up. 'Now, when you're ready, call me.'

She wrinkled her nose. 'But why are you going in there?'

'Because every lady should be allowed to dress in private, of course.' He winked at her, went into the en suite and closed the door.

He was almost afraid to look round and he sent up a silent prayer that his suspicions would be unfounded.

For someone who didn't have much time for God he was doing an awful lot of praying these days. He took a deep breath and turned round slowly, letting out an audible sigh of relief when he saw that the room was empty. He had been so sure he was going to find Hazel drowned in the bath or with her wrists cut and the room drenched in blood. But the fact remained that she was missing and had been for hours. He knew that she'd often slipped out to capture a sunrise when Gracie was asleep, but she always made sure to get back before the child woke up. Still, she was so preoccupied lately, she might have lost track of time.

'PJ, I'm ready,' Gracie called.

He went in and smiled at the sight of her with her top on back to front. 'Perfect,' he said and scanned the small room. His heart fell when he saw Hazel's art bag and easel behind the door. Still, she could be out sketching. His eyes searched the room again until they landed on the pad on the bedside table. The top page had something written on it but he couldn't make out what without his glasses. Hesitating only for a second, he tore it off and shoved it in his pocket before taking Gracie by the hand and leading her downstairs.

Studiously ignoring Sandra, PJ sat Gracie at her usual table and went into the kitchen. Rai was cleaning a pan, but when he came in she immediately stopped and dried her hands.

'Is everything okay?'

'I'm not sure,' he admitted. 'Look, I know this is a lot to ask but do you think you could entertain a four-year-old for a few minutes?'

'Gracie?'

'Yes. If you could just feed her, make a fuss of her – not for long, I promise. I wouldn't ask only—'

'It's fine,' Rai told him and led the way back into the dining room. 'Hello, Gracie. Tell me, do you like pancakes?'

The little girl nodded.

'Do you know how to make them?'

Gracie frowned and shook her head.

Rai pulled a face. 'That's a pity. Would you like to learn?'

'Yes please!' Gracie said, hopping to her feet.

'Great. Sorry, PJ, you'll have to excuse us,' Rai said. 'We have some serious cooking to do.'

PJ looked at her in admiration. He was really beginning to take to this girl. 'Have fun,' he said, winking at Gracie. Then, going back up to his room, he found his glasses and pulled the note out of his pocket. To his surprise it was addressed to him. With a sense of foreboding, he started to read.

Dear PJ,
I'm sorry for all the subterfuge but when I couldn't talk to you last night, asking you to come to my room seemed the next best thing.

He stopped, frowning. When had Hazel asked him to come to her room? He hadn't seen her since Sunday. Shaking his head, he read on.

I had made up my mind, you see. I decided that this was the best, the only, way forward and I was afraid that if I waited I would lose the courage and change my mind. So, PJ, by the time you read this I'll be long gone.

'Mother of God,' PJ muttered.

Gracie is better off without me and, though it's taken me a long time to admit it, she will be happier with her father. I know you're probably shocked but I think you'll agree when you meet him. Please call him as soon as possible, PJ, for Gracie's sake. It would be great if he arrived before she even started to realize I was gone. Please, please, please, look after her until he gets there; I would trust no one else.

Try not to think badly of me, PJ. I haven't been a very good mother and this may be the best and kindest thing I can do for my daughter.

Thank you for your friendship, PJ. Gracie and I have had some of our happiest moments in Dunbarra, and most of that was down to you.

X

Hazel

Underneath she'd printed a name, Des Tiernan, and a phone number.

PJ lowered the page, his hand shaking. What had she done? Dear God, what had the girl done? He'd have to act quickly, he realized. She'd been gone for at least four hours, maybe more. 'Please don't let me be too late,' he said, hurrying out of his room.

Twenty-Eight

PJ was in the hall with the phone in his hand, staring at Hazel's painting when Erin and Ronan came in.

'Hi, PJ. How are you?' When he didn't answer Erin moved around to face him. 'PJ?'

'Is everything okay?' Ronan said, as he came in and closed the door.

PJ seemed to come out of his reverie. 'No, I'm afraid it isn't. Hazel Patterson has left.'

'Left? When?'

'Early this morning.'

Erin heard laughter coming from the direction of the kitchen. 'But I can hear Gracie.'

PJ met her eyes. 'Gracie's still here.'

'Then Hazel can't have gone far. She's probably gone for a walk or is off doing some painting—'

'She left a note.'

Erin stared at him. 'What kind of a note?'

He pulled a piece of paper from his pocket and handed it to her. Ronan read it over her shoulder.

PJ searched their faces. 'What do you think? Does that sound like a, a . . .'

Erin shook her head. 'It's not a suicide note, PJ, of course it isn't.'

'We should phone the police,' Ronan told them.

'Do you think that's necessary?' PJ asked, his voice weak.

Ronan held his gaze. 'We don't have any choice.'

'They probably won't do anything,' Erin told him. 'She's an adult and we know she hasn't been abducted.'

'She's abandoned her child,' Ronan pointed out. 'That has to be an offence.'

'Hardly abandoned,' PJ protested. 'She left a note and a contact number for the child's father.'

'Have you called him?'

'Not yet.'

'Why not?' Ronan asked.

PJ's face darkened. 'I don't know. What kind of man could he be if she ran away from him? I wouldn't be surprised if he's the reason Gracie stopped talking.'

Erin pushed her hair out of her eyes and scanned the letter again. 'That's unlikely. She's asked you to call him and quickly. She wouldn't do that if she didn't trust him to look after Gracie.'

He sighed. 'I suppose you're right. But what about Hazel, Erin? She could be in the lake for all we know.'

Erin patted his arm. 'I'm sure she isn't.'

'Are you?'

Erin sighed. 'Okay, let's call Gracie's dad and then the police.'

'You do it.' PJ took his jacket from the stand in the hall. 'I'm going to start looking for Hazel.'

Erin put a hand out to stop him. 'You can't, PJ. You have to stay here. She asked you to look after Gracie, remember?'

He looked at her, frustration and worry creasing his face. 'But I have to.'

'Erin's right,' Ronan said. 'You should stay with the child. It's only a matter of time before she starts asking questions. I'll look for Hazel.'

Erin shot him a grateful look. 'Thanks, Ronan.'

PJ put his coat back on the stand and looked almost fearfully towards the kitchen. 'What will I tell Gracie?'

'Lie,' Erin and Ronan said together.

When she was alone in the hall, Erin started to dial the number on the letter, but she hung up three times before finally allowing it to ring. As she waited, she realized that it would be the second time this week that she had to deliver bad news.

'Hello?'

The voice threw her and she was at a loss for words for a moment.

'Hello?'

Erin swallowed back her nerves. 'Hi, may I speak to Des Tiernan, please?'

'Speaking. Can I help you?'

It wasn't the sort of voice Erin had been expecting. He sounded pleasant, nice, not at all the ogre that PJ seemed to think he was. Still, anyone could have a nice voice. He could be a drug dealer for all she knew.

'Hello? Are you still there?'

'Yes, sorry. Look, my name is Erin Joyce, but you don't know me. I own a bed and breakfast in Offaly. Your wife and daughter have been staying here.'

'Gracie! You have Gracie?'

Erin smiled. There was no mistaking the joy in the man's voice. 'Yes, she's here.'

'Can you give me your address and directions? Hang on, just let me get a pen. I can't believe this. Thank you so much for calling me.'

Erin held the phone away from her ear as he dropped the receiver. He was back again in seconds.

'Okay, go ahead.'

'Mr Tiernan, about Hazel—'

'Don't worry about her,' he said, his voice hard. 'I'll deal with her.'

Erin bristled. Perhaps he wasn't so nice after all. 'No, Mr Tiernan, you won't. Hazel isn't here.'

'What do you mean, she isn't there? Where the hell is she?'

'She disappeared early this morning. She left a note asking us to call you.' There was a silence, and though Erin waited he said nothing. 'Hello? Mr Tiernan? Look, I'm sure she's fine and there are people out searching for her right now. But I think we should call the police.'

'You think she's committed suicide, is that it?'

'No, of course not! Please try not to worry—'

'The only person I'm worried about, Ms Joyce, is my daughter. To be perfectly honest with you, it would probably be best for everyone if Hazel did kill herself.'

Erin didn't know what to say to that and when Des asked again for her address, she gave it and hung up. Then she picked up the phone again and dialled 999. 'Police, please. I need to report a missing person.'

'Put the phone down, Erin.'

She spun round to see Sebastian standing in the doorway. 'What?'

'Put the phone down.' He crossed the hall, took the phone from her and put it back in its cradle.

Erin looked up and saw Sandra at the top of the stairs, watching them. 'Let's go into my office.'

Sebastian followed her and Erin shut the door firmly, then turned to face him. 'What the hell is going on?'

'Hazel is perfectly safe, you don't have to worry.'

'But where is she? No,' she held up her hand, 'wait until I get PJ.' She went out to the kitchen where he was watching Rai and Gracie making pancakes. 'PJ, could I grab to you for a minute? And save me a pancake, Gracie. They look gorgeous!'

PJ followed her back into the hall. 'Any news?'

'Yes, and it's good,' she told him, waving him into her office.

'Sebastian?' PJ frowned. 'Do you know where Hazel is?'

Sebastian nodded.

PJ collapsed into a chair. 'Well, thank God for that.'

'So?' Erin sat down behind her desk and looked expectantly at Sebastian.

He looked at his watch. 'She'll be boarding a plane to London about now.'

'What?' PJ's eyes widened. 'Why? And what about Gracie?'

'You asked me to help her, PJ, and I tried but I was getting nowhere, so I did the only other thing I could think of: I offered to pay for her to go into a clinic I know well. She agreed.'

'But why did she have to go without telling anyone?' Erin asked.

'And how could she leave that poor child alone in their room? Gracie was in an awful way when I found her. And I mightn't have gone up at all only Sandra complained about her crying.'

Sebastian frowned. 'I don't understand that. Hazel said she left a message asking you to come to her room first thing.'

'But I didn't get any message,' PJ told him.

Erin closed her eyes and sighed. 'That was my fault, PJ. Hazel came to see you last night, and when I wouldn't let her disturb you, she asked me to get you to drop in to see her first thing. But I wasn't here, of course, and I completely forgot. I'm sorry.'

'But I still don't understand why she couldn't just have told you all that she was leaving, or, at least, say a proper goodbye to Gracie.'

Sebastian shrugged. 'I can't explain that, I'm afraid. She was adamant that she didn't want anyone to know and she said she couldn't face telling Gracie that she was deserting her – her words not mine.'

'I think Hazel has a love of the dramatic,' Erin said, her face hard.

'She's obviously not thinking straight,' PJ excused her. 'Have you phoned the husband?'

Erin nodded. 'Yes, he's on his way.'

'Well, that's something, I suppose. Will I tell Gracie?'

'Why not let it be a surprise?' Erin suggested. 'It might distract her from the fact that Hazel has disappeared.'

'And if she asks me where she's gone?'

'I think you should leave it to Des to explain.' She looked at Sebastian. 'He won't be impressed. With Hazel, or with you for helping her.'

'I just can't win, can I?' Sebastian muttered, turning to go.

'Wait. What am I supposed to do with the rest of her stuff?'

'Leave her room exactly as it is,' he told her. 'She'll come back for her things when she gets out.'

'But when will that be?' Erin persisted.

'No idea, but I'll write you a cheque to cover the cost.'

PJ looked at him suspiciously. 'That's very generous of you, after all you hardly know the girl.'

'Like I said, PJ, you did ask me to help. And when I couldn't, I threw money at the problem.' He gave a tight smile. 'People don't usually object.'

'Well, you're not in Hollywood now,' PJ muttered. 'Irish people have their pride. But,' he added hurriedly, 'I'm grateful to you for helping Hazel. It's more than I was able to do.'

After Sebastian had left them, PJ went back out to the kitchen to check on Gracie, and Erin phoned Ronan to tell him the news.

'I'm glad she's okay but I have to tell you, Erin, you have some weird guests.'

She laughed. 'Don't I know it. I'm so sorry, Ronan.'

'Hey, it's not your fault. I'm glad you called, though. I was about to call in reinforcements.'

'I'm so glad you didn't; that would be truly embarrassing.'

'Indeed. Right, I'd better get back to work.'

'Okay, then. I'll phone you later and let you know the latest developments.'

Erin went out to the kitchen where Rai was alone, cleaning up the substantial mess made by Gracie. 'Hey, you don't have to do that.'

Rai looked up and smiled. 'It's no problem. Is everything okay?'

'Yes, fine. There was just a bit of a misunderstanding.' 'You can head off now, and thank you so much for standing in for me again this morning.'

'That's okay.' Rai picked up her jacket. 'Serving breakfast to Sebastian Gray isn't exactly a hardship.'

'I suppose not.' Erin smiled.

When Rai had left, Erin finished tidying the kitchen and went to check on PJ and Gracie. She found them picking runner beans, although PJ was doing most of the work while Gracie watched, her large eyes sad. 'Hello, there. Are you working hard?'

'We are, but I was just saying to Gracie that maybe we'd take some time off to do a bit of fishing.'

'Fishing, eh? It's a nice day for it.'

Gracie looked up at the sky and frowned. 'But it's cloudy.'

'Sure, the fish love clouds,' PJ explained. 'When it's sunny they're afraid to swim too near the surface in case they're seen, but when it's cloudy they're practically jumping out of the water!'

'I'll have to ask Mummy first. She says I should never go near the water unless she's with me.'

PJ's eyes met Erin's over the little head. 'Quite right too.'

'Has she come back yet?' Gracie asked in a small voice.

'Not yet, darling,' Erin said softly.

Gracie's lip wobbled. 'She's never gone away without saying goodbye before.'

'I'm sure she had a very good reason,' PJ told her. 'Tell you what, why don't we finish picking the beans and tomatoes, and maybe by that time your mum will be back and you can ask her about the fishing?'

'That sounds like a plan. See you both later.' Erin smiled and went back inside. As she did, the phone was ringing and she ran to answer it. 'Oh, hi, Nora.' She looked at her watch. 'Have you been delayed?' She listened for a moment and sighed as her cleaner gave her the news that, yet again, she wouldn't be able to come in. 'Fine, Nora, I hope you feel better soon. Bye.' Muttering to herself, she gathered the mop and bucket and basket of cleaning stuffs and took them upstairs.

As she crossed the landing she looked out of the window and paused when she saw Sandra and Sebastian having what seemed to be a heated conversation. *Now, what's that about?* she wondered, her curiosity piqued. Ronan was right. Her guests were definitely quite a weird bunch at the moment. She had been surprised that Sandra hadn't hung around earlier to find out what all the fuss was about. Perhaps she was quizzing Sebastian and he was telling her to mind her own business. That must be it, she decided, and went in to clean PJ's room.

Chapter Twenty-Nine

Erin had just finished upstairs when she heard a car pull up outside and she hurried downstairs to answer the door. She didn't know the car or the man who got out of it but she recognized the smile and the eyes. This was definitely Gracie's dad. She went down the steps to meet him. 'Mr Tiernan?'

He came forward to take her outstretched hand. 'It's Des.'

'And I'm Erin.'

'Where is she?' he asked, his eyes darting around the place.

'She's in the garden, but could I have a word before I take you to her?'

'Sure.'

They went into the house.

'I'm sorry about what I said on the phone,' Des said. 'It must have sounded cold and heartless.'

'A bit,' she admitted.

He sighed. 'I didn't mean it. But she's hurt me so much over the last couple of years.'

They went into the sitting room and closed the door. Erin gestured to a chair and then sat down opposite him.

'Then one day I came home and she'd gone and taken Gracie with her,' he continued.

'But why?'

'I was angry and frustrated because she wouldn't take her medication. I threatened to leave and take Gracie with me. But she beat me to it.'

'I'm sorry, I didn't know. That must have been terrible.'

'It was. Oh, she phoned that night to let me know they were okay, but she wouldn't tell me where they were and she said that I'd never see Gracie again.' He looked up at her and there were tears in his eyes. 'And I haven't. Thank you so much for calling me.'

'Hazel left a note asking us to call you,' Erin told him.

'I suppose that's something. Have you phoned the police?'

Erin shook her head. 'It turns out that one of our other guests helped her and knows where she is.'

Despite his anger towards his wife, Des looked relieved.

'She's gone to a clinic in London.'

'Oh! Well, that's good news but how on earth will she afford that? We don't even have health insurance.'

'This other guest is paying. He's quite rich.'

'He?' Des flushed an angry red. 'Is this a lover? Has

she been living with another man in front of my daughter?'

'Oh, no, nothing like that!' Erin assured him. 'Hazel has become quite close to two other guests. PJ Ward is an older man who lives here and looks after our market garden. Gracie has become very fond of him and he spends a lot of time showing her how we do things here.' She smiled.

'So he's paid for Hazel to go to this clinic?'

'No. PJ was worried about Hazel. He could see that she wasn't well and he talked to this other guest about it. Sebastian had bought a couple of Hazel's paintings and knew her slightly better than the rest of us. When PJ got worried about her, he turned to Sebastian for help. I was on the point of phoning the police when Sebastian walked in and told me that she was on her way to London. Apparently he tried to talk to her, but when he couldn't make any headway, he offered to send her to this clinic for help.'

'This is all a bit strange.'

As Erin talked she'd been thinking the same thing. 'I'll introduce you to both Sebastian and PJ and you'll get a clearer picture of the situation.'

He stood up. 'Right now I'm more interested in seeing my daughter.'

Erin stood up too. 'I'm sure she'll be thrilled to see you.' She led him out of the front door, across the lawn, through the orchard and down towards the greenhouses. Spotting a flash of pink, she veered right, in the direction of the cabbage patch, and then stopped. 'Would you like to go on alone?' she asked Des, pointing to where his daughter was kneeling beside PJ, digging.

'Please,' he said, and walked on towards the pair. 'Gracie?'

The child turned round and Erin would never forget the sheer joy that flooded the child's face. She scrambled to her feet and ran to him. 'Daddy!'

He held her close. 'Gracie! My Gracie. You're talking!'

PJ rose to his feet, smiling. 'Hello.'

Des gave a curt nod and then pulled back so he could look into his daughter's face. 'How are you, Gracie?'

'Fine. This is my friend, PJ. PJ, this is my daddy.'

'Nice to meet you,' Des said stiffly.

'And you,' PJ replied, sounding equally uncomfortable.

'Gracie, why don't you take your dad into the front garden and I'll bring you both a snack?'

PJ came to stand next to Erin and they watched as father and daughter walked away, hand in hand. 'Well, what do you make of him?' he asked.

'He seems okay. He's had a tough time, PJ. Hazel ran out on him too. He hasn't seen Gracie since.'

'Lord, God. This is an awful mess altogether.'

'Not really. Hazel is getting help, Gracie is talking again and she's been reunited with her father. I'd say things are finally looking up.'

'I suppose, when you put it like that.'

'I've tried to explain to Des about your friendship with Hazel and Gracie and also Sebastian's involvement, but I think it would be best if you had a chat with him yourself later.'

'No problem. After all I'm the one really responsible for the girl deserting Gracie.'

'That's not true. It was a grandiose gesture by Sebastian Gray.'

PJ shot her a sidelong glance. 'I thought you two were, er, friends.'

She sighed. 'We are, sort of, but he has a habit of doing things without considering the consequences. I think it's all part of being a celebrity. He's used to others clearing up after him.'

They went into the kitchen and Erin put on the kettle.

'So what's he going to tell Gracie about Hazel?'

'I've no idea,' Erin admitted. 'He was anxious to see Gracie so we didn't have time to discuss it.'

'We'd better watch what we say around the child, then.' PJ sank into a chair.

'True.' Erin prepared a tray of milk, biscuits and coffee and carried it out to the father and daughter.

PJ followed and hovered in the hall, watching anxiously. 'Well, how's it going?' he asked, when she returned.

Erin shrugged. 'I didn't hang around to find out. I just told him that we'd be in the kitchen when he was ready to talk to us.'

PJ nodded. 'Fine. What about Gray? We'd better let him know that he's here. Will I go?'

'No, I'll do it.' PJ shot her a sharp look and she sighed. 'Don't worry, PJ, I'll only be a minute.'

When Sebastian opened the door and saw her, he turned away with a groan. 'Oh, please, don't give me any more grief.'

'I'm not going to,' she said, stepping inside and closing the door. 'I just wanted to let you know that Hazel's husband, Des, has arrived.'

'I suppose he's going to have a go at me too.'

'I'm not sure,' she admitted. 'But I think he's more interested in his daughter. Although, when I was trying to explain your involvement, he assumed that there was something going on between you and Hazel. I put him right straight away,' she added hurriedly.

He looked at her in amusement. 'Did you, indeed? But you've had your own suspicions, Erin.'

'And I was wrong and I'm sorry, okay?' She turned to go, but stopped at the door. 'Please don't go anywhere, Sebastian. Not until you've spoken to Des.'

He gave her a mock salute. 'Yes, Ma'am!'

Shaking her head, Erin left the cabin and went back around to the front of the house. Des was still sitting on the bench, Gracie on his lap. Relieved that the child seemed so comfortable with him, Erin went back into the house.

PJ was now in the sitting room, reading a news-paper. He lowered it when she walked in. 'Well?'

'I've asked him to stay put until Des is ready to talk to him.'

PJ nodded. 'Do you think Des will take Gracie home tonight?'

Erin sat down. 'I don't know.' She looked at him. 'You'll miss her.'

'I suppose I will.'

'It's better this way. You said yourself that Hazel wasn't able to look after her any more.'

He looked at her. 'You're annoyed with Hazel, aren't you?'

'Yes. No. Oh, I don't know. She's probably not responsible for her actions at the moment but I feel so sorry for that poor kid. I mean did Hazel have to leave in such a dramatic fashion? Would it have hurt to call Des and then say a proper goodbye to Gracie after he'd come to pick her up?'

'I don't understand that either,' PJ admitted. 'And I don't know why Sebastian couldn't have told us what was going on. I wonder how he's going to explain that one to Des.'

Erin looked out of the window and saw Des and Gracie approach the house. 'They're coming. I suppose I should look after Gracie and let you two talk.'

'Would you, darling?' PJ stood up.

'Sure. You take him into the kitchen and I'll put on

a video for Gracie. And find out what he's told her, PJ, and what his plans are.'

PJ nodded and the two of them went into the hall just as Des and Gracie walked in. The child immediately ran to PJ's side.

'Mummy's gone into a special hospital and they're going to give her new medicine to make her better.'

He smiled down at her. 'Well, isn't that great?'

Her face fell. 'But it means I have to go home with Daddy tomorrow.'

'Well, won't it be nice to sleep in your own lovely bed and play with your toys?' he said.

'And you'll have friends to play with,' Erin pointed out.

The child brightened at that. 'I have missed my friends.'

'Maybe you'd like to watch some cartoons while your dad packs your things,' Erin suggested.

The child looked to her father and Des nodded, with a grateful smile at Erin. 'That's fine, sweetheart.'

Erin led the child into the sitting room and closed the door. PJ turned to Des. 'Could we talk?' he asked. Des nodded and PJ took him through to the kitchen. 'How did Gracie take the news?' he asked, sitting down at the table.

Des took the chair opposite. 'She was a little tearful but I think she's relieved too. She's had to live with Hazel's strange behaviour for a long time.'

'Has she suffered from depression for a while, then?'

Des turned his head to look at him. 'Depression? Is that what she told you? Hazel has bi-polar disorder. It's like depression only a lot worse, but it can be successfully controlled with the right treatment.'

'We didn't know. And Sebastian said Hazel wasn't taking her tablets.'

'Who is this Sebastian guy?'

'Sebastian Gray. He's another guest here.'

Des frowned. 'It's not *the* Sebastian Gray?'

'The actor? Yes, it is.'

'What on earth is he doing here?'

'His sister runs the restaurant up the road. He's quite a private man, but when he saw Hazel's work he took an interest and actually bought a couple of her paintings.'

'So she has been working?'

'Oh, absolutely. For the first few weeks you couldn't get her out of the garden. She and Gracie spent most of their time out and about, painting; Gracie seemed to love that. When the weather was nice, Hazel packed a picnic for them. And when Gracie was in bed, Hazel would sneak out first thing to paint daybreak, or at night to do sunsets. She was turning out paintings at an incredible rate. She did the one hanging in the hall, the one of the Gatehouse.'

'Well, I'm glad of that. When did it change?'

'I've been thinking about that a lot and I think it was when Hazel approached a retailer in Mullingar in the hope he'd be interested in selling her paintings.

He wasn't. It was just a souvenir shop and the oul eejit would only have been interested in commercial landscapes of the place. It was completely the wrong setting for her work. I tried to explain that but she took it very badly. And then I got an idea. I know a woman who runs an art gallery and I showed her one of Hazel's paintings – the one hanging in reception – and she thought it was wonderful. She said it was the best and most original work she'd seen in years.'

'Wow, that's great.'

'I know, and it wasn't enough for her to just sell the paintings – she wanted to give Hazel her own exhibition. I tell you,' PJ chuckled, 'I practically flew home to tell her, I was that excited.'

'She must have been thrilled.'

'I thought she would be, but it was like she didn't even hear me. She seemed fixated on being turned away by the other fella. When I tried to talk to her about it, she started to avoid me, and she became really withdrawn so I backed off. She still let Gracie spend time with me but she kept her distance. And she stopped painting. She seemed to spend most of her time in bed, to be honest. That's when I started to get really worried and I asked Gray to have a word.'

'And did he?'

'Yes, but he didn't have much success. He said Hazel told him about the depression and that she was supposed to be on medication, and then she told him—' PJ stopped, realizing that Des might not know.

'What?' Des looked at him. 'It's okay, PJ, there's nothing you can say that will shock me; I've seen it all.'

'Apparently she tried to take her life at some stage.'

'Oh, that. Yes, I know all about that.'

'So it's true?' PJ asked, not sure he wanted to hear the answer.

'She took some tablets. I'm not convinced it was a serious attempt but it confirmed that she needed help. I tried to get it for her but she wouldn't listen to me either.'

'So I suppose we should be happy that she's gone to this clinic. If Gray organized it, you can bet it's the best. But I still don't understand why it was such a big secret. Why all the subterfuge?' PJ scratched his head, baffled. 'I mean we wanted her to get help, we would have been happy for her.'

Des sighed. 'That's classic Hazel, I'm afraid. She gets it into her head that everyone is working against her.'

'So what will happen when she gets out?'

Des shrugged. 'I don't know.'

'Would you not let her come home, Des?'

'Absolutely not. The first thing I'm going to do when I get back to Dublin is get custody of Gracie and try to ensure that Hazel never gets to see her alone again.'

'Ah, but, Des—' PJ started.

Des held up his hand. 'No, PJ, I'm sorry, but I can't do it any more. I've lived with this illness for years and I stood by Hazel every step of the way. But then she decided that I was the enemy and she took Gracie away from me. I have woken up every morning for the last four months wondering where my daughter was. I won't ever let Hazel do that to me again. And I don't care what help she gets in a fancy clinic. If she goes off her medication again she is capable of anything, and that makes her an unfit mother. I have to think of Gracie's safety. You must see that.'

PJ nodded sadly. 'I do. It's a tragedy and I wish it were otherwise, but I know you're right.'

'Thanks. And thanks for all your kindness to Gracie. She's going to miss you.'

'And I'll miss her,' PJ told him getting slowly to his feet. 'When will you leave?'

'If it's okay with Erin I'd like to stay the night and then head off straight after breakfast. Will you be around?'

'I'll make sure I am,' PJ promised.

Chapter Thirty

Despite Erin, PJ and Ronan playing down Hazel's abrupt departure, word still leaked out. Rai chattered on and on about it as she, Sean and Marguerite got ready for service.

'I thought she was a bit odd from day one,' Rai confided.

Marguerite shot Sean an exasperated look.

'She's safe and well and that's all that matters,' Sean retorted.

'I just wish I knew why my brother got involved,' Marguerite murmured. 'Ah, speak of the devil.' She smiled when she saw Sebastian in the doorway and quickly went to embrace him.

'Nice holiday?' he asked, kissing her.

'Lovely, little brother.'

Rai stood staring at the two of them. 'Brother?'

Sebastian nodded at Rai. 'Hello again.'

She continued to stare at him and Marguerite. 'He's your brother?'

Marguerite laughed. 'Half-brother. But you have already met, *n'est-ce pas*?'

'Yes, but I didn't know you were related. That's so cool.'

Marguerite shot her brother an amused glance. 'You think, eh? So, Sebastian, are you going to stay for lunch?'

'Yes, why not? I believe you have a new chef who's much better than you.'

Rai's cheeks flamed. 'I never said that, Marguerite!'

'Don't mind him, Rai. He likes to tease. You go and get started and I'll take his order.'

Rai hurried out to the kitchen and Marguerite led Sebastian to a table in the corner. 'Now tell me everything,' she commanded.

'What do you mean?' he asked, innocently.

'You know exactly what I mean. Why did you send that girl off to this London clinic and what were you thinking of, not telling anyone?'

'Marguerite, please don't blow this out of proportion. Your friends have completely over-reacted.'

She raised her eyebrows. 'You think worrying about a woman who walks out on her child is an overreaction? Tell me, how would you feel if Vanessa walked out and left Toby and Jess alone in a strange place?'

He pulled a face. 'Okay, point taken. But I knew that the mystery would be cleared up within a matter of hours. I'd asked the reception to call me as soon as Hazel was checked in.'

'But why did you do it, Sebastian? Why did you get mixed up with that girl? I thought you came here because you wanted to get away from people.' And then she sighed. '*Mon dieu*, you're not lovers, are you?'

'No, we're not.' He laughed.

'Then why?' she persisted.

'PJ was worried about her and the child. He thought that maybe I could help, that she would talk to me.' He gave a self-deprecatory laugh. 'I don't know why. Anyway, she didn't so I offered to pay for her to go and get help from someone a little more qualified. It's a good place, Marguerite. They will sort out her treatment and give her counselling too.'

Marguerite patted his hand, her smile warm. 'You're a good, kind man.'

'I don't think your friends agree.'

'I'm sure they will once they get over the shock of yesterday. But you have drawn a lot of attention to yourself. Rai dropped into Paddy's coffee shop on her way in and said everyone was talking about it.'

He frowned. 'About Hazel.'

'It's only a matter of time before they hear of your involvement.' Marguerite pointed out. 'That woman Sandra is very good friends with Paddy and she is a terrible gossip.'

He shrugged. 'What can I do about it?'.

'You could get away from here. You could go home.'

'I suppose so.'

She looked at his dejected expression. 'But you don't have to. We could tell everyone you'd gone and you could lie low for a while. I'm sure Erin would be happy to play along.' Something she said amused him. 'What?'

He shook his head. 'Nothing.'

'So what do you think?'

'I'd like to stay a little longer,' he admitted. 'I've grown quite attached to the place. I thought I was coming to a quiet backwater and instead it's a hive of intrigue. I wonder what will happen next; maybe there'll be a murder.'

'There will be if you don't order some food, and quickly. Rai is peeking out at us looking positively desolate.'

He laughed. 'Then let's eat.'

Rai had re-plated Sebastian's lunch three times now and Sean was losing patience. 'Oh, for God's sake, love, he's not royalty,' he groaned.

'No, he's much more important.' Rai cleaned the edge of the plate.

'Haven't you already served the man breakfast?'

'It's not the same. Does that look okay?'

'It looks fine. It looked fine the first time. I've never known so much fuss over a bloody lunch.'

'Sean, this man has probably eaten in some of the best restaurants in the world.' Rai gave the dish a final wipe and then pushed it across the counter. 'Be careful with it, and hurry. I don't want it to get cold.'

He shook his head as he picked it up. 'And is Marguerite not getting fed at all? Only, she might not be a movie star but she is your boss.'

'Shit, yes, it's here.' Rai turned to get the smoked fish salad and handed it to him. 'Watch his face as you give it to him.'

He stared at her. 'Why?'

'Because I want to know his first reaction, of course,' she said impatiently.

'Of course,' he said and took the food into the dining room.

Rai ran to the door and peeped through the crack but Sean was in her line of vision and she couldn't see Sebastian's face. 'Move,' she muttered, chewing distractedly on a nail.

Sebastian laughed at something Sean said, making her frown. 'You'd better not be laughing at my food,' she growled.

When he came back in she was waiting for him, arms crossed and foot tapping. 'Well?'

'Table three want one special and one shepherd's pie.'

'I don't care what table seven want; what did he say?' she hissed.

'Who?' Sean blinked.

'Tell me or I swear I'll stab you with a skewer!'

'Now, that's not very friendly,' Sean said and then laughed as she advanced on him. 'Okay, okay. He smiled and said that it smelled nice.'

'And?'

He shrugged. 'That's it.'

'But he was laughing. You said something and he laughed.'

'Oh, yes, I said that he was lucky to be fed at all given the chef was so star-struck.'

'You didn't.' She looked at him, horrified.

He grinned. 'No, I wished him a drama-free lunch.'

'I still can't believe that he's Marguerite's brother!' She went back to the door. 'He's eating it,' she said excitedly.

'That is the general idea,' Sean said drily. 'Now, can you please see to table seven or you won't be working in this restaurant for much longer.'

Rai took a last look at Sebastian and returned to her workstation. 'I can't get my head around the fact that Sebastian Gray is hanging out in a tiny town in the middle of Ireland.'

'Amazing.'

'Does he spend much time in Dunbarra?' she asked, trying to sound casual.

'No, this is his first proper visit.'

'And has he been here long?'

'What is this, twenty questions?' Sean grumbled.

'Humour me,' Rai wheedled.

Sean sighed. 'He's been here a couple of months.'

'You're kidding? And he's staying in a poxy bed and breakfast?'

'I doubt Erin would call it that. And, by the way, she's Marguerite's best friend.'

'I didn't mean anything. I like the Gatehouse but, let's face it, he must be loaded; he could stay in the best of hotels.' Rai stopped chopping onions and grinned at him. 'Hell, he could probably buy a hotel.'

'True, but I think it was the peace and anonymity of Dunbarra that attracted him and, of course, Marguerite.'

'Are they close?'

'They seem to be.'

'He'll probably leave now, won't he?' Rai said sadly.

'Why?' Sean frowned.

'Well, all this business with Hazel will draw attention. It's only a matter of time before someone phones a newspaper to tell them he's here.'

'You'd better not.'

'As if.' She looked at him as if he were mad. 'The last thing I want is for him to go.'

'Would you look at you going all dewy-eyed. Sure, he's probably old enough to be your father.'

'I quite like a more mature man,' Rai told him.

Sean wriggled his eyebrows. 'Do you indeed.'

Rai grinned. 'I said mature not decrepit.'

'You watch your tongue, my girl.' Sean walked to the door and took a look out. 'Is that order ready yet? Table seven are beginning to look a bit restless.'

'Ready.' Rai added some dill to the fish dish, sprinkled parsley on the pie and pushed the dishes towards him. *'Et voilà*, as our boss would say.'

Sean picked up the plates and carried them to the door. 'No time for any more daydreaming,' he called back over his shoulder. 'A party of six just walked in.'

'No problem,' Rai said, hurrying over to the door for another glimpse of Sebastian. He had finished eating and was in deep conversation with his sister. God, Rai thought, he really is gorgeous. He must be bored out of his mind around here. Maybe he's ready for some company. She wondered how to engineer a meeting when she wasn't on duty. Marguerite wouldn't be impressed if she flirted with him when she should be working. In fact, Rai thought Marguerite probably wouldn't approve of her flirting with him at any time. But he was a free agent and so was she and she was determined to contrive a meeting with him one way or another.

PJ was digging potatoes when he heard footsteps behind him. He straightened, wiped his forehead on his sleeve and looked back to see Erin with a mug in her hand.

'You haven't stopped for hours. Please take a short break. I don't want you to get sick.'

'I won't get sick,' he told her, taking the mug and leaning against the fence to drink it.

'It's quiet without her.' Erin hoisted herself up on the fence beside him.

'Gracie?' He smiled. 'I was just thinking the same thing. Isn't it strange, she wasn't exactly a loud child, was she?'

'I wonder how Hazel's doing.'

PJ sighed. 'Well I suppose she's in the hands of the professionals so that's probably a good thing.'

She looked at him. 'But?'

He shrugged. 'I can't help thinking she'd be better off with people who love her.'

'Except she doesn't have anyone, does she?'

'No and Des won't take her back.'

'You can't really blame him, PJ.'

'I don't, darling, I don't. He's only trying to protect his daughter. But I keep wondering what will happen to Hazel when she gets out of that place. If she does-n't have Gracie and she doesn't have her painting, what reason has she got to go on?'

'Don't think like that, PJ. Sebastian says this is a great clinic. They won't let her out until they're sure she's going to be okay. Try not to worry about her and please come inside for something to eat; you must be ravenous.'

He handed her his mug and picked up the spade again. 'I'd like to finish this first and, to be honest, I'm trying to avoid Sandra.'

Erin laughed. 'Now that, I can understand. Just be glad she spends so much time at Paddy's. Though I'm amazed she didn't stick around today to quiz us about Hazel and, indeed, Sebastian. In fact, now I come to think of it, she never shows much interest in him. Isn't that odd?'

'I suppose so.'

Erin looked at her watch. 'I'd better get back. Don't stay out here too long, promise?'

'I won't,' he said and returned to his digging, but as soon as Erin was out of sight, he stopped and leaned heavily on his shovel. He felt so tired and so broken; he was a different man from the one who'd woken up on Monday morning. 'Oh, Isabelle, what will I do without you?' he said aloud, looking up at the sky.

And then as if he wasn't miserable enough, Gracie had thrown herself into his arms this morning and clung on to him, sobbing her little heart out. He and Des had to promise her – and cross their hearts – that she could visit some time soon. He thought his heart would break when her father finally prised her away from him, and he'd never forget those big, mournful eyes looking out of the car window as Des drove her away.

It was in that moment that he realized just how sick Hazel must be. How could she choose to leave her little girl? It must have torn her apart. He knew there'd be those – no doubt Sandra among them – who'd presume she'd been fed up with a kid hanging around and just dumped her. And the fact that Gray was involved would really get tongues wagging. He couldn't listen to it, not at the moment. He'd lose his temper and lash out and that wouldn't do.

So, for the moment, he intended to stay close to home. Perhaps some fishing with Mark would help. He wouldn't get the same comfort from the vegetable garden as he used to. His eyes drifted to the patch he'd made for Gracie. It just wouldn't be the same without her.

Chapter Thirty-One

Erin ran through her list one more time, threw an eye over the baskets and bags in front of her and, satisfied that she'd got everything, went out to open the car. She frowned at the sight of a van in the driveway and two men standing against it, smoking and chatting. 'Can I help you?'

'Howaya, love, do you work here?'

'I own the Gatehouse,' she replied, scenting trouble.

'Oh, right, great, so is he here?'

Erin remained expressionless. 'Is who here?'

'Sebastian Gray?'

'No. So please leave.'

He grinned and sidled closer. 'That's okay, love,' he said and pulled out his wallet. 'I don't expect nothing for nothing.'

She raised an eyebrow. 'Oh, really?'

'Absolutely. Why don't you make me a nice cup of coffee and we can discuss terms?'

Erin smiled at him and leaned closer. 'Why don't

you and your friend get off my property before I call the police?'

He frowned in annoyance. 'You're making a big mistake. If he's here, I'll find out. Someone will talk.'

She shrugged and started to walk away. 'Good luck with that.'

'If he wasn't here you'd say so to get rid of us,' he called after her. 'But don't you worry, we can wait. It's all part of the job.'

By the time Erin had finished loading the car, they'd left and she hurried around the side of the house to the cabin.

Sebastian opened the door wearing only a towel and a smile. 'Well, this is a surprise.'

Erin looked away, scowling. 'It might be an idea to put something on before you come to the door. The press were just here.'

His smile disappeared as he looked past her. 'What?'

'I threw them out but they won't have gone far. I was offered money to give them my story.' Her lips twitched. 'I was sorely tempted.'

'And what a story that would be,' he murmured, leaning against the door jamb and letting his eyes run over her.

'Stop that,' she muttered, shifting self-consciously. She could feel her face flush and cursed her body for the way it gave away her feelings. Sebastian never looked uncomfortable or embarrassed, she realized. The only time she'd ever seen him emotional was when he talked about Marina. Even Hazel didn't seem to move him. 'Have you heard from Hazel?' she asked, to divert him as much as anything.

'Still jealous, eh?' he teased.

'Jealous of a sick woman? Hardly. But I do think your behaviour is a little odd. It was good of you to help her, but why all the secrecy? Poor Gracie didn't deserve that.'

His expression hardened. 'Most people would think I did a kind and charitable thing but you manage to make it sound Machiavellian.'

She sighed. 'I'm sorry, I didn't mean to but it all just seemed unnecessarily cloak and dagger.'

'I agree, but that was the way she wanted it. From my brief conversation with her husband, that was entirely in keeping with her condition.'

Erin nodded. 'You're right. Sorry. I must go and do my deliveries. I just wanted to warn you about the press.' She turned to go.

'Erin?'

She stopped and looked back at him.

'Thank you.'

'No problem.'

'I miss you,' he added quietly.

'I doubt that.'

'Why's that, Erin?'

'You don't need anyone, Sebastian. You're completely self-sufficient.'

'I didn't say need, did I?' He looked amused.

'I have no time for your games today,' she retorted and walked away.

Damn him, Erin fumed as she drove off on her rounds. She shouldn't have sent that journalist away. She should have pointed the man towards the cabin and let him do his worst. Then she'd be rid of Sebastian Gray and his taunting ways. Except she didn't want to be. She sighed. While he was around there was an air of excitement in her life that hadn't been there for quite some time. And while it was dangerous and wrong to want him to stay, she couldn't help it. But she had no illusions that it would amount to anything more than a brief affair. In fact, if he asked her to come and live with him in America she would be appalled. Flattered, but appalled. She would never want to be a part of that fake world with its double-zero women and perfect, white smiles. She couldn't imagine living anywhere other than Ireland. In fact, she couldn't imagine ever even leaving Dunbarra. And perhaps that was why Sebastian fascinated her. He was like an exotic bird that had flown into her very ordinary garden. He was a creature of beauty and wonder, but he didn't belong and soon he would return to his own world and life would go on as before.

When she reached town she wasn't surprised to see the press van parked outside the coffee shop. No doubt they would get plenty of stories there, not all of them true. Sandra and Paddy would be in their element. Spotting Ronan's jeep outside the hardware shop she pulled in behind it and waved as he emerged from the shop.

He came over and stuck his head in the window to kiss her. 'Hello, you.'

'Hiya.'

'A word of warning. There are some journalists hanging around, asking questions.' He nodded towards the van.

'Yes, I just threw them out of the Gatehouse; they'd camped in my driveway.'

'Cheeky buggers.'

'They offered me money to spill the beans,' she told him.

Ronan grinned. 'So why didn't you?'

'I don't think Marguerite would be very impressed with me, do you?'

'No, I suppose not. Gray will probably leave now that his cover is blown.'

Erin looked away from his searching gaze. 'Yes, probably.'

'He hasn't said anything?'

'No.' She made a show of looking at her watch. 'I must get on. I'm only halfway through my rounds.'

'Okay. Fancy going for a drink tonight?'

'Not with that lot around.'

'We could go to Dijon. They won't dare go in there.'

'There's a thought. I wonder if they know that Marguerite is his sister.'

'If they don't now, they will before the afternoon is out,' Ronan assured her. 'Most people in Dunbarra know that even if not all of them realize who Sebastian actually is.'

Erin sighed. 'Then I think we should definitely go to Dijon. We need to warn her about what's going on.'

Ronan watched as one of the journalists walked out of the coffee shop, talking into his phone, and made his way across the road to the pub. 'I have a feeling that by the time we see her, she'll have heard all about it.'

Dijon was surprisingly busy for a Sunday evening. 'It seems we've got celebrity status,' Sean said with a grin.

'Oh, dear.' Erin sat up on a stool. 'So word has got around, then?'

'Indeed it has. Everyone's dying to get a look at the movie star.' Sean laughed. 'It's gas. Yesterday, Sebastian was just this weird foreigner that wandered the countryside at all hours of the day and night. Today, he's a superstar and everybody wants to see him. And Marguerite, well, she's famous by association.'

Ronan laughed. 'Rai must be delighted she works here.'

'It's her day off.' Sean chuckled. 'She'll be furious she missed all the fuss. So are you two having dinner?'

'No, we just dropped in for a drink. We were afraid to go to the pub.' Ronan looked at Erin. 'Shall we share a bottle of wine?'

'Sure, why not?'

'The Chilean merlot, please, Sean. And if Mark's around tell him he's welcome to join us.'

'I think he might be upstairs. Just let me take table five's order and then I'll give him a shout.'

'No, don't bother, I'll go.' Ronan told him and went through to the back.

Sean went off to look after his other guests and then came back to open the wine.

'So how are you and Rai getting along?' Erin asked.

'We don't do too badly. She's a great cook and a hard worker but sometimes she can be so –' he searched for the right word and then grinned – 'young!' He opened the wine with a flourish and poured some for her to taste.

'That's lovely,' she told him.

'And she's completely star-struck by Sebastian. She can't stop talking about him.'

Erin laughed. 'If she had to live with him for a couple of months she'd soon find out that he has feet of clay.'

Sean filled her glass . 'Do I detect a note of bitterness?'

'No,' she had a quick look around before continuing, 'but I'm just getting a bit fed up of having long-term guests. And to be fair, Sebastian isn't the worst.'

'Ah, you're talking about the redoubtable Sandra Bell.'

Erin raised her glass. 'The one and the same.'

'She's not so bad,' Sean said with a chuckle. 'I think Paddy is quite smitten. She's put a spring in his step and totally reinvented the coffee shop.'

'I suppose she has,' Erin agreed. 'He'll miss her when she goes.'

Sean winked at her. 'Maybe she won't.'

Erin stared at him in horror.

'What's wrong?' Ronan asked sliding back on to his stool.

'Sean's suggesting that Sandra might not go home.'

He laughed. 'Well, look on the bright side. At least if she marries Paddy she won't be staying at the Gatehouse any more.'

'But I'd see her practically every day – for ever! And we could never go near the coffee shop. She'd be passing gossip around to beat the band. Could you imagine?'

'She's a lonely woman,' Sean told her. 'She has nothing in her life so instead she immerses herself in other people's. It's sad really.'

'And harmless,' Ronan added.

Erin looked at him. 'I don't agree. Gossip can

hurt a lot of people especially when it's spiteful. PJ can't stand that woman and he's a great judge of character.'

'How is PJ?' Sean asked.

'He's a bit upset that Gracie, the little girl, has gone home,' Erin told him. 'They were great pals.'

'And he was already very down when he returned from the funeral,' Ronan added.

'He'll be fine; you know PJ. He always bounces back,' Erin said, uncomfortable with the way this conversation was going.

'I'm off Wednesday evening,' Sean told her. 'I'll take him for a game of snooker or I could arrange a poker night; that would cheer him up.'

Erin made a face. 'I don't know, Sean, I think he wants to stay close to home at the moment. He's not in a very sociable mood.'

Sean shrugged. 'Well, maybe next week.'

Erin smiled. 'Great.'

Sean went off to take an order and Erin turned to Ronan. 'Isn't Mark joining us?'

'He'll be down in a minute. Why are you being so protective of PJ? Sean's a friend and I'm sure a night out would do PJ good.'

'He's not interested, Ronan. He doesn't want to see or talk to anyone right now. You'd probably be exactly the same in his position.'

Ronan twisted his face as he thought about this. 'No, I think I'd want you all to make a fuss of me. You, now, you're different. I can see you retreating into your shell. You and PJ are a lot alike.'

'Mark!' Erin jumped up to kiss the big man and pulled a stool over for him to sit on. 'How are you? I haven't seen you since you got back from France. How did it go with your mother-in-law?' She wrinkled her nose. 'What's the French for mother-in-law?'

'*Belle-mere*,' he said, straight-faced.

'Doesn't that mean beautiful mother?' Ronan said, pouring Mark a glass of wine.

'It does. Now there's an oxymoron for you.'

'Don't let Marguerite hear you say that,' Erin warned.

'Don't worry. As far as she's concerned I'm a devoted, loving son-in-law.'

Ronan grinned. 'Is she that bad?'

Mark put his head on one side. 'I'm hoping that she's like a good wine and will get better with age.'

Erin laughed and turned to Mark. 'Do you think it would be okay for me to go in and see Marguerite?'

'Sure. If she's too busy to talk, she'll tell you, or else she'll give you an apron.'

Erin slipped off her stool and picked up her glass of wine. 'No problem. I won't be long,' she told Ronan.

'Don't believe it,' Mark told him.

'I don't,' Ronan assured him, topping up both their glasses.

Marguerite looked up and smiled when she saw her. 'Erin, how are you?'

'Fine. Can you talk or are you too busy?'

'I'm a woman.' Marguerite shrugged. 'I can do both.'

Erin smiled and took a seat in the corner, well out of her friend's way. 'Do you want me to do anything?'

'No, everything is under control. I believe you had a visitor today.' Marguerite threw a steak into the pan.

Erin waited for the sizzle to die down before replying. 'The press. Did Sebastian tell you?'

'He phoned, giving me my instructions.' Marguerite added wine to a fish dish and checked the vegetables roasting in the oven.

'Which are?'

Marguerite looked up and smiled. 'To say nothing.'

'No comment.' Erin nodded. 'Unfortunately there will be others only too happy to speak. I'd say it was Sandra Bell that tipped them off.'

But Marguerite was philosophical. 'He has only himself to blame. If he had kept his head down and not involved himself in that girl's life, none of this would have happened.'

'You're right. Do you think maybe he did it on purpose? Perhaps he's missing the media attention. Perhaps he's ready to go back.'

Taking the steak out of the pan, Marguerite slipped it on to the hotplate. 'I don't believe so. I suggested that it might be time he went home or moved elsewhere but he seems to have grown quite attached to Dunbarra.' She smiled. 'Just like the rest of us.'

Erin couldn't help wondering if it was the place or if it could be something, or someone else. The thought made her pulse quicken and she felt filled with guilt at the thought of Ronan sitting at the bar waiting for her, unaware of her treachery.

'Erin?'

She looked up to see Marguerite watching her. 'Sorry, what was that?'

'I asked if you could do me one more favour.'

'If I can. What is it?'

'Just let me serve up and then we'll talk.' Carefully, Marguerite plated the food and then rang the bell for Sean.

He came in laden down with dirty crockery. 'Table six haven't turned up yet so you can have a break.'

'What about table three, don't they want dessert?'

'They want to wait for a while.'

'*Eh, bien.*' Marguerite fetched a bottle of water and sat down on a stool next to Erin.

'So?' Erin prompted her once Sean had left.

'I thought that maybe we could *tell* everyone that Sebastian had left but that he could stay on for a while.'

'It would never work, Marguerite. Everyone connected with the Gatehouse would know he was there.'

'Perhaps he could stay in the cabin for a few days.'

'I'd still have to feed him,' Erin pointed out.

'You are right. It's a terrible idea.' Marguerite sighed.

'But,' Erin mused, 'it might work if he actually left.'

Marguerite clapped her hands excitedly. 'We tell everyone he's going. They take photos of him getting into a car or arriving at a hotel in Dublin . . .'

'Or getting on a plane,' Erin added.

'And then when the fuss had died down, he comes back.'

Erin frowned. 'Except whoever tipped off the press the first time, will do it again.'

Marguerite's smile faltered. 'Oh, Erin, what can we do? He wants to stay. I think, maybe, he needs to stay.'

'Then,' Erin said simply, 'we'll find a way.'

Chapter Thirty-Two

Rai checked her appearance in the mirror one more time and then tugged on Mark's huge anorak. It came to her knees and the hood completely covered her face so no one would recognize her. Picking up the quiche that she'd slaved lovingly over all afternoon, Rai set out for the Gatehouse. As she'd expected there were a couple of guys from the newpapers hanging around outside the bed and breakfast. 'Howaya,' she said in her gruffest voice as she passed by.

They nodded at her and carried on talking. Given how tall Sebastian was there was no way anyone would mistake her for him. But they were crap at their job. Surely they realized a man as handsome and famous as Sebastian would have visitors? If they'd been at all observant they would have noticed that she was wearing silver wellies. They didn't deserve to get a scoop. If she had no luck with Gray though, maybe she'd consider giving them something for their stupid papers.

Walking past the main entrance, Rai went around

the bend and ducked into the hedge and on to the path that Gracie had shown her. Who'd have thought babysitting could be the source of such useful information? She swung around the front of the house, keeping her head down in case that nosey yank was about, although in this gloom and with this disguise Sandra would never recognize her. Still, knowing that woman she'd come down for a closer look. Rai hurried down the path, and pressing herself up against Sebastian's door she rapped on it with her knuckles. No answer. She panicked briefly wondering if he could actually be out after all her planning. And then she realized that, given the press were in town, he was unlikely to answer his door at night when he wasn't expecting anyone. 'Sebastian, it's Rai Price,' she called as loudly as she dared. 'I've brought you some supper.'

There was nothing for a moment and then she heard footsteps and the door opened a fraction. 'Rai?'

She let her hood fall back from her face and smiled up at him. 'Hi.'

He looked around and then back at her, a slightly bewildered expression on his face. 'Hi,' he said, not moving.

'I thought you might be under siege so I brought you something to eat.' She held up the container.

'Oh, thanks.'

He held out his hand and Rai realized he planned to take it and close the door in her face. 'I need to heat it up for you,' she said, holding on tightly to her passport.

He raised an eyebrow. 'I wouldn't be able to do that myself?'

Rai grinned. 'Maybe you could but as I've come all this way, I may as well do it.'

He hesitated for a moment and then opened the door wider and stood back. 'Come on in.'

Almost fainting with happiness, Rai squeezed past him, revelling in the brush of his body against hers, brief though it was. She made straight for the kitchen and turned on the oven.

He followed and leaned in the doorway, watching her. 'You seem to know your way around.'

'I was your housekeeper a couple of times while Erin was away,' she explained as she carefully removed the quiche and transferred it to a baking tray.

'That looks delicious,' he said, 'but there's an awful lot for one person.'

'Well, you could always keep some for tomorrow or . . .'

'Or?'

She smiled at him from under her lashes. 'I could stay and share it with you.'

'You haven't eaten?'

She shook her head.

'Well, as you've come all this way it would be very ungrateful of me to send you away with an empty stomach.'

She beamed at him 'Very,' she agreed and popped the tray into the oven.

He looked at her in amusement. 'Then let me take your coat and pour you some wine.'

'Great.' Her eyes holding his, Rai pulled down the zip of the anorak and shrugged it off her shoulders to reveal the cropped black top that barely covered her pert breasts and showed off her silky brown midriff and the red stone twinkling in her navel.

His eyes travelled down her body and then back up to meet hers. 'You didn't say you'd brought dessert.'

She moved towards him and slid her arms up his chest and around his neck. 'Did I mention it will be about twenty minutes before supper's ready?'

Rai was at once thrilled and slightly shocked by Sebastian's lovemaking. They didn't even make it into the bedroom. Instead he pressed her down on the rug in the tiny living room. And though it was fantastic and he was every bit as hot as she'd imagined, she was a little disappointed at how quick and impersonal it had been . . . until Sebastian stood up and held out his hand to her. 'Now let's try that again in slow motion,' he said.

Shivering with anticipation, Rai followed him. 'The quiche will be ready.'

He led her to the bed, smiling. 'I need to work up an appetite. How about you?'

'Good thinking,' she whispered before his lips came down on hers once more.

When they finally came up for air, Rai got up to get dressed. Her legs were shaking and her mouth and face were on fire from the stubble on Sebastian's chin.

He came up behind her as she studied herself in the mirror. 'I'll have to shave the next time,' he murmured, bending his head to kiss her neck.

Rai closed her eyes and let her head fall back against him. 'Is there going to be a next time?'

He turned her round and looked into her eyes. 'Do you want there to be?'

'I don't want to leave,' she told him, holding his gaze. It was a dangerous move that might put him off completely but he knew exactly why she'd come here tonight. It was a bit late to play the shrinking violet.

'Then don't,' he said and pushed her back down on to the bed.

It was after midnight when they finally got around to eating. Sebastian sat on the rug, his back to a chair, wearing only jeans. Rai, dressed in his T-shirt, served him. 'It's a bit dried out,' she said as she handed him a plate.

'A small price to pay,' he assured her.

Rai smiled as he ate hungrily. 'You seem to have found your appetite.'

'Watch out,' he told her. 'I'll have lots more energy after this.'

'At your age, no chance,' she teased.

'I'll bet I have a lot more stamina than the pimply youths you're used to.'

'How do you know what I'm used to?'

'You're very mature for your years,' he observed, finishing his food in double-quick time and settling back with a can of lager.

'I know what I want,' she said, taking a delicate bite of quiche and then licking her lips.

'You do, don't you? I must say, I find that a real turn-on.'

Rai put down her plate carefully then came across the room on her knees and climbed on to his lap. 'I'm finished, how about you?'

'I'm only just starting,' he muttered, his voice ragged as he grabbed her hair, pulled her head back and kissed her hard.

By the time Rai finally left she was satisfied that Sebastian would be coming back for more. He had thought to shock her with his appetite and strength but she had matched his ardour and knew how much that had excited him. Tonight she had ignited something in him that would ensure this was not a one-night stand. It was the best possible outcome she could have hoped for.

High on adrenalin and wine, Rai ambled down the

driveway as dawn broke, at peace with the world. She looked up and smiled at a blackbird singing in a tree, her hood falling back unheeded, and she never heard the sound of the camera shutter closing or noticed the accompanying flash.

It was mid-morning and Erin was working in her office when Sebastian appeared in the doorway. He hadn't been in for breakfast and she felt a flicker of irritation that he thought he could arrive late and she'd just drop everything she was doing to look after him. 'Good morning,' she said. 'I'm afraid you've missed breakfast.'

He closed the door and leaned against it. 'I don't want breakfast,' he said, his face grim. 'I want you.'

Erin looked at him, waiting for the punch line but he seemed deadly serious. 'You can't have me,' she said with as much conviction as she could muster.

'You want me too, I know you do.'

'I'm with Ronan.'

'What's that got to do with it?' he said impatiently. 'What's that got to do with us?'

'Well, you might be happy to sleep around but I'm not.'

He gave her a lazy smile. 'You seemed more than happy to me, every time.'

'That doesn't make it right.'

He advanced on her and pulled her out of her chair

and into his arms. 'Life's too short, Erin.' He cupped
her face in his hands and looked into her eyes. 'Don't
throw away what we've got. It may be short-lived, but
it may also be the last time that either of us will feel
anything this intense.'

Erin was mesmerized by his eyes and the way his
thumbs were gently stroking her neck. 'You're not
good for me, Sebastian,' she said weakly.

His smile was sad. 'I know.'

'Erin? Erin, where are you?'

She sprang away from him. 'That's PJ.' She opened
the office door. 'Coming,' she called before turning
back to Sebastian. 'You have to get out of here.'

He sat down on the edge of her desk and crossed
his arms. 'Not until you promise you'll come over to
the cabin as soon as you've dealt with him.'

'Sebastian, I have a business to run,' she protested,
but he just sat there, looking at her. 'Okay! I'll come
over, but I can't stay long.'

He pounced on her for one brief, hungry kiss and
then went out through the door, grinning happily.
'Don't be long,' he called and was gone.

She shook her head and looked round to see PJ
standing at the other end of the hall. How long had
he been there, she wondered. Too long, judging from
his grim expression. 'What's up?' she asked with an
innocent smile.

PJ ignored the question. 'What did he want?'

'He spilled some coffee on his duvet and asked me

to change it.' Erin was amazed at how easily the lie tripped off her tongue.

PJ grunted. 'Oh. I was just wondering if you wanted me to plant in the spinach and garlic.'

Erin frowned. 'Well, I suppose so, but if you wait till tomorrow we can do it together.'

'I'd prefer to get started on it now,' he said, turning away.

'PJ, don't you think you're doing too much?' she suggested, worried at how gaunt and drained he looked.

'I'm fine. Don't fuss, Erin,' he said brusquely and left.

Erin stood looking after him for a moment and then remembered her promise to Sebastian. She sped up to her bedroom to freshen up, and was about to walk out of the door when she remembered to collect some fresh bed linen. She reddened, thinking how embarrassing it would be if she met PJ on her way to Sebastian's and she was empty-handed.

He opened the door almost the instant she knocked, wearing only jeans. 'It might not have been me,' she pointed out.

'But it was,' he said, drawing her inside and closing the door.

'You love this, don't you?' she murmured, dropping the linen and running her hands over his chest. 'You love the danger, the ducking and diving. That's what turns you on, not me.'

'Don't be so self-deprecating,' he told her, pushing up her top so he could look at her breasts. 'I'm constantly turned on by you. When you're bending over pouring me coffee every morning I have to sit on my hands to stop myself grabbing you.'

'That would give Sandra Bell something to talk about,' Erin grinned.

'Speaking of talking,' he said, pulling her down on to the rug, 'we're doing way too much of it.'

As usual she felt riddled with guilt. But not enough to say no to him, she thought as she showered. But she couldn't carry on like this. Marguerite wanted Sebastian to stay and so did she. If he did, they would carry on like this and it wasn't fair to Ronan. No, it was time for a decision. One of them had to go. And that someone was Ronan.

It was crazy, as there was little or no chance of a future with Sebastian. But she knew that any time Sebastian clicked his fingers, she'd hop. Be it tomorrow, next month or next year, she would always make herself available to him because she simply didn't know how to say no. It made her feel embarrassed and ashamed. He was like an addiction that would harm her, the way all vices did eventually. But maybe, for just a while, they could be happy. LA wasn't that far away and other people made long-distance relationships work.

'Oh, who am I kidding?' she muttered, towelling

herself vigorously. Sebastian probably wouldn't give her another thought once he went home. But as long as Marguerite lived here there was a chance he would return. Erin had visions of herself growing old waiting for him, just like his own mother had waited for his father. The thought was a sobering one.

She stared at her reflection in the mirror. It wasn't too late. Ronan didn't know. She could still do the sensible thing and say nothing. She could treat this thing with Sebastian as simply a holiday affair and enjoy it for what it was. And then when he went home life would go on as before. And if Ronan didn't know, he couldn't be hurt.

The argument continued in her head for the rest of the day. But when Sebastian stopped to say hello to her when she was in the orchard with PJ and surreptitiously slipped his hand into the back of her sweatpants, Erin knew what she had to do.

Chapter Thirty-Three

It would be easier if they were somewhere private, Erin thought, looking around the busy pub. Still, at least it wasn't their local and she couldn't spot anyone she knew. She watched Ronan as he stood at the bar ordering their drinks and chatting with the barman. He was a fine-looking man and so clever and funny. Why wasn't that enough? She didn't have the answer. Perhaps she should wait. It was a mistake rushing into this; she probably wasn't thinking straight – she rarely did after a session with Sebastian. Just thinking about it was enough to make her feel hot and bothered.

'What's wrong, Erin?'

She looked up to see Ronan standing over her, frowning. 'What?'

He put the two beers down and then pulled up a stool. 'Don't pretend,' he said wearily. 'I know you better than you think. It's Gray, isn't it?'

'What are you talking about?' Erin stared at him, stunned, but she feel the flush creeping up her neck and into her cheeks.

'Don't try to deny it, Erin. I'm not blind and I'm not stupid.'

'I know you're not,' she murmured, feeling awful. 'I'm sorry.'

He looked at her in disgust. 'Is that it? You're sorry?'

She flinched at the viciousness in his voice. 'Maybe we should go.'

He sat back and folded his arms. 'I'm not going anywhere until you tell me everything,' he said, his voice deliberately loud.

Erin shrank in her seat, aware that he'd drawn some curious looks from the people around them. 'I'm sorry. I didn't plan any of this. It was just one of those things—'

'Oh, please, spare me. I knew there was something going on. In my gut, I knew it. But I tried to convince myself that you would never do that to me. I told myself that you had way too much class to behave like that.'

'I'm sorry,' Erin said again.

'You two must have been having a great laugh at my expense.'

'Of course not.'

'So what's the plan, Erin? Are you selling up and moving to Hollywood?'

'Don't be silly. I'm not going anywhere.'

'So, let me get this straight. You've given up what we had for a quick roll in the hay with Sebastian Gray.'

She looked down at her hands and said nothing.

He stood up and grabbed his jacket. 'I hope he was worth it,' he said and walked out.

'Me too,' she mumbled, staring into her drink, oblivious to the stares of those around her. She didn't think it was possible to feel even worse than she had before, but she did. Ronan had exposed her for the cheat she was and she felt cheap and ashamed. She'd given up on a great relationship because she couldn't resist Sebastian's charm. She had never considered herself sex mad before, but she figured she must be. How else could she explain her behaviour? She wondered how Sebastian would react to the news that Ronan knew about them and had dumped her. She had a horrible feeling that he would see it as some sort of victory. If he did, she hoped he had the sense to hide his feelings because they would be really hard to take. And the thought of succumbing to his charm if she didn't even like him very much – well, that would mean she had reached a new and all-time low even for her. Maybe she was more like her mother than she realized.

*

Rai woke up early so she decided to treat herself to a nice, rich latte on her way to work. She nipped into the corner shop to pick up a newspaper so she could read her horoscope and catch up on celebrity gossip. She wasn't aware of the curious stares in the shop but she definitely noticed the sudden hush in conversation when she walked into Paddy's Burke's.

'Hi, can I have a latte, please?'

Paddy winked at her. 'Of course you can.' He set up the machine and turned back to her still grinning like a lunatic. 'So how are you settling in, love?'

'Fine.' Rai nodded. She'd been here ages – why was he asking her that? Apart from giving her a grilling the first week, he'd hardly said a word to her since. What had changed?

'Nice to have a cuppa and a read before the day begins, isn't it?' he was saying now. 'I love to read what all the celebs are getting up to.'

Rai grinned back. 'Yeah, me too,' she said, her smile faltering at the titter that went around the room. 'Is there mascara on my nose or something?'

Paddy smiled kindly and pushed her coffee across the counter. 'No, love. You just enjoy your coffee and the paper.'

There was another giggle, which Rai ignored as she took out her money.

Paddy shook his head. 'That's okay; it's on me.'

She stared at him. 'Oh. Thanks.' She took her coffee to the bar at the window, where she could turn her back to the room, and unfolded the newspaper. Her gasp was audible, giving rise to another ripple of laughter. A picture of her, wearing Mark's enormous anorak, was on the front page. And there was no doubt that it was her. The hood had fallen back and she was smiling, completely unaware of the camera. No wonder they were all laughing. There was a smaller photo of Sebastian and the headline read: *Is this the New Woman in Seb's Life?* Rai didn't know whether to be pleased or horrified. She was aware of all the eyes in the room on her and she turned and smiled. 'Not a bad photo,' she joked.

A couple of women in the corner frowned in disapproval and turned away but Paddy laughed. 'You look gorgeous. But sure, you'd look grand in a sack.'

'Thanks, Paddy.' She turned back to read the article but found there were no further details and they didn't know her name. They also didn't seem to know that Marguerite was his sister, which was incredible. Rai wondered what Sebastian would make of this. Would he pack up and leave and, if so, would he tell her first? She wasn't sure. Maybe she should be the one to tell him the news and that way she could at least get a phone number from him before he left. She couldn't believe that she hadn't got it that night, but then she hadn't exactly been thinking straight. She smiled. She couldn't stop thinking about Sebastian and wondering if there would be a repeat performance. While her gut had told her yes, she'd been filled with doubt since. Maybe this was an opportunity to rectify the situation. Of course it could backfire. Sebastian might be furious that she'd got caught or think she'd done it deliberately. Well, Rai, you're just going to have to convince him otherwise, she told herself, draining her coffee and heading for the door.

'Are you off?' Paddy called after her, looking disappointed.

She grinned. 'Yeah, I have to go to work today but hopefully not for much longer. Bye!' Rai walked out laughing. That probably wasn't wise, it would no doubt turn up in a tabloid tomorrow, but she couldn't resist it. It was hilarious that anything she said might prove to be celebrity gossip. Her problem now, though, was that she had to talk to Sebastian. But how? She was due at work in ten minutes, and if she waited until she finished it might be too late. And then it came to her and its simplicity was mind-blowing: he could come to her.

'But it's you!' Marguerite looked from the newspaper to Rai and back again. 'They've made a mistake. We'll call them at once and they'll have to print a retraction immediately.'

'They haven't named me, Marguerite, and it's not a mistake.'

Marguerite stared at her. 'Pardon?'

Rai gave her a cheeky smile. 'What can I say?'

'*Mon dieu*,' Marguerite muttered, 'what has he done?'

'What have *we* done,' Rai corrected her. 'I'm not a child.'

'You are, Rai, you are.' Marguerite cried. 'What

were you thinking of? Have you any idea how old Sebastian is?'

'Thirty-something?' Rai shrugged. 'So what?'

'What he did was wrong and I shall tell him so.'

'Well, I don't agree, but I think you should call him and ask him over here. I'd prefer he heard about this from me – us.'

'I'll call him. In the meantime, get started on lunch.' Marguerite gave a weary sigh. 'We still have a restaurant to run.'

Rai nodded and went out to the kitchen, peeved at being dismissed so easily. She was no longer just the employee, after all. Mind you, in Marguerite's mind she was probably worse. For the first time Rai wondered how this news would affect her position here. If Sebastian left without a backward glance she was going to need this job. In fact, she wanted this job. Donning her whites, Rai decided to make this the best lunch ever. She would do well to remind her boss exactly how good she was.

Marguerite put her head in about an hour later. 'Sebastian will be dropping in to see us after lunch.'

'Okay.'

'Can you manage without me for a while? I have to go out.'

'Everything's under control,' Rai assured her. 'You take as long as you want.'

Marguerite gave her a wan smile. '*Au revoir.*'

Well, at least he was coming, Rai thought, breathing a sigh of relief. She wondered how much Marguerite had told him and if he knew that this was going to be a three-way meeting. She was suddenly overcome with nerves. What if he was horrible about it all and laughed it off as unimportant and meaningless? That would be so humiliating. But underneath the Hollywood glitz, Rai thought that Sebastian was still an English gentleman at heart. At least she hoped so.

Erin fidgeted with her phone while she waited in the fast-food joint in Mullingar. It was the only place she could think of where there was no chance of bumping into either Ronan or Sebastian. She had slept badly, dreaming fitfully of Ronan, and when she woke up feeling tired and miserable there was only one person she wanted to talk to. Marguerite had sounded distracted when she phoned but she must have detected the anxiety in Erin's voice because she agreed to meet immediately.

'I have something to tell you anyway,' she added somewhat cryptically and rang off, leaving Erin wondering if there was something wrong.

She didn't have long to wait and she smiled when her elegant, attractive friend walked in looking totally out of place among the jeans and tracksuits. They kissed and Erin offered to get her a coffee.

Marguerite made a moue of disgust. 'God, no, I couldn't drink that shit. Do they have bottled water?'

'I think so.' Erin laughed and went to get some.

'So what is the problem?' Marguerite asked as she opened the bottle and took a delicate sip.

'Ronan and I have split up.' Erin pulled a face. 'Well, no, to be honest, I suppose he dumped me.'

'Oh, Erin, that's terrible. But why, what happened? Everything was going so well, you seem so happy together.'

'It's a bit complicated. I've been seeing someone else and Ronan guessed as much.'

Marguerite's eyes were like saucers. 'No! Who?'

Erin felt her cheeks start to burn. 'I thought you'd have guessed.'

'No, I've no idea . . .' She trailed off and then shook her head slowly, her expression, horrified. 'Not Sebastian. Please, tell me it's not Sebastian.'

'Why?' Erin said, immediately on the defensive. 'Would it be so wrong?'

Marguerite dropped her head in her hands. 'Oh, this is terrible. Wait until I get my hands on him—'

'Don't be silly, Marguerite, it takes two. I'm a big girl so you can't blame Sebastian. I didn't have to sleep with him and I didn't have to tell Ronan the truth. Only, I did. I've been so miserable. It's best that it's out in the open. I couldn't have gone on like this for much longer.'

'When did all of this happen?' Marguerite asked, looking grim.

'Just last night. You're the first person I've told.'

Marguerite closed her eyes and groaned.

'It's not the end of the world, Marguerite. Don't you think you're overreacting a little?'

Again Marguerite didn't answer the question. 'So what next, Erin? Do you see a future for you and Sebastian?'

'Not a normal one,' Erin admitted with a rueful smile. 'I can't see myself leaving Dunbarra, never mind Ireland, and I somehow doubt he'll give up Hollywood for me. But we can visit; others do it.' She met Marguerite's worried eyes. 'I realize it's an almost impossible scenario, but I also know that any time he did come back I'd want to be with him. So how could I keep deceiving Ronan?'

'Oh, Erin,' Marguerite looked at her with eyes full of tears.

Erin looked at her in alarm. 'Hey, come on, there's no need for that.'

'I'm so sorry, Erin.'

'Why are you sorry? What do you mean?'

With a sad shake of her head, Marguerite pulled something from her bag and pushed it across the table.

Erin unfolded the newspaper and frowned. 'Rai?' She read the headline and gave an involuntary gasp, then smiled in understanding. 'It's a mistake. They just got the wrong woman.'

Marguerite looked at her with pity. 'I'm so sorry I brought him into your life, my friend.'

'No, honestly, Marguerite, this is a mistake.'

'I talked to Rai, Erin. It's no mistake.'

Erin still wasn't convinced. Marguerite didn't know how intense her relationship was with Sebastian. Perhaps he flirted with Rai. That wouldn't be a surprise; she was beautiful and completely star-struck. 'Marguerite, your brother came to me yesterday morning, telling me how much he needed me.'

'I just can't believe he's behaved so badly.'

'Marguerite, you're not listening.'

'I am, Erin. But I am sorry to have to tell you that this photo was taken early yesterday morning as Rai left the Gatehouse after spending the night with Sebastian.'

Erin stared at her. 'He wouldn't,' she whispered.

Marguerite's eyes were hard, her expression one of disgust. 'He would and he has. And you have given up Ronan for a man like this.'

'I can't believe it. I mean, I know he's no angel, but this is incredible. Has he seen this?' Erin asked, looking back at the newspaper.

'He hadn't when I talked to him an hour ago. I've told him to come to Dijon after lunch. Rai thought we should tell him before someone else did.'

'How very thoughtful,' Erin scoffed. 'She probably engineered the whole thing.'

Marguerite frowned. 'I don't think so. If she'd done that then they would have a lot more than a grainy photograph. They don't even know her name.'

'They'll know it by now. All they'll have to do is show that photo around the pub or coffee shop and someone will tell them.' Erin tried to smile. 'On the bright side, you'll probably have a full restaurant with them all trying to interview her.'

Marguerite groaned. 'And Sebastian will walk right into the middle of it. Perhaps I should call him and arrange to meet somewhere else.'

'Just go to the Gatehouse,' Erin advised. She didn't like the idea of Sebastian, Marguerite and the beautiful Rai sitting down for a nice cosy chat anyway.

'Yes, that's what I'll do.' Marguerite began to stand up and then hesitated. 'What about you? Will you be okay?'

Erin forced a smile for her friend's sake. 'Yes, although I feel very stupid.'

'Maybe you should talk to Ronan—'

'Absolutely not. If there's one thing I know for sure it's that I've burned my bridges there. Anyway, he's a good man, he deserves better.'

'He loves you.'

'I'm not so sure about that any more.'

'I'd better warn Sebastian to stay well out of his way.'

Erin nodded. 'That might be wise. Ronan isn't

usually the violent sort, but he doesn't like to be made a fool of. Oh, Marguerite, I've really screwed up, haven't I?'

'It's not your fault, it's Sebastian's. And I will tell him so.' Marguerite leaned over to embrace her. 'Take care, my poor friend. I'll call you later.'

Chapter Thirty-Four

Rai went on with what she was doing when the phone rang, knowing that Sean was around somewhere. Minutes later he stuck his head into the kitchen. 'That was Marguerite. She said to tell you that she's going to see Sebastian and won't be back until later this afternoon.'

Rai stopped and looked up at him. 'She's going to see Sebastian?'

'That's what I said.'

'But why? He's supposed to be coming here.'

He held up his hands. 'No idea, I'm just the messenger.'

He left Rai cursing silently over her risotto and wondering what had happened to make Marguerite change the plan and where exactly it left her. For all she knew, Marguerite might drive Sebastian straight to the airport and Rai would never see him again. But no, she wouldn't. Marguerite would at least make him call. Rai grimaced. She didn't want anyone to have to make him do it. She wanted him to race over here to see her and tell her everything was going to be fine. Rai snapped back to reality just in time to rescue the risotto. She stirred it quickly and added more stock. This was no time to screw up. If she had lost Sebastian, she needed to at least hang on to her job.

Marguerite fumed all the way to the Gatehouse. She was furious with her brother and embarrassed that he could treat her friend so badly. First, getting involved with Erin when he knew she was already in a relationship, and then to spend the night with Rai – and the girl not even twenty yet. It was disgraceful; he was so like their father.

There was no answer when she knocked on his door and she was about to leave when she realized he was probably being cautious, given there were journalists hanging around. 'Sebastian, open up, it's me, Marguerite.' She was right and almost immediately he opened the door, surprised.

'Marguerite, I thought we were meeting at the restaurant.'

She marched past him and when he'd shut the door and joined her, she shoved the paper into his hands without a word.

He sighed. 'What is it now?' and looking at the paper he smiled slowly as he recognized Rai. 'You've got to admit she looks gorgeous even in that ridiculous coat.'

'I know about Erin.' Marguerite said, filled with fury and disgust.

'Ah.'

'Is that all you've got to say?'

He shrugged. 'What do you want me to say?'

'You make love to my best friend, even though she was in a steady relationship, and then you cheat on her with a girl who's little more than a child, so I expect you to say quite a lot. You came to me looking for refuge and this is how you repay me?'

He looked at her, frowning, seeming genuinely puzzled. 'But this hasn't anything to do with you, Marguerite.'

'Erin is my friend!' she shouted at him. 'I begged her to take you in and not only did she do it, she gave you her own apartment so that you would have total privacy. And Rai, in case you'd forgotten, works for me, so this, *mon frère*, has everything to do with me. And now Erin and Ronan have broken up, so that's another good friend of mine that you have managed to hurt.'

'What did you say?'

'You heard. She told Ronan about you last night and was greeted by this –' she slapped her hand across Rai's image – 'the very next day.'

'I never asked Erin to finish with Ronan.'

'No, of course you didn't. In fact, probably the only reason you were interested in her was because she was already taken. But Erin is a much better person than you. She couldn't continue to deceive Ronan and so she told him the truth.'

He put his head on one side. 'I'm not sure if that makes her noble or stupid.'

Incensed, Marguerite raised her hand and struck him across the face.

Looking more surprised than shocked, Sebastian put a hand to his reddening cheek.

Immediately she was filled with remorse. 'I'm sorry, Sebastian, I shouldn't have done that but you make me so mad. How can you be so cruel and heartless?'

'You're always ready to think the worst of me, Marguerite. Erin was the one in a relationship, not me, and as a grown woman she could have said no. As for Rai, she arrived on my doorstep half naked under that coat so don't blame me for giving her what she came for.'

She shook her head, sad that this was what he'd become. 'I don't know you at all, do I, Sebastian? If you had any sense, you would be begging Erin's forgiveness. She is a better woman than any you'll find in your fake, pretentious world, and your life would be enriched with her in it. Now I think you should leave before things become any more sordid than they already are.'

He shrugged. 'If that's what you want.'

'It is,' she told him and walked out.

She found Mark scrubbing the deck of the boat with a heavy wire brush and whistling while he worked. She stood on the jetty, watching him and waiting for him to notice her. He was a good man and she was lucky to have found him. She'd thought Erin equally happy and lucky, but obviously not. How strange it was that you could know someone so well and yet not really know them at all.

When Erin first came to Dunbarra she'd been very wary of people. It had taken a while for Marguerite to win her over and a little longer before they grew close enough to share a confidence. It had taken Marguerite by surprise the first time. She had remarked on what a lovely couple Erin and Ronan would make and Erin had told her in no uncertain terms that she was not interested in anything heavy. 'I'm no good at relationships. I take after my mother. We're both tarts,' she'd joked. Marguerite had left it at that but over time Erin had fed her titbits about how her life had fallen apart after the death of her father and her mother's revelation that he wasn't her father after all. But, though Marguerite could understand it had been a difficult time, Erin was a different person now and she and Ronan were a perfect match. She had been disappointed when Erin had turned down Ronan's proposal.

'Give him a chance,' she'd urged but Erin had been resolute.

'I won't marry him or any man,' she had said and

that was the end of that. Things had cooled between the couple for a while but then it seemed Ronan decided that it was better to have Erin on her terms than not to have her at all, and it appeared to work. Had it really or had she only seen what she wanted to see? Marguerite wondered. Maybe it was the same with her brother. Sebastian had always been a womanizer, but she'd thought it was because he loved women. Now she wondered whether, in fact, he hated them.

'Hello, this is a nice surprise!'

She looked up to see her husband leaning on his brush and smiling down at her. 'Hello.'

'Want to come aboard, Madame Hayes?' He winked at her.

'Only if I can have a very big hug from the captain.'

'I think that can be arranged.' He reached out and pulled on the rope tying the boat to the jetty so that he could bring it closer for her to climb up, and then helped her on board.

She snuggled into his arms and rested her head on his chest. 'Oh, Mark, I love you.'

He lifted her chin and kissed her. 'And I love you too. Now, what's wrong?' he asked, his eyes searching hers.

She sighed. 'So much I'm not sure where to begin.'

'Oh. This sounds serious. Why don't we go into the cabin, share a little glass of brandy and you can tell me all about it?'

'The bastard. I'm sorry, Marguerite, I know he's your brother, but really.' They were curled up on the tiny divan with tumblers of brandy and Marguerite was telling him about her morning.

'I know. I agree,' she assured him. 'I told him he had to go.'

'What did he say to that?'

'I didn't wait around to find out, but why would he stay? Rai says the place will be crawling with press before the week is out.'

'I'm afraid she's probably right.' Mark smiled. 'Paddy Burke will be thrilled. They'll be lining up outside to buy his coffee and cakes and he'll be able to gossip to his heart's content.'

'How can you laugh?' she reproached him. 'Poor Erin, poor Ronan.'

'I do feel sorry for Ronan but I'm glad Erin told him what was going on. He's better off without her.'

Marguerite turned to look at him. 'Mark!'

'I'm sorry, love, but I think she's behaved abominably.'

'It's Sebastian's fault. He's just like our father. Women cannot resist him.' She sighed. 'Perhaps you should go and see if Ronan's okay.'

'I'm not so sure. He'll be licking his wounds and he won't want an audience. I'm just glad that it was Rai on the front of that newspaper and not Erin; that would be very hard for him to take.'

'True. No one knows anything about Erin.'

'I thought she was happy with Ronan,' Mark said with a sad shake of his head.

'She probably was, in so far as she's capable of being happy in any relationship.'

He looked at her. 'What a cryptic comment. What exactly do you know about the woman that I don't?'

'She's just like the rest of us, Mark; she has a past.' Marguerite put up a hand to caress his cheek. 'There was a time when I didn't think our marriage would survive.'

He put a finger over her lips. 'Don't.'

She held his hand to her mouth and kissed it. 'It's okay. I won't get upset. It may have been the worst time in my life, in both our lives, but I think it made our marriage stronger.'

'I know it did,' he said, his voice soft. 'But I still wish it hadn't happened.'

Marguerite turned round and lay back in his arms. 'Our lives would have been so different if he'd lived,' she said dreamily. 'I'd have stayed at home and been a full-time mother and you would have worked long hours at that silly bank so you could buy him everything his heart desired.'

Mark chuckled. 'I'd have spoiled him rotten.'

She smiled sadly. 'We both would have.'

'Am I enough for you, Marguerite?' he said after a moment. 'Can you ever be truly happy with just the two of us?'

She twisted round again and took his face in her

hands. 'I am happy, my sweet, sweet man. You are my family. You are all I need. You are all I want.' And she kissed him and set about showing him that she meant every word.

It was almost time to open for dinner when Marguerite finally got back to Dijon and an anxious Rai ran to meet her as soon as she walked in the door. 'Did you see him? What's happening? What did he say?'

Marguerite gave her a weary look as she took off her shawl and hung it on a hook by the door. 'Not much. I've told him he must go home.'

Rai's face fell. 'And what did he say?'

'I didn't wait for an answer. Oh, Rai, you are so young and you have your whole life ahead of you. Don't waste it on someone like Sebastian. He will play with you and then he will move on to the next girl. I've seen it all before.'

Rai scowled but said nothing. How could Marguerite possibly know what she and Sebastian had shared?

'You are a good chef and one day you will be a great one. Follow your dream,' Marguerite urged her. 'Don't throw it away on something that isn't real.'

'It is real,' Rai burst out, unable to stop herself.

'Oh, really? And what would you say if I told you that Sebastian slept with another girl in Dunbarra?'

Rai tried to shrug as if she didn't care. 'I suppose

he's the kind of guy who could have anyone he wants. And he has been here for months. He only met me a few days ago.'

Marguerite sighed and put a hand on her shoulder. 'He slept with this girl only yesterday, Rai.'

Rai felt as if she'd been kicked in the stomach but she tried to laugh it off. 'I doubt that very much.'

'Believe me, it's true.'

Rai shook her hand off and glared at her. 'You're just saying that to drive a wedge between me and Sebastian. You don't want him to be with me. What is it? Am I not good enough, Marguerite?'

Marguerite just gave a tired shrug. 'You must believe what you want but I am not lying to you.'

Rai felt tears prick her eyes but she was damned if she was going to let Marguerite see her cry. She turned on her heel and headed for the door. 'I've got to go. Everything is prepped for dinner. See you tomorrow.' And grabbing her bag and jacket, she fled.

Chapter Thirty-Five

Erin stayed out working in the garden for the remainder of the day and, when it grew too dark to work, she went into the shed and started to clear it out. It didn't really need it but she wasn't ready to go inside; she couldn't bear the thought of having to talk to people and behave normally. As she tidied shelves and checked stocks, Erin thought about the events of the last few months and how Sebastian was so often the central character. He had come here to heal. He had come in search of peace and privacy. And yet he'd managed to affect her life, Hazel's and now Rai's. By design or accident? She wasn't sure, but she hoped the latter. She couldn't bear to think otherwise. And yet for him to have slept with Rai then come to her the next morning telling her he wanted her . . . And, unable to resist him, she'd obediently gone to him and lain where Rai had lain only hours before. That must have given him some kind of thrill. But she couldn't absolve herself of all responsibility. There had been times when she had searched him out and it seemed Rai had done the same. But she was just a kid. Erin didn't have that excuse. She had made a total fool of herself and hurt Ronan in the process. She was damn lucky that it wasn't her photo on the front of a tabloid newspaper.

Erin realized that she need never have told Ronan about Sebastian. He'd have been relieved to see that the actor was involved with Rai and delighted to see him pack his bags. And then they could have gone on as before. That was impossible now and Erin vowed to keep out of his way for a while, although she supposed he was entitled to have a good laugh at her humiliation. She hoped that he and Sebastian didn't come face to face; it didn't bear thinking about. It would be best if Sebastian did what Marguerite told him, and went home. She wondered if he was packing right now.

She finished tidying the shelves and got to work with the broom.

The door opened and PJ stood blinking in the light.

'Erin! I saw the light and thought we had intruders.'

'There aren't many thieves interested in fertilizer,' she said, smiling.

'No, but there are a lot of kids who'd be interested in some of the solvents.'

'I hadn't even thought of that,' Erin said with a shudder.

'Everything okay?' he asked, leaning against the doorpost and watching her as she continued to sweep.

'Fine.'

'You seem to be keeping your head down.'

'You can talk,' she retorted with a grin.

'The difference is you know why.'

She stopped brushing and looked at him. 'Ronan and I have broken up.'

He sighed. 'Because of Sebastian?'

'Yes.'

'Oh, Erin.'

'It gets worse, I'm afraid.'

'Go on.'

'There was a photo on the front page of one of this morning's tabloids. It was of a woman leaving Sebastian's room yesterday morning.'

He looked horrified. 'Not you?'

Erin shook her head. 'It was Rai.'

'Rai?' PJ shook his head in confusion. 'The little one from Dijon?'

Erin nodded, deciding not to tell him about her subsequent visit to the cabin; that was one embarrassment too far.

'But she's little more than a child,' he protested.

Erin shrugged.

'I never liked him,' PJ muttered unnecessarily. 'But why did you finish with Ronan?'

'He guessed there was something going on,' Erin explained. 'and when he asked me, I couldn't lie to him.'

PJ's eyes were full of compassion. 'That's an awful

pity. Sure, when Ronan heard about this photo he wouldn't have been suspicious any more.'

'Ronan knows me very well. That photo knocked me for six, PJ, and Ronan would see that.'

'I'm sorry, darling. You know I didn't approve of you messing around with that fella but I wouldn't wish this on you for anything.'

'I'll survive. I just feel a bit foolish. I knew that he wasn't going to propose but I really felt there was a connection between us. He confided in me, told me things he wouldn't tell Marguerite. I suppose that made me feel important.'

'It was probably meant to,' PJ said in disgust.

'No, PJ.' She shook her head. 'You saw what the guy was like when he first came here; he was a wreck, emotionally and physically. He wasn't capable of such subterfuge.'

'And yet look at how he was with Hazel. He seemed to worm his way into her life too.'

'What are you saying?'

'Just that he never bothered with any of the men,' PJ pointed out.

'Well, everyone who's ever heard of Sebastian Gray knows that he loves women. That's not news.'

'I suppose not. So what will you do now?'

'Nothing. Keep my head down and concentrate on my work. I was considering closing the guest house early, what do you think? Sebastian will probably leave in the next couple of days and I can give Sandra a week's notice.'

'It would be nice to have the house back to ourselves,' he admitted. 'But can you afford to do that?'

She made a face. 'The two families that were booked in for the end of the month have both cancelled. It would probably be wiser to close. I could put more money into the market garden and spend all my time working in it.'

'It's an idea. Let's sit down tomorrow and have a proper chat about this. I'm sure we can come up with some ways to cut costs and increase productivity.'

'Yes, okay. If nothing else, it will at least distract us from our other problems for a while.'

'I doubt it,' he smiled sadly, 'but sure, we can give it a try. Now come on, you've done enough for one day. Let's go.'

'Just let me finish up here.' He hesitated, looking at her, his green eyes full of concern. 'Really, PJ, I won't be long.'

He left and she continued to work. A few minutes later she heard the door open behind her. 'I'm nearly finished, PJ.' She looked up and saw Sebastian standing in the doorway. 'What do you want?'

'Marguerite told me that you and Ronan broke up. I'm sorry.'

'Are you?'

'Yes. I didn't want to hurt anyone.'

She looked at his confused expression and believed him. 'I think the problem is that you don't really think about other people at all, do you, Sebastian? Is that because you lost Marina or have you always been like this?'

His eyes slid away from hers. 'I have no excuses.'

'Just go, Sebastian,' Erin said, feeling weary and sad. When she had seen him in the doorway she'd thought that maybe he'd come to tell her that she was the one he really wanted.

'Not without saying goodbye,' he murmured, coming closer.

Erin looked at the sexy smile and those gorgeous eyes and thought, why not?

He bent and kissed her long and hard and then raised his head, his eyes teasing. 'You don't really want me to leave.'

'You're right, I don't,' she said, pulling away from him and crossing to the door. 'Now go.'

He shrugged and smiled. 'Goodbye, Erin,' he said, and walked past her into the night.

'Goodbye, Sebastian,' she whispered and steeled herself not to run after him and beg him to stay.

When Erin finally went into the house it was to find Sebastian and Sandra ensconced in the living room, deep in conversation. Sandra looked slightly embarrassed. 'I'm sorry, Erin.'

Erin looked at her in confusion. 'About what?'

Sandra shot Sebastian a questioning look and he just shrugged.

'Excuse me, it's been a long day,' Erin said and fled into the kitchen.

PJ was sitting at the table, drinking coffee and working on a crossword. He took off his reading glasses and looked up at her. 'Did you see the two of them inside?'

Erin went to the sink to wash her hands. 'Sebastian and Sandra? Yeah. What's going on?'

'Who knows, but they've been in there arguing for the last twenty minutes.'

'Arguing? About what?'

'I've no idea. In fact, I don't think I've even seen them talking together before now. What on earth could that be all about?'

'I'm too tired to care, PJ.'

'Will I make you a coffee?' he asked gently.

'No, I need something a little stronger.' Erin dried her hands and went over to the wine rack. 'Want to join me?'

'Why not?'

Rai curled up in bed and put on the TV. She couldn't believe the noise outside. The town was full of bloody journalists. Her first inclination had been to walk straight up to them and tell them who she was, but something stopped her. Instead she retraced her steps, went around the back lane, and tapped on the window of the flat next door to ask them to let her in.

Now she stared blankly at the quiz show on the box wondering what to do. She had no intention of going home to Dublin with her tail between her legs, that was for sure. Her mother would read her the Riot Act. Rai could imagine her horror when she saw that photo; she probably already had. There were six messages on her phone but she hadn't bothered checking them. As for Sebastian, she was convinced that he'd probably already left Dunbarra, if not the country. She could cry with frustration. To have managed very successfully to seduce him and then lose him again so quickly wasn't just unlucky, it was a downright tragedy. But, if Marguerite was telling the truth, then maybe it was over as soon as she walked out through his door. It was mind-blowing and less than flattering that he had been with some other woman just hours later. Who could it possibly be? Rai couldn't figure that out at all. Dunbarra wasn't exactly full of attractive young women. Erin was reasonably pretty in a girl-next-door kind of way but she was definitely the wrong side of thirty and everyone knew that Sebastian liked his women young. Marguerite probably lied in order to put her off. Rai was immensely cheered by the thought, although that still didn't solve her problems. If she stayed in Dunbarra there was a small chance of Sebastian getting in touch again; if she left he'd have no way of tracing her. If she stayed she'd be considered a minor celebrity by some and a slut by others. If she stayed, and she crawled back to Dijon, she could continue with her dream as Marguerite had advised, and when she had enough experience she'd be able to leave on her own terms. Rai decided, in a rare moment of sensible and rational thought, that this was the best course of action, although having to work with a frosty Marguerite and mocking Sean would not be easy. But she was tough, she could cope with them. She could cope with whatever was thrown at her if it meant reaching her goal.

The buzzer on her door went and she froze. At this hour of night it could only be a bloody journalist, but surely they wouldn't be that cheeky. It buzzed again but she continued to ignore it. Next minute there was a rap on the door. It was her neighbour.

'Rai, answer the door. It's a pizza-delivery guy.'

'I didn't order pizza.'

'Tell him yourself, I'm going back to bed.'

Rai pressed the buzzer. 'I didn't order pizza.'

'Good, because I didn't bring any.'

'Sebastian!' Rai threw open the door and flew down the stairs to let him in.

Chapter Thirty-Six

Sean was sitting at the bar in Dijon, eating a bacon sandwich and reading the latest instalment about Rai and Sebastian, when Marguerite came down. 'Howaya!' He smiled broadly while trying to slide the paper under the *Irish Times*.

'It's okay, Sean, you don't have to do that.'

'Don't pay too much attention to it, love. I'm sure most of it's lies. Paper doesn't refuse ink, as my father always used to say.'

She smiled. 'Thanks, Sean, but as it's about Sebastian, there's probably a fair amount of truth in it. Is Rai in yet?'

He shook his head. 'It's early. Why don't I make you a nice cup of coffee and you can relax for half an hour?'

'I would love a *café au lait*.'

'Coming up,' he said and went through to the kitchen.

Marguerite sat down in his place and pulled out the paper, a different tabloid from yesterday's. There was a small piece on the front page and a link to two pages inside. '*Mon dieu,*' she murmured, and with some trepidation she turned to the relevant pages. Apart from a grainy photo of Rai outside the restaurant and an even worse one of Sebastian walking away, all the photos were old ones of him with various women. There was a chronology of his affairs and how long they had lasted. Most of them had been ended by Sebastian. It seemed he had left a string of heartbroken or angry women in his wake. Marguerite read with interest. Some she knew of, but many she didn't. She scanned down the page in search of his most recent relationship and found a name that caused her to stop and think. According to the author, the current woman in Sebastian's life was Lexi van Dere, a rich, twice-divorced socialite from New York. She read and reread the article but could find no mention of Marina, the girl who had died. Marguerite began to feel uneasy as she remembered her initial suspicion when Erin had told her Sebastian's story. But perhaps this girl had been so special he had kept her completely hidden from the public eye and had used this Lexi as a decoy.

Sean emerged with a large cup of coffee and two chocolate biscuits in the saucer. 'For energy,' he said with a wink.

'Sean, what would I do without you?' She took a grateful sip from the steaming cup.

He leaned against the bar and crossed his arms. 'So,

what now? Do you think Rai will stay with us? More to the point, do you want her to?'

'I'm not sure how she will feel about it but I'm happy for her to continue here. She's so young, Sean. We can't blame her for being swept away in the romance of sleeping with a movie star. If anyone is to blame it's Sebastian.'

'I suppose you're right and she's a good little worker. Mary is thrilled that my hours are reduced and, I must admit, I do feel better for it.'

She patted his hand. 'If she leaves, I promise I'll find someone else.'

He groaned. 'I hope it doesn't come to that. I'd hate to go through all that initiation period again.'

She smiled. 'We'll cope.'

He walked to the window that looked out on the car park. 'Speaking of coping, what do you want to do about them?'

'Who?' She stood up and went to join him. 'Oh, really, this is ridiculous!' There were three vans out front and people were standing around in groups, chatting cameras at the ready.

'Do you want me to threaten them with the police?' he offered.

'Give me a moment.' Marguerite went out to the telephone in the hall. Erin answered immediately, sounding somewhat subdued. 'Erin, it's me.'

'Hi, Marguerite.'

'Is he still there?' she asked.

'No.'

'Good. Can I come over? I need to talk to you.'

'Please don't tell me I'm in the papers this morning,' Erin begged.

'No, *chérie*, you are not.'

'Then I'll put on the coffee.'

Marguerite went back in to Sean. 'I'm going over to the Gatehouse, Sean. And, on the way out, I will give them the bad news that my brother has left.'

'Thank God for that, but they'll probably hang around anyway to see Rai.'

'They can hang around some place else and I shall tell them so. Do you mind if I borrow your paper?'

Sean shook his head. 'Help yourself.'

Marguerite tucked it under her arm. 'Thanks, Sean. I'll be back in time to do lunch.'

Erin never heard the door. She was sitting at the kitchen table, the breakfast dishes were piled up in the sink, she hadn't cleaned the pans of grill and there was a mountain of laundry in the utility room waiting for her attention. To cap it all, when Nora had phoned with yet another excuse as to why she couldn't come to work, Erin had told her not to bother coming in at all any more and hung up.

The back door opened and Marguerite came in. 'Here you are! I've been standing on your doorstep for the last five minutes. What if I had been a customer?' she teased.

'I'd say, "Go away."'

Marguerite sat down opposite her and sighed. 'My brother has much to answer for.'

'It's not because of him – well, not entirely. I'm closing the bed and breakfast at the end of the month. I've had a couple of cancellations so it's not worth my while staying open, especially as I've just fired Nora.' Erin stood up and went to pour the coffee.

Marguerite stared at her. ''I don't believe you have finally seen sense and got rid of that useless woman.' Her eyes travelled around the dishevelled kitchen. 'But how will you manage without her?'

'I've been managing without her for years,' Erin said, smiling. 'Wasn't that your point? Anyway, once I close I'll just have to keep the rooms dust-free, it will be easy.' She turned and caught Marguerite's sceptical look. 'This is different.' She waved a hand around her. 'This is just me feeling sorry for myself. Twenty minutes and I'll have it gleaming again.'

'Let me help.' Marguerite started to get up.

'No. Sit. Here's your coffee.' Erin carried the two mugs to the table while Marguerite cleared a space.

'So did you get any answers from my brother before he left?'

Erin shook her head. 'I didn't ask. To be honest, I'm not sure I care, although I am curious about Sandra's involvement.'

'Pardon?' Marguerite looked at her, confused.

'Oh, sorry, I forgot you don't know. When I came in

last night, Sandra and Sebastian were in the sitting room, arguing about something. From what I can gather they know each other. In fact, I think they actually came here together.'

'No, that doesn't make sense. Sebastian has never even mentioned her. And what about her husband?'

'I don't know, Marguerite. But she came to me this morning and asked me to make up her bill. She's leaving later today.'

'But that is very strange. Aren't you curious, Erin?' Marguerite looked incredulous. 'Don't you want to know what's going on?'

Erin dragged her hair back from her face with tired fingers. 'What difference does it make? He's gone now and that's an end to it.'

Marguerite looked down at her hands and said nothing.

Erin's eyes narrowed. 'Why did you want to see me, Marguerite?'

She raised her head. 'I did not lie. There is nothing about you in the papers.'

'But?' Erin prompted.

'There is rather a lot about Sebastian and the women he has been with.' Marguerite pulled the newspaper from behind her on the chair. 'There is no mention of Marina.'

For a moment what Marguerite said didn't really register with Erin. She felt so tired she didn't think she was capable of rational thought. 'So?'

'She was the reason he had a breakdown, the reason he came to Dunbarra. Isn't that correct?'

Erin nodded.

'But, according to the paper, he is currently dating some rich socialite.'

'They got it wrong. Newspapers get things wrong all the time, Marguerite,' Erin reminded her. 'Especially rags like this one.'

'It is strange there is no mention of her at all,' Marguerite insisted. 'I'm beginning to wonder if she ever existed.'

'That's ridiculous, Marguerite. You must remember the state of Sebastian when he first came. He was completely distraught and he looked like hell. Marina was real and her death had to be quite recent.'

Marguerite nodded. 'Yes, I know, and so I thought perhaps he protected her from the press and they led a quiet life together. That maybe this socialite was some sort of decoy.'

'He told me that Marina didn't like his life,' Erin remembered, 'and that she hated it when they were photographed together or were hounded by the press.'

'Ah, well, then, it makes sense.'

'No. no, it doesn't. You see, because she felt that way, he threw lots of parties so that all his friends could meet her in his home, away from the spotlight.'

'So?' Marguerite asked.

'If all these people knew Marina then they would have known about her addiction and they certainly would have known about her death.' Erin looked down at the two-page spread and then back at Marguerite. 'So why isn't it in the newspaper? How could Sebastian possibly have kept it a secret?'

Marguerite put a hand to her mouth and shook her head. 'He couldn't,' she said simply, and stood up.

Erin watched her cross to the door. 'Where are you going?'

'To fetch Madame Bell. I have a feeling she may be able to enlighten us. Which room is she in?'

'Number three, second door on the right.'

Marguerite came back down alone and obviously fuming. 'She refused to tell me anything until she talked to Sebastian. The nerve of the woman!'

'So what now?'

'She's calling him.'

'How?' Erin looked at her watch. 'He'll be at the airport and he doesn't have a mobile phone.'

'Apparently he does.'

'So I was right, then. Sebastian and Sandra do know each other.'

'Definitely.'

'How strange. What on earth can all of this be about?'

'I don't know, Erin, but I am so sorry I let Sebastian come here. Can you ever forgive me?'

Erin turned to her. 'Don't be ridiculous, Marguerite, you are not responsible for Sebastian. You were just trying to do the right thing.'

'Yes, and I feel that he has tricked me. I won't be happy until I know exactly why he did come and what on earth Madame Bell has to do with it.'

'If you make me a coffee, I'll tell you,' Sandra said from the doorway.

Erin stood up. 'Marguerite, why don't you and Sandra go into the dining room and I'll bring the coffee?'

When she brought in the tray, the two women were sitting in silence, waiting for her. Erin set out the mugs, sat down and looked at Sandra. 'We're listening.'

Sandra took a sip of coffee and looked at each woman in turn. 'I'm sorry about this and I'm furious that Sebastian put me in this position, it was not part of the plan.'

'Plan?' Marguerite said, and frowned.

'I'm an acting coach,' Sandra explained.

Marguerite shook her head in disbelief. 'Sebastian has been acting for years. He is one of the highest-paid actors in Hollywood. Why would he need a coach?'

'You are right, he is hugely successful,' Sandra agreed. 'But he has been approached to do a play, and the stage is a completely different animal.'

'Pardon?' Marguerite looked even more confused.

'Sandra is helping him prepare to play a stage role,' Erin explained. She looked back at Sandra. 'But why all the secrecy? Why did you pretend to come here with your husband? Why did you and Sebastian pretend not to know each other?'

'One thing at a time, please. Sebastian's agent approached me, asking me if I would help him prepare for the role. I wasn't keen, to be honest. Not many actors are successful when they move from celluloid to stage. And if he bombed, well, it would reflect badly on me.'

'But you were persuaded,' Erin said grimly.

Sandra smiled and shrugged. 'The fee was generous. But I told him, straight off, that it would only work if we got right away from Hollywood. We needed to go somewhere where he could get into character and, preferably, not be recognized. Well, you can imagine, it's not easy to find a place like that. Sebastian's face is well known all over the world. Then he told me about Dunbarra, saying that even if anyone did recognize him they wouldn't care. I thought it sounded perfect although he was worried that you, Marguerite, would smell a rat. He said you knew him too well, that he wouldn't be able to fool you.'

'Why not just be honest with her?' Erin asked.

Sandra shook her head. 'He would never be able to get into character if she knew it was all an act; it would totally defeat the purpose. So Sebastian went to a clinic in New Mexico for a couple of months before he came here. We got some photos taken there and his agent has been drip-feeding them to the press over the last few months to cover his absence.'

'But why was he in a clinic?' Marguerite asked, mystified. 'Is he sick?'

'No, we wanted him to lose a few pounds so he'd look the part. The weight loss, the haircut and a few nights with no sleep . . .' Sandra grinned. 'Well, you saw for yourselves how effective it was.'

Erin felt sick. 'You mean he deliberately made himself look like that just to fool us?'

'Sure. Actors do that kind of thing all the time. He was pretty convincing, wasn't he?'

'He certainly was,' Marguerite muttered, looking furious.

'But he was still nervous you'd see through him, Marguerite. That's why he never talked to you about Marina. He wasn't convinced that he could carry it off. You were going to be his final test before he left. When he felt he could make you believe in her, then he'd know, we both would, that he was ready for the stage role.'

Erin looked at Sandra. 'So instead you chose me to . . . practise on.'

Sandra completely missed the hurt in Erin's voice and smiled. 'That's right.'

'Where does Hazel come into this? And, for that matter, Rai?' Erin asked, avoiding Marguerite's gaze. The kindness in her friend's eyes would be enough to destroy her composure, and she couldn't let that happen. It seemed that Sandra didn't know the extent of her involvement with Sebastian, which was something.

'Neither of them was part of the plan,' Sandra assured her. 'But Sebastian liked Hazel and her work. He also thought that being around someone so damaged would help him practise his empathy.'

'What?' Marguerite's eyes widened in horror.

'I know, I thought it was a bit of a stretch.' Sandra nodded solemnly. 'But he did pretty well, I think.'

'That's preposterous,' Erin protested. 'You can't play around with people's emotions like that, especially someone as vulnerable as Hazel.'

Sandra's expression grew defensive. 'I told you, it was his idea. Anyway, it all worked out fine in the end. She's being treated in the best clinic in the UK, thanks to Sebastian. He's a very generous guy.'

'How much longer was Sebastian planning to stay?' Erin asked quietly.

'Another month, probably less. Rehearsals start in November. But Sebastian was in no hurry to leave; he's a perfectionist and wanted to keep practising.'

'Yes, but practising what?' Marguerite murmured.

Sandra frowned. 'I warned him: no sex. But that guy just can't keep his pants zipped.'

Marguerite was careful not to look at Erin. 'At least it was just once and, like you said, he was about ready to go home anyway.'

'We should have left as soon as he moved Hazel into that clinic, but he didn't want to go.' Sandra looked at Marguerite and smiled. 'I think he enjoyed being here with you.'

Erin met Marguerite's eyes. 'So was Marina a total fabrication?' she asked.

'She was,' Sandra admitted with an apologetic smile.

'And your husband?' Marguerite asked.

Sandra chuckled. 'I've been divorced for five years but I invented a husband because I thought it might look odd, a middle-aged woman travelling alone to a small town in the middle of nowhere and staying for so long.'

'And why were you so interested in everyone's lives?'

'Mainly to distract you from Sebastian,' Sandra explained, 'and to stop you making the connection between us.'

'What about Paddy?'

'What about him?' Sandra glanced at her watch. 'So, ladies, is that it? Can I go now?'

'You're not going anywhere.'

The three women looked up to see PJ in the doorway.

Chapter Thirty-Seven

Sandra groaned. 'I've told Erin and Marguerite everything. If you have any questions, ask them.'

Erin looked worriedly at PJ's face. He was flushed, there were beads of sweat on his forehead and he was clearly furious. 'Sit down. I'll get you some coffee.'

He shook his head. 'No. Thanks, Erin, but I think I'd choke on it.'

'Don't get my hopes up,' Sandra drawled.

He glared at her. 'You and Sebastian have abused the trust of everyone in this town,' his eyes flickered to Erin, 'some more than others.' Then he looked at Marguerite. 'I'm sorry, my dear, but your brother has behaved abominably.'

'Don't apologize, I completely agree,' Marguerite assured him.

'And to play around with Hazel's feelings like that, was criminal,' he continued.

'You asked him to talk to her, to help her,' Sandra reminded him, 'and he did.'

'I wanted him to be a friend to her, not use her.'
Erin looked at him with concern as his voice rose. 'PJ,
calm down.'

'Yes, PJ, calm down,' Sandra agreed, with a mocking smile. 'What are you getting so worked up about?
Are you upset that Sebastian could help her and you
couldn't? I must say, I'm surprised. I thought it was
the kid you were into—'

'You bad-minded bitch.' PJ took a step towards
Sandra and raised his hand to strike her, but
Marguerite blocked his way.

'No, PJ, don't.'

He slumped against her and Marguerite stumbled
under his weight. 'PJ?'

Erin caught him from behind and eased him down
gently on to the floor. His eyes were closed and his
face was grey. 'PJ? PJ, can you hear me?'

His head lolled back and Erin put her fingers on his
neck, feeling for a pulse.

'Is he breathing?' Marguerite asked.

Erin looked at her with frightened eyes. 'I'm not
sure.'

'Dial 999,' Marguerite barked at Sandra, 'quickly.'

Sandra ran from the room as Marguerite loosened
PJ's collar. She put her head on his chest to check for a
heartbeat. 'I can't hear anything.'

'Oh, my God. PJ, come on, wake up, talk to me!'
Erin said, rubbing his hands between hers.

'Do you know CPR?' Marguerite asked.

'I'm not sure. I think so.'

'Watch me carefully. When I get tired, you will take over. It could be fifteen minutes or more before an ambulance gets here and we must keep it up until then. Erin, do you understand?'

'Yes. I'll do whatever you say.'

It seemed like hours before they were finally relieved by the emergency services. Sandra had disappeared, so Erin had left the front door open. When she heard the ambulance pull up outside, she ran to the door. 'In here,' she called and returned to where Marguerite continued with the CPR. The two paramedics were hot on her heels.

The girl crouched down beside Marguerite. 'I'm Valerie and that's Ciaran. How long has he been down?'

While Marguerite filled her in, Ciaran turned to Erin. 'Has he any history of heart disease?'

'No.' Erin frowned. 'At least I don't think so. He never said anything. I'm afraid I've only known him a few years.'

'Okay, don't worry about it.' He smiled at her. 'Do you know if he's on any medication?'

'Yes, he takes something for blood pressure.'

'Good. Do you think you could find those tablets?' Erin nodded and turned to go upstairs. 'And bring back any other tablets you find, or any prescriptions,' he called after her and then knelt down beside PJ. 'Hi.' He nodded at Marguerite. 'Are you his daughter?'

She shook her head. 'No. PJ is a guest here.'

'Is there any family we should contact?'

Marguerite frowned. 'I'm not sure. I don't think so. Erin will know.'

Valerie looked up at him. 'We're going to have to shock him.'

'Move back, please,' Ciaran said, and opened up the defibrillator.

Marguerite stood up and backed away.

Erin came into the room, brandishing the medicine she'd found. She pulled up short when she saw what they were doing. 'Oh, God, he's going to die, isn't he?'

'Not if I can help it,' Valerie assured her. 'Clear!' she called and pressed the paddles to PJ's chest.

Erin and Marguerite clutched each other and watched as PJ's body jolted.

'Come on, PJ,' Valerie muttered, but Ciaran listened with the stethoscope and shook his head.

'Go again,' he said.

'Please don't die,' Erin sobbed as Valerie picked up the paddles again.

'Clear!'

Ciaran put the stethoscope to PJ's chest, nodded and smiled up at Erin. 'He's back.'

'Oh, thank God,' Erin gasped, tears streaming down her face. 'Is he going to be all right?'

'It's too early to say,' Valerie said as they hoisted PJ on to the trolley. 'Anyone want to come with him in the ambulance?'

'I will,' Erin said immediately.

'I'll follow in the car,' Marguerite promised.

At the hospital, Erin was shoved into a tiny room to wait while PJ was wheeled off down the corridor. It was about ten minutes before someone came to talk to her. She whirled around. 'Is he okay?'

'Mr Ward is comfortable. Are you a relative?'

'I'm his daughter, Erin,' she said, looking him straight in the eye.

'Dr Nugent.' He shook her hand and then waved her to a seat while lowering his long frame on to a stool. 'Your father has had a massive coronary and there is a lot of damage to heart muscle. Also, three of his arteries are partially blocked.'

'But you can fix him.'

'We need to carry out a triple-bypass.'

'That's a very successful operation, right?'

'It is, but I'm afraid your father has been unconscious for some time so there are no guarantees. And if he does come through the operation there may still be brain damage.'

'When will you know?' she whispered.

'Not until he wakes up, I'm afraid.'

'When are you going to operate on him?'

'As soon as a theatre becomes free. As his next of kin you'll need to sign this release form for me.'

'No problem.' Erin took it and scrawled her signature on the bottom.

'Would you like to sit with him?' He gave her a kind smile.

Erin swallowed. 'Yes, please.'

'Come with me.'

Marguerite found her sitting in a cubicle, PJ on a trolley beside her, wires coming out of him all over the place. A nurse stood on the other side of him, writing up a chart. 'Can I come in?' she whispered.

The nurse waved her in and then turned to Erin. 'They should be coming for your father in the next ten minutes or so,' she said and left.

'Father?' Marguerite sat down on PJ's other side.

Erin shrugged. 'They don't tell you anything unless you're a relative.'

Marguerite nodded her understanding. 'So what's happening?'

'They're going to do a triple-bypass but they don't know if that will be enough. He was out for so long—' Erin broke off.

'He is going to be fine. Don't doubt that. Is there anything I can do?' Marguerite looked at Erin, her eyes full of compassion.

Tears filled Erin's eyes. 'I wish there was.'

'Shouldn't we call someone? Surely he must have some family somewhere.'

'He does, Marguerite.' Erin smiled through her tears. 'And I'm right here.'

Marguerite stared at her, but before she could say

anything, the nurse returned with a porter to take PJ down to theatre.

'I need a cigarette,' Marguerite said, as they watched them wheel him away. 'Come on.' Putting a gentle arm around Erin, she guided her outside. 'Want one?' she asked when they were in the sheltered smoking area next to the car park.

Erin nodded, took the cigarette with shaking fingers and cupped her hand around it as Marguerite lit it.

Marguerite took a long drag before she spoke. 'Are you PJ's daughter, Erin?'

Erin nodded.

Marguerite gasped in suprise. 'I can't believe it. But I don't understand. Why is it a secret? Don't you want people to know?' Her face fell. 'Or doesn't PJ?'

'He doesn't know, Marguerite.'

'It sounds like this could be a long story.' Marguerite looked around and saw a bench a few feet away. 'Let's sit down.'

When they were sitting side by side on the stone bench, Erin started to talk. 'My father died just over a year before I came to Dunbarra.'

'Yes, I remember you telling me that.'

'He was a good, gentle and quiet man, Marguerite. I adored him. After the funeral, when everyone had gone, my mother told me that he wasn't actually my father at all.'

'*Mon Dieu*, what was she thinking?' Marguerite shook her head, her eyes wide.

Erin sighed. 'I think in some sort of misguided way she thought it would be a comfort to me to know that my real father was still out there somewhere, but I was just devastated. It turned out my father was a bit too quiet for her and she'd had an affair, with PJ. Well, it wasn't really an affair by the sounds of it, more of a quick fling.' She shrugged. 'I didn't know what to make of it. I was so angry with her and disgusted and furious with PJ too, for messing about with a married woman. The only consolation was that at least my father didn't know. It would have destroyed him. He worshipped my mother. I couldn't deal with it at all, Marguerite. I was grieving for my father, angry with my mother, curious about PJ. I was basically a mess and my work suffered.'

'Was that when you were working in the small hotel in Dublin?' Marguerite asked.

'Yes, that's right. I'd forgotten I told you about all this.'

Marguerite raised an eyebrow. 'Not all, it seems.'

Erin pulled a face. 'Sorry. So, yes, I was drinking too much and generally behaving badly. In the middle of all that my mum found herself a new man. That was the final straw.'

'Is that when you started to date the married man?'

'Date is a kind word, Marguerite.' Erin laughed. 'I don't think we ever actually went anywhere together other than bed. He was rich, successful, at least twenty years older than me and, yes, married, but I didn't care. I seemed to want to court danger. Of course the inevitable happened. We were caught, unfortunately by his wife, and my boss suggested that maybe I should "consider my future".'

Marguerite frowned. 'You lost your job?'

Erin nodded. 'That's when I decided to go and look for PJ. It wasn't hard. Mum knew quite a lot about him and I soon discovered where he was living. It was in a small village outside Newbridge in County Kildare. You should have seen me, Marguerite,' she laughed. 'I was like some kind of second-rate PI. I would park down the street from his house, slouch down behind the wheel, and watch him coming and going. I did that a couple of times a week for months but I never had the courage to go up and knock on his door. Most of the time I just saw him; his wife didn't seem to go out that much. And then one day I saw her being taken away in an ambulance. I followed them to this clinic. She never came out again and PJ visited every day. I watched him grow older and wearier before my eyes. He didn't seem the villain that I'd created in my head. He was just a broken man whose wife was sick. At this stage I started looking for a new job. My mother was getting very agitated by my strange behaviour – I never told her where I went when I disappeared – and I knew I couldn't live off her indefinitely. I got a temporary position in a hotel in Newbridge. I didn't go near PJ for a couple of weeks as I settled into the job. By the time I got a chance to check on him again, there was a For Sale sign up outside his house.'

Marguerite put a comforting hand on her arm, but said nothing.

'I waited for ages, but there was no sign of him and so I went to the clinic and was relieved to see his car there. When he eventually came out, I followed him. He didn't go home, though. He drove for over an hour, all the way to this guest house on the far side of Mullingar.'

Marguerite's face lit up. 'The Gatehouse!'

Erin smiled. 'Yes. The new job took up a lot of my time and I didn't go to spy on him as much. The contract was coming to an end and I had applied for a couple of other jobs but I couldn't find anything suitable. To be honest, I wasn't trying very hard.'

'It is understandable. But why didn't you approach him, Erin? With his wife in hospital it was safe without knocking the apple cart.'

'I know, but he seemed to have enough on his plate and I was still annoyed with him. But not annoyed enough to upset him. I couldn't tell him who I was, not then.'

'So what happened next?' Marguerite prompted.

'I finished up at the hotel in Newbridge, I told my mother that I was going on holiday and the next day I checked in to the Gatehouse.'

Marguerite hugged her. 'I thank God for that day! You have become my very good friend.'

Erin hugged her back. 'I'm glad too.'

'So then you got to know PJ?'

'Yes. He persuaded Ivy to let him plant some vegetables and I pretended an interest in gardening as a way of getting to know him better. And not only did I discover that the man was pure gold,' she chuckled, 'I actually got to like gardening too. The more I got to know PJ, the less I could understand how he'd ever got involved with my mother. She really wasn't his type at all.'

'Oh, Erin, you know what men are like. They don't always use their heads to make the decisions!'

Erin laughed. 'No, they don't, but he just seemed so crazy about his wife.'

'And I'm sure your mother loved your father but,' Marguerite was philosophical, 'these things happen.'

'Anyway, he finally told me his story and how he had to sell his home to pay for Isabelle to stay in the nursing home.'

'What was wrong with her?'

'Alzheimer's.'

Marguerite winced. 'That is sad. Was she very serious at this stage?'

'There were days when she knew him but more when she didn't.'

'But why did he move so far away?'

'He couldn't stand his old friends and neighbours asking about her, sympathizing with him, pitying him; it made things more difficult. He had this idea that if he moved somewhere where nobody knew him or Isabelle, he could be stronger for her.'

'So he made the Gatehouse his home.'

'I don't think that was his original plan. I think he meant to move even further away once she had died. But he fell in love with the garden. He was a horticulturist by trade, you know.'

'Yes, I knew that.' Marguerite nodded.

'And when he was working he was able to forget about his problems for a while.'

'Now that, I can understand,' Marguerite said softly. 'I spent morning, noon and night in the kitchen after our baby son died. I don't think I'd have made it through otherwise.'

Erin squeezed her hand. 'You would have been a wonderful mother.'

Marguerite sniffed. 'It was not to be. And if my son had lived, Mark and I would not have moved to Dunbarra and opened Dijon. *C'est la vie*. But why do you think PJ told you his secret when he has kept the truth from everyone else?'

'Ivy had announced she was selling up. PJ and I were both distraught but for very different reasons. He had found a new home of sorts and I couldn't bear the thought of losing him. I told him about Dad dying and about losing my job in Dublin and that I didn't want to return. And he told me about Isabelle.'

'I see.'

'And that's when he suggested that I take over the

Gatehouse. Well, at first I thought it was a ridiculous idea but, once he'd planted the seed, I couldn't stop thinking about it. I'm not naturally the kind of person who can just sit around doing nothing, and I was beginning to feel restless. Also, I could see that the Gatehouse had a lot of potential. So I went home and talked to my mother about it. I think she was relieved that I wanted to do something constructive. She agreed to put up half the money and I got a loan from the bank for the other half.'

'I remember the day you told us.' Marguerite smiled. 'We were so glad that you were making Dunbarra your home.'

'It was the happiest I'd been in a very long time,' Erin admitted. 'I finally felt that I was doing something useful with my life. And it was such a bonus that PJ was going to be a part of it. He couldn't afford to invest in the Gatehouse, but it was his idea to develop the garden into a proper business and we are equal partners in that.'

Marguerite looked at her in surprise. 'I didn't know that.'

'He won't take a penny from me, though, even though the profit more than covers his bed and board.' Erin shrugged. 'He didn't want people to know he was involved. I'm not sure why. But he's always been quite a private person. I agreed immediately, anyway, simply to keep him close. I never expected it to be such a success.'

'And still you didn't tell him you were his daughter.' Marguerite shook her head. 'Why not?'

'I don't really know. Somehow, with Isabelle so sick, it seemed wrong to remind him of a time when he'd cheated on her.'

'But she's dead now. There's nothing stopping you telling him the truth.'

'He's just had a heart attack, Marguerite. I think the last thing he needs right now is a shock like that.'

Marguerite looked at her in amusement. 'He's lost his wife, thinks he's alone in the world, and you think that finding out the girl that he obviously loves is, in fact, his daughter will be a shock? You are going to make him the happiest man in the world. You are going to give him a reason to get better, a reason to live.'

Erin thought of how PJ had already lost Hazel and Gracie and how down he'd been lately. Perhaps Marguerite was right. Perhaps it was time to tell PJ the truth.

'Don't worry about it now, my friend,' Marguerite said, standing up and stretching. 'You've waited this long, a little longer won't do any harm.' She pulled Erin to her feet. 'Let's go to the hospital chapel and say a prayer.'

Erin looked at her in amazement. 'I didn't know you were religious.'

'Isn't everyone at times like these?'

Erin took her arm. 'You're right. Let's go.'

Chapter Thirty-Eight

When they emerged from the chapel, Erin persuaded Marguerite to go home. 'You have the restaurant to think of and there's nothing you can do hanging around here.'

Marguerite agreed reluctantly. 'But I'll be back,' she assured Erin.

After seeing Marguerite to her car, Erin went back into the hospital, roamed the corridors for a while, glanced through a magazine that a kindly nurse had lent her and forced down a sandwich in the canteen. She even returned to the chapel, finding the peace somewhat calming.

Then she went back to the waiting room that she'd come to hate. There was something so depressing about its bland decor, and garish red plastic chairs. She wondered how many families had sat here waiting for news and how often it was bad. The door creaked open and she looked up to see Ronan standing there.

'I thought you could use some company,' he said.

'Oh, Ronan.' She stood up, and when he opened his arms she stepped into them.

He held her tightly, patting her back as if she were a child. After a moment, Erin stepped away and smiled through her tears. 'Thanks, I needed that.'

'Isn't there anywhere else we can go?' He looked around the room, frowning. 'This place is bloody depressing.'

'I was just thinking the same thing when you came in,' she said, laughing through her tears. 'Fancy a cup of rather average coffee?'

'Why not?'

Erin stopped off at the nurses' station to let them know where she'd be and then led Ronan downstairs to the canteen.

'Marguerite called me after she left you,' he told her when they had found a seat. 'I told her not to bother coming back, that I'd come.' His eyes held hers. 'Is that okay with you?'

'More than okay,' she told him, tears welling up again.

'You've had quite a day.'

'Oh, Ronan, if it hadn't been for Marguerite, I don't think PJ would have made it this far.'

He squeezed her hand. 'I'm sure he'll pull through, Erin. He's a strong man.'

'He has to. I don't know what I'd do without him.'

'I sent one of the lads round to water the garden,'

Ronan told her. 'He'll come again in the morning so you can give him a list of what needs doing.'

'Thanks, that's really good of you, but are you sure you can spare him?'

'No problem.' he said, with a humourless grin. 'I got a call last night. Fenton's have gone into receivership.'

'What?' Erin stared at him, trying to take in what he was saying. Fenton's was one of the biggest chains of supermarkets in Ireland and Ronan's main customer.

Ronan sighed. 'I know, I couldn't believe it either. Still, when I heard about PJ it put things into perspective.'

'But what will you do?'

'In the short term I'll send all the younger birds off for processing. I can't afford to feed and keep all of them and they will fetch the most money.'

Erin searched his face, noticing for the first time how tired and anxious he looked. 'And in the long term?' she asked.

'I'm not sure, but I may have to cut my losses and get out of the business altogether.'

Erin's eyes widened. 'And do what?' Ronan loved his farm. She couldn't imagine him doing anything else.

'I honestly don't know, Erin, but I think we're all going to have to be creative to get through this recession. I was talking to Mark earlier and he's concerned about Dijon and the fishing business, too.'

'But they're doing okay, aren't they?'

'At the moment, yes, but Mark thinks that as people tighten their belts they won't eat out as often and fishing trips will become a luxury that people will do without.'

Erin sighed. 'I think we're all in for tough times. The Gatehouse hasn't done so well this season but I thought I could rely on the market garden for a steady income, but who knows?' She looked at her watch. 'I need to get back upstairs. PJ should be out of surgery soon.'

'I'll come with you,' he said as they stood up.

'Are you sure?'

He looked into her eyes and nodded. 'I'm certain.'

'Thanks, Ronan.' She gave him a shaky smile. 'I'm not sure I could do this alone.'

He put a protective arm around her shoulders. 'You don't have to.'

As they approached the nurses' station, the surgeon was there, still in his greens. Erin stopped and clutched Ronan's sleeve. 'That's him. That's the surgeon who operated on PJ.'

'Then let's go and talk to him.'

But Erin couldn't move. This doctor could be about to give her great news or the worst news in the world. But she knew that he wouldn't have to say a word. She'd know, just by looking into his eyes, how the surgery had gone. The nurse turned and spotted her and pointed. The surgeon spun round and smiled, and Erin felt her legs start to give way. 'Oh, thank God,' she murmured as she fell.

Ronan caught her before she hit the ground and lifted her in his arms.

'In here.' The nurse led him into a ward and waved to an empty bed. The surgeon followed.

Erin was already feeling better and she tried to sit up.

'Take it easy,' he told her. She looked up at him and he smiled. 'It's good news, Erin. The operation was a success.'

'So he's going to be okay?'

'He regained consciousness for a few minutes and was making perfect sense, which is a very good sign.'

'Can I see him?' she asked.

'He's still in recovery but they will transfer him to ICU soon and then you can go in for a few minutes. Why don't you rest here for a while and I'll get someone to bring you a nice cup of sweet tea?'

'No, no tea. I've enough caffeine in my system to keep me awake for a week.'

'No wonder you fainted.' He laughed and strolled away.

Ronan came to sit beside her. 'You see,' he smiled. 'I told you he was going to be fine.'

Erin pushed back her hair and smiled at him although there were tears rolling down her cheeks.

He wiped them away with gentle fingers. 'Don't cry, Erin. Everything's going to be fine now.'

She looked at him. 'Is it?'

'Are we still talking about PJ?' Ronan asked.

'No.'

He looked away. 'Let's just get through today, Erin.'

'So it's not okay, is it?' she said, through her tears. 'You'll never be able to forgive me. I don't blame you, you know. I can never forgive myself—'

He put a finger to her lips to stop her. 'Give me time, Erin. I'm here, aren't I?'

She nodded, smiling.

He stood up. 'So would you like that cup of tea or can I get you anything else?'

'Nothing,' she said, sitting up and swinging her feet to the floor.

'Where do you think you're going?' he asked.

'I'm going to find a ladies' room so I can tidy myself up. I can't let PJ see me in this state, now can I?'

When PJ opened his eyes and saw Erin at his side he smiled. 'If Marguerite hadn't stopped me hitting Sandra, she might have been lying here instead of me,' he croaked.

'And you would have been in a jail cell,' she retorted. 'How are you feeling?'

'A bit woozy. What time is it?'

'Almost eight.'

'At night?' He shook his head in disbelief. 'I hope you haven't been here all this time.'

'Where else would I be?'

'Looking after your guests and watering the plants. You're going to have a lot on your plate while I'm in here, Erin.'

'Stop worrying, PJ. Ronan has sent a lad over to help out tonight and we can have him for as long as we need him.'

Despite his grogginess PJ looked at her with a twinkle in his eye. 'Did he indeed? Wasn't that very good of him?'

'It was. He sends his best, by the way. They would only let you have one visitor.'

'He's here?' PJ's eyes widened.

'He's here.'

PJ sighed. 'He's a good man.'

'Yes.'

'Don't muck it up this time, darling.'

'Don't go jumping to conclusions,' Erin warned him. 'He's doing it for you as much as for me.'

'He's a good man,' PJ repeated, his eyes closing.

A nurse approached and put a hand on Erin's arm. 'Your dad should really get some rest now.'

'He's not my dad,' Erin said, avoiding the nurse's eyes.

'More's the pity,' PJ said with a sleepy smile.

'Well, no daughter could have been more caring,' the nurse assured him. 'She's been worrying herself sick about you all day.'

He held out his hand and Erin took it. 'Go home, darling. Get some rest.'

She bent to kiss him. 'I'm so glad you're all right, PJ. I don't know what I'd do if—'

'Now, now, none of that,' he said as her eyes filled up. 'I'm not going anywhere.'

'Good. I can't afford a gardener,' she joked. 'See you tomorrow.'

Ronan stood up as she came out of the ward. 'How is he?'

'Good.' She nodded and tried to smile but began to cry again.

'Hey, you're supposed to be happy,' he said, putting an arm around her.

'I'm sorry. I suppose I'm just tired and emotional.'

'Come on, I'll take you home.'

She looked up at him. 'Are you sure?'

'What kind of a silly question is that?' he asked, and taking her hand he led her towards the lift.

Ronan led her out to the jeep, sat her into the passenger seat and put on her belt. She let him, hardly aware of her surroundings as she relived the events of the day.

'You know it's going to be a while before he's back on his feet,' he said when they were on their way home.

'I'm just relieved he's alive. I hadn't really thought beyond that.'

'Well, like I said, you can have Billy for as long as you need him.'

'Thanks, Ronan. It won't be for long. Now that –' she was about to say Sebastian but quickly corrected herself – 'my guests have all left, I'm going to close the guest house for the season and concentrate on the market garden.'

He looked over at her. 'And who'll look after PJ?'

She sighed. 'We'll manage.'

He swung the car into the driveway and pulled up in front of the house. 'You're not alone, Erin,' he said, turning in his seat to look at her.

She smiled.

'There are lots of people in this town who'll be glad to help,' he continued.

Erin swallowed hard and nodded. 'Do you want to come in?' she asked in a small voice.

'No, you're tired. Get a good night's sleep. You'll feel better in the morning.'

Erin reached across to kiss him and he turned his head slightly so her lips grazed his cheek. She pulled back and climbed out of the jeep. She opened the front door and then looked back at him. 'I'm sorry, Ronan, for everything.'

He nodded. 'I know,' he said and drove away.

Feeling exhausted, Erin closed the front door and began to lock up. She went into the kitchen to check the back door and jumped when she saw the figure at the table. 'Sandra! Dear God, you frightened the life out of me. I thought you'd gone.'

Sandra rose to her feet, looking pale and haggard. 'I couldn't leave until I knew if PJ was okay.'

'He'll live, no thanks to you,' Erin retorted.

'I'm so sorry, Erin. I've been reliving those moments all day and I can't believe that I said those things.'

Erin relented when she saw tears fill Sandra's eyes. 'His heart was damaged. You're not responsible for that. He could have had a heart attack at any time. I'm just grateful it didn't happen when he was alone in the garden. As it is, he's just had a triple-bypass and it seems to have been successful.'

'Thank God,' Sandra whispered. 'And thank you for telling me, Erin. I'll go now.'

'Don't be silly, Sandra. Stay the night.'

'Are you sure?' Sandra looked down at her.

Erin nodded, and going to the fridge she took out a bottle of wine. 'Fancy a drink?'

'Are you kidding?' Sandra gave a throaty laugh.

Erin filled two glasses. 'To a hell of a day,' she said, raising hers.

'Amen.' Sandra downed half her glass. 'God, I needed that. I don't suppose you have any cigarettes?'

Erin smiled. 'Sorry, no.'

'Just as well. I gave up two years ago. This is the first time I've felt tempted.' She sighed. 'My ex always said I had a tongue that would cut a man in two. Today proved him right.' She took another drink. 'I have to admit, that man rubbed me up the wrong way, but if I could take back those words . . .'

'We all say things in the heat of the moment that we don't mean. To be honest, I think the problem was that you were coming from a completely different place this morning and that enraged all three of us.'

Sandra frowned. 'I don't understand.'

Erin searched for the words to explain what she meant. 'You and Sebastian were so caught up in your acting project that you forgot you were meddling in real lives. The thought that Sebastian was thinking of a part when he was dealing with Hazel and her very serious problems was completely shocking to us.'

'But it's not true,' Sandra protested. 'Sebastian was worried about Hazel. I kept telling him not to get involved. We were here to do a job and he was getting distracted.' She stopped at the look of disgust that crossed Erin's face. 'Yes, I realize that makes me sound like a cold-hearted bitch, but I was only doing what Sebastian had hired me to do. And trust me, Erin, I've worked with actors a long time and when things go wrong, they look around for other people to blame. But I was wasting my time. Sebastian wouldn't listen to me and insisted on helping Hazel. He's not a bad person,' she added. 'He's just been in the limelight so long he thinks he's God.'

Erin couldn't help smiling at that, but she wasn't ready to let Sandra off the hook just yet. 'And what about Paddy Burke? You were the one to get involved there. You were here to work with Sebastian. You didn't have to involve yourself in any of our lives the way you did.'

'No, That's true. But I get bored easily. Don't worry, though, I won't be losing touch with Paddy.'

'You won't?' Erin stared at her.

'I've left him signed photos of Sebastian and I've promised him a mention on Seb's website. Also, I'm going to send him memorabilia from some of the other stars I work with. He's going to turn that coffee shop into a little piece of Hollywood.'

'So you two aren't an item, then.'

Sandra threw back her head and laughed. 'Jeez, no! Even if I did go for his type, Paddy wouldn't be interested. He's the most contented old bachelor I've ever met.'

'Perhaps it's because he's surrounded by people all day,' Erin mused. 'When he closes, he's happy to have some time to himself.'

Sandra drained her glass. 'Who knows?'

'Thank you for waiting to talk to me,' Erin said.

'What else could I do? PJ and I never hit it off but I'm not totally heartless.' Sandra stood up.

'Still, I appreciate it and I know he will too.'

Sandra smiled. 'Goodnight, Erin, and thanks for everything. It's been . . . an experience.'

Chapter Thirty-Nine

Marguerite worked alone and in silence. Erin had phoned with the good news that PJ was going to be fine but she still felt shaken by the day's events and embarrassed and disappointed by Sebastian's deceitfulness. Mark and Sean were incredulous when she told them. Rai kept her head down and said nothing. When Marguerite told her that she would be working just out front today she had simply nodded. Marguerite didn't mean to be hard on her, she just couldn't bear to work with the girl. She was a constant reminder of Sebastian's disgraceful behaviour.

'Why don't you go to bed and let Rai finish up here?' Mark said from the doorway.

'I'm fine.'

'You are far from fine,' he said, coming in and perching on a stool.

Marguerite looked at him with sad eyes. 'I just feel so embarrassed, Mark. How could he have done this to me?'

'He didn't do anything *to* you, love. He just did it. I doubt he even wondered if or how it might affect you.'

She put her hands on her hips. 'Is that supposed to make me feel better?'

He chuckled. 'Sorry.'

Sean arrived and stuck a chit on the board. 'Table four's desserts.'

'And then we are finished?' she asked hopefully.

'That's it, we're done.'

'Thank God,' she muttered, going to the board and reading the order.

'Why don't you let Rai do that?' Sean suggested.

'You're wasting your breath,' Mark warned him.

'Thank you, gentlemen, I know you mean well but just let me be.'

Mark stood up. 'I'm going.'

Sean followed and Marguerite carried on with her work. When the desserts were ready, she rang the bell. Rai came to collect them but she hesitated before taking them into the restaurant.

'What is it?' Marguerite snapped.

'I need to talk to you,' Rai said in a small voice.

'I'm really not in the mood. Please get on with your work.' Rai didn't move and Marguerite looked up, frowning.

'I need you to come back to the flat with me after we close.'

'Why on earth would I want to do that?'

'Because Sebastian's there.'

Marguerite stared at her. 'What?'

'He hasn't gone yet. He wanted to talk to you first.'

'So he spent the night with you.'

Rai blushed and looked away.

'*Incroyable!*'

'So will you come?' Rai asked.

'I most definitely will, but I want to talk to him alone.'

Rai nodded her assent and carried the desserts into the restaurant.

Abandoning her work, Marguerite went upstairs to tell Mark.

'That's good, isn't it?' he said.

'I suppose so,' she said, pacing the floor. 'I'm just afraid I might hit him.'

'Don't be afraid. Give him a punch for me.'

Marguerite stopped and smiled. 'What would I do without you?'

He put his arms around her and gave her a kiss. 'I know you want to give him a piece of your mind, love. Just remember to listen to him too.'

'I will.' Marguerite sighed. 'Though I'm not sure that I will like what I hear.'

When they got to the flat, Rai opened the door and stood back. 'I'll wait outside.'

'Thank you, Rai.' Marguerite gave her a small smile and went inside.

Sebastian was sprawled on the bed, reading, but he dropped the book and stood up when he saw her. 'Hi. I'm glad you came.'

She nodded but said nothing.

He looked uncomfortable in the face of her silence. 'Sandra tells me that she filled you in on our project.'

'Project. An interesting word but not the one I would use,' she said, quietly.

'But Sandra said she explained to you that it was an acting exercise,' he said, looking confused.

'And were Hazel, Erin and Rai part of your project?'

Sebastian groaned. 'We've been through this. I've told you I helped Hazel because I liked her and because I could. As for Erin, she's a grown-up. I didn't force her to do anything she didn't want to do. And Rai?' He smiled. 'Hell, I'm only human.'

Marguerite glared at him. 'How could you bring this "project" into my life? How could you do that to me, Sebastian?'

'I didn't do anything to you, Marguerite.'

As Marguerite looked at the exasperation and confusion on his face, she realized that Mark was right. Her brother hadn't given a thought to how his behaviour would affect other people, even her. 'When I met you at the airport, I got the fright of my life.'

He smiled. 'Losing all that weight was a master-stroke, wasn't it?'

'No! No, it wasn't, Sebastian. I was worried sick

about you. I haven't stopped worrying since you phoned me, asking to come here. So don't tell me that you didn't do anything to me.'

He looked at her. 'I never thought.'

'*Précisément*, Sebastian. You never thought.'

'I'm sorry, Marguerite. I'm a selfish bastard.'

'We agree on something.'

'I just get so caught up in a role that I don't think of anything or anyone else.'

'Erin and Ronan have split up. PJ is lying in hospital. Tell me, was it worth it, Sebastian?'

'Yes. I mean no.' He sighed. 'It was a great experience for me and I really think this exercise will help me give a better performance. But I'm sorry if I upset you, Marguerite. You know that was never my intention. I'd never hurt you deliberately.'

And she knew that was true. Sebastian was guilty of being thoughtless, self-obsessed and insensitive, but she knew he had meant no harm. 'You must explain yourself to my friends,' she said at last.

'Sure, I'll visit Erin before I—'

'No!' She glared at him. 'You will do no such thing. You can write to her and to PJ.'

'Don't you trust me, Marguerite?' His eyes twinkled in amusement.

'No, I do not.'

'And what about Rai?' he asked.

'She does understand you are leaving, doesn't she?'

'Of course.'

'And she is staying?'

He laughed. 'Of course!'

She sighed. 'Good. In that case I may be able to forgive you. But only if you leave Dunbarra now.'

'I am going in the morning.'

Marguerite held his gaze. 'Tonight.'

He held up his hands, smiling. 'Okay, tonight.'

'And, Sebastian?' Marguerite walked to the door.

'Yes?'

She looked back at him. 'Don't hurry back.'

'But you said you weren't going till morning,' Rai protested, as he zipped up his bag and sat down to put on his trainers.

'My plans have changed.'

'What's going on, Sebastian?' Rai asked. 'What did Marguerite say?'

'Nothing that concerns you.'

She recoiled at the irritation in his voice, but when he looked up and smiled she figured she must have imagined it.

'It's a few hours earlier than planned; what difference does it make?'

Rai sat down on his lap and put her arms around his neck. 'Well, I haven't given you your going-away present yet,' she murmured and kissed him.

'Oh? Is it something nice?' he asked.

She nodded and started to unbutton her top. 'It's something that will help you remember me.'

Sebastian's eyes followed her hands. 'Rai, I'm never going to forget you.'

'I'd like to make sure,' she said, her hands going to his belt.

'I suppose another hour wouldn't hurt,' he said and pulled her top off.

'An hour?' she pulled him back on the bed. As he watched, she stripped off and then climbed on top of him.

'Maybe two,' he murmured, his hands spanning her waist.

'That might be long enough,' she allowed. 'I'm not sure.'

'Will you just shut up and kiss me?'

Rai smiled, excited at the urgency in his voice. 'You shut me up,' she told him.

'Happy to oblige,' he said, and pulled her to him.

Chapter Forty

It was almost Christmas before PJ started to feel really strong again. His recovery had been hampered a little by loneliness; he couldn't believe how much he still missed Isabelle. And though he was getting stronger every day, his brush with death had left him feeling more vulnerable. But he was cheered by occasional visits from Gracie, by a letter from Hazel telling him that she was doing much better, and by the fact that Erin and Ronan seemed to be getting past the Gray incident, as he'd come to think of it. They were still tiptoeing around each other but PJ noticed that Erin treated Ronan differently, showing him more respect than she once had.

But he worried about her and the business. Erin had closed the Gatehouse and with Ronan's help had concentrated on the market garden. Despite their efforts, though, profits were down. PJ had tried to talk to her about what steps they should take to deal with the recession but she brushed off his concerns. He knew it was because she didn't want him to worry but it had the opposite effect and just served to make him feel frustrated and useless.

Finally he decided to confront her and one evening after dinner, instead of retiring to his room to watch a bit of telly as he usually did, he poured them both some wine and produced a notebook.

'Should you be drinking?' Erin frowned.

He glared at her. 'Stop nagging, Erin, I want to talk to you. We need to figure out a way of beating this recession.'

'There's no way to beat it, all we can do is ride it out,' she told him and stood up.

'If you don't sit down this minute and listen to me, I'm moving out.' She turned and looked at him, her expression a mixture of hurt and dismay and he immediately felt bad. But he knew he had to say something drastic to get through to her. 'I mean it, Erin,' he said, holding her gaze.

She sank into the chair and folded her hands on the table in front of her. 'I'm listening.'

'Good.' He opened his notebook and ran through a list of ways of cutting costs and boosting productivity. She nodded solemnly but said nothing. When he'd finished he topped up their glasses, ignoring her disapproving look, and sat back in his chair. 'Or we could do something a little more radical. We could join forces with Ronan.'

'Excuse me?' Erin stared at him.

'Hear me out,' he told her, holding up his hand. 'It's

not as crazy as it sounds. If Ronan moved his farm over here we could share costs and he could sell or rent his own place. The businesses complement each other. They are both organic operations, after all, and we could expand and become more inventive. For example, we could have a market each weekend and sell directly to the public. Marguerite might like to get in on the act and sell breads or preserves and Mark, fish. I haven't thought through all the details, Erin, but we need to work together to get through this difficult time. Dunbarra needs to develop a plan to fight this battle and, as three of the main businesses in the area, we should lead the way. I have an idea about the Gatehouse too. We could advertise it as a venue for conferences, small weddings, that kind of thing. It's a beautiful house, in a wonderful location, with accommodation –' he threw up his hands – 'what more could anyone ask for?'

We'd have to hire a cook, a good cook and extra staff,' Erin pointed out.

'Team work,' PJ replied. 'It's a project that you could get Marguerite in on. You look after the organization and she takes care of the food. Also, you're going to have your pick of local staff, what with White's closing and the other businesses that have been cutting staff numbers. This is only the tip of the iceberg, Erin. We need to talk to Ronan, to Marguerite and Mark, and to all the other local employers and pool ideas. I'm sure they'll come up with much better concepts.' He searched her face for a reaction but saw nothing. 'You think it's a terrible idea.'

'Not at all. I think it's ingenious.'

'Really?'

She nodded. 'Really. And even if Ronan or Marguerite aren't interested in going into business with us, we'd be mad not to form some sort of Dunbarra action group.' She shook her head. 'I've been coming at this all wrong. I've been thinking in terms of survival while you're thinking about going on the attack. But tell me, where could Ronan possibly put a few thousand chickens?'

'I've thought about that too.'

'I thought you might have,' she teased.

He ignored her. Now that he'd finally got her to listen, he couldn't wait to tell her all his ideas. 'That field beyond the greenhouses would be the perfect spot. The land is useless for farming because of its proximity to the lake, and it would be far enough away from the house so that guests wouldn't be bothered by noise or smells.'

'Sounds good. I must say I love the idea of a weekly market,' Erin told him. 'I can't see how that could fail.'

'Me neither,' PJ agreed. 'There is little investment involved and we could advertise it through the parishes.'

'And you know what else we could do?' Erin said, getting carried away by his enthusiasm. 'We could run an annual fair with prizes for largest vegetables or best jams. And you could run courses teaching people how to grow their own.'

PJ's eyes twinkled. 'Now you're thinking outside the box, as the Yanks would say.'

Erin looked thoughtful.

'What?' he prompted.

'I'm just thinking about Mark. His business is suffering too but he's another one that could turn to teaching. He could get a few small dinghies, canoes, that sort of thing, and run courses. I'd imagine his highest cost would be insurance.'

'And he'd love it.' PJ grinned at her in delight.

'Oh, PJ.' She sighed.

PJ's smile faded when he saw that there were tears in her eyes. 'What is it, Erin? What's wrong?'

She shook her head. 'Not a thing. I'm just so happy that you're all right. I feel I can get through anything with you by my side.'

'Well, what a lovely thing to say,' he said, touched by her words. 'I think I'm the lucky one, though. No one could have looked after me better than you have these last few weeks. You're like the daughter I never had.'

She held his gaze. 'I am the daughter you never had, PJ.'

He smiled and nodded.

'Do you remember a woman called Darina Callaghan?'

He frowned. 'No, I don't think so.'

'You knew her a very long time ago – thirty-two years ago, to be precise. You landscaped her garden.'

'Why yes, of course, Darina!' He sighed. 'A beautiful woman. I thought maybe she might be the one but it turned out she belonged to another so I quickly moved on.'

'And you belonged to Isabelle,' Erin reminded him.

'Oh, no, my darling, that was before I even met Isabelle. I was still a bachelor in those days.' He chuckled. 'But how do you know Darina?'

Erin looked at him for a long moment before she answered. 'She's my mother.'

His mouth fell open and he stared at her. 'But she didn't have any children then. She said she and her estranged husband had tried but they hadn't been blessed.'

'PJ, I'm thirty-one.'

He still stared at her, not allowing himself to read anything into her words. Instead he noticed the flecks in her hazel eyes that reminded him of his father's and the way her mouth turned up at the edges when she smiled, just like her mother's had. 'Thirty-one,' he mumbled.

'Matthew Joyce, Darina's husband and the man I thought was my father, died a few years ago. The night he was buried, my mother told me he wasn't my dad. My real dad was a man by the name of PJ Ward.'

PJ stared at her. 'Really, Erin?' he whispered.

She nodded, her eyes searching his face. 'Really.'

'I don't know what to say.'

'I was hoping you'd say that you were happy,' she said with a shaky smile.

'Happy? I'm over the moon!' he assured her, grasping her hands in his and kissing them. 'I just can't quite believe it. But how do you feel about it, Erin?'

'I was angry at first. I couldn't believe she'd been unfaithful to Dad – he never deserved that – and I was furious with you for taking advantage of a married woman.'

'But I didn't know, Erin,' PJ told her. 'She told me that she was separated.'

Erin closed her eyes. 'I should have guessed. It's typical of her to leave out an important little detail like that.'

'It was a long time ago,' PJ consoled her. 'Don't fall out over this.'

She shook her head. 'Don't worry, I'm used to her. And it doesn't come as much of a surprise. She's always had an eye for the men, and she's completely lost the run of herself since Dad died. Sadly they seem to get steadily younger.'

PJ chuckled. 'Good luck to her. Sure, life is short. Tell me, is she still beautiful?'

Erin nodded. 'And maddening and irritating but it's hard not to love her. Anyway, the one thing in her favour was that, having committed adultery, she decided to turn something wrong into something right. She told Dad they were going to have a child –

they'd been trying for years and pretty much given up – and he was over the moon. He was a wonderful father.'

'I'm glad but, I have to be honest, I'm also jealous. I'd give anything to have known you when you were little.'

'It's such a relief that you feel this way.'

He looked at her in astonishment. 'My darling girl, how could you think that I would feel any other way? I've loved you almost as long as I've known you. To find out that you're my daughter – my daughter,' he said again, savouring the words. 'I'm the proudest man in the world.'

They talked long into the night and she told him stories from her childhood and how she'd tracked him down and followed him around for months. He told her about his brief affair with her mother, his subsequent meeting with Isabelle, with whom he fell head over heels in love at first sight, and his devastation when she was diagnosed with Alzheimer's.

When they were finally ready to retire after copious cups of tea – Erin refused to allow him to drink any more wine – PJ, though tired, felt ten years younger. He gathered her into his arms and held her tightly, tears filling his eyes. 'I can't believe that I could be this lucky. Thank you, Erin. Thank you for finding me. Thank you for taking the time to get to know me. Thank you for telling me the truth.'

She smiled up into his face. 'I love you, PJ.' She frowned. 'Is it okay if I still call you that? It's just that Dad doesn't seem right, somehow.'

'Call me whatever you like, my darling. But I must warn you that I'm going to call you my daughter at every opportunity.' He laughed then stopped abruptly. 'Or is this just going to be our secret?'

'I've had my fill of secrets,' she said with feeling. ' I want everyone to know the truth.'

Ronan was feeding the chickens the next morning when his mobile rang. He looked at the display and smiled. 'Hi, Erin, you're up and about early. Is everything okay?'

'Never better,' she told him. 'Can you come over for breakfast?'

'The works?' he asked.

'The works,' she told him.

'You haven't cooked breakfast in weeks, what's the occasion?'

'There's someone I want you to meet.'

'Who?' he asked.

'You'll just have to wait and see. Is nine okay?'

'Perfect.'

'Great. See you then.'

'What's all this?' PJ pushed open the door of the kitchen and licked his lips.

Erin left her place by the cooker to come over and

kiss him. 'Good morning. I've invited Ronan to join us for breakfast. Sorry, but I couldn't wait to introduce him to my dad.'

PJ smiled. 'Thank God for that. I was afraid I'd dreamed the whole thing.'

'You didn't,' she assured him.

He looked past her at the bacon sizzling in the pan. 'So, am I actually allowed a real breakfast for a change?'

'Yes, but it's not going to be a regular thing,' she warned him.

'I'd settle for occasional. There's only so much bran a body can take.'

She laughed and was cracking eggs into a pan just as the doorbell rang. 'Let Ronan in, would you, PJ?'

'Will do.'

'But don't say anything yet,' she called after him.

'I won't,' he promised, still not able to believe that last night had really happened. 'She's my daughter,' he said aloud, and was smiling broadly as he opened the door. But it wasn't Ronan standing there.

'Hello, PJ.'

PJ hadn't thought it was possible to feel happier. 'Hazel! Come in! How are you?'

'Fine,' she said, with a shy smile, although when she hugged him back it was a good firm hug.

He studied her for a moment. Her eyes were clear, her hair shone and she'd put on some weight. 'You look wonderful.'

'So do you. How are you keeping?'

He frowned.

'Des told me,' she explained.

'So you're in touch?' PJ smiled.

'We are. He's been great. In fact, I'm going to tea with him and Gracie on Sunday.'

'That's wonderful, Hazel. I'm delighted for you.'

'I have Sebastian to thank. I'm not sure where I'd be now if he hadn't talked me into going into that clinic.'

PJ pulled a face. 'You won't find many people around here with a good word to say about that man.'

She shrugged. 'I'm not trying to change your mind or anyone else's. I just know he saved my life.'

'PJ, Ronan, hurry up, breakfast is ready,' Erin called from the kitchen.

'Sorry, I won't keep you,' Hazel told him. 'I just came for the rest of my stuff.'

'Oh, right.' PJ nodded. 'So where are you off to?'

Hazel shrugged. 'I'm not sure yet.'

'PJ, what on earth's keeping you?' Erin pushed through the door into the hall and pulled up short at the sight of Hazel. 'Hazel, how are you?' She came forward and embraced the other girl. 'Silly question, you look absolutely marvellous.'

Hazel looked slightly taken aback by the effusive welcome. 'Hello, Erin. I'm fine. How are you?'

'I'm great. You're just in time for breakfast.'

PJ turned surprised eyes on his new-found daughter. 'Are you sure?'

She kissed his cheek. 'Positive.'

Hazel glanced from one to the other. 'I don't want to intrude . . .'

'You're not intruding,' Erin assured her and then, looking past her, she smiled. 'Ronan.'

'Sorry I'm late. Hello, Hazel.' His smile widened in surprise. 'So you're the reason for this impromptu breakfast.'

Hazel frowned. 'No, I don't think so.'

Erin looked at PJ and he looked at her.

Ronan shook his head. 'What's going on?'

'I'm not saying anything until we're sitting down.' Erin told him. 'Come on, Hazel, I'll set another place.'

PJ put his arm around Hazel and they all followed Erin into the dining room.

'Wow.' Ronan's eyes widened as he took in the table that Erin had spent half an hour decorating.

'Take care of the Buck's fizz, would you, Ronan?' Erin asked. 'And not too much fizz for PJ.'

'Spoilsport,' PJ said, with a good-natured chuckle.

'Okay, I am dying of curiosity now,' Ronan admitted as he popped the champagne cork. 'But who is this celebrity guest? And why is the table set only for three?'

Erin quickly organized another place setting. 'All will be revealed,' she promised, before going back into the kitchen.

'This is all very mysterious,' Ronan said, pouring wine and juice into four champagne glasses.

'I shouldn't be here,' Hazel said, looking embarrassed.

'Nonsense,' PJ told her. 'You've made it even more special. I've been so worried about you.'

'We all have,' Erin confirmed, coming through the door with their food. 'Really, Hazel, you are very welcome.'

'Thanks.' Hazel smiled, and sat down next to PJ.

When they were all seated, Ronan looked expectantly at Erin. 'Well? We have the champagne glasses ready. Who is this person you wanted me to meet?'

Erin shot a look at PJ and then lifted her glass. 'My dad.'

Ronan frowned. 'But you told me your dad was dead.'

Erin nodded. 'The man who raised me is dead, but my father is alive.'

'Oh?' Ronan raised an eyebrow. 'Oh!' He looked around. 'Is he here?'

Erin smiled. 'Yes, I'm happy to say he is.'

PJ stood up and made a slight bow. 'Hello, everyone, nice to meet you.'

Erin laughed and clapped her hands.

'Oh, for God's sake, what are you two up to?' Ronan asked, smiling at their antics.

Erin stood and put her arm through PJ's. 'It's true. PJ is my dad.'

'And this,' PJ smiled fondly at Erin, 'is my daughter.'

Ronan stared. 'You're kidding.'

'Really?' Hazel gaped from one to the other.

'Really,' Erin and PJ said together.

'This is amazing!' Ronan stood and shook PJ's hand and kissed Erin. 'I don't know what to say.'

'I'll explain everything,' Erin promised, 'but first sit and eat before the food goes cold.'

'Good idea.' PJ sat down and tucked enthusiastically into his breakfast.

'Should you be eating this stuff?' Ronan asked, helping himself to toast.

'He shouldn't,' Erin said, 'but I don't suppose it will hurt just this once.'

'Once?' PJ looked at her in dismay. 'You said occasionally.'

'It's open to negotiation.'

'Good.' He caught Hazel's eye and winked. 'So, Hazel, you timed your visit perfectly. I can't think of anyone I'd rather hear our news first than you, Well, maybe your daughter.'

Hazel laughed at that, and PJ and Erin proceeded to tell their story over breakfast.

'It's like something out of a novel,' Ronan said, pushing away his empty plate and accepting a refill of coffee from Erin.

'It's all true, I promise,' Erin assured him.

'It'd better be. My heart couldn't stand it if you said you were joking,' PJ warned her.

Hazel stood up. 'I'm happy for you both. Now, I'd better go up to my room and pack my things.'

'Of course.' Erin smiled and went to get the key. 'No one has touched your things,' she promised. 'And Sebastian paid for the room until the end of February, so it's all yours if you want to stay.'

'Are you serious?' Hazel stared at her.

'Dead serious.' Erin smiled.

'Please stay, Hazel,' PJ added.

'I'd like that,' Hazel told them.

'Excellent.' PJ beamed at her.

When she had left them to settle back in, Erin turned to PJ. 'You know, PJ, I think art lessons could feature in our new project.'

PJ's eyes lit up. 'Well, that's an excellent idea.'

'Art lessons?' Ronan frowned.

PJ locked eyes with Erin and then turned to Ronan. 'We've been playing around with some rather different ideas that might help us combat the recession,' he explained. 'We were hoping to involve you too. Are you interested?'

'Absolutely.' Ronan nodded and then looked over at Erin, his eyes searching her face. 'After all, we're all in this together, right?' He reached for her hand.

Smiling, Erin took it. 'We certainly are.'

POCKET
BOOKS

Colette Caddle
Between the Sheets

Dana De Lacey, bestselling romance novelist, has the world at
her feet. The words on the page flow easily, an exciting new
book deal beckons, and life at home in Dublin is good.

But Dana's self-confidence and success depend on one person:
her gorgeous husband Gus. Without him, she has no fall-back.
No children, no close family of her own to call upon. When
Gus leaves her, she is devastated. The words fail to come.
The alcohol flows too freely. She cannot sleep.

Then her estranged brother Ed arrives out of the blue to take
care of her and memories that she has kept buried for many
years start to rise to the surface. Forced to face up to the past,
can she find the real Dana, recover her career, and try
to make Gus love her for the person she really is?

ISBN 978-1-84739-332-6
PRICE £6.99

POCKET
BOOKS

Colette Caddle
It's All About Him

*If you were given the chance to confront the man
who ruined your life, what would you do?*

With the health of her son always an issue and bills constantly
flooding in, the last thing Dee Hewson needs is to open her
front door one day and come face to face with the childhood
sweetheart who broke her heart and abused her trust.

Though she was devastated by his betrayal, she has triumphed
over all the odds and pulled the pieces of her life back
together. Through love and a lot of hard work, Dee has
changed adored son Sam from being a delicate toddler into
a feisty and fun-loving four-year-old. Her money worries may
finally be receding and there are wonderful new business
opportunities on the horizon. She has even dared to
find love again – with strong and reliable Conor.

So is Dee really prepared to jeopardize all this simply
to give Sam the chance of having a father?

With great warmth and an unerring eye, Number One
Irish bestseller Colette Caddle makes Dee's dilemma
acutely real as she explores the fragility of family
and friendship in today's fraught world.

ISBN 978-1-41652-194-5
PRICE £6.99

POCKET
BOOKS

Colette Caddle
The Betrayal of Grace Mulcahy

*Interior betrayals, Venetian blinds; this warm,
wise and affecting novels unravels the numerous
betrayals we make upon even those we love*

The life and marriage of Grace and Michael Mulcahy has all
the signs of being a successful and fulfilled one: a daughter;
rewarding jobs; plenty of friends. But when Grace discovers
that Miriam, her partner in her interior design business, is
embezzling her, the seeds are sown for Grace's bind. When
confronted with her betrayal, Miriam begs Grace not to tell
anyone in order to preserve Miriam's marriage which will fall
apart if the truth outs. Grace agrees to keep quiet but finds it
leads to all sorts of complications and misunderstandings that
put a strain on all of her relationships both professional and
personal. By the time she notices how close things are to
crumbling, is it too late to piece together the ties
that bind her to those she loves?

ISBN 978-1-41652-193-8
PRICE £6.99

POCKET
BOOKS

Colette Caddle
Changing Places

Anna and Rachel Gallagher, two sisters close in age
but very little else. Ten minutes in each other's company
and they are at each other's throats.

Anna is the elder, the pretty one, working her way up
the career ladder as an estate agent, married to Liam
and happy to wait for his assured promotion at work
before they start a family.

Rachel, by comparison, feels lumpy and grumpy. Mother
to five-year-old Alex, keeping her second pregnancy a secret
even from her husband Gary, she is the stay-at-home
younger sister, tired out and lonely.

Caught in the middle is Jill, forever trying to be peacemaker.
She has her own problems, at work and at home, but, with a
confident smile and a spring in her step, she tries
to take them all in her stride.

In her warm, wise and wonderful new novel, Colette Caddle
takes us right to the heart of family relationships and all the
contradictions. When Anna's husband loses his job and
Rachel is in danger of losing her husband, will blood
really prove thicker than water?

ISBN 978-0-74346-885-5
PRICE £6.99

POCKET
BOOKS

Colette Caddle
Red Letter Day

Recently married to Dermot and tipped as Ireland's hottest
new designer, Celine Moore is relaxed, happy and looking
forward to an exciting future. Why then, just five years later,
is she barely able to hold her head up high in her local Dublin
neighbourhood, at odds with her father and sister-in-law
and accepting a job in a second hand clothes shop?

Celine's life changed the night Dermot failed to return from
work and his violent death destroyed all her happiness and
ambition. Aching loneliness and anger took their place, and
without thinking through the consequences, Celine embarked
on an affair with a married man. Now, desperate to put some
distance between herself and the local gossips, a new start
in a new place and a new job seems like the
perfect opportunity to start again.

But it's not long before she realizes that however much you try
to run away, your past has a habit of always
catching up with you in the end …

ISBN 978-0-74346-884-8
PRICE £6.99

**POCKET
BOOKS**

This book and other **Pocket Books** titles are available from
your local bookshop or can be ordered direct
from the publisher.

Praise for Colette Caddle

'If you like Marion Keyes, you'll love Colette Caddle' *Company*

'Will have readers laughing and crying every step of the way' *Irish Times*

'An engaging, warm slice of life with which all women will be able to identify. Highly recommended' *Publishing News*

'A warm, irresistible Irish author for all ages. Heaven knows how they do it, but they have that special magic' *Bookseller*

'Caddle seems to know instinctively what women readers want' *Ireland on Sunday*

'Skillfully written, by an accomplished Irish author, the characters are intriguing and the story is deftly paced . . . you will enjoy this one!' *Irish Independent*